THE HERESY OF DR DEE

THE HERESY OF DR DEE

*Being edited from the most private documents
of Dr John Dee, astrologer and consultant
to Queen Elizabeth*

PHIL RICKMAN

CORVUS

Published in hardback and trade paperback in Great Britain in 2012
by Corvus, an imprint of Atlantic Books Ltd.

10 9 8 7 6 5 4 3 2 1

A CIP catalogue record for this book is available from the British Library.

Hardback ISBN: 978 1 84887 276 9
Trade paperback ISBN: 978 1 84887 277 6
E-book ISBN: 978 1 84887 278 3

Printed in Great Britain by TJ International Ltd, Padstow, Cornwall

Corvus
An imprint of Atlantic Books Ltd
Ormond House
26–27 Boswell Street
London
WC1N 3JZ

www.corvus-books.co.uk

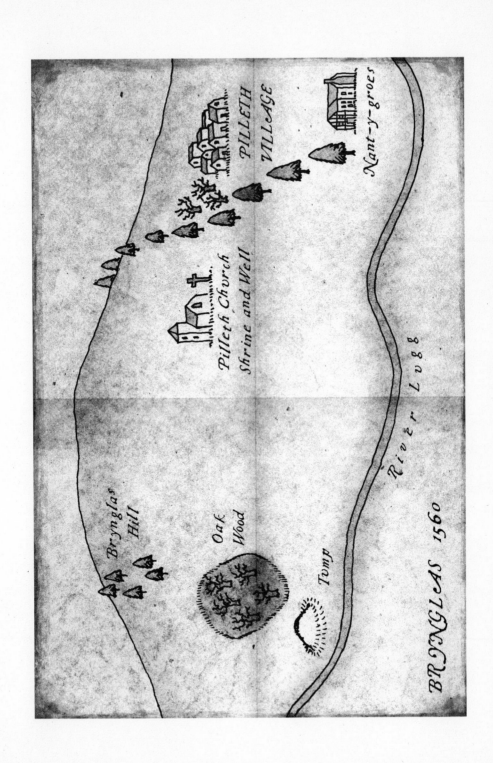

Nant-y-groes

PILLETH VILLAGE

Pilleth Church
Shrine and Well

Brynglas Hill

Oak Wood

Tomp

River Lvgg

BRYNGLAS 1560

JOHN DEE

The early history

Born in 1527, John Dee grew up in the most volcanic years of the reign of Henry VIII, at whose court his father was employed as a 'gentleman server'. John was eight when the King split with Rome, declaring himself head of the Church of England and systematically plundering the wealth of the monasteries. Recognised by his early twenties as one of Europe's leading mathematicians and an expert in the science of astrology, John was introduced at court during the short reign of Henry's son, Edward VI.

When Edward died at only sixteen, John Dee was lucky to survive the brief but bloody reign of the Catholic Mary Tudor. Mary died in 1558 and was succeeded by the Protestant, Elizabeth, who would always encourage John's lifelong interest in what he considered science but others saw as sorcery. Caught between Catholic plots and the rise of a new puritanism, he would feel no more secure than Queen Elizabeth herself, who was fending off the marriage bids of foreign kings and princes.

1560 began what biographers have seen as John Dee's 'missing years.' A dangerous period, especially after the mysterious death of the wife of Dee's friend and former student, Lord Robert Dudley, thought by many to be the Queen's lover.

PART ONE

All my life I had spent in learning... with great pain, care and cost I had, from degree to degree, sought to come by the best knowledge that man might attain unto in the world. And I found, at length, that neither any man living, nor any book I could yet meet withal, was able to teach me those truths I desired and longed for...

JOHN DEE

I

Source of Darkness

IT WAS THE year of no summer, and all the talk in London was of the End-time.

Even my mother's neighbours were muttering about darkness on the streets before its time, moving lights seen in the heavens and tremblings of the earth caused by Satan's gleeful stoking of the infernal fires.

Tales came out of Europe that two suns were oft-times apparent in the skies. On occasion, three, while in England we never saw even the one most days and, when it deigned to appear, it was as pale and sour as old milk and smirched by raincloud. Now, all too soon, autumn was nigh, and the harvests were poor and I'd lost count of the times I'd been asked what the stars foretold about our future… if we had one.

Each time, I'd reply that the heavens showed no signs of impending doom. But how acceptable was my word these days? I was the astrologer who'd found a day of good promise for the joyful crowning of a woman who now, less than two years later, was being widely condemned as the source of the darkness.

By embittered Catholics, this was, and the prune-faced new Bible-men. *Even the sun has fled England*, they squealed. *God's verdict on a country that would have as its queen the spawn of a witch* – these fears given heat by false rumours from France and Spain that Elizabeth was *pregnant with a murderer's child.*

God's bollocks, as the alleged murderer would say, but all this made me weary to the bone. How fast the bubble of new joy is pricked. How shallow people are. Give them shit to spread, and they'll forge new shovels overnight.

All the same, you might have thought, after what happened in Glastonbury, that the Queen would seek my help in shifting this night-soil from her door.

But, no, she'd sent for me just once since the spring – all frivolous and curious about what I was working on, and had I thought of *this*, and had I looked into *that*? Sending me back to spend, in her cause, far too much money on books. Burn too many candles into pools of fat. Explore alleys of the hidden which I thought I'd never want to enter.

Only to learn, within weeks, that heavy curtains had closed around her court. Death having slipped furtively in. The worst of all possible deaths, most of us could see that.

Although not the Queen, apparently, who could scarce conceal her terrifying gaiety.

Dear God. As the silence grew, I was left wondering if the End-time might truly be looming and began backing away from some of the more foetid alleyways.

Though not fast enough, as it turned out.

II

Rooker

September, 1560. Mortlake.

IT WAS TO be the last halfway-bright day of the season, but the scryer had demanded darkness: shutters closed against the mid-afternoon and the light from a single beeswax candle throwing shadows into battle on the walls.

'And this…' Dithering now, poor Goodwife Faldo looked at me over the wafer of flame and then across the board to where the scryer sat, and then back at me. 'This is my brother…' her hands falling to her sides and, even in the small light, he must surely have seen the flailing in her eyes '…John,' she said lamely.

'John Faldo,' I said at once.

And then, seeing the eyes of my friend Jack Simm rolling upwards, realised why this could not be so.

'That is, her *husband's* brother.'

Thinking how fortunate it was that Will Faldo was out with his two sons, gleaning from his field all that remained of a dismal harvest. Had he been with us, the scryer might just have noted that Master Faldo was plump, with red hair, and a head shorter than the man claiming to be his brother.

Or he might yet see the truth when he uncovered what sat before him. It made a hump under the black cloth as might a saint's sacred skull. My eyes were drawn back to it again and again. Unaware that the scryer had been watching me until his voice came curling out of the dark.

'You have an interest in these matters, Master Faldo?'

A clipped clarity suggestive of Wales. Echoes of my late tad, in fact.

Jesu... I met his gaze for no more than a moment then looked away towards the crack of daylight betwixt shutters. The Faldos' dwelling, firm-built of oak and riverbed daub, was but a short walk from Mortlake Church which, had the shutters been open, would have displayed itself like a warning finger.

'The truth is,' I mumbled, 'that I'm less afraid of such things than my brother. Which is one reason why I'm here. And, um, he is not.'

The scryer nodded, appearing well at ease with his situation. Too much so, it seemed to me; the narrow causeway 'twixt science and sorcery will always have slippery sides and in his place I would ever have been watching the shadows. But then, that, as you know, is the way I am.

I studied him in the thin light. Not what I'd expected. A good twenty years older than my thirty-three, greying beard tight-trimmed to his cheeks and a white scar the width of his forehead. Well-clothed, in a drab and sober way, like to a clerk or a lawyer. Only the scar hinting at a more perilous profession.

He'd introduced himself to us as Elias, and I was told he'd been a monk. Were this true, it might afford him protection from whatever would come. Certainly his manner implied that we were fortunate to have his services.

'And the other reason that Master Faldo is not with us?'

He smiled at me, with evident scepticism. I was silent too long, and it was the goodwife, alert as a chaffinch, who sprang up.

'My husband... he knows naught of this. He's working the day long and falls to sleep when he comes in. I...' She lowered her voice and her eyelids, a fine and unexpected piece of theatre. 'I was too ashamed to tell him.'

She'd already paid the scryer, with my money. I'd also been obliged to meet his night's accommodation at the inn – more than I could readily afford, especially if I were to make a further purchase. Served me right for starting this game and involving the goodwife in the deception.

Brother Elias smiled at her with understanding.

'So the treasure you want me to find... would be your wedding ring?'

Goodwife Faldo let out a small cry, hastily stifled with a hand. How could he possibly have known this by natural means? I stiffened only for a moment. It was no more than a good guess. He must oft-times be summoned to locate a woman's ring or a locket. It was what they did.

'What happened...' Goodwife Faldo displayed her fingers, one with a circle of white below its joint '...I must have taken it off. To clean out the fire ready for the autumn? Laid it on the board, where you're...' Peering among the shadows on the board, as if the missing ring might be gleaming from somewhere to betray her. 'And then forgot about it until the night. And it... was gone.'

'You think someone stole it?'

'I'd not *want* to think that. We trust our neighbours. Nobody

7

here bolts a door. But… yes, I do fear it's been taken. Been many years in my husband's family, and has a value beyond the gold. Can you help me?'

'Not me alone, Goodwife. Not me alone.'

Brother Elias speaking with solemnity and what seemed to me to be a first hint of stagecraft. Goodwife Faldo's stool wobbling and the candlelight passing like a sprite across her coif as she sat up. Like many women, my mother's neighbour was much attracted to the Hidden, yet in a half-fearful way – the joy of shivers.

'I can only pray,' she said unsteadily, 'that whatever is summoned to help you comes from the right… quarter.'

This, I'll admit, was a question I'd primed her to ask. No one should open a portal to the Hidden without spiritual protection. There are long-established procedures for securing this; I wanted to know if the scryer knew them.

'Oh, it must needs be Godly,' Elias assured her confidently. 'If it's to find this ring for us. However…' his well-fed face became stern '…I must make it clear to you, Goodwife, that if the ring *has* been stolen and we are able to put a face to the thief, then it's your business, not mine, to take the matter further.'

'That's, er…' I coughed '…is another reason why *I'm* here.'

Me, the fighting man. *Dear God.*

'And what *are* you, Master Faldo?' the scryer said, but not as if he cared. 'What's your living?'

I shrugged.

'I work at the brewery.'

The biggest employer of men in Mortlake. *Tell him you work at the brewery*, Jack Simm had said to me earlier. And then, looking at my hands. *Dealing wiv orders.*

'And you…' the scryer turned to Jack, '…were once, I think, an apothecary in London?'

'Once.'

Jack stubbornly folding his arms over his wide chest as though to ward off further questions. *Get on with it.* The scryer cupped his hands over the black-draped object before him, drew a long breath, as if about to snatch away the cloth… and then stopped.

'It's not mete.'

Pulling his hands away from the mounded cloth, stowing them away in his robe.

A scowl split Jack Simm's lambswool beard.

'What?'

'I regret it's not mete for me to go on,' Brother Elias said. 'The crystal's cold.'

Speaking with finality, where most of his kind would be smiling slyly at you while holding out their grubby hands for more money. Maybe it came to the same. Elias's apparel showed he'd already prospered from his trade.

Yet I felt this wasn't only about money. The air in here had altered. The hearth looked cold as an altar, the room felt damp. I became aware of the fingers of both my hands gripping the edge of the board as the scryer reached to the flagged floor for his satchel.

'We should light a fire?' Jack Simm said.

Halfway to his feet, angry, but Elias didn't look at him.

'If you want this to have results,' he said quietly, 'then I must needs go back to the inn and rest a while. I'll return shortly before nightfall. That is, if you wish to continue with this…'

… comedy? Was that what he thought?

Did he suspect false-play?

Look, I wanted to say, *if we've insulted your art, I beg mercy, but I feared you'd be a rooker. Back-street scryers, I thought all they sought was a regular income. That they had no aspiration to walk in the golden halls of creation and know the energies behind their art. I thought that all that mattered was that it worked. And if it didn't, you faked it. I want to know where the fakery begins, to separate artifice from natural magic. I want to watch what you do, observe your methods. And... I want to know where to obtain the finest of shewstones.*

Should I identify myself, accept a loss of face?

No. I held back, watching him shoulder his satchel and make his stately way to the Goodwife's door, wondering if he'd return or vanish with my money.

'Oh,' he said mildly. 'I have one question.' He opened the door and the light washed over him. 'Why am *I* summoned to Mortlake?'

From outside came the scurrying of birds.

'Why *Mortlake*?' the scryer said. 'When Mortlake's surely home to a man more qualified than I?' He looked at each of us in turn. 'Or is the good Dr Dee too busy conjuring for the Queen these days to waste his famous skills in service of his neighbours?'

Jack Simm glanced at me. I knew not how to respond.

'Dr Dee,' Jack said, 'doesn't scry.'

Hmm... not yet, anyway.

III

Call Them Angels

JACK SIMM WAS a gardener now. He'd abandoned his London apothecary's shop during Mary's reign, when the agents of Bishop Bonner had been scouring the streets for signs of Protestants and witches alike, and anyone else who might be deemed an enemy of the Catholic Church.

Like many a poor bastard who'd burned in Bonner's purge, Jack had been neither, but the scent of roasting flesh singes the soul. And he had a young wife and so chose to pursue his trade in a quiet way, from his home on the edge of the village, growing herbs in other people's gardens as part-payment for his services. Growing certain mushrooms for me, to bring about visions. Not that they'd worked, but that wasn't Jack's fault.

I'd tell him he had no need to be a secret apothecary any more. It was a new reign. Everything was changed for the brighter. Kept telling him all this, but he was wary yet.

Particularly wary when, about four weeks previously, I'd asked him to find me a good scryer and perhaps a shewstone for sale.

For pretty much the same reason I'd wanted the mushrooms.

✠

'You ain't a *complete* fool, Dr John,' Jack had said, 'but you're ever running too close to the bleedin' cliff-edge.'

We'd been walking the pathway through the wood behind his dwelling. An unusually muggy day – a sneer of a day, a taunt at a drear summer's end. My shirt had been sweated to my spine while my boots were yet soaked from the puddles.

Look, I'd been aware of the scrying profession most of my life, my tad oft-times making mock of it – all furtive foreigners and gypsies who'd gaze into a stone or a mirror and tell you where your missing property might be recovered or how many children you'd have. Or, if you underpaid them, exactly when the children could expect to inherit your worldly goods.

Rookers to a man, and they oft-times conduct their trade through an apothecary, who takes a cut of the fee.

'I *could* find you one, no problem,' Jack had said. 'When I was in town, we must've had a dozen or more of these bleeders in the shop. Wanting me to put 'em in touch wiv the sick and the bereaved or anyone who needed somebody to talk to the dead on their behalf, intercede wiv angels. I'd kick their arses down the street. And been cursed for it a few times. But I'm still here, ain't I?'

He'd been gazing out between the heavy, dripping trees towards the swollen river and his voice was damp with disdain.

'Why?' he said. 'That's all I'm asking. I ain't getting it, Dr John. I've watched men and woman staring into stones and seeing fings I can't see. And if I can't see it…? You know what I'm saying?'

'Everything's open to abuse,' I said.

'But you're a… a whatsit, natural-philosopher… a man of bleedin' *science*.'

'Well, exactly,' I said. 'Knowing the science behind crystal-gazing makes all the difference.'

I could have told him then precisely why I was, of a sudden, interested in the art of scrying. But, although I trusted him more than most, it wasn't the time. And I'd have to admit that I'd been as sceptical as he was until, at the university of Louvain, I'd been given sight of a rare manuscript by the scholar and cabalist Johannes Trithemius of Spanheim. Which explained why certain stones, if used with knowledge and reverence, could give access to the very engines of heaven.

'A stone's a *stone*, Dr John.'

'Never dismiss what's beneath your feet, Jack. Crystals will absorb and reflect celestial rays. If employed at certain times – on certain days, under specific planetary configurations – they'll open up the inner rooms of the mind ...to levels of existence normally denied to us.'

Jack kicked a lesser stone into the grass.

'Spirits, is it?'

I sighed. A very loose word, oft-times misused.

'Three spheres, Jack: this earthly plane and, above that, the astral, where earthbound spirits linger, the place of ghosts. And above and beyond all... the supercelestial... the over-realm, the furnace room of Heaven.'

As a scholar of Hebrew I'd studied in depth the Cabala which, through mystical symbolism, offers a stairway to the sublime. It makes logical, mathematical sense and, although Jewish in origin, can be practised just as effectively through Christianity. The *Christian* cabala would be my shield against the earthbound spirits and the kind of demonic entities which might enter a shewstone and possess the unguarded scryer.

13

As distinct from the higher spirits, the good spirits.

Call them angels.

'In Europe,' I said, 'the shewstone is seen as a legitimate method of penetrating the higher mysteries. In England, it's yet a joke, at best. At worst, the devil's own mirror.'

'You told them this in Europe?'

'Hell, no.'

Not for me to confirm their opinion of England as a land of Philistines – or to confess my own ignorance. I'd read and re-read the works of Agrippa and what I could of Trithemius, but my personal experience was, at best, thin and always would be until I seized the nettle and took steps to acquire my own shewstone.

A good one. A good crystal, with which to carry out exper-iments. But what kind, what colour, how big? These were fundamentals I ought to have known about but did not, for opinions varied.

'You're an innocent soul, Dr John.' Jack Simm standing among the roots of a venerable oak and facing me like a father, hands sunk into the pockets of his jerkin. 'You fink fings is different, now nobody gets burned. The Queen smiling, all gracious. Oh, yea, folks can believe what they like, long as they keep it to themselves. Like we ain't heard all *that* before.'

'Times change, Jack.'

'Kings don't change. Nor Queens. It's religious freedom one day then, in a blinking, it's all about how to prove you ain't a witch's daughter.'

The Queen's mother, Anne Boleyn, executed by the Queen's father for treason and adultery, had been possessed of a sixth finger and a furry growth on her neck. How much evidence did you want?

'Now how's the Queen *do* that?' Jack said. 'She makes war on witchcraft, and her advisers look around for somebody well-known to execute to make it look good.'

A dead twig had snapped under his boot, making me start as he sprang away from the oak, forefinger aimed at my chest.

'Go on… tell me it's wivout bleedin' precedent. And you may mention the late King Harry.'

I wanted to laugh, but it wouldn't come. This queen was different. This queen had an acute intelligence and questing mind fascinated by alchemy and the cabala. This queen was powerfully Protestant while celebrating the Mass in deep privacy.

'Heresy.' I'd shrugged. 'All science is heresy. Now… can you help me?'

He'd paced a slow circle around the oak.

'Yea, well,' he'd said at last, 'I suppose you oughter have somefink to take your mind off what's happening downriver.'

He'd meant London. Becoming known in Europe as Satan's city. And not, at this moment, a good place to be if you were a friend of Robert Dudley.

IV

The Smoke of Rumour

WHEN BROTHER ELIAS had made his stately departure to the inn, we ate bread and goatcheese with Goodwife Faldo.

It had been Jack's idea that she should play the pigeon so that I might observe a scrying without giving away my identity. Goodwife Faldo, who'd once taken my mother to see a cunning woman in the hope of asking my dead father if there was money hidden anywhere, had agreed at once to accept me as her brother for the day.

After our meal, she said she'd walk out to the meadow to suggest to her husband and sons that, rather than disrupt our sitting, they might eat at the inn tonight. I gave her my last shilling to pay for their meat and small beer, and then Jack and I walked down to the riverside where casks of fresh-brewed ale were being loaded into a barge. The air was cooling fast these evenings and the ambering sky above the distant city was smutted and heavy from first fires. And the smoke of rumour.

I hadn't ventured into London for more than a week, but the gossip had been drifting down to me like black flakes from a lamp-scorched purlin. The city all atremble in the glitter of a dangerous lightning.

'What were they saying when you were in town?' I asked.

One reason I'd come to trust Jack Simm: he was a man of intelligence but without ambition.

Without ambition. What a blessed state that must be. Ofttimes, my mother had accused me of it – far from the truth, of course, I *did* have ambition, though it related not to the attainment of high office so much as the acquisition of high knowledge. Not easy, however, without the level of protection that only wealth and position could provide.

Thus far, the Queen's patronage had given me freedom to pursue my studies but not the means, for the fingers gripping the royal purse were famously held as tight as the rectal muscles of the ducks upon the river. Having calculed, by the stars, a smiling day for her coronation, I'd hoped for secure office, but nothing had come. And if things went wrong I could soon, as Jack had warned, be dangerously out of favour. In many ways, the daggers-out world of political advancement was far simpler than mine.

We'd moved away from the beer-barge, back into the wood, but I still kept my voice down low.

'What *were* they saying?'

'About Lord Dudley? You really want to know?'

'In truth, I suspect not, but...'

'Here it is: nobody I spoke to, from the pieman to the pamphlet-seller, finks he didn't murder her. Although the pieman reckoned killing your wife to make room for the next one is only part of a great Tudor tradition, so he's just getting in some practice for his future role as—'

'Oh God, enough of this!'

'You asked.'

'Yes,' I said wearily. 'I asked.'

I'd barely seen Robert Dudley since he'd journeyed with me to Glastonbury in search of the bones of King Arthur, through which to strengthen the Queen's majesty as Arthur's spiritual successor. A quest with mixed success.

I've been hearing all about your journey to the West, she'd said on my one visit to the court since that mission. *The horrors of it! Lord Robert was so very appreciative of your assistance in this matter.*

My assistance, *Highness? That's what he said?*

John... She'd laid a white and fragrant hand on my arm. *He's told me everything.*

The lying, self-promoting *bastard.*

'He's never been mightily popular since she made him Master of the Horse, has he?' Jack Simm said. 'The lavish festivities, the arrogance, the preening.'

'Behind all that,' I said, not without doubt, 'is a man of... integrity. Who's seen much death.'

The execution of his father, the Duke of Northumberland, for the support of Jane Grey, the shortest-lived queen in history. Then his own confinement in the Tower under a death sentence, later withdrawn.

And all this time coming closer to the Queen than any man. Grown up together, locked away in the Tower at the same time during her sister's reign. Always an understanding betwixt them. And the carnal attraction. As Master of the Horse, he took her hunting. Knew how best to entertain her – make her laugh, which she loved to do. Little doubt they'd have wed. *If...*

Jack shrugged.

'Maybe he's seen so much of death, it's trivial to him now.

Man who has his wife pushed down the stairs to get his paws on the Queen—'

'Not proven.'

'Nah, and never will be after they bribe the coroner. He'll walk away in a pomander haze, but it won't make no difference, will it? Still be the dog turd on a platter of sausages. And the closer *you* are to him…'

He was right, of course. But Dudley and I went back too long. Though only a few years older, I'd been appointed by his father to teach him mathematics and the mapping of the heavens, and he it was who'd sought my astrological advice on the coronation date.

Now, in the lowest alehouses – and some higher places, too, by all accounts – they were saying John Dee had taught Lord Dudley the blackest arts of sorcery, to win the Queen for Satan.

Never underestimate the malice of the common man.

I sank my hands into the pockets of my doublet and, in one, found a hole. I could never forget that, while in Glastonbury and rendered delirious by a fever, my friend had confessed that he'd wished his wife dead.

And now she was. Found at the foot of some stairs at a house called Cumnor Place in Berkshire where she was 'staying with friends'. Dumped there by Dudley because the Queen wouldn't have wives at court. Least of all, his.

My hands felt cold. *Bess and me, we're twin souls*, Dudley had said when he was recovered from the fever. As if convinced that a marriage to the Queen was ordained by the heavens, though he'd never dared ask me to confirm it through astrology. Dear God, never in all history had there been a better reason for a man to kill his wife.

'And what's your thinking, Jack?'

Jack Simm leaned against an ash tree's bole, smiling faintly.

'*I fink*... if the Angel of the Lord come down on top of the Tower and proclaimed that Lord Dudley never done it and, while he's here, that Dr John Dee ain't a sorcerer... they'd all be waiting for his bleedin' wings to drop off.'

'Thank you, Jack.'

'Now ask me why the scryer's had to go back to the inn to warm his crystal.'

Were a shewstone to be used to reach the angelic, extensive preparation would be needed: days of purity, fasting, abstinence from alcohol. In this instance, I could think of three more practical reasons for the departure of Elias to the inn.

'He wants to ask what John Dee looks like. What apparel he wears. And if Will Faldo's brother works at the brewery. But... he's not quite a rooker, is he?'

Or, if so, certainly of a higher grade than the lowlifes who hang like ravens around the taverns of Southwark.

'Well,' Jack said, 'he did come recommended by a chaplain of the Bishop of London.'

'*Did* he now?'

A good apothecary is ever well-connected.

'Oh, he's well-patronised. That's why he costs. You still want me to ask him if he has a fine crystal to sell?'

'For... an un-named customer of yours?'

'Yea, yea. Dr John, look, he won't learn noffing at the inn. This is Mortlake and he's a stranger. They all remember your old man, whatever he done, and they like your mother. And, as long as you're welcome at court, they like you.'

'The wizard in his cave?'

'They try not to fink too hard about that. Or the owls what goes *woo woo*. But they ain't forgot when the Queen come to visit you at Candlemas, and how much the inn raked in, refreshing all the pikemen and the boys what carried the banners and the rest. Don't make light of what you done for Mortlake, Dr John.'

I shook my head, bemused.

'Just don't bleedin' ruin it now,' Jack Simm said.

V

The Ingle

A WAXING MOON's the best time for it.

This was what I'd read, and it makes good sense to anyone who has stood on the edge of a tranquil pond and observed moonlight shivering in the water. Even more to those of us who watch and chart all the bright spheres of the heavens.

Reflected light. As above, so below. To hold a perfect crystal sphere in your hands is to enclose earth and heaven.

Dear God... to what level is this the truth?

✢

The sun's last stain lay upon the river when the scryer returned with his wood-framed cloth satchel.

This time, we truly had need of the candle, and I leaned into its halo to watch him unpack his bag, carefully taking out his treasures, all swathed in layers of grey and black cloth.

'Have you eaten, Brother?' Goodwife Faldo asked.

'Goodwife,' he said softly, 'one must needs *fast* before a scrying.'

Which could be true; fasting prepares the body and keeps the spirit light and permeable. This man's pomp and solemnity continued to imply a degree of learning I'd not expected. I watched him laying out his bundles on the board, his back to the empty ingle and the door to the winder-stair.

Then I stiffened when, from the most shadowed end of our bench, Jack Simm spoke.

'And did you find Dr Dee?'

All dark in this simple, square farmhouse hall, except for the white of Jack's beard and the goodwife's coif. I felt her black cat rubbing his head against my left calf and reached down to stroke him, as if this discussion was no concern of mine. The scryer looked up, his eyes still.

'If I *were* looking for Dr Dee, I'd be disappointed. Not often here these days, it seems. Appears to spend much of his time in the Low Countries, giving lectures. When he's not at court teaching magic to the Queen.'

'So now you see,' Jack said, not looking at me, 'why us lowly folk have no dealings wiv him.'

'Though we do see his mother,' Goodwife Faldo said.

I made murmurs to the cat. Brother Elias took out the shrouded stone and set it down before him and lowered the satchel to the stones behind his stool.

'Hard to believe that bodged place is his family home.'

'They say appearances have little value for the doctor,' Jack said. 'Not a man for whom a display of wealth—'

'If wealth he has.'

'The house is very tidy inside,' Goodwife Faldo said. 'Very tidy indeed.'

'A man with neither wealth nor honour.' Elias had unwrapped a pair of eyeglasses which he balanced on the bridge of his nose without looking up. 'You'd think, given his position as the Queen's primary advisor on the Mysteries, he'd be *Sir* John by now.'

I could almost hear Jack Simm inside my head, screaming at me to say nothing.

'He's good to his mother,' Goodwife Faldo said, firm-faced.

'And she to him, apparently, Goodwife. From what I'm told, without his mother he'd have no roof over his bed.' Brother Elias chuckled absently and then looked up at last. 'But then that's no affair of mine. Let's now proceed, shall we?'

The stone lay before him, still covered. Father Elias placed his palms together above it, closed his eyes.

'*Oh, God, author of all good things, strengthen, I beseech thee, thy poor servant, that he may stand fast, without fear, through this work. Enlighten, I beseech thee, oh Lord, the dark understanding of thy creature, that his spiritual eye may be opened to see and know thine angelic spirits descending here into this crystal.*'

He laid both hands upon the shrouded stone, and my stomach tightened as if he'd touched me.

For I'd read these words, this entreaty. Written them, even.

'*Oh be sanctified and consecrated, and blessed to this purpose, that no evil phantasy may appear in thee... or, if they do gain ingress they may be constrained to speak intelligibly, and truly, and without the least ambiguity, for Christ's sake. Amen. And forasmuch as thy servant here desires neither evil treasures, nor injury to his neighbour, nor hurt to any living creature, grant him the power of descrying those celestial spirits or intelligences that may appear in this crystal...*'

My hands went cold upon my thighs below the board top. I'd translated it myself, in the past year, from unpublished writings I'd borrowed in Antwerp.

'*... and whatever good gifts, whether the power of healing* *infirmities, or of imbibing wisdom, or discovering any evil likely to afflict any person or family, or any other good gift thou mayest be pleased to bestow on me...'*

I threw a glance at Jack Simm but could not make out his eyes.

'... enable me, by thy wisdom and mercy, to use whatever I may receive to the honour of thy holy name. Grant this for thy son Christ's sake. Amen.'

'Amen,' Goodwife Faldo said faintly.

Outside, the leaves on the trees were astir, the evening shaking with the last birdsong. When the scryer bent to his bundles I now knew exactly what he'd unveil. I saw an ebony pedestal and a golden plate and knew it would carry the engraving of the divine name, *Tetragrammaton...* and the names *Michael, Gabriel, Uriel, Raphael*, the four archangels ruling over the Sun, Moon, Venus and Mercury.

A continued tightening in my chest, a cool sweat upon my face and forehead. Trithemius had written that the names and characters must be drawn in order... the names of the seven planets and angels ruling them, with their seals or characters.

Let them be all written within a double circle, with a triangle...

Silence, now, and an odd sense of sacrament. I watched Elias place the crystal, still shrouded, upon its pedestal, becoming aware of Goodwife Faldo's rapid breathing.

... this being done, thy table is complete and fit for the calling of the spirits...

I watched the scryer's hands pulling away the cloth and saw, for the first time, the sphere.

✝

What had I expected?

Scrying crystals – I'd seen some during my work abroad. But I'd been a mathematician, sometimes a teacher, sometimes a student, therefore interested only in their perfect geometry. There hadn't been *time* then to approach their deeper mysteries. Nor had I been entirely convinced of what was said of them.

A stone's just a stone.

At what point this night I became afraid, I'm not quite sure. To a scholar, fear arrives with a certain shame, akin to the shame a soldier feels, holding himself back from the heat of the fray as his comrades are cut down before him.

Not that I'd know. Unlike Dudley, I've never been a soldier, the kind of knowledge I hold having preserved me from bodily conflict. A bargain with the Crown which decrees I must stride out, wearing knowledge like armour, the questing mind thrust forward like to a sharpened blade.

Soon blunted tonight. I'd set out from my mother's house believing that my own knowledge would far exceed that of the man I was to meet. Now I knew it wasn't so and I suppose the fear came out of this. Yes, I'm a man of science and natural philosophy, skilled from years of study in mathematics, geography, celestial configuration, theology and so on. And no, I don't believe this is the End-time, far from it. In fact, signs everywhere I look are telling me that this is the beginning of a new enlightenment, an explosion of spiritual light such as the Earth hasn't seen since the days of old Greece and the ancient Egypt of thrice-great Hermes, who walked the night sky as if it were his kitchen garden.

As above, so below.

Elias's hands were lifted and, for a brief moment, it was as though the candleglow shone from the hollows of his palms.

Below them, the true source of it, a small planet of light.

It was no bigger than a cider apple. Beryl, I guessed, a gemstone which comes in several colours and the shewstone possessed all of them: now a lucent brown, like the brown of an eye, now the soft ambered pink of a woman's cheek.

It was as though the wan light had been expanded by some substance in the air, making everything more vivid, and I considered how this might be done, what theatre the scryer might employ to render us all dizzy with delusion.

I watched his plump hands as they spread apart either side of the stone, as if they were holding light like some solid object. I watched his lips forming words I could not hear and thought him to be summoning some spirit from the ether. I wanted to kill my fear by rising up and screaming at him, *Tell me its name!*

… and then time had passed, maybe faster than I knew, in a hollow of muttering and liturgy, and Elias was whispering, not to me but to Goodwife Faldo.

'Hold out your hand.'

When she held it up, hesitant, he reached out quickly and seized her wrist and pulled her into the light, and I half-rose, fearing for some reason that he would feed her fingers into the candle flame.

But his own hand fell away, and hers stayed in the air, as if held there by strong light. As if detached from Goodwife Faldo at the elbow. Had she met his eyes? Did he have the ability, which I've marked in others, to hold her in thrall?

Or even all of us. I shook myself, blinking wildly, fearing that long minutes may have passed in a state where my senses were not my own. I saw that the scrying stone was duller now but seeming to quiver, like to a toad, on the boardtop, and I didn't notice that the ringless hand had gone until I heard Jack Simm draw breath, sharply, as if aware of an alteration in the air.

Did I feel that, too? Maybe. I found I was gazing not at the shewstone but into the ingle, where a fire of logs and coal would soon be lit that would last all winter long. The warm core of the house where a stewpot would hang, the air pungent with cooking herbs grown by Jack Simm and the mellow crusting of bread in the side-oven.

But now, in this thin, uncertain, peripheral time between seasons, it was only a mean cavern of ill-dressed rubble-stone, and cold.

A cold reaching out of the ingle along with a stillness which could be felt, like to the rancid, waxen stillness of a stone chapel where a corpse lies before burial.

I liked it not. I tell myself I don't fear death, but the presence of the dead conveys no sense of peace to me, and there can be no beauty without life.

Clack.

Something wooden falling to the floor.

A stool. Rolling away under the board, and the cat rushed between my ankles and I heard a poor cry, of the kind made without breath, and saw that Goodwife Faldo was backed against the wall by the shuttered window. Her face shadow-lined and stretched in agony, her coif dragged back, and she was pointing at the maw of the ingle and whimpering like an infant.

As if in another world, the hands of Elias were held apart, two inches from the globe, as though his fingers were bathed within its aura.

He said, with mild curiosity, 'Tell me what you see, Goodwife.'

I followed her wretched gaze, heard her hoarsened voice.

'Death.'

'In what form?'

'Oh my dear Lord!'

Both hands over her face, peering through her fingers, the candleglow cold as a haloed moon.

Her voice was held in my head and then faded as if it had lain down and died there. Panicked, I lurched to my feet and tried to follow her gaze into the ingle. All I saw there was packed rubblestone fading into the blackness of soot.

Nothing more.

Nothing. Jesu, have I ever felt more worthless than when I stood there, sightless, hearing the returning voice of Goodwife Faldo, an arid panting.

'Does this mean death for us? Oh please God, make it go away. *Please God, Father, I've two sons!*'

One moment, her body was bowed over in anguish upon a sob, and then she was twisting around, squirming upright and stumbling into the ingle where I could hear her fumbling about and then the muffled clang of the bread oven's door.

When she emerged, her hands were clasped together as if she held a baby bird. Holding it out to Elias, hands shaking.

'Please,' she whispered. 'I beg mercy, Brother. I've sinned.'

Her shadow skating on the wall, she opened out her hands and the ring clinked upon the board next the crystal.

Goodwife Faldo, scrabbling after it, shoulders still hunched and heaving. Snatching it up and ramming it on her finger.

Losing her coif as she tumbled away across the room and dragged the shutters wide to expose the purpling dusk.

VI

Cousin

IT WAS LIKE to the air after a storm has blown itself out. The candle extinguished, the hall draped in a drabness of brown and grey. I felt weakened in a way I could not have anticipated, and saw faces everywhere, staring in from the unshuttered window and over the threshold where the door had been flung wide.

And one was my mother's.

Jane Dee stepping through the doorway, dark-gowned, full of a fury seldom seen and so not easily dismissed.

'*Your* doing!'

'Mother—'

'What have you *caused*?'

A tall woman of sixty years, admirably unbowed by circumstance, but ever dismayed by what I did and pained that my meagre earnings were spent more on books than repairs to the house my late tad had half-built.

However, Jane Dee was never more formidable than when bleeding from another's wound.

'Goodwife Faldo's in bitter distress.'

'Yes,' I said tightly. 'I know.'

'What have you brought into her house? You tell me, *now*, John, what have you *done*?'

We were alone. Goodwife Faldo had not returned, and I looked around for Elias, but he too was gone, along with Jack Simm and the shadowed faces at the open door and the window. Some of them melting away upon the arrival of my mother, who, like my father, had been a good Catholic but now mistrusted the miraculous.

Was it? Was the miraculous ever so mean, cold and squalid as what seemed to have happened here this night?

'On second thought, don't tell me,' my mother said.

I let go a sigh.

'It's gone, anyway.'

As if I knew. As if I was in any position to state that what I'd never seen was now no more. But my shivers recalled the deep bone-cold which no fire can reach because it's forever beyond this life, beyond the air that we breathe. And I did not want to look again into the ingle. And see nothing.

'... believing her family will perish for her sins,' my mother was saying.

'Any sin this night,' I said, almost angrily, 'is mine.'

'John,' she said sadly. 'As if I didn't know that.'

The way she'd spoken to me when I was six years old.

'Mother,' I said wearily, 'I beg mercy, but it wasn't—'

'Don't beg mine, beg hers.'

'Yes... yes, I'll do that.'

Gladly, for Goodwife Faldo was a good and generous woman, and I must needs make it clear to her that there was nothing for her to fear. And would have tried to explain it to my mother if I'd thought that, for one silent minute, she'd listen.

It had been no more than we'd deserved. I knew that now and profoundly regretted involving Goodwife Faldo in this

32

conceit. Even the protective prayers intoned by Brother Elias would have been ineffective because our sitting was built upon deception. Any summoning not grounded in full honesty attracts only that which thrives on lies, confusion and all the lower longings of humanity which remain undissolved by death.

And I knew I'd get no sleep this night if I'd failed to find out what form it had taken. What they'd all seen and I – *Oh, blood of Christ* – had not.

'Here.' My mother drew something from a fold of her gown. 'This was delivered.'

Placing on the board a thin letter with a seal which – Oh my God – I recognised at once. I picked it up and knew the paper.

Of all the times for *this* to be delivered...

'Mother, when did this arrive?'

'Not ten minutes ago. It's why I was coming to find you... amid all the clamour and upset.'

I carried the letter to the window and broke the seal, tension quickening my blood as, in the fading light, I read,

Dr Dee
There is a need to speak with you on behalf of our Cousin.
My barge will dock in Mortlake tomorrow at eight

Unsigned, yet I knew, my heart all aquake, that it was from Mistress Blanche Parry, my elder cousin on my father's side. But that the cousin referred to in the letter was someone to whom neither of us was related. This term had been used before to disguise the identity of she whom Blanche served as

Senior Gentlewoman. It was significant that this was far from a formal missive. It meant I was to be consulted in confidence.

'Mother, the messenger... he's not waiting for a reply?'

My mother, who also knew that seal, shook her head and then found a strained smile – any kind of summons to court would renew her hopes of me finding a stable income. She was of good family and had barely spoke to me for a week after I turned down the offer of a permanent lecturer's post at Oxford.

'I shall go now, John – left too quickly, with neither cloak nor lamp. You'd best come home. When you've brought your... small comfort to Goodwife Faldo.'

When she was gone, I took several long breaths and then knelt before the ingle. Alone here now and held in dread, for all my book-fed knowledge, of what I could not see, I said a fervent prayer to banish all unwanted spirits from this house. And then, espying under the window the coif shed by Goodwife Faldo, I picked it up and left.

This end of the village was quiet now, the sky pricked with first stars over the darkening river which linked us, better than any road, with London. I wondered if it would be Mistress Blanche in that barge tomorrow, or the Queen herself.

Then turned, knowing where the Goodwife would be.

✝

St Mary's, Mortlake, is a modern church, towered but without steeple – a misjudgement in my view, for a steeple conducts to earth divers rays from the firmament. When worshipping

34

here, however, I tend to keep opinions like this to myself. A wisehead is seldom welcome in the house of God.

A single candle was lit upon the high altar, Goodwife Faldo bent in mute prayer on the lowest chancel step. I walked quietly along the aisle and knelt alongside her, leaving a seemly distance betwixt us.

I held out the coif. Marking the dawning of grey in the strands of her freed hair, a sheen of tears on her cheeks as she looked up at me, a pale smile flickering in the candlelight.

'Why can we never leave well alone, Dr John?'

Tucking her hair into the white linen. I knew what she meant, but the idea of it was well beyond the imagining of a man who lives only to meddle.

'It's gone,' I said, hoping to God I was right. 'All gone now.'

'Where?'

A good question, but this was hardly the time or place to serve up a treatise on the nature of the middle sphere.

'Back into the stone,' I said. 'And the stone is back in the scryer's bag. Where it should have stayed.'

'Oh fie, Dr John!' Lifting herself to the second step, which she sat upon. 'The first mention of it by Master Simm, and I was hooked like an eel.'

She gazed beyond me, into the darkness of the nave.

'When I was a child, I loved to go into church and feel it all closing around me. I felt cloaked in colours... and the sweetness of the incense. And all the Latin, like to the sound of spells being uttered. More... more magic than I could hold.'

'Yes.'

The church had been all about magic, then, if we'd but known it.

35

'And then the King made God smaller,' Goodwife Faldo said.

I looked at her with an admiration that surprised me. Her tear-streaked face shone like an apple in the warm candle-light. I turned quickly away and looked up at the long panes in the stained window above the altar. Bright coloured glass reduced by the night to the dull hues of turned earth.

'Don't let them stop you, Dr John.'

'Who?'

'The Puritans, the Bible men. They're taking hold. Get one of *them* as king and the world will be a grey place.'

'This Queen won't see that happen. The Queen loves magic and wonder.'

'Yes. So we're told. But she must have care. As must you. Small people like me – no-one cares any more what we believe, as long as we turn up at church on a Sunday and say the right words. I wouldn't be taken away any more for letting a scryer into my house. Would I?'

'Frances,' I said. 'What did you see?'

'I lost my mind.'

'I don't think so.'

'There was a change in the air such as I've never felt since I was a child.'

'There was. I felt it.'

'The presence of something that wasn't... I can't put it into the best words, I'm only a farmer's wife and I don't read very well, and I...'

'Tell me.'

'I'd hid the ring in the bread oven. And of a sudden I felt a terrible guilt about that, as if it was the worst thing I'd ever done. As if I'd lied to God. And it came into my head that I must face a terrible penance. And the worst of all penance to me would be...'

Holding back tears.

'The loss of your family,' I said.

She nodded.

'And that was when I saw the figure of a pale man. Not clear at first – as though made of dust motes. The bones... the bones were more solid and had their own—'

She shuddered. I looked for her eyes.

'Bones?'

'The bones had their own awful light. As though it were *not* light.'

'Where were these bones?'

'He was holding them. One in each hand, clasped to his chest. Death... death's heads.'

'Skulls? More than one?'

'How can I ever sit before that hearth again?'

'You can. It won't happen again, Goodwife. Not there. Not ever again. None of it' – Putting it all together in my head as I spoke – 'none of it was real. Only pictures conjured from the crystal, which... held us all in thrall. Changed your head around so that you took your worst fears and made them into... pictures.'

She nodded, yet uncertain.

'Ephemeral,' I said firmly. 'Illusion. Nothing was there. You didn't lie to God. Only to the scryer. And you admitted it to him. You put things right.'

It took away the magic, but I felt it was what she wanted to hear at this moment.

'And there's been no plague this summer,' I said.

Watching myself forming words while I was somewhere else. Somewhere grey and foetid and full of bones.

'I feel so much calmer now,' Goodwife Faldo said and laughed lightly. 'Thank you, Dr John.'

VII

Coincidence and Fate

MORTLAKE HIGH STREET. Sticky, blurred lantern-light, echoes of the cackle and whoop of roistering from the inn and, presently, the spatter of piss against a wall.

No place to look up at the stars or the new-born moon.

After walking Goodwife Faldo to her door, I should have gone home and slept, to be refreshed and fully sentient at the riverside on the morrow. But how could I sleep now?

The inn was ahead of me. Recently extended to offer five bedchambers, two with glass in their windows for the moneyed traveller, but yet a rough place after dark. I slowed my steps, recalling a night when, for no clear reason, I'd been given a beating by men unknown to me, although it was clear they knew who I was. *Smash the conjurer down. Smash him down in the name of God!*

Soft footsteps behind me and I turned. A light shining out in my path, and I froze into stillness as it rose level with my face.

'Go quietly, Dr John.'

'Jack.'

He carried one of the candle lanterns you could borrow from the inn if you were deemed sober enough to remember where to return it.

I said, 'Where is he?'

'Abed, I assume.'

'Then I'll wake him up.'

'No need,' Jack said. 'We shared half a jug of small beer in the back room.'

'And?'

'He said it happens. On occasion, when the stone's active, spirits that manifest in the crystal can be... fetched out of it and into the air.'

'Astral forms?'

'Apparitions. Creatures of the air. The scryer must never allow himself to become distracted by them. That's their aim, he says. To distract him. All they seek's attention. His, anyway.'

He gestured back up the street and I followed him back towards the church. We stood in the shadow of the coffin gate, where Jack put the lamp on the ground.

'Elias has a reputation, going back to days as a novice at Wenlock Priory. Up towards Shrewsbury?'

'Yes.'

'Where he... caused some concern.' Jack paused, sniffed. 'Visions.'

I said nothing, and he began to rhyme them off, without emphasis, as if listing ingredients for a stew.

'Holy martyrs stepping from the stained glass. Noises in the night. Words mysteriously etched on the walls of locked chambers. Cracks in statues. Well, this was the time of the Reform. Not what anybody wanted, then. So when the abbot finks about maybe having him exorcised, he's off. Takes to the road. Where the gift of vision, once kept under the board, becomes his living.'

40

'Evidently a good one.'

'When he fetches up in London, sure.'

'Where he has patronage?'

If he was recommended to Jack by a chaplain to the Bishop of London, might that not mean he had the protection of the bishop himself?

'Somebody's looking out for him, that's for sure,' Jack said.

I picked up the lantern and asked, because I had to,

'What did *you* see this night? What did you see in the ingle?'

No reply. Back down the street, some man was retching.

'Jack—'

'Ah, how can we ever know?'

'What did Elias see in the crystal?'

'Wasn't a ring, that's for sure. Look, he wouldn't talk about it and I didn't want to come over too pushy. He says it don't matter what he sees, he never questions it. He's only the middleman.'

'And *you* saw...?'

'Me? I dunno... bones? Hazy grey man-shape, wiv bones. I didn't like it.'

'Marked?' I said urgently, before I could stop myself. 'Marked here?' Snatching up the lantern, holding it to my face and raising fingers to my cheeks. 'And here?'

'Keep your bleedin' voice down. Marked how?'

'Black lumps. As seen in places where sheep are farmed, wool gathered...'

Hell, I knew this was a far cry from scientific inquiry, that the last thing I should do was prompt him. But I was tired and overwound.

'Who you got in mind, Dr John?'

41

'There *was* a man I met in Glastonbury. A trader in what he claimed were holy relics. But they were just old bones. He had hundreds of bones. If they were digging up a graveyard for more burials he'd be there with his bag. In the end, he was able to give me the intelligence I needed about the bones of Arthur. This was just before he died. Of… of wool-sorters' disease. Face full of foul black spots.'

Benlow the boneman. I recalled, with a sick tremor, how this man, an obvious buck-hunter, had tried to attach himself to me. *Never thought I'd meet a man as famous as you, my lord.*

'He wanted to come to London. Wanted me to bring him back with me. I… may have… implied that this would be possible.'

'You made a bargain wiv him?'

'I suppose I was in his debt. But if he thought we had a bargain… it was one I couldn't keep.'

Benlow crouching amid the smashed shelves of his grisly warehouse, having attempted, in his agony, to take his own life by cutting his wrists and his throat, but too weak. Dying eventually surrounded by the detritus of death, the bones he'd offered for sale as relics of the saints. A rooker in every sense, but in the end I'd felt pity for him and some measure of guilt.

And now he haunted me? Wanting me to know he was there, even though I could not see him – worse, it seemed to me, than if I could. The injustice mocked me daily – the learned bookman, heaven's interpreter, cursed by a poverty of the spirit. I knew more about the engines of the Hidden than any man in England, but I could not *see* except, on occasion, in dreams.

And maybe in a scryer's crystal?

I looked up at the night sky, in search of familiar geometry, but it had clouded over and there were neither stars nor moon.

'Jack… erm… did you, by chance, ask him…?'

'Where one might be obtained? A shewstone? Course I asked him.'

'But?'

'It ain't simple, Dr John. And it ain't cheap.'

☦

Brother Elias had said there was always a few around, but most of them were of little value to a scryer, full of flaws and impurity. The more perfect of them were hard to come by and cost more than a court banquet.

'And might be dangerous,' Jack Simm said.

'How?'

'For a novice, he meant. The more perfect ones have been used by men of power. A man what's never scryed might find himself driven into madness. It would take a man of knowledge and instinct to… deal wiv what it might… bring into the world.'

'Hmm.'

'A responsibility. Laden wiv obligation – *his* words.'

'Of course.'

'Like to a wife,' Jack said. 'You must take it to your bed.'

'Go to!'

'I'm telling you what he *said*. There must needs be a close bond 'twixt the crystal and the scryer, so you might sleep wiv it under your bolster. Bit bleedin' lumpy, if you ask me, but monks is fond of discomfort.'

There was logic here. Crystal possesses strangely organic

43

qualities; crystal spheres change, grow, in response to unseen influences. The stone in the Faldos' hall this night, the way its colours changed, the way it seemed to tremble or crouch like a toad...

Ripples in my spine.

'Oft-times you don't choose the stone,' Jack said. 'The stone chooses you. He said the right one might come along when you ain't looking for it.'

'And does he have one he might sell?'

'Reckons he's offered crystal stones wherever he goes, but most of 'em's flawed and there's – aw, Jesu, I could see this coming a mile off – apart from his own, there's only one other he's coveted in years. Odd that, ain't it?'

'Go on...'

'The kind you don't find anywhere in Europe. Maybe a treasure from some ancient people of the west. A history of miracles and healing. But the man who has it, he'll want a fair bit more gold than Brother Elias could put his hands on. And Brother Elias, if I don't insult you here, Dr John, is a richer man than you.'

'Jack,' I said sadly, '*you* are a richer man than me. Where did he see it?'

'Abbey of Wigmore. Not a long ride from Wenlock, out on the rim of Wales. That's where he *said* he seen it.'

I did know of this abbey. It was close, in fact, to where my father was born. Dissolved now, of course.

'Was it your impression that Elias might be an agent for whoever has the stone?'

'Could be. Told him I was inquiring for a regular customer. But I reckon he knows.'

44

'He was certainly asking questions about the extent of my wealth,' I said. 'Maybe he thinks I keep it abroad.'

'Whatever, it don't give me a good feeling. He ain't a rooker in the normal sense, but it's all too much like... coincidence and fate.'

I knew what he was saying, but I was in a profession which dismissed neither fate nor coincidence, only sought the science behind them.

'Who owns the stone?'

'He was being close on that, but I had the impression it was the last abbot. Gone now, obviously, and the abbey passed through the Crown and into private hands long ago.'

'Easy enough to find out whose. But the abbott – is he even in the vicinity any more?'

'*Blind me*, you don't bleedin' listen do you, Dr John? You could sell your house and put your mother on the streets and you still couldn't afford it. I don't understand none of this. I don't see why the scrying stone – any scrying stone – is suddenly become so important for you. They've been around forever. Why now?'

Above the coffin gate, a single planet – the great Jupiter, inevitably – had found a hole in the nightcloud, as if to remind me of my insignificance and the pointlessness of concealment. I could sit on the truth of this matter, keep it to myself, take it to my grave...

'Because— *Oh God,* because the study of its properties, notably in the matter of communion with angels, was... suggested to me.'

'By whom?'

'Is it not obvious?'

Jupiter seemed to pulse as if sending signals to me and was transformed into the sun in the pure glass of a tall window in a book-lined chamber at the Palace of Greenwich, where a light, merry voice was asking me had I thought of *this*, and had I looked into *that*?

'Bugger,' Jack said. 'That's *all* you need.'

I hear the French king consults one owned by the seer, Nostradamus, which is of immense benefit in planning campaigns. And winning the support of the angels. Do you have a shewstone of your own, John? Will it give us communion with the angels?

Well... obviously, I do, Highness, and intend to spend some time assessing its capabilities, but...

Perhaps worth more attention, John, don't you think?

'Jesu, Dr John,' Jack Simm said. 'You really know how to put yourself between heaven and hell and a pile of shite.'

'We all walk a cliff-edge,' I said.

'She'll forget, though, won't she? She got too much to worry about.'

I blinked Jupiter away. Of course the Queen would not forget. Unless by design, she forgot nothing.

'Yea, well...' Jack Simm tossed the heel of a hand into my shoulder. 'Leave it alone, eh?'

'I fear I shall have to,' I said.

'Good.' He picked up his lantern. 'It's a wasp's nest. Go to your bed and fink not of ghosts.'

I nodded, resigned. This was not a night to remember with satisfaction, not in any respect.

'Thank you,' I said. 'But—'

'Just... *piss off*, Dr John!'

I nodded. Passed through the coffin gate to the churchyard and the path to our house.

Even made it up to the rickety, stilted terrace before turning around to make sure I was not followed by the sickly shade of Benlow the boneman.

How much easier we could all sleep, now that Lutheran theologians had assured us that, with the abolition of purgatory, ghosts were no longer permitted to exist.

VIII

Favoured

THAT NIGHT IT rained hard and my sleep was scorched by dreams.

Lately, I'd been welcoming journeys through the inner spheres and would keep paper and ink at my bedside to write down their substance upon awakening. But these... these I made no notes upon, because I dreamed not, as I'd feared, of Benlow the Boneman...

...but – *oh God* – of Eleanor Borrow with her green eyes and her soft body so close that I could feel its eager heat and had thrown out my arms in a feral desire. One of the few dreams I'd wished never to awake from, even if it meant, God help me, embracing death.

But I had, of course, awoken at once, and Nel's warm body was gone to cold air, as if she'd been no more than a succubus, some siren of sleep sent to taunt me. I may have cried out in my anguish. In the pallid dawn only the pain in my heart was real. For, since Nel in Glastonbury, I'd not lain with a woman. And, before her, never at all.

It would have been wrong to feel a bitterness about this, for my waking life had been given over to study. My father had not oft-times been a wealthy man. He'd been proud to see me at Cambridge at the age of fourteen and, in order to repay him sooner, I'd eschewed strong drink, carousing and even sleep.

And now my poor tad was disgraced and dead and, while my scholar's knowledge of mathematics and the stars had brought me some small fame in the universities of Europe, in England I was regarded by many as little more than—

Jesu! I rolled from my bed in a rush of anger.

—as little more than a rooker myself. I had few friends, not much money and no wife.

And oh, how my perception of this last condition had changed. The hollow emptiness of the single man's life was something I'd never felt before my time with Nel. A constant raw longing which, for virtually all my sentient years, had applied only to knowledge.

Dear God, what am I become?

✝

At the breakfast board, my mother said, 'The hole in the roof that you attempted to mend last week is a hole once more.'

Holding up the painted cloth which had hung in the hall. Soaked through, now.

I closed my eyes, with some weariness. She'd probably been up since well before dawn, preparing sweetmeats with Catherine, her only servant. Making sure the house was as fit as ever it could be to welcome the woman closest to the Queen.

Hardly for the first time, I felt a strong pity for my mother. Something in that terse letter had told me it was unlikely that Blanche would even leave her barge this day. Just as with the visits of the Queen, all my mother's work would be wasted.

49

'It's been a summer of endless rain,' I said, 'And I've never pretended to be any kind of builder. Builders are... men we should employ. When the money's there.'

'When the money's there' – My mother's voice was flat – 'you buy more books.'

I tore off a lump of bread. It was true enough. But I *needed* books, and all the knowledge therein, and more. All the knowledge that was *out there*. Needed to be ahead of the others, or what hope was there for us?

'Another winter's coming.' My mother pulled her robe close about her and came out with what clearly had long been in her mind. 'By the end of the summer, I'd rather expected you to have been... favoured.'

There could be no happy reply to this. I suppose I also had expected... well, *something*, by now. Not necessarily a knight-hood – Sir William Cecil, as the Queen's chief minister, inevitably would advise against the ennoblement of a man still considered by many to be a common conjurer.

What I needed, far more than social status, was a secure supply of money. Oft-times, the Queen had sent for me and would receive me pleasantly, and we'd talk for two or more hours about the nature of things. If she truly valued what I provided, both as an astrologer and a cabalist, then surely something with a moderate income would not be out of order... something to replace the rectorate of Upton-upon-Severn, awarded by the short-lived King Edward only be to taken away in Mary's time.

More than a year and a half had passed since Elizabeth's coronation, held on a day calculed by me, according to the stars, as heralding a rewarding reign. And such, for the most part, it had been.

Until the death of Amy, wife of Dudley.

I rose, brushing a few crumbs from my fresh doublet and the ridiculous Venetian breeches my mother had had made by a woman in the village. There was nearly an hour to spare before Blanche's barge was due, but, almost certainly, she'd be early. A severe and efficient woman, my cousin, and usually disapproving of me.

Until she wanted something.

+

My mother had insisted I should be at the riverside over half an hour before the royal barge was due to arrive from Richmond Palace. But, as I had no wish to draw attention to what I guessed would be a discreet visit, I used the time to go to the inn to leave a letter for the post rider.

My dream of Nel had reminded me of the journeyman mapper, John Leland, who might have been her father, and I'd gone into my library early this morning and taken down his *Itinerary* to confirm that Wigmore Abbey was within a few miles of my tad's birth-home, Nant-y-groes. With this in mind, it had seemed worth writing to my cousin, Nicholas Meredith, who lived in the nearest small town.

I'd never been to the town or met Nicholas Meredith but had received a letter of congratulation from him after the Queen's coronation on the date calculed by me – this being widely spoken of at the time. We'd exchanged a few letters since, so I felt able to ask him, in confidence, if he knew anything of the present whereabouts of the former Abbot of Wigmore, whom I wished to consult on a matter of anti-quarian interest.

It had been madness to lie to the Queen about owning a shewstone and the only fortuitous aspect of the current turbulence at court was that she hadn't asked me to bring it to her. Yet.

I hear the French king consults one owned by the seer, Nostradamus.

Hmm. It seemed unlikely that the crystal consulted by the well-favoured and undoubtedly wealthy Nostradamus would be the kind of minuscule, flawed mineral that *I* could afford. I'd wondered if I might see Brother Elias at the inn and if it might be worth revealing my identity in hope of learning more about the Wigmore stone. It was a relief, I suppose, to find he'd gone at first light. Which left only one other man in London who might know of the stone or at least be able to direct me to someone who did. Maybe I could see him tomorrow – for at least I knew where *he* was.

The river lay brown and morose under dour cloud, wherries busy, as I waited at the top of the stone steps. A black barge was moored where the beer had been loaded yesterday, several men sitting in it as if waiting for cargo. But the river traffic was nearly all London-bound. No sign of flags or the glint of helm and pike blade. Nor, I guessed, would there be.

My poor mother. I looked back towards the house, my only home now, and thought I marked her face, all blurred in the window of her parlour. River water lay in shallow pools around the stilts supporting the parlour and hall. Far from the most distinguished dwelling, this, even in Mortlake.

Saddening to think that several properties had once been owned by my father, who had first come to London as a wool merchant, progressing to the import and export of cloth. This was before his appointment as gentleman server to the King, who also made him packer of goods for export – and that paid a good income. Oh, an important man, my tad, for a while. Until the financial collapse which left him with a cluster of riverside outbuildings bought cheaply and linked together to form a most eccentric dwelling which yet looked temporary.

From the river steps I could see, to one side of the house, the orchard and the small pasture rented for crumbs to William Faldo. It was yet my aim to use part of it to extend the house for further accommodation of my library – consisting at this time of two hundred and seventy-seven books, many of them the only editions to be found anywhere in England. I'd offered them to the Queen and to Queen Mary before her, for the foundation of a national library of England. But a monarch would ever rather spend money on war than learning. Unless, of course, it was the kind of learning that might effectively be used in war.

One thing was sure. If there was no improvement in my situation, then, God help me, I might have to sell books to repair the roof and find work teaching the sons of whichever of the moneyed gentry were prepared to employ an infamed conjurer.

'Dr Dee?'

Two men had climbed from the black barge at the river's edge and were approaching the steps. I was fairly sure I knew them not and made no reply.

'Sent to fetch you, Doctor.'

'Oh?'

Naturally, I was wary. I'd heard of men who'd been taken aboard such vessels as this, robbed and killed for their valuables and their remains thrown in the river. And no, the irony was not lost on me.

I didn't move. When the first of them reached the top step, I saw that he was young, small-bearded and well-clad, in rusted doublet, high leather boots and good gloves. He looked impatient.

'The circumstances of your appointment have now been changed, Doctor.'

'My appointment?'

He let a low breath through his teeth.

'Mistress Blanche… has been called away to attend to the Queen's majesty but expects to be free to speak to you by the time we reach Greenwich.'

'I see.'

'Well then…?'

He stood aside, extending an arm to where his companions and the oarsmen waited in the black barge. I had no choice but to follow him down the steps. At the bottom, he stood back while I boarded the barge, and then leapt in after me, and the oarsmen pushed us hastily from the bank.

Too hastily, it seemed to me. I yet felt all was not right and stood close to the bow of the vessel.

'Sit down, please, Doctor,' the young man said.

It sounded more like an instruction than an invitation, but there were good cushions to sit on. Though hardly luxurious, this clearly was not a cargo barge, and I was not alarmed until, as we moved downriver towards the steaming midden of Southwark, it was steered sharply away from another barge coming out of London towards Mortlake.

This one had no flags, but there were at least seven armed

men aboard. And one woman, subduedly cloaked and gazing ahead of her.

When I thought to hail my cousin and half-rose, I heard movement behind me and, twisting round, I saw the first man reaching to his belt.

'Either you hold your tongue at this moment, Dr Dee,' he said pleasantly, 'or I must needs slice it off at the root.'

PART TWO

I have no way to purge myself of
the malicious talk that I know the
wicked world will use

ROBERT DUDLEY, in a letter to

his steward Thomas Blount

IX

The Summoning of Siôn Ceddol

Autumn, 1560. The Welsh Border.

MY FATHER GREW up in a modest farmhouse below the hill called Brynglas, at Pilleth on the border of England and Wales – the Welsh side.

The house, Nant-y-groes, is now the home of Stephen Price who, until recently, was Member of Parliament for this area, thus spending much time in London. More than was necessary, if truth be known, for Master Price was much taken with the excitement of London life and, on his increasingly infrequent returns home, would tend to find the place of his birth rather dull and – for the first time – strange.

Now he's home for good. Fighting the drabness of his life with ambitious plans for his farm, but finding that life at Pilleth soon brings out the negative aspects of his essentially choleric temperament.

He's dismayed, for example, when the village men won't help him build his new barn. He has – intentionally, perhaps – forgotten how, below Brynglas, even the most commonplace activity is oft-times governed by custom and ritual.

'I *can't*,' he says, when Pedr Morgan, the shepherd, tentatively offers him advice. 'I'm supposed to be— I *am* the *squire*.' He twists away. 'Anyway, the boy's the lowest kind of idiot. I can hardly be seen to consult an idiot before initiating something as fundamental as building a barn.'

Master Price likes to use some of the longer words he picked up in Parliament. This will not last.

Pedr Morgan shrugs his scrawny shoulders, no doubt wishing he were somewhere else – this is common on Brynglas at twilight.

'It's just what he does,' Morgan says, uncomfortable. 'You knows how it is.'

'I know how it *was*,' Master Price says with resignation. 'Well, my thanks to you, Morgan, but I'll have men brought in from Off. Local boys don't want my money, that's their choice, ennit?'

Pedr Morgan nods. He won't press the matter and won't be telling anybody what Master Price has said about Siôn Ceddol. Has no wish to stir up resentment against his master, but, hell, it must be some Godless place, that London. Sodom and Gomorrah and London, that's how the new rector puts it. The rector's this bone-faced Bible-man, and he doesn't like Siôn Ceddol either, and that's not good *at all*… for the rigid attitudes of a bone-faced Bible man will never bend.

Stephen Price stamps irritably away, and Pedr Morgan, thin and tired, most of his hair gone before its time, looks down to where his wife is waiting by the bridge with their three young children. She won't follow him up the slope of Brynglas at close of day, any more than she'll pass the earthen grave of the old dead. Even the sheep flee this hill before sunset.

And Price *knows* all that, at the bottom of him. But he's been away too many times. He's seen the shining towers of the future, and the future looks not like Pilleth. None of the fine towns he's

seen on his travels has risen out of old fear and clinging superstition. This can lead only to a mortal decay – the decay that
Pilleth wears like a rancid old coat which no one must tear from
its body lest the body itself falls away into rotten strips.

Pedr Morgan raises a hand to tell his wife he's coming down,
then turns briefly towards the church of St Mary, set into the
hill halfway up, and crosses himself as he always does.

Except when the rector's there.

✛

I suppose I too was inclined to be dismissive and superior
when my father spoke of his birthplace, putting on the accents
which, he would say, might vary from country English to
country Welsh within a mile.

For I was younger then and deep into my studies of
Mathematics and Greek and the works of Euclid and Plato.
Convinced that all knowledge and wisdom came from the
Classical world, long gone. Unaware of the rivers of the divine
and the demonic which rush invisibly through and around
places like Pilleth.

And I suppose my tad's fond memories of the border were
shaped around the knowledge that he was unlikely ever to be
going back.

✛

A month has passed. Stephen Price has new cattle in the lower
field, the first frosts cannot be far off. Yet only foundations for
the new barn have been dug – painfully and laboriously by
himself and his sons, assisted fearfully by the servants at Nant-
y-groes.

To his fury, Price has failed to recruit skilled labour in Presteigne, the prosperous assize town a few miles from here – every man he's approached claiming an obligation to work elsewhere or some affliction that renders him incapable of heavy labour.

It's those great shelves of rock, found less than a foot down, that finished it. After three long days of struggle and the wrenching of a muscle in his back, he finally walks out to find Pedr Morgan, the shepherd.

Grumpily requesting him to talk to Mistress Ceddol about the employment of her damned brother.

He says nothing to his wife who, during his time as an MP, preferred to live down the valley with his older brother's family. Joan doesn't like it here and probably hopes that all his plans will fail so they don't have to stay.

☩

On the morning Siôn Ceddol comes, the land appears luminous, the shaven hay-meadows all aglisten from the rain following a thunderstorm which broke over Radnor Forest in the early hours, awakening the whole wide valley before dawn.

The strangeness soon becomes apparent to Stephen Price. It's as though the summoning of Siôn Ceddol has set into a motion some ancient engine.

People come, as if to prepare the way. First to appear is the new Rector of Pilleth, full-robed and carrying his prized copy of the New English Prayerbook. Arriving at sun-up, he stands alone in the shorn grass, the prayer book open in his twiggy hands. His lips are seen to be moving although his voice is so hushed, rapid and intense that nobody hears the substance of it. Approaching him, as he knows must be expected of him, Price is wishing to God that Father Walter had not died when he did. Father Walter was no papist but he understood the ways of Pilleth.

The rector's look would turn fresh apples black.

'That *you*, of all men,' he says, 'would bend a knee to Satan...'

'And you'd have all my cattle dead by Christmas, would you, Rector?'

'If God wills it.'

If God wills it, Price thinks, feeling his face redden, *likely we'll have a new rector by All Souls Day.*

Stephen Price stands his ground. For all he dismisses superstition, he carries no candles for a God with all the pity of a Norman baron.

After a few minutes, the rector throws back his bony head and, with the book under an arm, walks stiffly away in the direction of the hillside church. At the same time, villagers begin appearing on the boundaries of Stephen Price's ground, like the risen dead.

'Master Stephen... he's yere.'

The housekeeper, Clarys, at his elbow. A woman who was at Nant-y-groes long before Stephen Price and may even have been known to my tad. Clarys nods towards the lower gate that gives entrance to the Presteigne road and the river bridge. Two figures stand behind it, male and female.

Stephen Price raises a weary hand towards the gate and beckons once before thrusting the hand away, embarrassed. When the two people pass through, one is walking an irregular path, watching the ground, like a dog responding to a scent.

It's the first time Stephen Price has seen Siôn Ceddol. He doesn't even know how the boy and his sister came to be in Pilleth village. They seem to have arrived during one of his periods in London, the mad boy apparently receiving the blessing of Mother Marged, the wise woman, before her death.

Through the sunhaze, he marks a scrawny boy of some sixteen years, wearing an ill-fitting jerkin and a red hat. When the boy reaches the platter of land on which the barn is marked out, he stops and turns the hat around on his head and sniffs the air like some wary animal. Never once looking at Stephen Price or anyone, and when he speaks it's only to the woman with him and is neither in English nor Welsh, but some language of his own which ranges from mumbling to screams and yelps, like to a fox. Price has been told that many people believe this to be a faerie language.

Yet are drawn to him, it's said, like night-moths to a taper. Already the people on the southern boundary hedge number twenty or more, watching the idiot boy pacing rapid circles in the grass.

'This is madness,' Price mutters.

Drawing a sharp look from the one person here who appears to understand what Siôn Ceddol is saying.

Anna Ceddol, the boy's sister. Who speaks both English and Welsh and also, it seems, faerie. She's approaching twenty-nine years and unmarried – because of her brother, obviously. An old maid in waiting. Their parents are dead, she's all he has. And who would have the mad boy?

And so no one has her. Which is a crime against all creation, Price thinks, marking how lovely she is, in a way not of her class. Head held high, hair brushed back and eyes wide open, unafraid to the point of insolence.

'What's he doing?' Stephen Price demands of her.

Speaking roughly, no doubt to ride over a surging of desire – as Siôn Ceddol teeters on the edge of the nearest of the foundation trenches and then jumps down into it.

'Wait,' Anna Ceddol says. 'If you please, Master Price.'

And so they all wait, Stephen Price and his sons behind him and his servants behind them, as Siôn Ceddol's red hat is seen bobbing along the top of the trench, suggesting that surely he can only be crawling along the bottom.

I was not, of course, there, but I can feel the air, as I write, all aglow with trepidation and awe. And an unnatural excitement – the soul of a village briefly lit by the glow of its disease.

After some minutes, the boy emerges crawling, like to a spider, from the trench. Kneeling, he takes the hat off his tousled black hair, beating it against an arm and then turning it in his hands as if to make sure it's clean of mud before replacing it on his head.

'Ner,' he says.

His bottom lip thrust out, sullen.

'Nothing there,' Anne Ceddol tells Stephen Price.

The boy has stepped back from the trench and now walks towards the beginnings of another, his hands splayed in front of him, stiffly at first and then aquiver, as he reaches it. It's not a warm day – few of those this summer – but the sun is well aloft and lights the shallow trench as he drops into it, then disappears from sight, and there's the sound of scratting, and a mist of earth flies up.

'Fetch him a scratter.'

Stephen Price tosses the instruction to his eldest son, annoyed that he can't take his eyes away from the place where Siôn Ceddol disappeared. When a trowell is produced Anna Ceddol accepts it and takes it to her brother and returns to Price.

'Thank you.'

She stands so close that her beauty must be disturbing the hell out of him. Can't avoid marking the form of her breasts, where her overdress is worn thin. The dress is the colour of the soil-spatter thrown up from the trench before a screech like to a barn-owl drives the people back in a panic of excitement.

And now Siôn Ceddol's on his feet again, his face lit with a broad, pink grin.

Though not, it must be said, as broad as the grin of the earth-browned human skull now held up, clasped tightly between the boy's eager hands to keep the jaw attached.

✠

Weeks hence, when his barn is built and the summoning of Siôn Ceddol is raised one market day in the new Bull Inn at Presteigne, Stephen Price may be heard making dust of it. How the idiot boy was putting on a show of searching the ground, foot by foot, when he knew all along where the bones lay... having, Price is convinced, buried them there the night before. Either him or that sister of his who oft-times disturbs Price even more and in ways he'd rather not tell you about.

Well, he says in the Bull, to Bradshaw and Beddoes and Meredith, en't as if they'd have had difficulty finding bones on Brynglas. Like to a charnel house this year.

'An omen, they're saying, the villagers. Like the weather. A reminder.'

Bradshaw eases his weight upon the bench and farts.

'Don't they know of the capture of this man Gethin? Is that not a good sign for them?'

'Hell, no.' Stephen Price almost laughs aloud. 'It's another sign that it's all coming back, the blood and the fire, and they're unprotected.'

'Well, it'll be good for us,' Bradshaw says. 'They've never recognised us in the west, as the county town. Now we're settling their score for them.'

Stephen Price says nothing. Bradshaw's from Off. Crossed the border to swell his fortune. He thinks wealth is the balm for all wounds.

Price buys more wine he can ill afford this year, to dull the fears that chatter in his head like the restless sprites that he's sure no one he met in Parliament believes in. Blanking out the image of the skull the boy found. One eye-hole twice the size of the other, where the blade went in.

The night before last, Stephen Price woke in a sweat from a dream where he saw a man lying, all cut about, on his back, in his own blood, on the side of Brynglas Hill, with another man standing above him twisting the squat blade of his pike round and back and round again in that left eye while the dying man screams to heaven.

Price drinking harder to drown out the voice of the new and forbidding rector, the narrow, white-faced man arching his spine, peering into his face, asking him, *Master Price, why* do *you let the devil have rein in Pilleth?*

X

Begins in Joy

THE COLD RAIN was lashing us by the time I was led to the scaffold.

More rickety than the last time I'd been here, some of the frame hanging loose. It might bear the weight of a man, but not for long. Clearly had not been used for some time, and its poor condition seemed in keeping with the rumours I'd heard.

'Why did you not say where we were going?'

Angry now, but the man in the rusted doublet ignored my question, as he had every one since we'd left Mortlake. We passed under the scaffold to the front door, opened as we reached it, by an armed servant.

And then up the stairs. I knew the way. The owner used to call it his *cottage*. It was three storeys high and now had several new-made windows taller than a man. When last I'd been here, builders had been intensively at work on the scaffold, seemingly engaged on turning this into the finest house on the Strand. But rumour had suggested this might not be the London home of the secretary of state for much longer.

'Was to have been another large window in the master bedroom by now,' the secretary said mournfully when I was shown into his work chamber. 'Foolish of me to wait for fine weather in a summer like this.'

'Anything else, Sir William?'

The man who'd brought me loitered in the doorway until Cecil raised a dismissive hand from the folds of his drab robe.

'No, no, thank you, Fellows. I'll send for you when Dr Dee's ready to leave.'

'No need,' I said curtly. 'I'll hail a wherry.'

Cecil peered at me.

'Sit down, John?'

I stayed on my feet, behind the proffered chair. The usual mean coal fire smouldered in the hearth behind me and the rain rattled the panes. Whenever I was here, there would be rain.

'If I'd refused to step into that barge, Sir William, would they have brought me here in chains?'

Cecil's guard-dog eyes widened fractionally.

'You think chains would have been necessary to restrain you? Taking more exercise nowadays, is it?'

'Bigger books,' I said. 'Higher shelves.'

He didn't laugh. For Cecil, banter was never indulged in for its own sake, only to grant himself more time to think. I noticed he'd put on more fat since last I'd seen him, as if to make himself harder to shift. Fewer than forty years behind him, but you'd have thought at least fifty.

'John, I regret that we haven't spoken a great deal since your return from Somerset with the, ah… remains of King Arthur.'

'The Queen—' I cleared my throat. 'The Queen believes it was Dudley's mission. I was there to hold his bridle while he resolved matters.'

I wouldn't normally have passed this on, but I was tired of being undervalued and thus underpaid and guessed that, for the first time, this man, who had survived service to three successive monarchs, would begin to understand.

'Oh *really*,' Cecil said mildly, 'What else would you have expected?'

There was considerable tension this year between Cecil and Dudley, whose star had grown brighter in the royal firmament than Venus at dawn. Cecil, meanwhile, had been deemed a disappointment for his failure, in negotiations with the French, to regain Calais for England. This had ever been unlikely, but the idea that it was even possible had been put into the Queen's head by... Dudley, of course.

I said nothing. The word was that Cecil had felt himself abused to the point where he'd tendered his resignation to the Queen. But then Amy Robsart, who had become Amy Dudley, had died and something had snapped like an over-wound crossbow.

Cecil went to sit down behind his trestle. The great window's lower frames were barricaded from outside by the builders' scaffold, but when he leaned back, tilting his oaken chair on two legs against the sill, at least half the spires of London were, once again, at his elbows, blurred by rain.

'John, would you happen to know why Mistress Blanche wanted to see you?'

'Would you?'

'I might.'

'However,' I said, 'when she – and, presumably the Queen – find out that you physically prevented the meeting taking place, as arranged—'

'She'll simply realise that you didn't receive the letter. I gather it was left with your mother, you being absent at the time.'

How the *hell* did he know all this?

'Having gone off on one of your… expeditions in search of the Hidden.' Cecil leaned forward until the front legs of his chair met the floor. 'Do you want to know what this visit may have been about, John?'

And what was I supposed to say to that? Cecil half stood to pull off his bulky black robe, revealing a doublet in what was, for him, the somewhat frivolous colour of charcoal. He tossed the robe across the wide trestle in front of him.

'Now *sit down*,' he said.

✝

The people of the Welsh border take a long path to the point. My father loved to explain that this was because, in an area ever riven by conflict between the Welsh and the English, they would need to know precisely where a visitor's allegiances lay before entrusting him with even the most trivial intelligence.

I'd oft-times marked this approach in the manners of Blanche Parry, who retained her accent, but was inclined to forget that the family of William Cecil – from whose tones all trace of Welshness had long ago been smoothed – had once spelled its name *Seisyllt*.

'Did you know Amy Robsart, John?'

'I wouldn't say I knew her. She tended not to come very much to town.'

An understatement. The Queen was not exactly approving of wives brought to court, or even to London. Especially Dudley's wife, obviously. In the absence of a Dudley country mansion, Amy had spent most of her married life as a guest of various friends of her husband. A dismal existence.

'Met her once,' I said. 'On one of her rare visits to Dudley's house at Kew.'

'And what thought you of her?'

At last I sat down. Truth was I'd thought Amy quite beautiful. Also intelligent, lively and warm. In my view – was this treason? – as a wife, the Queen would not quite compare. God help me, I'd even caught myself, wishing that circumstances had been such that I might have met her before Dudley.

'You're blushing,' Cecil said.

'Heat of the fire.'

Cecil laughed.

'What a waste, eh, John? As I oft-times think about a carnal marriage—'

'Starts in joy, ends in tears?'

Cecil frowned. I'd gone too far.

'A perceptive saying of yours oft-times retold,' I said, in placation.

He made a steeple of his fingers. His own first marriage may even have been a carnal union, but his second one, to the severe Mildred, could only have been founded on a need for reliability and circumspection. Cecil was a man long wed to his career.

'Do you know when he last saw her alive?'

I did but said nothing, remembering something else I'd noticed at my one meeting with Amy. While she was – of necessity, no doubt – fairly compliant, there was a certain equality in her union with Dudley. She was not nobility, merely the daughter of a country squire, yet seemed in no awe of the son of the Duke of Northumberland. To his credit, he seemed to like that about her.

'It was over a year ago,' Cecil said. 'Over a year before she died.'

'A long time.'

Too bloody long.

'Distance,' Cecil said, 'can bring about a cooling.'

'Sometimes.'

I'd never have left Amy for even a week. When I was called to Europe, I'd have taken her with me.

'Let's not walk around the houses, John.' Cecil let his hands fall flat to the trestle. 'I was ever fond of Robert Dudley, but never deluded about the extent of his ambition. He wants the highest role possible for a man not born to it. His whole life has been a play performed for the Queen. Whose side he's scarce ever left.'

'And she wished him away?'

Cecil was silent. Poor Amy's fate, in these circumstances, saddened me more than I could say. The inquest had been opened three days after her body was found at the foot of a short stairway. And then adjourned *sine die*. Nobody knew how long before the jury would reach its verdict but when it came it seemed likely to be one of Accidental Death.

Nobody to blame. I pointed out to Cecil that Dudley had gone to great pains not to be seen as having or attempting to have an influence on the jury, calling for men who were unknown to him to serve on it.

'Unknown? Is that what you think?'

I said nothing. Dudley had sworn to me his wife's death from a fall had been a bitter shock to him, and I'd very much wanted to believe that. Although he'd said, on an earlier occasion, that she'd shown signs of unhealth and once had told him

73

she might not have long to live, I'd refused to accept the dark stories, dating back some months before her death, that attempts had been made to poison her.

'Not that it matters.' Cecil half turned away from me to peer out over the shiny roofs of London. 'The Queen herself is young, impulsive and will remain' – Cecil swung round of a sudden to turn his mastiff's gaze on me – 'conspicuously besotted with a man now infamed and likely to remain so for the rest of his life.'

'But if the inquest verdict clears him of blame—'

'It doesn't *matter* what the inquest verdict is. Enough men hated him before this to make even his return to court a slight against all decency. As for the thought of a Queen of England wed to a murderer... how does that play across the capitals of Europe? And if the Queen thinks everyone here will forget, in time, then she's not as close to the mind of her country as she likes to believe.'

'*I* don't...' I was shaking my head, 'I *can't* believe that Dudley's a murderer.'

'Well, not *directly*, no.' Cecil spread his hands. 'No one's suggesting he planted his foot in her spine and kicked her down the bloody stairs. But whether he ordered it to be done, in his absence, is another matter entirely. Never be proven, but what's that worth in Europe? Especially if, after however length of time, the Queen does something blindly foolish. She's had suitors of her own standing in France, Spain, Sweden... and keeps them at arm's length. At home, she has the Earl of Arundel waiting with his tongue hanging out...'

'No hope for him, surely?'

'*I* know there's no hope, *you* know there's no hope, but the old bladder peers blearily into the looking glass, sees a face twenty years younger and tells himself it's only a matter of time before the Queen sees the sense of it.'

I nodded in wry agreement. It was well-enough known that Cecil's own choice as a husband for the Queen was the Earl of Arran. A resident of France from a Scottish family with no love of Elizabeth's cousin, Mary, the Queen of Scotland, who was also, since her marriage, Queen of France. In terms of a lasting peace in the north, Arran had much in his favour and would be a satisfyingly severe blow to French hopes of putting Mary on the throne of England.

But the lure of a carnal marriage. Twin souls since child-hood. The power of the heart…

'The Earl of Arundel would have had Dudley dead years ago,' I said. 'Or so it's said.'

Cecil let a silence hang and the rain ceased as if he'd commanded it.

'Arundel's too old and too vain, but he's hardly alone,' he said at last. 'Think of Norfolk. Think of those who conspired to get John Dudley topped and now fear Robert's vengeance if he's in a position to wreak some. Let me be honest. If he's betrothed to the Queen, no matter how long after his time of mourning, Dudley must needs be looking over his shoulder all the way to the altar. Indeed, if a messenger was to come knocking on *my* door now with news that he'd been cut down… or shot… or skewered in a crowd…'

My hands had tightened around the seat of my chair. The rain had begun again.

'Why are you telling me this?'

'What did Mistress Blanche want with you?'

75

'I don't *know*.'

'Oh, come now, John. Who does the Queen trust more than Mistress Blanche to conduct business of a highly personal nature? And what personal business might concern you, as a long-time friend and confidant of Robert Dudley?'

'I don't know, I can't—'

'Think you not that the Queen might wish you to perform, in secret, a similar task to the one you did before the coronation?'

The sound of rain against the good glass panes was like to a cackling laughter. I felt my heart lurch.

'You mean… she might want me to choose, by the stars, a day that's mete for…?'

'A royal wedding,' Cecil said. 'Indeed.'

XI

Dark Merlin

BY NOW I'D learned that Cecil never ventured an opinion without a degree of secret certainty. It was said that his ambitious young fixer, Walsingham, had agents at court who didn't even know of each other. Spies who spied on spies.

I leaned back, gazing at the window. London had misted, the steeples no more than indents on a bedsheet.

A terrible logic here. The Queen, for all her will and vigour, was ever indecisive, changing her mind three times in as many hours. Would make a firm decision then sleep on it and awake uncertain again. Dudley was no longer someone to play with. She would have accepted that the urging of her heart would not be enough. Might well seek some indication of heavenly affirmation, the design of destiny.

Might seek a date, however many months hence, which the stars found fortuitous for the announcement of a betrothal which at present would be abhorrent to so many.

Behind me, the coal fire hissed as rainwater dripped down the chimney. I took in a slow breath.

'How does Blanche feel about this?'

Cecil smiled and made no reply. Which may have been an answer in itself. Blanche was a cautious and watchful woman who only lived to keep the Queen secure. No wonder she hadn't turned her head this morning as her barge had glid past.

'If the Queen's determined on this, then she'll try again to have Blanche reach me,' I said. 'What then?'

'That, John… is precisely why we're having this discussion.'

'I can't refuse. You know I can't.'

'Of course you can't.'

'And if what Dudley says about the coincidence of their times of birth is correct, then their destinies may indeed appear interwoven.'

'Oh, *please*.' The trestle groaned as Cecil leaned forward. 'I have no doubts about your ability in this regard. Which is why I don't want you and your fucking charts within a mile of the Queen at this time.'

'I see.'

Cecil leaned back, folding his arms, giving me silence in which to consider my situation. I recalled how, on our return from Glastonbury, I'd been summoned here and shown a pamphlet handed out free on the streets. It was heralding a second coming – the birth of the child of Satan, the Antichrist, in the new black Jerusalem. Which was London, the fastest-growing city in Europe.

False prophecy originating from France, seedbed of the campaign to put the Queen of Scots on the English throne. I myself had been named as some kind of dark Merlin, canting spells at the lying-in of Queen Elizabeth, pregnant with the bastard child of Robert Dudley. Elizabeth, daughter of the adulterous witch, Anne Boleyn. They were now saying that the Queen – thanks, some said, to the magic and prayers of the French prophet and magus Nostradamus – had miscarried the babe. But the devil would not give in so easily.

I said at last, 'What would you have me do?'

Cecil rose and put his robe back on, like a judge about to pass a hard sentence.

'As I see it there are two approaches to this problem. One is for you to spend some time with your charts and return with the information that the stars at present are frowning on the prospects for a union of two people born under their particular signs.'

'Which, as I've already said—'

'Would be unlikely, yes.'

'Sir William, I spent more than a year teaching mathematics and the elements of astrology to Dudley. One of the subjects he showed most interest in. What I'm saying is that to convince Dudley – and even the Queen, who's far from ignorant of planetary movement – that the stars disapprove of their match—'

'Or might better approve of them under some heavenly configuration not due to take place for... say, five years?'

A lot could have happened in five years. The Queen's infatuation might have lost some of its fire. Or equally it might be proved beyond all reasonable doubt that Dudley had not killed his wife. Who could say?

I shrugged.

'If it was not the answer she sought... I'm far from the only astrologer in England. All it needs is for one of them to go to another and my competency would be called into question. Also my integrity and all of my past work, and worse than that—'

'All right. We'll go no further down that road. Examined and rejected. This leaves the second path... from which you disappear.'

Cecil rose, sweeping his robe behind him, and picked a single lump of coal from the scuttle with tongs and dropped it on the fire.

'I mean on one of your ventures in search of the Hidden. We spoke of this earlier. Wouldn't be the first time, would it? Were you to be gone even for a matter of weeks, that might be sufficient.'

'Oh.'

I felt a momentary relief. For one instant in time, I'd thought he'd meant that it was to be permanent, and the air betwixt us had seemed, of a sudden, cold with menace.

'*Do* you have a matter of, ah, science, requiring your specific and immediate attention?'

'I don't know. Maybe.'

'Preferably in some place at least two days' ride from London.'

Dear God, this man thought he could move anyone around, like a chesspiece, to suit his purposes.

Which, of course, he could. After a period when his advice had rarely been sought, Amy's death looked to be putting him back where he was certain he belonged. And maybe he was right; I could think of no one at this time who was fit to replace him.

Replacing the tongs, Cecil went back to his chair.

'Methinks this expedition of yours should begin at once. Would you agree?'

'Sir William—'

'Which means you won't be lying at your mother's house tonight.'

'But my mother—' I rose to my feet. 'My mother has need of me. The fabric of the house wants repair, the roof leaks.'

I'd used this one before, but it was no less true for that.

'Your skills extend to roofing, John? I'd hardly think so. But we'll see to all of that. I'll have a number of men dispatched to Mortlake to mend whatever needs mending. Your mother will scarce know you're missing.'

He was right. My mother would be in delight.

Bastard.

'My barge will take you back briefly to collect your bag, but I'll want you away by nightfall.'

'That's impossible.'

'Two days, then. Maximum.'

'Sir William, if the Queen thinks I'm making distance between myself and—'

'My problem, not yours. Two days. And stay out of London, meanwhile.'

The discussion over, Cecil rose.

✝

Enshrouded in a damp dismay, I stumbled out onto the cobbles and knew not which way to turn. The Strand, once the home of senior churchmen, was now rosy with the new brick of London's richest homes. Not a place which the secretary, his building work yet incomplete, would want to leave.

The rain had stopped and the brightening sky had brought out the chattering wives of the wealthy with their servants and pomanders, though this was hardly an area where nostrils might be assailed by the stink of beggars. Amongst the throng, I espied the unsmiling, unseasonably fur-wrapped Lady Cecil, out shopping with their two glum-faced daughters. Suspecting she'd be among those who considered me little more than a common conjurer, I turned back to walk the other way and thus glimpsed a man discreetly sliding through Cecil's doorway.

Dark bearded, dark clad and instantly admitted to the house. Unmistakably Francis Walsingham, the Oxfordshire MP known to serve the Privy Council on a confidential level. A coolly ambitious man whom I was more than inclined to mistrust. The very sight of him made me wonder if I were followed and I pulled down my hat, threw myself into the crowd and then slipped into an alley, where I stood with my back to the rain-slick brickwork and found myself panting.

Fear? Very likely. I'd persistently refused the offer of Cecil's barge, recalling the man who'd been beaten, robbed and drowned. If it could happen once this year, then it could happen again, and who'd question it?

You think me suffering from some persecution sickness? All I can say is that you weren't with the secretary this day. A man who'd felt himself slipping into the pit and now was scrambling back up its steep and greasy sides.

And was, therefore, less balanced and more dangerous than ever he'd been.

I thought of Dudley, once his friend, fellow supporter of Elizabeth from the start. And then Dudley, drunk on his status at court, unable to do wrong in the Queen's eyes, had seen himself as her first advisor, damaging Cecil. Now Dudley was sorely damaged and Cecil would seize his chance to...

...*what?*

Thrusting myself from the wall, a sweat on my brow, I followed the alleyway into another, this one ripe with the stench of rotting meat. I waited, listening for running footsteps above the distant bustling and chattering, the barking of dogs, the cries of street traders, the grinding of cartwheels and the clacking of builders' hammers on brick and stone.

No one coming. I walked on, through the mud and stinking puddles, across an inn yard and along a mews, with its more friendly stench of horseshit, until I saw the glitter of the river.

I stood beneath an iron lamp on its bracket, Cecil's voice in my head.

Do *you have a matter of, ah, science, requiring your specific and immediate attention?*

There *was* a man I would have visited on the morrow.

On the morrow, I was now commanded to be out of London.

I walked, with no great enthusiasm, out of the mews, to hail a wherry to take me not to Mortlake but across the river into Southwark's seething maw. Not a place I've oft-times visited, having little taste for gambling, whoring, bear baiting or street-theatre. But, then, I didn't have to go far after leaving the wherry.

A solid building close to the riverbank, like to a castle or my old college in Cambridge, but still a place I feared, like all gaols, as a result of having myself been held in one. At the mercy, as it happened, of the man I now thought to visit.

But… there are gaols and gaols, and it might have been Jack Simm who once had described the Marshalsea as the finest inn south of the Thames.

Now the official residence of the former Bishop of London, known in his day as Bloody Bonner.

XII

Blood and Ash

SHUTTING THE DOOR behind us with his heel, he set down his jug of wine on the board and then rushed to clasp my right hand.

'John, my boy...' Letting go the hand, stepping back and inspecting me, beaming. 'And, my God, you're still *looking* like a boy. Some alchemical, eternal youth thing you've contrived?'

In truth, I must look as worn and weary as I felt. I removed my hat. He was just being kind.

Yes, yes, I know. Kind? Bishop Bonner? I still could barely look at him for long without recalling some poor bastard's crispen feet, black to the bones in the ashes of the kindling... or the savage flaring of hell's halo as the hair of another Protestant took fire. I'd oft-times wondered how many nights Bonner might lie awake in cold sweat, accounting to God for all the public burnings he'd ordered during the years of blazing terror after Mary had restored the Roman faith.

How many nights? Probably not one. Even now, in a bright new reign, when stakes were used more for the support of saplings, he seemed to believe that there'd been a moral substance to what he'd done. How could I possibly have grown to like this monster?

'And what think you of my dungeon, John?'

His grin displaying more teeth than he deserved.

'It's not the Fleet, is it?' I said.

Bonner sniffed.

'*You* might think it looks not unpleasant, my boy, but you aren't here when the brutal guards come at nightfall and hoist us in chains from iron rings on the walls.'

Inevitably, I looked up at the conspicuously unbloodied walls until his laughter seemed to crash from them like thunder. *Haw, haw, haw.* Then I heard a key turned in the lock on the door and spun around.

'Don't worry,' Bonner said. 'They lock me in for my safety. I'll see you get out. Before the week's end, anyway.'

I smiled cautiously. We had history, Bishop Bonner and I. When first we'd met it had been in my own cell, back when I was falsely accused of working magic against Queen Mary and also of heresy. The good man I'd shared it with was already become cinders and even though I'd overturned the primary case against me in court I'd no cause to believe I'd escape the same end.

But Edmund Bonner had been curious about my reputation as a scholar of the Hidden. Wanted to know what mystical secrets I might have uncovered at the Catholic university of Louvain.

And so, against all odds, I'd been allowed to live, even serving for a time as his chaplain – the inevitable guilt that haunted me tempered by the discovery that, just as Bloody Mary was said to have been surprisingly soft-hearted, Bloody Bonner had a learned and questing mind and was – God help me – good company.

'Wild tales abound,' he said, 'of what you and Lord Dudley found in Glastonbury.'

'Can't tell you about it, Ned. You know that.'

'Pah.' He waved a hand. 'It can be of no consequence now, anyway. As long as dear Bess was happy with you.'

She was far from happy with Bonner. Yet, even now, all he had to do to regain his freedom was to recognise her as supreme governor of the Church. While admiring his steadfast refusal, I guessed that, in his own mind, he already was free. Only the bars outside the window glass were evidence of a prison. Almost everything else was recognisable from the cramped chamber he'd occupied while under house arrest at his bishop's palace: the chair and board, the looking glass and the books on the shelf, with Thomas Aquinas prominent.

Yes, it was fair to say the Marshalsea had not the squalor of the Fleet – none that could be seen, anyway. Established to confine maritime offenders, it now also housed debtors and those convicted of political crimes... and thrived upon a strong foundation of corruption. Prisoners with money could buy good meals and wine, and others without money were allowed out by day to earn some to hand over to their gaolers.

For Edmund Bonner, it was a life of no conspicuous discomfort. He'd expressed joy at my visit, offering to entertain me in the cellar where wine was served. But there were too many of his fellow prisoners in there, some with their wives who came and went unchallenged, especially if they brought money. Impossible for us to talk with confidence here so, taking with us a jug of wine, we'd gone upstairs to his cell.

There was a stool for me to sit on, while Bonner, clad in the robe of a humble Franciscan monk, poured wine for us.

'I was *told*' – eyes aglint with mischief as he stoppered the jug – 'that after the demise of Dudley's poor, wretched little wife had become known, the Queen would be seen around the court all in black attire—'

'As was everyone at court.'

'—with a dance in her step and a lovely, joyful smile upon her face that remained immovable for days. Is it still there?'

His own face – which, with his history, you might imagine moulded into a permanent rictus of hate – was, as ever, plump and benign as he handed me a cup and lowered his bulk to the edge of his pallet.

'I understand that the smile,' I said, 'is now a little strained.'

He nodded, looking me steadily in the eyes.

'I also heard that, some days before your friend Dudley was widowed, the Queen confided to the esteemed Spanish ambassador, Bishop La Quadra, that Lady Dudley would very soon be departing this life. Have you heard that, too?'

Yes, and wished I hadn't.

'When it first came to my notice,' Bonner said, 'I couldn't help but wonder if it was you who'd happened to see this impending tragedy in the stars.'

I considered this unworthy of reply, but it didn't stop him.

'Because, as you must see, John, the only other possible explanation of the Queen's foreknowledge of the death of Amy Dudley is that she was, herself, party to the disposal of the woman preventing marriage to her childhood sweetheart.'

'There are many explanations,' I said firmly, 'and one is that the Spanish Ambassador is lying.'

'A bishop of the Roman Church?'

'As part of his campaign to win the English queen for the Spanish king – again.'

'Well yes.' Bonner nodded. 'Indeed, it was my hope too that

she'd see what God wanted of her and choose Philip of Spain for herself.'

'Her sister's widower? Was that ever truly on the cards?'

'Was for him. And think of the benefits – we'd be back with Rome before the year's end, and I'd be brought out of here in glory and made Archbishop of Canterbury.'

For a moment he looked almost serious and then a belch of laughter made his body rock.

'In truth, I suppose I'll die within these walls. Never mind.' He took a slow sip of wine. 'But methinks you didn't come here to discuss the arrangements for my funeral.'

'Or the marriage prospects of the Queen.'

'Then what?'

I sipped some prison wine, which proved better than ours at home.

'Wigmore Abbey,' I said.

'Where's that?'

'In the Welsh Marches. Not far from where my father was born.'

'Ah yes. Of course it is. Or was. Is it *was*?'

'So I believe.'

'Never went there, John. Horrible journey, I hear. Best thing your father did, getting out of that wilderness, or you'd've been born into a life of penury and ignorance.'

He sat for some moments peering into his cup, then looked up and beamed.

'Ah,' he said. 'It's come to me, now. *John Smart.*'

I waited, guessing it had not come to him at all. It had ever been there, in the catacombs of his impressive mind.

'Last Abbot of Wigmore. Got himself reported to Tom Cromwell, on a list of charges as long as my cock.'

'What charges?'

'As I *recall*… simony on a grand scale. Smart was littering the place with new-made priests. While also growing rich on the sale of abbey treasure. What a rogue the man was. Hunting and hawking with his canons. Poking maids and goodwives over quite a wide area. Ah… I see your ears are already awaggle.'

'Abbey treasure? Gold? Plate?'

'Doubtless.'

'What else? Precious stones?'

Bonner frowned.

'Methinks, before we travel further down this road, it would be as well for you to enlighten me as to our destination.'

I was hesitant. Bonner drained his cup and placed it on the board at his bedside.

'John, I may have blood and ashes on my hands but I'm not known for breaking confidence.'

I nodded. What was there to lose? I took my wine over to the window, with its view, between bars, of the river, and told him what I knew about the shewstone of Wigmore Abbey.

✠

I admit to being captivated by what I'd been told about this wondrous crystal with its *history of miracles and healing*. But talking to a cynic like Bonner could sometimes bring you sharply to your senses.

And the more I heard about the last Abbot of Wigmore, the more I wondered if he and the scryer, Brother Elias, were not, as Jack Simm had suspected, working together. Abbot Smart, an Oxford graduate, had been appointed Abbot of Wigmore by Cardinal Wolsey. Although there were rumours, Bonner said, that he'd paid for it. His rise had been rapid. In the years before the Reform he was also become suffragen Bishop of Hereford and accumulating endless money, most of it directly into his purse, by appointing over fifty candidates to Holy Orders.

'Ho, ho,' Bonner said. 'What a holy knave the man was. Many attempts were made to unseat him, of course, but he always wriggled away, with the help of a small coterie of thoroughly reprehensible followers. While the abbey, both physically and morally, was rotting around him.'

'But he escaped the dissolution with his life,' I said.

'And with a pension, for heaven's sake! But then… who knows what favours he did for Lord Cromwell? A man who'd bend the law to have you hanged for stealing a spoon and sprung from a murderer's death-cell if you were a friend he could use.'

If the shewstone was amongst his treasures, it seemed more than likely that he knew Elias and that both were well connected.

And well informed. In the right atmosphere, and with a good foundation, the power of insinuation is near limitless and may take on a life of its own. What had happened during our time in Glastonbury was surely talked about over a wide area of the west and beyond. It was not unlikely that Elias's path had crossed with that of some fellow priest – even the garrulous Welsh vicar of Glastonbury – who had known of my passing association with Benlow the boneman. Unlikely, but not impossible.

'You truly believe,' Bonner said, 'as a philosopher and a man of science, that it's possible to achieve communion with the angelic hosts by means of a reflective stone?'

'By means of celestial rays and the human spirit. There's a long tradition of it.'

'There's a tradition of reading the future in the entrails of a chicken, John, but it still sounds like balls to me.'

'Comes from a stimulation of the senses,' I said. 'Like to prayer and meditation in a church under windows of coloured glass, while the air is laden with incense. Sometimes a cloth is pulled over the head to shut out the world, so that, for the scryer, the crystal becomes luminous.'

Like to a small cathedral of light. I tried to find words to explain how attention to the light-play within the crystal might alter the workings of the mind, rendering it receptive to messages from higher spheres, and Bonner didn't dismiss it.

'But would you also accept,' he said, 'that a true mystic has no need of a scrying stone or any such tool?'

'Of course.' I looked over to where his rosary hung by the window. 'But while a mystic accepts what he receives and dwells upon it—'

'—you, as a man of science, must needs explain the process?'

'Yes,' I said. 'That's how it is.'

Bonner smiled.

'With which archangel do you seek to commune?'

'Michael,' I said at once.

His ancient sigil appearing in my mind, where I must have drawn it more than a hundred times in the past year, to summon courage and the powers of reason.

Which told me now to say nothing to Bonner about the

91

Queen's interest in communion with the supercelestial and the pressure upon me which would almost certainly resume when those deceitful mourning clothes were put away.

'Methinks,' he said, 'that you imagine this stone might… awaken something in you?'

This would be the lesser of two admissions but I said nothing.

'The great sorrow of your life,' Bonner said, 'is that you yourself, with all your studies and experiments, your extensive book-knowledge of ancient wisdom and cabalistic progression through the spheres are… how shall I put this…?'

'Dead,' I said. 'Dead to the soul.'

Exaggerating, in hope that he'd contradict me.

'Poor boy,' he said.

+

I'd hoped he'd be able to tell me more, but all he could recall were this man Smart's alleged crimes against both Church and Crown. Crimes for which, in earlier times, he would have roasted. The fact that he seemed to have survived suggested he knew men of influence.

So where was he now? Still at Wigmore? Bonner thought he might be able to find out if I could come back, say, in a week?

I supposed I could find accommodation in some part of London well away from the court and Cecil, but I'd forever be watching my back, and anyone, from a street-seller to a beggar, might be one of Walsingham's agents.

And why would I take the risk of discovery for something I'd never afford?

I shook my head, Bonner regarding me from his pallet, a pensive forefinger extended along a cheek.

'What else are you not telling me, John?'

Kept on shaking my head. I'd been drawn into circumstances I'd had no role in shaping. However the matter of Amy's death and her own marriage was resolved, the Queen would remember that I'd not been here when she had need of my services. And Dudley... Dudley would also remember. If he survived.

... if a messenger was to come knocking on my door now with news that Dudley had been cut down... or shot... or skewered in a crowd...

I saw Cecil's narrow, long-nosed face and dark, intelligent eyes, flecked, for the first time in my experience of him, with what seemed a most urgent need.

And then he'd said,

Were you to be gone, even for a matter of weeks, that might be sufficient.

For what? Sufficient for circumstances to alter so that Dudley's marriage to the Queen was no longer a possibility...

... due to his death?

Was I mad to think thus?

'Dudley, eh?' Bonner said.

As if he'd tapped into my thoughts. I stared at him, startled.

'Poor Dudley,' he said. 'Exiled from court, compelled to keep his burrowing tool out of the royal garden. Do you see him these days?'

'I had... a letter from him, in which he told me that his wife may have fallen because her bones were made brittle through a malady in her breast. He'd spoken before of her illness.'

'Interesting. I was told that the malady related to her humour. An advanced melancholy. Bodily, she appeared in good health... apart from the sallowness and loss of weight symptomatic of such a condition.'

'Who told you that?'

'Ah...' Bonner shrugged. 'You'd be surprised at the people who come and go from the Marshalsea. However, that's neither here nor there.'

Something pulsed within me, and I knew what I had to do.

'Ned, how do you get letters out?'

'From here? There's a guard who'll collect them, for a consideration, and take them to a stable lad who, for another consideration—'

'Nothing more private than that?'

'An approach to the stableman himself is usually found safer for those of us allowed out of here. He's at an inn round the corner. Offers a first-stage post-horse service. You want to send a letter?'

'If you can spare me paper and ink.'

'Where to? May I ask?'

'Not far. Kew.'

'He'll do that by mid-afternoon. Paper and quill are in the box under the bookshelf. Sealing wax and ink, too. If it's gone hard, add a little wine.'

'Thank you.'

I sat down at the board with paper and quill and ink and kept the message short, asking only for a meeting. Bonner evidently didn't feel the need to inquire who I was writing to, knowing full well who lived at Kew.

I sanded the ink and sealed the letter it with wax. He may

not want to meet me at this time, but at least I would have tried.

'I assume you know what you're doing,' Bonner said.

'Not really.'

'I'll pray for you, then.'

'Now I know I'm dead.'

But neither of us was laughing as I stowed the letter away in my doublet. Bonner arose and clasped my hand a final time and then brought out from his robe a single key with which he unlocked the door of his cell.

'You have a key to your own prison?'

'For reasons which escape me,' Bonner said, 'I yet seem to be less than popular in some quarters. It would not help the mood of the Marshalsea were I to be set alight in my own cell.' He held the door open. 'Good luck to you, John, in all your quests.'

'Thank you, Ned.'

'And should you ever come to possess the stone,' Bonner said, 'perchance you might bring it here one day. And we shall see what we shall see.'

I nodded and walked away along a short passage and down the stairs towards the darkness of the day.

XIII

Court Clown

ALREADY, HE WAS saying, her ghost had been seen on those stairs at Cumnor Place. The little stairs, the too-short stairs.

'All in white,' Dudley said, 'but with a grey light around her, like to a… a dusty shroud. Walking off the top step, gazing ahead of her and then… then she vanishes.'

His body stiffening as if to forestall a shiver, and then he was pouring more wine, as though to prove to himself that his hand was not shaking.

'But never coming to me,' he said. 'Why not to me?'

He didn't drink.

'I don't know,' I said. 'I never see them either.'

The weak sun had begun to fade into the river at the bottom of my mother's garden. A garden which, like Dudley's beard, was less tended these days. He looked hard at me, his skin darkening – stretched parchment held too close to a candle, as though the rage in him were burning through the grief.

Was it grief, or was there a suppressed excitement? How could I be sure? But the rage was ever there, and some of it might have been directed inwards.

He must have called for a horse the minute my letter had arrived. Five men had ridden with him to Mortlake – John Forest, his lieutenant, Thomas Blount, his steward and three men armed as though for war. Blount and Forest were in the old scullery, probably reducing my mother's larder to crumbs, but two armed men were outside and one guarded the door of my private workroom, where Dudley and I now sat.

'You know about these matters,' he said. 'If I murdered her, why's she not haunting me?'

He spoke roughly, and then sat back, as if ashamed. Both of us silent now. Early evening light cowered in the murky glass behind my finest owl. Through a system of pulleys, this owl could flap his wings and make hoot but now stood like a sentinel in the small window.

'Your men are all laden with weaponry,' I said. 'One with a firearm?'

'You noticed that.'

Dudley rolled his head wearily, black hair still sweated to his brow from the vigour of the ride. The horses had been taken around the back, to what remained of our stables, but their arrival here would hardly have gone unobserved, and I knew I was imperilled by their very presence.

I said, 'You've had threats to your life?'

'There's ever been threats to my life. I'm a Dudley.'

I'd met him just once since our return from Glastonbury. This was before Amy's death, and he'd displayed a feverish hunger for life. It had seemed no time at all since his father, John Dudley, Earl of Northumberland, had hired me to teach his sons mathematics and astronomy. But, he was right, death and the Dudleys were bedfellows.

Robert Dudley was twenty-eight years old.

Five years younger than me, ten years younger than Sir William Cecil.

And of an age equal to the Queen. To the day, he'd claim. Even to the hour.

Twin souls.

Would he kill his own wife for her?

I'd stared hard at this question, night after night, and my most brutal conclusion was: yes, he might. If he scented destiny. If he saw himself as the only man who could save the country from France and Spain and a Catholic resurgence. If he thought Amy was ill and would not live long. If he—

Dear God, I must needs put this from my mind. I arose and went to the window, standing next to the owl, symbol of Athena, goddess of wisdom, and I'd rarely needed it more.

'I was taken this morning to Cecil,' I said.

Watching his fingers curl, the knuckles grown pale as I explained about the heralded visit to me of Blanche Parry and the act of near-piracy that had taken me to the Strand. And some of what I'd learned there.

Dudley drained his wineglass.

'Cecil believes he's doing what's best for the Queen, but he's fighting for his own future. And that, for once, makes him fallible. Vulnerable.'

'And dangerous,' I said.

'You think he scares me?'

'He should. By God he should.'

Seeing now that *both* these men were at their most dangerous. Each guessing that only one of them would come through.

'Cecil's served and survived, thus far, three monarchs,' I said. 'If I were a gambling man my money would not be on you.'

'John, you don't *have* any fucking money.'

I said nothing. The air was still. The first beating of horse-hooves had sent my mother, in a hurry, to the Faldos' house. At one time she'd been impressed by my friendship with Dudley but now, although she never spoke of it, it was an evident source of trepidation.

'Is it true,' I asked him bluntly, 'that Blanche had been sent to have me choose a date for your wedding to the Queen?'

A rueful smile.

'Nothing so exact. It was hoped you might find some suggestion from the heavens that one match in particular might be... more propitious than any of the others. And... Yes, all right... that there might be a most suitable time to announce to the people of England a betrothal.'

He toyed with papers on my long board. The rough copy, made in Antwerp, from the writings of Trithemius of Spanheim, lay open next to some notes for my book of the Monas Hieroglyph which would explain in one symbol all I knew about where we lodged with regard to the sun and the moon and the influence of the planets. I'd been working on it, in periods, for nearly three years, knowing it must not be hurried.

I said, '*Who* hoped?'

'What?'

'Who hoped I might do these charts?'

Well, obviously, Mistress Blanche Parry would seek my services on behalf of only one person, but I wanted to hear him say it.

He said nothing. He lowered his head into his cupped hands on the boardtop and stayed thus, quite still, for long seconds. A man widely condemned as arrogant, brash, impulsive, never to be trusted… and I supposed I was heartened that he didn't think to hide the less-certain side of himself from me.

At length, he raised his head, dragged in a long breath. The chamber was dimming fast around us. We might have been in a forest glade, with the owl watching us from the fork of a tree.

'Very well, John,' Dudley said. 'Let's get this over.'

✝

What the hell had kept us friends? A fighting man and prolific lover who thrived on hunting stags and watching, with an analytical excitement, the baiting of bears by dogs… and a bear-sympathist who hunted only rare books and had lain with only one woman and could not sleep for the longing.

I spun away from the window.

'You hadn't seen her… for a whole *year*.'

'John—'

'You self-serving *bastard*.'

Recoiling from myself. I rarely shout at anyone. Dudley bit off his response, sat breathing hard, his hands pushing down on the board.

'Mercy.' Holding myself together and banishing an image of Amy Robsart whom I feared I could have loved. 'Yes, I do fully understand the Queen's policy on wives at court.'

'She wanted' – he didn't look at me – 'to see me there every day. *Every* day.'

'And every night?'

He was silent.

'You told me you thought Amy was ill,' I said. 'You told me even she thought she'd die soon.'

'That was what she said, yes.'

100

'You brought a doctor to her?'

'Several.'

'Robbie… you ever think that was simply to test where your thought lay? See how badly you wanted her soon to be dead and out of the way of your ambition? Do you not think it possible that the only sickness she suffered was a malady of the mind?'

'For a man of books, you seem to know a surprising amount about the ways of women.' Dudley turned his head at last towards me. 'Or was she ill because she was being slowly poisoned? I stayed away because I was having her poisoned and would rather not be there to watch it happening.' Staring at me now, his eyes ablaze. 'That's what you think – I'd have my wife poisoned?'

'I didn't say that. You did.'

'But one way or another I'm behind her death. Jesu, John, even I'd think I was behind it. Who had more to gain?'

'Or more to lose.'

He said nothing. Would only have talked of twin souls, astrology.

Or all the dangerous marriages, any one of which might be forced on the Queen if she got much older unbetrothed. I was aware of a dark abyss below me.

'You loved her once. Amy.'

Thinking that if there was any time he might leap up and strike me it was now. I didn't step away. Would even, God help me, have taken the blow. But he didn't move, except to lean back a little on the bench.

'A squire's daughter. And I was… nobody in particular. Not then. With ambition, of course, but in some ways just glad to be alive. Glad to have survived. We were happy. We were a pair. I… destroyed her.'

I stiffened. He was very still. The air was fogged on the cusp of night, Dudley's voice toneless.

'But I didn't kill her. I didn't pay anyone to kill her.'

This time I let the silence hang. I wanted to say I believed him, but the words would not quite come.

I could take this matter no further. Went and sat down opposite him and heard him swallow.

'You know why Bess trusts you, John? *Do* you?'

I had no answer to this. I knew the Queen believed in me and what I did – she who'd learned eight languages, maybe more, and had once told me how she saw her reign as a magical period, framing a great tapestry of human progress.

'I'll tell you,' Dudley said. 'It's because she knows that, for all your extensive knowledge of the vastness of things, you're a simple soul without political ambition. You want only to buy more books. That so makes her laugh.'

'I'm so glad,' I said, 'to be awarded the much-coveted status of Court Clown.'

'God's bollocks, John!' Dudley bringing down a fist on the board, almost splitting one of its poor pine panels. 'She has no fears about your *fidelity*, that's all I'm saying. And knows she'll get from you only the unwaxed truth as you see it… and that your vision's far-reaching. And right now that's worth a lot.'

So why doesn't she pay me a lot? Or even anything.

Dudley looked at his empty cup, but I didn't offer to refill it. Couldn't anyway – we had no more wine.

'Now tell *me* the truth,' he said. 'Why precisely did you ask to see me? What am I doing here?'

'Because I would not have been able to live with myself if I returned to find you'd been—'

102

'Returned from where?' He looked up quickly. 'Where are you going?'

I saw no reason to avoid the truth. I told him I must needs fulfil a promise to the Queen. In relation to her professed interest in scrying through a shewstone. Spoke aloud, it sounded almost foolish, but he, if anyone, would know that it wasn't. He was already nodding.

'She talked of that. She was... enthused.'

'When was this?'

'Not long ago.'

Avoiding my eyes, which seemed to confirm a long-held suspicion of mine that there'd been a least one meeting between Dudley and the Queen since Amy's death. A guarded meeting, no doubt, away from court. Hooded figures in a palace garden, a covered barge on the river.

'I told the Queen I'd acquired a crystal sphere. And would be working with it. And that I'd report back to her.'

I saw Dudley looking around the darkening workplace.

'You won't see one here,' I said. 'God knows, I've been trying to *find* one.'

Dudley began to laugh.

'You mean one you can afford?'

'The ones I can afford would probably be useless for my purposes. You're right, I'm a clown. However...'

Told him, in some detail, about the crystal sphere last heard of in a former abbey in the Welsh borderlands. Finding I had his full attention.

'So you don't know if it's still there and you're fairly sure you wouldn't be able to afford it, but you're planning a long and arduous ride to find out?'

'Haven't decided yet. But the fact remains that Cecil wants me out of town for a while.'

'You mean out of the reach of Blanche Parry. Can't help wondering if Cecil wasn't told about the plan to consult you by Mistress Parry herself – his fellow Welshie. Who may also disapprove of Bess's taste in men. She's polite to me, is old Blanche, but ever somewhat distant. Uncommon that, for a woman of whatever age.'

'Robbie, she's distant from *me*, and I'm her cousin.'

'*Cousin*. Half of Wales is your cousin. Look at that bastard – isn't *he* a cousin? The notorious villain, Thomas...'

'Jones. Thomas Jones.'

'Who robbed his betters on the road. Almost openly. *Is* he your cousin?'

'Betrothed to my cousin, Joanne. And I don't ask what he did or to whom. He was young then. Reformed now, anyway. A scholar, with a doctorate. And given a royal pardon.'

Dudley snorted.

'Bess is quite ridiculously tolerant towards the Welsh.'

'Perhaps because she *is* Welsh.'

'She is *not* Welsh! Her grandfather was Welsh. Partly. So you think Cecil might try and have me slain, do you?'

The sky momentarily was shadowed by a flock of birds going to roost, the dimmed window glass turning Dudley's fine doublet from its mourning indigo to black.

'He likes you,' I said. 'But he might not shed tears over your corpse.'

His lips tightened, vanishing into his once-proud moustache, now straggled and uneven.

'I... had a servant die, John. Couple of days ago. A kitchen maid. Spasms of the gut, and dead within an hour. I... ordered all the meat in the house taken out and buried.'

'You're thinking poison?'

'If *I* died from it, people would say it was no more than divine justice.' He stared up at me, his face twisting into wretchedness in an instant, the way a child's does. 'They can all say what the hell they like, now I'm exiled from court, and nobody visits me for fear they'll come away soiled by second-hand guilt. Maybe' – pushing himself back from the board, the bench-feet squealing on the flags – 'you can summon Amy's spirit into a fucking shewstone to tell us precisely how she died.'

Did I mark tears in his eyes? Finally? Tears for Amy? Tears for himself? Did he even know the difference?

'What should I do?' he said at last.

'Not for me to say, Robbie. We're acting on different stages now.'

'You're still my friend.'

I suppose I nodded, though I'd rarely been less sure of it.

XIV

God and All His Angels

SHE'D BEEN IN a wild mood that day, the day not so long ago when they'd talked of knowing the future and having communion with angels. Red hair all down around her shoulders, the pale sun on her pale face, a faerie light in her amber eyes... and Dudley wanting her so badly that he'd fallen to his knees in the island garden at Richmond, burying his head in the grass 'twixt her feet.

Remembering now how she'd insisted that God and all His angels must surely be on her side.

Our side, Dudley had wanted to say, but didn't. Telling me he'd been thinking of all they'd come through, both of them losing a parent to the block. Imprisoned side by side in the Tower, not knowing if they, too, would end up there.

But how will we know, she'd said, and he recalled her voice grown thin, *when what we do fails to please them, and God and all His angels begin to turn away? How will we know when evil's at the door?*

'Do you see?' Dudley said to me. 'Do you see where this goes?'

'No,' I said.

Although of course I did and was filled with a mixture of alarm and excitement, as Dudley arose and picked up the

106

smaller of the two globes given to me by Gerardus Mercator, with whom I'd studied at Louvain. Holding it up to the last of the light, as if it were a symbol of his destiny.

✠

'Spirits,' Dudley said. 'A shewstone can bring forth spirits. Good spirits… evil spirits?'

I watched him slowly turning Mercator's globe. Geography is one of my less-dangerous obsessions.

'I'm a cabalist,' I said, 'and also a Christian. Therefore any spirits called into the stone by me must needs be touched by the angelic.'

'Good enough,' Dudley said. 'So far. Go on.'

'The Queen knows her reign could see the meeting point of science and the spiritual. A wondrous thing. If barriers are not raised against it.'

'Ah… that old question of religion.'

'Not an *old* question at all,' I said ruefully. 'When I was a boy, mystery was all around us. Christ was full-manifest in the Mass. Every baptism was an exorcism of evil spirits. The world *vibrated with magic*. And… and if men like me sought divine inspiration in the cause of making new discoveries, it would be a long time before someone cried *heresy*.'

'Except possibly the Pope.'

I nodded sadly.

'We get rid of the Pope, and what happens? In no time at all, we've gone too far the other way. Christ is *not* manifest in the Mass. It's all theatre. Let's strip it away, the new Bible-men cry, not for us to ask questions. The will of God is the will of God, and you either accept it or you go to Hell. You explore *nothing*.

Jesu, I— I'm a Protestant, Robbie, I believe in the Church of England... and yet know it could take us back centuries.'

Both of us knew where the Queen stood on this. There would be no persecution of Catholics if they worshipped privately.

Or she'd be persecuting herself.

'Tell me how it works,' Dudley said. 'The shewstone.'

'I don't *fully* know how it works. I know that planetary rays are drawn into the stone through ritual and the focus of the scryer, who must needs enter an altered state to perceive the flow of messages.'

'If this French bastard Nostradamus can do it,' Dudley said, 'then you can do it.'

Dear God, I'd wish for a half of his confidence. I'd met Nostradamus just the one time and didn't believe him a rooker. Not entirely. Envied him, I'd have to admit, for his standing at the French court and the monetary favours that came his way. The way he was venerated and left to experiment unmolested by Church or Crown.

'We're both reaching for the same things,' I said. 'Though my own feeling is that his prophecies are a little too... poetic. Not the best poetry, either.'

'And shaped to the French cause.' Dudley was yet nursing the globe. 'This clever stone... *does* Nostradamus have one?'

'Don't know. He claims he's a natural scryer who needs only to look into a glass of water to connect himself to channels of prophecy. But I'm a scientist and must needs have proof. Scrying stones have been around throughout history, but only now do we have the means and the knowledge to subject them to proper scientific study.'

'What are we seeking here, John?'

We? I sought a careful answer.

'Knowledge of the hidden engines that power the world? The workings of the mind of God?'

Jesu, that wasn't careful at all, was it?

'*The mind of God*, John?'

Dudley took breath in a kind of shudder, and I endeavoured to back away.

'I just don't believe we can do anything of significance alone. All great art comes through divine inspiration. Advances in science... the same.'

Told him what I'd gleaned from Bishop Bonner about the former Abbot of Wigmore, John Smart.

'Bonner? You consulted *Bonner*? And the fat bastard's going to keep his mouth stitched?'

'I believe he will.'

'You're an innocent, John.' Dudley shaking his head in feigned wonder. 'All right, tell me about the mysteries of divine inspiration.'

I told him that while we could hardly aspire, either side of the grave, to a direct approach to God, there were... intermediaries.

'Angels. Archangels – Gabriel, Michael?'

'Just names, Robbie. Just names for whatever moves the celestial forces which make us what we are. Just names for the controlling—'

'Good enough for me, John. How much does this man want for his stone?'

'Probably more than I have in the world.'

I looked away in sudden apprehension, heard Dudley stand up.

'But not, presumably,' he said, 'more than *I* have.'

Oh God help me... Shutting my eyes in dismay. Had this been what I'd been hoping for all along? Was this, in truth, why I'd writ the letter to him in Bonner's cell?

'All right, we'll both go,' Dudley said. 'You and I. We'll make a good bargain with this man, in the noble cause of expanding the Queen's vision.'

We? The way *we* brought back the bones of Arthur?

'Her stone,' Dudley said. 'Dedicated to the Queen's majesty. But as you're the only one who knows how to make it speak, you can keep it here and study it and caress it in your bed, whatever it takes, and bring it regularly to Bess at Richmond or Windsor. Present to her whatever you see within it. Or consider it *advisable* to see.'

What? I drew back across the chamber, hard against the door to the library, something twisted like a knife in my chest. I began to panic.

'Robbie, we don't know he still has it.'

'We don't? I thought you were of the opinion that the scryer had deliberately conveyed to your apothecary friend just enough information to tempt the infamous Dr Dee.'

'What if it's a rook?'

'Then we have the abbot brought back and thrown in the Fleet. *Jesu*, John, I have to do something. I'm sick to my gut of confinement at Kew, everyone regarding me with half-veiled suspicion... barred from court for the sake of appearances. What's the matter with you? Suddenly you don't think yourself worthy to know the mind of God? Listen to me...'

It felt as if the surging of his energy was taking away the air, and I found it hard to breathe. A half moon, ridged by cheap glass, shone behind the owl, and Dudley's voice rose in the darkness as if from the hollows of a dream. Talking of responsibility towards his heritage… all that his father had died for… the beheading of Jane Grey and all the other cruel deaths, the ashes of martyrs from which Elizabeth had arisen like the fresh and glistening spirit of a new age. Repeating her words from the island in the garden at the Palace of Richmond.

… how will we know when what we do fails to please them? How will we know when evil's at the door?

And over this I heard the voice of Brother Elias, the scryer, repeating the exhortation of Trithemius of Spanheim.

'*… and whatever good gifts, whether the power of healing infirmities, or of imbibing wisdom, or discovering any evil…*

Did I sense in Dudley this night a manner of madness? The haste with which he'd seized on this had made me wonder if truly he did fear for his life if he remained in London. Feared public assassination or a sordid, squirming death by poison. Or even a faked suicide. If so, what I'd told him about Cecil would scarce heighten his confidence of survival… unless…

Unless.

Across the board, his shape had almost gone to black and only the savagery of his smile shone through to show me he was afire.

☩

Five days later, Sunday, as I returned, with my mother, from church, a letter was delivered to me by Dudley's senior attendant John Forest who, along with Thomas Blount, his steward, seemed to have replaced his murdered servant Martin Lythgoe in the position of *most-trusted*.

111

The letter was to detail our itinerary, through Gloucester and Hereford, to the Welsh Border.

> *We shall be riding with a judge sent to preside*
> *over an assize court trial at Presteigne. In the*
> *border lands, in sombre attire, we should*
> *be inconspicuous in this company.*
> *It seems likely the judge will be returning to*
> *London within a few days, which should give us*
> *ample time to conduct our business.*
> *Until the company leaves,*
> *knowing of your problem, I should be glad to*
> *accommodate you here at Kew.*
> *Please tell Forest if this is what you wish.*

We were to travel with a judge on his way to preside over a trial? I guessed Dudley would be blind to the irony.

Still, it seemed a good and safe way to make the journey. Presteigne, county town of the new shire of Radnor, was within a few miles of my father's old home, and my cousin Nicholas Meredith lived in the town. The invitation to stay at Kew also made sense, as long as I didn't leave the house. And yet...

That evening, as the sun's last amber strips tinted the river, I packed a bag with a change of doublet and my hand-scribed copy of the writings of Trithemius relating to the rituals of scrying.

Outside, Cecil's builders, who had arrived this day to begin repairing my mother's roof, were packing up their tools, loading them on to their cart. As it was pulled away, I stood in my workplace, next to the owl, feeling lost and solitary. Last night, I'd lain too long awake, trying to divert my thoughts from the coming journey by thinking of Nel Borrow who, in my mother's eyes, would have made a most unsuitable wife – what Cecil would call, in contempt, *a carnal marriage*.

As distinct from the most dangerous of all marriages which beckoned Dudley. In writing to him from Bonner's cell, I'd followed only my conscience, but was now become part of the engine which powered his determination to wed the Queen in the belief *that it was right*... for England and thus for the world.

Your Highness, the archangels Gabriel and Uriel both send their respects and what look to be dread warnings of what may happen if, to gratify the political ambition of others, you turn away from love...

Oh, you might think my part in it would be no more than smoke. For everyone who calls me a sorcerer there's another who scorns me as a pretender to powers I don't have. And they, God help me, may be closer to the truth.

Was I then supposed to remind Dudley that, for all my learning, I could not make the leap from the written page into the void? That the birthcharts I'd drawn were craft not prophecy, the dreams I'd so assiduously written down upon awakening were invariably mundane? That even the ghost which had travelled in my baggage all the way from Glastonbury to London was apparent to everyone but me?

That I was afraid to my gut that if we acquired the shewstone of Wigmore it would not speak to me?

And would that, anyway, stay his hand?

Last night, after my prayers, I'd told all this to Eleanor

Borrow, wherever she lay. Nel, who would forever be a part of my past.

The full truth of this broke, as if the walls of our poor house were collapsing around me, and I stood with my back to the window and the owl and found myself to be weeping.

PART THREE

*The shameful villainy used by the Welshwomen
towards the dead carcasses was such as honest
ears would be ashamed to hear and continent
tongues to speak thereof*

HOLINSHED

Chronicles…

XV

The Hill of Bones and Ghosts

October, 1560. Brynglas at Pilleth on the Welsh Border.

A SINGLE EYE looks up at Anna Ceddol through a veil of shivering ground-mist, and all the rest is blood.

She's saying, 'Who is he?'

As if anyone could be sure. You must imagine Anna Ceddol clutching her woollen shawl tight across her breast but refusing to look away. Down the valley, the early sun hangs amid rusted coils of mist.

At first she could not understand what all the fear was about – Pedr Morgan's wife drumming with both fists on her door as the sky grew pink. A dead man found on Brynglas? Wouldn't be the first this year, nor the twelfth. All those forlorn heaps of browning bones turned up by the plough, all ragged with the remnants of leather jerkins and makeshift armour. Too many.

The dead are removed upon an old cart kept in a tumbledown sheep shelter halfway up the lower slope. Taken for reburial with small ceremony in the field beside the church where, even after a century and a half, their descendants come to pray and visit the holy well.

But anyone can see what's different about this one.

'Likely been yere all night,' Pedr Morgan, the shepherd says. 'But no longer than that. That's the point, isn't it?'

The stink of blood and shit will be wafting up at Anna, and still, I imagine, she does not turn away.

His face has been split open with a spade or an axe. One eye hanging out, laid upon the remains of a cheek, while the other has been taken, most likely by a crow. The naked chest and stomach have also been ripped and plucked by scavenging birds or foxes. Bands of glistening entrails left entwined like to a scatter of dull jewellery.

'We need the cart,' Anna says. 'He can't be left here much longer, or there'll be nothing left of him.'

She looks up at the church, Our Lady of Pilleth. Miraculous cures were once recorded here, under the statue of the Holy Mother above this shallow cauldron of empty hills. That was before a thousand men were shot and hacked to death. Before the sacred spring ran brown with blood and the church itself burned. There are more bones in the earth here than tree roots and no one wants to build over an unknown grave. Which is why they send for Siôn.

Maybe she's recalling how, when she was pulling on her shawl this morning, her brother began to howl piteously, his fingers clawing at the empty air. As if the terror of Goodwife Morgan was making divers pictures around him which he must needs rip away.

Anna has left him squatting by the fire, wrapped in a sheep-skin and hugging himself. He didn't want to go with her – as though he already knew what was here, just as he'd known what lay in the foundations of Stephen Price's new barn.

Siôn Ceddol. A miracle in himself.

✠

118

'No sign of his apparel?'

The shepherd shakes his head, closing his eyes, as though cursing the circumstance that had him born here, as he oft-times does aloud. In the valley, fresh smoke spouts from the chimney of an oak-framed house where new braces support an upper storey.

Nant-y-groes, where my father, Rowland Dee, was born, below the hill of bones.

'There's more, see,' Pedr Morgan says faintly, and Anna Ceddol stares at him. He turns to where the man with the ruined face lies on his back, half under a thorn tree. Its roots and bole are covered with vicious brambles, some of which have been dragged across the lower part of the body as if to conceal its male emblems.

Pedr Morgan pulls some of the brambles away to reveal a leg twisted at the knee.

'I'd not have my wife see this.'

Anna Ceddol almost smiles. She's grown used to being treated not as a normal woman. This, she knows, is because of the tasks she has to perform in the care of her brother. Their parents died within a year of one another, and so Anna has never married – too old now, at twenty-nine, she'll say, unless some widower is in need of comfort in his dotage.

But there's no hope of comfort with Siôn in the house – sixteen years now and terrifying to most.

'There's evil here,' Pedr Morgan says.

Anna Ceddol has borrowed Pedr's knife to cut away more brambles. When she glances up from the corpse, the shepherd is turned away, looking down the valley. She says nothing and bends to the brambles, working patiently and her hands do not tremble. She disregards the smells, seemingly unaware of the grace with which she undertakes such a foul task.

Both her hands bleeding freely from wrenching carelessly at the brambles. She slides a knife under a thick stem bristling with savage thorns and lifts. Up it comes, all of a sudden, bringing with it smaller shoots, and all is peeled away from the dead man's thighs.

'Oh,' Anna says.

Of course, she's heard the tales, still told in the alehouses of Presteigne, tales spat out like bile from the gut.

About what happened after the battle between Mortimer's cobbled-together army of untrained English peasantry and the hungry Welsh, serving their fork-bearded wizard. On windy nights, they say, the last cries of dying men still are heard, bright threads of agony woven into the fabric of the storm.

This hill of faith and death. This holy hill soiled by slaughter and an old hatred that never quite goes away because this is border country and its air is ever ajangle with bewildered, jostling ghosts.

Anna Ceddol sees the dead man's mouth is a mash of shattered teeth, though nothing parts them but a bloody pulp.

Betwixt his thighs, however...

Anyone can tell *that's* not done by the crows.

XVI

Pike-head

I WAS THROWN back at the sight of several dozen men with pikes and crossbows and a half-concealed firearm or two. And a dozen laden carts, all gathered under a whelk-shell sky in the field beyond London Bridge.

Seemed at first like an advance guard for the Queen, and it was only when I left the wherry that I marked the absence of flags, music or any hint of merriment. And saw that the shabby-clad man approaching me was Dudley.

'Dr Dee.' He shook my hand with formality. 'Master Roberts. Remember me?'

First I'd seen of him since that night in my workroom. When I'd taken up his offer for me to lie at his house in Kew until our departure for Wales, he'd been absent the whole time. A bedchamber had been prepared for me and my meals made daily by the servants, while I spent long hours in solitary book-study. No one in the house appeared to know where Dudley had gone.

Master Roberts?

The name he'd been known by on our mission to Glastonbury at the end of the winter. An indication that discretion was to be exercised on this journey, for him if not for me, and yet...

...*Jesu.* I surveyed the clattering assembly with dismay. This was his idea of discretion? Before I could question it, Dudley led me across the well-trodden field, away from the throng.

We stopped close to the bridge itself, where it was quiet.

I said, 'Have the trumpeters been delayed?'

The crow-picked head of a man had fallen from one of the poles and lay in the grass near our feet. I wondered if it had belonged to some executed traitor I might recognise, winced and looked away as Dudley kicked the head down the bank, then grinned.

'All this... it's not for me, you fool.'

Close up, I realised that shabby had been a wrong impression. If the mourning purple was gone and had not been replaced by his customary gilded splendour, his leathery apparel was still of good quality. Country landowner-class, at least, except for the exceptionally beautiful riding boots, possibly a small gift from the Queen at a time when there were no thousand-acre estates to spare.

'It's for the judge,' Dudley said. 'Sixty armed guards.'

He explained. It seemed the trial in Radnorshire was for some Welsh felon, of whom an example must needs be made. Dudley said a London judge had been requested by the Council of the Marches in Ludlow to make sure it was handled *efficiently and robustly.*

Well, I knew what that meant, but a *London* judge? Was that usual?

'It is,' Dudley said, 'when the local judiciary fears for the health of its wives and children and safety of its property.'

The man on trial was the leader of *Plant Mat*, a brotherhood of violent cattle-thieves, highway-robbers and killers lodged in the heart of Wales. Well organised, controlling trade, smuggling goods from France, running several inns at which travellers were habitually robbed or held for ransom.

'I've never heard of this. Plant Mat? Children of Matthew?'

Dudley shrugged.

'It's Wales. Where they seem to be regarded as heroes for the obvious reason that they've been preying, whenever they can, on the English. Or so they claim.'

'Hence the guard?'

'Procured with the full agreement of Cecil, I'd guess. Despite his being Welsh.'

I tensed.

'That means Cecil knows we're travelling with them?'

'Of course not. We're here through Blount's connections.'

Thomas Blount, his steward, was a former attorney.

'There's a handful of others also travelling with us,' Dudley said. 'All of them well-investigated, no doubt, to make sure none are too... shall we say *too Welsh?*'

When he smiled, I saw that his moustache had been trimmed close to his face, his beard cut back to little more than stubble. Hardly distinguished but it was wise enough, under these circumstances. A ransom for Lord Dudley would be not inconsiderable.

'Sure you're quite happy with this, Robbie?'

'Welsh banditry? God's bollocks, John.' Dudley sniffed in contempt and began to walk back up the field. 'Come on, we need to fix you up with a horse. Oh, and while I remember... if anyone should ask, Dr John Dee is journeying, as he often does, in pursuit of old books and also to inspect his family's property in the borderlands. Assisted by his old friend, Master Roberts, the antiquary. That sound plausible to you?'

123

Highly plausible, and it had worked in Glastonbury. Several dozen significant rare books and manuscripts in my library at Mortlake had come from the libraries of dissolved monasteries. When religious houses are plundered for treasure, either by common thieves or the Crown, the books are ofttimes flung aside as worthless.

I caught him up.

'Who knows the truth?'

'Nobody knows the *truth*, John. Though obviously Legge knows who Roberts is and can think what the hell he likes about my reasons for getting out of London for a while.'

I stopped, grasping his arm.

'Legge?'

'The judge.'

'*Christopher* Legge?'

'*Sir* Christopher Legge. If you paid proper attention to the lists you'd know these things.' Dudley scrutinised me. 'History here?'

'In a way.'

Five years back, when I'd been accused of conjuring against Queen Mary, several false charges had also been levelled against me by a lawyer, name of Ferrers, now himself held in suspicion after a printing press producing pamphlets full of French lies about the Queen had been found on his premises. Ferrers had oiled his way out of the Fleet by convincing the court he'd had no knowledge of the treasonous intent of a man renting his premises.

It seemed unlikely he'd yet have links with Christopher Legge who, as a young attorney, had helped process evidence against me for presentation to the Star Chamber. Evidence which, being qualified in law and so conducting my own defence, I'd assiduously broken to dust.

Legge was now a *judge*? He must be a couple of years younger than me, maybe not even thirty. We'd never spoken and there was no reason to suppose he bore ill will towards me, if ever he had. But, for the duration of this journey, I'd try to avoid him, nonetheless.

'He'll be on the Privy Council one day, from what I hear,' Dudley said. 'If he survives the trial.'

'Why would he not?'

'Just something I heard.'

He laughed, and I took the remark as being not too serious. Taking this opportunity to ask him where the hell he'd been while I was lying low at his house in Kew.

'Later,' Dudley said.

He walked away.

'*Robbie...*'

Dudley stopped ten or so paces short of the first cart, looked over a shoulder and lowered his voice to a hiss.

'Cumnor. I was at Cumnor.'

Rapidly, I caught him up.

'Was that advisable?'

To my knowledge, until now he'd never been back to the house where Amy died since she was found. Would not have been seemly. Might have suggested he had traces to cover. On the surface, he'd behaved impeccably, only sending Thomas Blount to record the circumstances on his behalf.

'Why?' I said. 'Why risk it, with the inquest still in process?'

'Could be months before the inquest returns its verdict. I'm to be held in purgatory till then?'

'And was it worth it? Did you learn anything?'

'Too much.'

Ahead of us, I could now see Sir Christopher Legge. Would not have marked him if I hadn't known he was here. He'd changed. Narrow features, which had been gawky when last I'd seen him, had hardened like a new-forged pike-head introduced to cold water. He was enclosed by a dozen attendants and minor attorneys but was somehow distant from them all.

'Well?' I said to Dudley.

Still unsure how far I trusted him.

'I'll tell you when there's privacy.'

He began to walk up the riverside field towards the company of men and horses. His gypsy's skin seemed darker under the pink-veined sky.

Of a sudden, he turned back.

'There's an evil here, John,' he said.

XVII

A Sense of the Ominous

WHEN FIRST I was known as the Queen's astrologer, my services were in big demand, mainly from ambitious people wanting my name on their child's birthchart. In the euphoria following the coronation there were more of these requests than I could easily deal with.

But a few others – and they still come, on occasion – related to the less-easily defined aspect of my role – *adviser on the Hidden.* And therein lies a dilemma.

These approaches are, as you'd expect, more discreet and come from men who feel their homes or their families to be cursed by enemies or menaced by demons and ghosts. Coming to me as if I'm believed equipped to dispel a nameless evil in the name of the Queen.

Dear God. Oft-times, I'll make an excuse and walk away, knowing there's confusion about the nature of my profession. While I'm no sorcerer, neither am I a proper priest.

When I was made Rector of Upton-upon-Severn, during the short reign of the boy king Edward, it was a lay appointment, designed to provide a firm income so that I might pursue my studies and also eat. Later, I did take Holy Orders and during Mary's reign could have passed as a Catholic priest – hence my time as Bonner's chaplain. But it seemed to me no more than a formality, little better than having conveyed a quiet gift of silver to someone like the former Abbot of Wigmore.

Even my mother fails to understand this and will, on occasion, berate me for giving up an income for life. But, dear God, I dread to think how many useless blessings have been given by unholy priests invested for money. What you must needs know is that I never believed myself to have been *called* to it, and thus have ever refused to accept responsibility for the cure of souls. Or the redemption of unquiet spirits.

A priest's approach to the unseen must needs be single-minded. He must deem all ghosts satanic, attacking them with a passion, assailing them with missiles of liturgy. And must never let himself become diverted from his task by tantalising and forbidden questions: *What is this? Does it exist only in my mind, or has it a chemical reality? What can it tell me about the afterlife? What knowledge can it pass on about the hidden nature of things?*

The questions of a natural philosopher, a man of science. Who may have a firm grounding in divinity and a full devotion to God, but should never in this world don the robes of a practising priest.

So I must have shown little enthusiasm when, as we came towards Hereford, one of the minor attorneys, a young man called Roger Vaughan, rode alongside me and asked if I were here to offer spiritual counsel.

✢

It was the close of our third day on the road. Such a company as ours – with ten carts and sixty armed men, for heaven's sake – would not hope to make good progress. Neither did my relations with Vaughan get off to the most promising of starts.

'*Siarad Cymreig*, Dr Dee?'

I'd picked up enough of the language from my tad to know what he was asking, but best for it to stop there.

'No,' I said. 'My father spoke some Welsh, but I don't. And never having been to Wales before—'

'*Never?* Oh.'

Vaughan was a solemn young man with a half-grown gingery beard and a mild Welshness in his voice. I knew his family was long-established on the border, claiming descent from princes – as, of course, did the Dees. Now he was telling me he'd been in London to study at the inns of court.

'Indeed I was also hoping to study with you, Dr Dee, but… I was told you were away.'

'I do spend a deal of time away. Which is one reason I've never had the time to visit Wales.'

Why would he want to study with me? Although qualified in the law, I'd never practised it except in my own defence. I steadied my horse before a small pond. With all the cattle drovers passing through here, you'd surely expect these roads to be among the best in England.

'You're also interested in mathematics, Master Vaughan? Astrology, perhaps.'

'I suppose… to a level. But that was not what I— That is, you're said to be better qualified than anyone in other areas of knowledge.'

The boy was almost as hesitant as I'd been at his age.

I said, 'You mean in matters of the Hidden?'

'Such matters,' Vaughan said, 'tend to provoke sneers at the inns of court. But not to someone born and bred in the Border country.'

'Some areas of life are not so easily manipulated as the law,' I said.

He laughed. I knew of the Vaughans through word of the Red Book of Hergest, a manuscript in the Welsh language, now nearly two hundred years old, containing the essence of the Mabinogi, the old Welsh mythology full of ancient wisdom and symbolism.

In fact, a good reason for one day learning Welsh.

'Your family still has the Red Book?'

'On occasion, attempts are made to have it taken deep into Wales, but we resist. The Vaughans… we're ever concerned with our heritage. Even have, as you may have heard, our own curse – spectral hound foretelling death in the family. However, this matter – the trial, that is – affects my family not at all. *Yours*, however…'

'*What?*'

'Please understand I'm not trying to pry or to intrude in any way.' Vaughan's face was now redder than his hair. 'I'm simply approaching you as a neighbour, your family home being but an hour's ride from mine.'

I had to shake my head.

'Master Vaughan, my family home is at Mortlake on the Thames. I was born in London.'

'Oh.'

'I'm here with my colleague to seek certain antiquities. The proximity of Nant-y-groes is purely coincidental. But if you're saying there's a problem there…?'

'Not as such, no.' Vaughan was looking directly ahead to where a spire had pierced the western clouds. God, the evasiveness of these border folk. 'Well… not so much Nant-y-groes itself as the nearby village. Pilleth. Which stands to the side of Brynglas Hill. The site of the battle?'

'The battle in which the English were, erm, slaughtered.' I stared at the churned mud ahead of us, itself like a battlefield. 'By the Welsh. Led by Owain Glyndwr.'

'And his general, Rhys Gethin,' Vaughan said.

My tad had spoken of this, though not in any great detail. Owain Glyndwr's campaign had begun as a dispute over the ownership of land and developed into a bitter war against England. Glyndwr had declared himself Prince of Wales and laid waste to the border and its strongholds. But this was a hundred and fifty years ago, in the time of King Henry IV.

I remembered from my Cambridge days learning how, as a young man, Owain Glyndwr had been well known at the English King's court. He was cultured, well educated, well qualified in the law... and also, it was said, in aspects of the Hidden. No one who knew him would have expected him to become such a ruthless and merciless opponent.

'A place where a thousand men have been slaughtered,' Vaughan said, 'is not exactly the easiest place to make a home.'

'But surely Nant-y-groes would have been there, in some form or other, before the battle?'

'However, the village was not. Only isolated farms existed before, and no one lived there for years afterwards. But then a few dwellings were built to house farm workers and their families, and—'

Of a sudden, he urged his horse forward as if to out-race an error, calling back over his shoulder, the wind whipping at his words.

'When you meet members of your family, please don't mention my approach to you.'

I caught him up, but the conversation was dead. Ahead of us, the spire was become the body of what I guessed to be Hereford's cathedral. Close by were the walls and tower of the castle, reddened not by the sun, as there was none, but by the nature of the stone itself.

Roger Vaughan looked up as an arrowhead of wild geese passed overhead. As if this might be an omen.

'Perchance there'll be occasion to talk again, Dr Dee,' he said.

☩

It had been a curiously muted journey from the start. Each night, we'd lain not at inns but at the country houses of well-off landowners, Justices of the Peace and county sheriffs, the guards all fed and bedded in their outbuildings, the horses accommodated in their stables. Everywhere, we were expected and bedchambers prepared. The talk over dinner was ever friendly but ever cautious.

Each morning, as we set out, there was, for me, a sense of the ominous. Accuse me, if you like, of living in the shadow of imagined persecution, but I could not believe that only Judge Legge knew of the presence amongst us of a suspected wife-killer believed to have bedded the Queen.

I watched Dudley riding ahead, with his man John Forest and the captain of the guard. He must have been known to at least one of the owners of the houses where we'd lain. Steps would have been taken to ensure discretion.

He'd yet told me nothing of what he'd learned at Cumnor Place. What he learned that implied *evil*.

Did Dudley prefer to ride at the head of the company because he was disinclined to be surrounded by unknown men with no cause to wish him a long life?

Unknown *armed* men. I flinched as a vision of the imagination ripped through me: riders all bunched together and then separating, leaving one man dangling from his horse, dragged by a boot in the stirrup through a river of his own blood.

And the next to die... the next would be me? The infamous conjuror said to trade with demons who would, if Ferrers and Legge had succeeded, have gone to ashes five years ago. Dear God, if I'd dwelt on this for long enough, I might have turned my horse around and galloped like a madman back into the heart of England.

Too late now. As if dropped from the sky, the city of Hereford was strewn about us, a damp untidiness of fenced fields and holdings and timbered shops and dwellings around a triangle of high-spired churches. A frontier town.

And a frontier in my life. I felt now, as I had these past three days, to be on an ill-made road leading not to the roots of my family but into somewhere far more foreign than France or the Low Countries, for at least I could speak their languages.

Guiding my mare between foot-deep puddles and mounds of rubble which had once been part of the old walls, I followed the train into a wide street, where people were gathered to watch us. One spired church lay behind us, the cathedral ahead, the last one in England. On the rim of twilight, its stones glowed the colour of the shewstone Elias had unveiled before Goodwife Faldo.

I thought of the Wigmore stone and could no longer

understand how the desire for it had lured me here. There were surely other stones to be found, as potent as this one.

Across the famous River Wye, a long line of hills lay on the western horizon. The *Mynydd Ddu* – Black Mountains. Where Wales began. The light from a now-invisible setting sun had bled into a symmetry of cloud which hung above these mountains like half-folded wings. Gilded feathers in a holy light. As we rode on, they came apart.

XVIII

Transcending the Mapper's Craft

We lodged that night with the Bishop of Hereford at his palace by the eastern bank of the Wye, deep and fast-flowing after this drear summer of persistent rain.

As ever, in a city new to me, I would have welcomed time alone to uncover its libraries and antiquities. I'd marked the once-proud Norman castle falling into ruin, as Leland had hinted in his *Itinerary*: greenery up the walls, parts of the tower gone to rubble, sheep grazing the one-time courtyards. Why am I ever drawn to ruins?

But no time for closer study. Salmon had been brought up from the Wye for our evening meal in two sittings in a near-monastic, white-walled refectory. As ever, it was polite but unjovial, most of us tired and aching from the ride. The talk was of little more than hunting, and, as soon as I could slip away, I did. Suppressing fatigue, I cornered one of the canons and asked if I might speak with the bishop.

His name was John Scory, once Protestant Bishop of Chichester, deprived of his status in Mary's reign, redeemed by Elizabeth. Yet sent out here into the wilderness, which seemed not much like redemption to me.

I was received into a crooked chamber with panelled walls of dark oak but no bookshelves. Only a Bible betwixt pen and ink and a wad of cheap paper on a narrow oaken trestle. A window was fallen open to the greying river.

Scory, plain-cassocked below his station, pulled out an uncushioned chair for me and went back behind his trestle, lit not by a candle but an old-fashioned rushlight. Possibly an indication of how brief he expected our discussion to be.

'Forgive me, Dr Dee, but do I recall you as Bonner's chaplain, once?'

For obvious reasons, this is not something I normally include in my *curriculum vitae*, particularly when dealing with Protestant bishops. I sought the short answer.

'Better than being burned for heresy, Bishop.'

'Oh, indeed. But why would Bonner choose to *employ* a man so narrowly spared from the flames? Do you mind the question?'

He was a wiry man of middle years, low-voiced for a bishop. He sat back in his chair, fixing on a pair of glasses as if fully to observe the quality of my response.

'I believe,' I said, 'that this was to enable Bishop Bonner to tap into what I'd learned in… what you might call the outfields of divinity.'

'Oh… keeping a *pet magician*?' In the sallow light, a wry smile was shaped in Scory's lean face. 'I do beg mercy, Dr Dee, but Bonner's a man who holds fast to his beliefs. If he'd signed to the Queen he'd be back on the streets, and the fact that he didn't and he isn't…'

'Suggests he feels safer living quietly behind bars,' I said. 'I wouldn't pretend to understand him, but behind the history of terror there's a questing mind. I… don't know why, given his deplorable history, but I can find things in him to like. Which makes me wonder about myself.'

He peered at me through his glasses, then snatched them off, and a full smile at last broke through.

'You're clearly an honest young man, Dr Dee. As I'd heard. Also, it's said, wondrous with numbers, more than conversant with the law, expert in geography, the arts of navigation...' Scory's eyebrows rose a fraction, and then he came forward, both elbows on the board. 'So what are you doing in such alarming company?'

'Alarming?'

'Biggest bloody hanging-party *I've* ever seen in this part of the world.'

Scory fumbled in a locker under the board and produced a good candle which he held to the dying rushlight until it flared. Evidently, the discussion was not to be as brief as I'd expected.

✠

Bishops have never been chosen for their nearness to God, but – unless, like Bonner, their working lives are over – most have kept close to prominent sinners. They'll bully harmless parish priests without mercy but, in dealing with influential laity, ever walk on eggshells.

Not Scory. Curiously, he was proving to be a man who gave not a shit for status.

'They're hardly going to offer him an amnesty, Dr Dee.'

'No,' I said. 'Erm... whom?'

'Believed to be a certain Prys Gethin.'

'Truly?' I said.

I'd never heard of this man, though the similarity of his name to that of Owain Glyndwr's general had not passed me by.

Scory was silent for quite a while. Through the opened window, I could hear a rising night-breeze on the river. Scory moved back from the candle to study me.

'Why do I have the feeling that you don't know what the hell I'm talking about?'

'Ah...' I shrugged uncomfortably. 'That's because I'm not part of the judicial company. Just a fellow traveller.'

'More and more mysterious. So what do you want from me, Dr Dee? Why would the Queen's advisor on all manner of extraordinary matters want to keep a tired old cleric from his bed?'

'Well, assuming your diocese includes the town of Wigmore, in the west, I wanted to ask what you knew about the abbey there. Whatever might be left of it.'

'Not much. Gone to ruin since the Reform, like most of them. The abbot's house is become a private home.'

'The abbot, yes,' I said. 'The former abbot was called John Smart? What of him?'

'I've only been here a year, therefore never encountered the man in person. Only by reputation.' Scory wrinkled his nose. 'Why do you want to know about Smart?'

'I gather that after the Reform, he was reported to the late Lord Cromwell for a number of crimes.'

'And that's unusual?'

'Simony, I heard. And lewd behaviour with local women. And misappropriation of abbey treasure?'

'And which of these might interest you?' Scory said slyly. 'Perchance... oh, let me think... the treasure?'

'Bishop,' I said. 'It's clear you have your own ideas where my particular interests lie. However—'

'Well, yes, I do, Dr Dee, but if what I've heard's correct we're not necessarily talking of gold plate. On that ground, it may well be that our definitions of treasure would, to an extent, correspond,' Scory said. 'Would you like to see some of mine before you retire?'

'Treasure?'

'A very rare treasure, to my mind, and I'd certainly welcome your opinion... as an authority in geography, navigation... and other matters.'

Response from the clergy to what I do falls into two groups: those who damn me as a sorcerer and those who wonder if my work and theirs might one day converge. Men like Bonner, this is, even though he kept his interests secret while publicly damning sorcerers and Protestants to hell.

And Scory?

Carrying a ring of keys, he led me out through a back door of his house and across the shadowed green to the cathedral itself... and into this vast red-walled oven of a building. Simpler in form and less-adorned than some I'd been into. A few lanterns were lit, and Scory unhooked one and I followed him across the misty nave and out through another door and into a cloister, where another lamp met us.

'Who's—?'

'Only me, Tom.'

'My Lord Bishop,' a shadow said.

'Taking our visitor to see the treasure.'

'Treasure, my Lord?'

Scory's laugh mingled with the jingle of the keys as he unlocked a door to our right and held the lantern high. I followed him into a square cell with one shuttered window and no furniture except for a wide oak cupboard on the wall facing us.

'I'd show you our library, too,' Scory said. 'If I wasn't too ashamed.'

'How so?'

'Disordered. One day we'll raise the money to pay someone to examine and list the books.'

'I'd do it for nothing.'

'If you had two years to spare.' He handed me the lantern and reached up to unlock the cupboard on the wall. 'Meanwhile, anything you can tell me about this...'

At first the doors jammed and then yielded and sprang open together and, by God, it *was* treasure. Couldn't take it in at first.

'Hidden away for years,' Scory said. 'Thought to be papist magic.'

'My *God*...'

The whole world was spread before us.

'How old?'

'At least three hundred years. Have you ever seen its like before, Dr Dee?'

He held the lantern close, slowly moving the lights around a thousand figures and images, etched in black upon a skin stretched over a wooden frame. I saw what seemed to be biblical figures surrounded by a monstrous bestiary of birds and fishes, serpents and dragons. Horned creatures and haloed men, robed and naked, amid a maze of towers and rivers and seas, hills and islands, all of them neatly labelled in Latin and enclosed by wedges of text.

'A map... of everything?'

'Of the world. As it was then known.'

'Was it made here?'

'Nobody knows where it was made or who made it or how it came to be in Hereford. Admittedly, a world that's less than the one known now.'

'Or more,' I said, thinking I could spend weeks in study of it. 'The knowledge we've gained is more than equalled by the knowledge we've lost.'

I stood transfixed, marking the figures of a mermaid and a lion with a man's crowned head and symbols I did not understand. Yes, primitive compared with Mercator's globe, yet I felt in the presence of something far transcending the mapper's craft. Evidently, the Welsh border had more secrets than I'd imagined.

'You should know that it does inspire a level of fear, even amongst some of the canons here. They say too much contemplation of it invites madness. I'm told there've been attempts over the years to burn it to a crisp. I'd guess there *is* an element of the occluded here. So for the present, I keep it locked away. Does it speak to *you*?'

Scory moved the lantern and the shapes on the map seemed to shuffle like playing cards into different patterns.

'Well,' I said. 'I doubt it was made by one man. More likely some closed monastic order. Look.'

I pointed at the centre of the map, where something of evident importance was represented by a cogged wheel.

'The centre of the world,' Scory said.

'Jerusalem.' I nodded. 'That could be of significance.'

I stepped back, half-closing my eyes, and new configurations began to form in the candlelight.

'Bishop, were the, um, Poor Fellow-Soldiers of Christ and of the Temple of Solomon... ever active in Hereford?'

'The Knights Templar?' Scory's eyes widened. 'Well... not in the city itself but, yes, there were several Templar communities within ten miles of here. My God, Dee...'

'Jerusalem obviously was the centre of the Templar world. They guarded the city against the Saracen for many years, had their headquarters on the site of the Temple and, it's said, had access to its most ancient secrets. Some of which might well be...'

I glanced at the map.

'Enciphered *here*?'

'I'd put extra locks on this cupboard... and on the door. That's assuming you do not consider the Templars to have been, um, satanic?'

Scory smiled.

'Part of my duty here, Dr Dee, is not to condemn but to protect what exists until such time as it might be interpreted. Well...' He let out a breath. 'What you say makes remarkable sense. I'd never thought of the Templars. This is, ah, better than papist magic, I think.'

'Potentially, beyond value,' I said. 'Which is why I'd recommend you make it even more secure.'

'I will. And, ah... some men, if I may say so, might have chosen to keep such a deduction about the map's origins... to themselves.'

'Why would they? It's in the best place.'

He put out his hand.

'Thank you, Dr Dee,' he said.

✠

As we walked back to the palace, Scory's mood was far more open. He told me he'd once been a Dominican friar. Possibly a reason he'd been given Hereford where, until the Reform, the Blackfriars had been popular residents in the heart of the city.

'Hereford might seem a lowly post after Chichester. But more important for being on the rim of Wales. The significance of which was made clear to me from the start – the importance of keeping Wales on the Queen's side.'

'The Queen's proud to be a descendent of King Arthur of the old Britons.'

'A descent beyond dispute, Dr Dee,' Scory said with what might have been mock gravity. 'Her grandfather's progress from out of Wales to the English throne is surely confirmation of the prophecy that Arthur would rise again. And all's been quiet on the border ever since.'

'It has?'

'More or less. Still recovering from the damage inflicted during the Glyndwr wars. And yet now... they're sending a small army to convict and hang one man. One *Welsh*man. Curious, don't you think?'

'I don't know enough about it.'

'No.'

He stopped, looking out over the river, moonlit now, and then walked down towards its bank.

'The Wye flows through a strange and individual place, Dr Dee – more so over the border. They have their own beliefs which continue regardless of the Church, whether it be Catholic or Protestant.'

'Oh?'

'It seemed to me that one could either respond with a Bonner-like ferocity or with a tolerance bordering on the spiritually lax.'

'Towards what?'

I followed him down to the edge of the river, a strip of silvery linen unrolled from the hills.

'I chose tolerance,' he said. 'Which is why I suspect that the behaviour of your Abbot Smart reflected no more than his own response to his bucolic situation. He feasted, he hunted, he chased after women. And caught some. Well... I'd be a fool to say that's not how some of my fellow bishops have behaved.'

'And the abbey treasures?'

'Such an extravagant way of life will ever demand a certain wealth,' Scory said.

'Do you know what they were, these treasures?'

'Never gone into it. What's the treasure you seek?'

'A gemstone. Said to have been at the abbey.'

'And you think you'll find it *now*?'

'A gemstone which is now, apparently, for sale.'

'Ah.' Scory smiled. 'Now *that* sounds like Smart. What kind of gemstone?'

'We think a beryl.'

'*We?*'

'The friend who's travelling with me.'

'And that would be...? Come now, Dr Dee, think yourself into my situation. Here I am, leading my quiet life, learning my Welsh to talk to the neighbours... when, of a sudden, I'm invited to accommodate a company including a prominent judge, the Queen's astrologer... and another man who, despite his dull apparel, I recognise from my time in the South as none

144

other than the Queen's Master of the Horse...' Scory leaned into the candlelight '... *at the very least.*'

I sighed.

'It is who you think, yes. Not the most popular man in London at the moment, for reasons you're doubtless aware of. But, I believe, falsely accused.'

Did I believe that? The candle in the lantern had gone out and I was glad of the relative dark.

'Nevertheless, a man not short of gemstones, I'd guess,' Scory said.

What choice did I have? I told him the beryl was famous as a spiritual device and heard him laugh.

'The magician arises. You've come all this way for a fortune-telling stone?'

'In the cause of, um, scientific study.' I was beginning to feel like a prating prick. 'The way such stones have been studied in Europe.'

He shrugged.

'I'll grant you that. I'm hardly in a position to dismiss miracle and magic when we have here in the cathedral the shrine of one of my distant predecessors, whose boiled bones seem to have cured thousands and still draw pilgrimages.'

He meant St Thomas Cantilupe. My library had several manuscripts on the tomb of this most famous bishop of Hereford and other healing shrines where tapers were lit and the bodies of the sick measured to the saints.

'Indeed,' Scory said. 'So a small brown stone dedicated in the names of several prominent angels which not only foretells the future but gives off healing rays—'

'So you know of it.'

145

'I've *heard* of it. But it's all gossip and myth and legend and I know not where it might be found. But I can tell you that if Smart has it, it won't come cheap. Unless you – or more likely Lord Dudley – are in a position to, ah, apply some physical pressure?'

'That was never my intention,' I said honestly. 'Do you have any idea where Smart might be found? Assuming he's still alive.'

'Oh, he'll be alive, unless the border's ridden with some vengeful plague I've not yet heard of.'

'How did he escape… well, at least imprisonment, when the charges against him were presented to Cromwell?'

I was thinking of poor pious Abbot Whiting of Glastonbury, who'd been hanged, drawn and quartered for less.

'Blood of Christ, Dr Dee,' Scory said, 'I didn't know, until this night, how you yourself escaped the stake at the hands of Bonner. And no, I don't know where Smart is, though I do hear word of him from time to time. If I were to say…'

His back hunched in deliberation, he walked along the moonlit riverbank, looking down at his entwined fingers.

'What *can* I tell you…? Except… as the rest of them are going to Presteigne, why not begin your inquiries there? The Abbey of Wigmore owned most of that town at one time.'

When I told him my cousin, Nicholas Meredith, lived there, Scory's laughter went skimming over the Wye like a hail of pebbles.

'And *Meredith*, I was about to say, owned much of the rest. And now appears to own even more. Oh, yes, he might be a *very* good man to talk to…'

'Bishop, I get weary of saying I don't understand, but—'

'No, no, no…' Scory moved away, separating his hands and wiping the air betwixt us. 'You'll get no more from me on this particular bag of adders. All I'll say is it's worth remembering that Presteigne still has its share of dark alleys. Anyway, you might see me there.'

'You?'

'The judge has asked me to give evidence to his court. Come along, Dr Dee. Past my bedtime, and past yours, too, if you don't want to fall off your horse tomorrow.'

'Evidence?'

'In the matter of witchcraft,' Scory said.

The river licked at the bank below my thin boots, like the sound of quiet, sardonic laughter, and I turned away from it and followed him back to his palace.

XIX

Dungheap

FOR A WHILE, the land was all red soil, as if the earth itself had been stained by the blood shed in the Glyndwr wars and the bitter battles through which the Tudors rose.

All was heavy under luminous grey cloud as we rode past the remains of castles, with towers like broken teeth, and bared mottes from which the stone had been stolen to build the farms in the valleys. And then the road was gloomed with forest to either side, dim as a church aisle at dusk, as we made our quiet and watchful way into Wales.

One day you'll go back, boy. One day.

My tad, Rowland Dee. All for Wales, but *he* never went back.

Welsh towns and villages… I'd learned that they were all stark and wind-flayed, their stone houses long and low and slit-windowed, as much against the weather as attack. Hard, cold houses occupied by the race of strong, sinewy men my father had spoken of.

Bending to the wind like hawthorn trees, boy, and no less prickly.

My tad describing all this to me as a child as though he, too, had been raised as a man of the mountains. As he was neither sinewy nor hard, I recall wondering if he'd been sent into exile for being insufficiently Welsh.

It was only when the road emerged from the forest and we crested a hill and I was at last looking down upon my family's local town... that I saw the dispiriting truth of it.

I urged my mare ahead to join Dudley, who was riding alone, having bid his man John Forest to remain in Hereford to receive any mail which might arrive from London and bring it on to Presteigne. Dudley had told me that Thomas Blount, at Kew, was on constant watch for anything new which might emerge in regard to Amy's death.

And something *had* happened. Something he could not even whisper about inside this quiet company of judicial strangers.

'John!' Dudley calling to me with unnecessary volume, as if to ridicule the silence of the company behind us. 'Will your letter have reached your cousin yet?'

'Who knows – can we ever rely on the post? If not we'll hope for an inn.'

'Plenty good beds in an assize town... all those fastidious fucking lawyers to accommodate.'

I felt the chilled silence of the attorneys behind us. By now, the wind had died back, but no one spoke above the measured clop of hooves and the creaking of the well-laden carts on the pitted track. Below us, across a quiet river, was tended pasture-land, farms and old cottages with frames of gnarled grey oak.

And this town. This *Welsh* town.

If the ghost of my tad were with us, I only hoped its face was red.

Lying low at the centre of the well-tamed land, snug as a ground-nesting bird, was this bright and modern country settlement, its buildings elegantly structured with red brick

149

and new timber-framing. I marked a proud, towered church with a flag of St George.

And sensed a glow about the place. A glow of… wealth… contentment?

What the *hell*?

I called across to Dudley.

'We didn't turn back upon ourselves somehow? This is… *Wales*?'

'What did you expect?'

'Didn't expect it took so much like… like England. More like England than anywhere we've passed since Hereford. And that *was* England.'

I looked out, as if cheated, towards wooded hills. Maybe Wales was a country of the mind that was never reached.

'Actually, I'm told it gets wilder the further west you go,' Dudley said. 'This *is* an English town in a way, grown rich on the wool trade. One of the canons in Hereford was telling me it's even on the English side of King Offa's dyke.'

Maybe a town built as a statement of future intent. The county of Radnorshire, its few sizeable settlements small and far-flung, has no history beyond the Act of Union in King Harry's reign. There are no ancient princes of Radnorshire, no great old families, no ancestral castles yet lived in. This is a county not as old as me, established quickly, out of expediency.

But if its county town was any indication of prosperity, nobody here would go back to the old days. It was like to a holiday. I was aware of a billowing excitement – cheers and halloos, bright flags drooped from ropes strung across the streets from gable to gable, all lurid against a sky swelling with unshed rain.

Of a sudden, my mare was rearing in fear at the sudden blast of jollity and I bent to calm her as our company thinned out to be fed into the town. Widening again as we entered a broad street leading down to the church and a bridge over the river. I marked a baker's shop, two alehouses, a tannery with a yard, a blacksmith's and an apothecary's, all well built with good signs.

To a gale of cheers, we came to a forced, untidy halt about halfway down amid a confusion of roadside stalls selling apples, plums, cherries and cold pies.

A juggler in a jester's cap sent up a spray of coloured woollen balls, while children tried to catch them. A smell of strong ale was loaded into the air and on the ground a great whooping press of townsfolk roiled and roared from the consumption of it, and I was reminded of the Queen's coronation, the happiest day of my life.

'*Get this rabble…*'

From behind me, a cultured voice, high and thin with fury, piercing the euphoria like an ornamental blade.

'*My Lord, it's—*'

'*Bring out the sheriff, sirrah. At once.*'

I looked over my shoulder, saw a press of armed guards around the judge and his men. Turning back to the street, I marked faces at windows, with and without glass, and then Dudley's horse was pulled alongside mine.

'You *do* know what this is *about*?'

'Some kind of harvest festival?'

'It's for us. Well, not *us*… the judge.'

I saw Roger Vaughan, the lawyer, sliding from his horse, elbowing through the crowd towards a big, walled and gated

151

house set back from the street. There was an inset door made small by a weight of ivy set into the high oaken gates, and Vaughan began to hammer upon it. A smittering of blood on his knuckles before it was opened.

'Where's the sheriff?'

The door was open barely a crack, and the voice from within no more than a mouse-squeak, so I heard not a word of it above the noise of the crowd. When Vaughan came back, the door was already being latched against him and the calm he'd shown on the road was gone.

'My Lord, I'm— The sheriff's gone with a couple of dozen men to fetch the prisoner from… from where he's kept.'

A horse was prodded out onto the cobbles, guards forcing the crowd back, and the judge, Sir Christopher Legge, looked down.

'They don't have a gaol here?'

'It's not the strongest, and there's fear that Gethin's brigands will attempt to free him. He's been kept in a dungeon in… in another place. Until the trial.'

'Forget the trial!' A man's voice from the street. 'Just hang the fucker!'

Whoops and laughter. Vaughan accepted the reins of his horse from one of the judge's men, stood like he knew not where to put himself. Clearly hadn't expected this. A single raindrop stung the back of my hand resting on the mare's neck.

'Remarkable.' Judge Legge rose up in his saddle. He was not tall, and his tight leather riding jerkin emphasised how lean he was, almost skeletal, his bladed face shadowed by a wide-brimmed leather hat. 'And what, pray, are we supposed to do until the sheriff returns?'

'My Lord, I—'

'This, I take it, *is* the sheriff's house?'

'It is, my Lord, but—'

'I believe… I *do* believe that I was told by my clerks that I'd be lying here for the duration of the trial.' Legge's voice seemed to prick at words like a bodkin. 'I do believe that I was told that. Now you are the…' He flicked a wrist, with impatience. '…local man, I forget—'

'Vaughan, my Lord.'

'Vaughan, yes. Well, perhaps you could go back, *Vaughan*, and tell the sheriff's servants to throw open the sheriff's doors. And the sheriff's gates. And' – he leaned forward, to the side of his horse's head, peered down at Vaughan, his voice brought down to a hiss – '*get us the hell out of this human dungheap.*'

'I'll do that now,' Vaughan said.

'Good of you.'

The sky was like to dark purple silk, all stretched. Legge leaned back in his saddle and looked up at it, with irritation, as if he might deflate it with his bodkin.

'I do believe it's about to rain,' he said.

And, by God, he was not wrong.

XX

Old Itch

It was as if the sky had split like a rotted water butt, releasing the kind of rain that joins clothing to skin in seconds. A rain that blinds. We watched its torrent in the milken glass in the parlour at the rear of the Bull Inn, forming rivers on the sills, dripping to the flags.

It was not yet five in the afternoon. The splattered street empty now.

According to Vaughan, the Bull was the best of the seven inns of Presteigne. Dudley and I had been told we'd have to share a bedchamber though not, I'd been glad to discover, a bed. A back parlour, plain but well-scrubbed, had been given over for our use and that of some attorneys who were not accommodated at the sheriff's house. Including Vaughan who came to join Dudley and me and a jug of small beer, explaining that the more senior lawyers were presently taking instruction from Legge.

'Evidently he wasn't expecting *that*,' Dudley said. 'I mean the crowd – not the weather.'

'Nor I, Master Roberts,' Vaughan said. 'For which I'll be held responsible for sure.'

I said, 'You're here to smooth the judge's path? Interpret the ways of local people?'

'Sent to him by one of my tutors. And making a cock of it.'

'Not the way of the Border, is it?' I said. 'All this fanfare.'

'We don't normally make a big noise about anything,' Vaughan said, letting the border into his voice. 'And we don't take sides till we knows who'll win.'

Well, I knew this – less from my father than my dealings with Cecil and, in particular, Blanche Parry, who'd walk thrice around some matter before dropping hints as to where she stood on it. And even then you wouldn't really know.

'This town's changed, see,' Vaughan said. 'New wealth and most of it from England. Big families in the wool trade come in from Ludlow. Experts in cloth-making brought from Flanders. And all the money from the Great Sessions – bedchambers and good food and wine for the lawyers and the judges. Like I say, it *en't* England… but it en't Wales either.' He lifted his cup, about to drink then lowered it again. 'As for free pies, free fruit…'

'*Free?*'

'A fresh mutton pie buys a good helping of merry cheer. In place of fear.'

He looked over to the window. A pool was spreading on the flags where rain was oozing between two badly-set panes. Dudley leaned forward on the bench.

'You're saying the merchants and the clothiers *paid* for that show of welcome for Legge? So he doesn't think he's come into a hostile Wales?'

'He's here to scratch a twenty-year-old itch, is what it is. Quick trial, nice long hanging.'

'Itch?'

I recalled what Bishop Scory had said about the biggest hanging party he'd seen hereabouts. Vaughan blinked.

'You do know, I take it, why the Sessions came to Presteigne?'

'Should we?' I said.

Preparing myself. Seemed to me that the Welsh border was like to a clinging midden, rotting history into legend so the twain could not easily be separated.

'Twenty years ago,' Vaughan said, 'all the courts were held at Rhayader. Out west.'

He looked at me in query. I'd never been to Rhayader, but knew of it. A town on the edge of the bandit-riddled wilderness which Vaughan said now had been more or less ruled by the brigand gang, Plant Mat.

There had been some resentment, it seemed, over the way justice was administered by the English judiciary, with only English spoken in court.

Plant Mat fed upon it.

Vaughan talked about the year 1540, four years after the Act of Union, when Plant Mat, lodged in the neighbouring county of Cardigan, were extorting regular payments from landowners to the west of Rhayader.

'If you didn't pay up they'd burn your winter straw. And if that didn't work it'd come to blood. Your stock then your family.'

I marked the suppressed rage roiling in Dudley's eyes as Vaughan talked about a judge sent to Rhayader for the Sessions. An old man and devout. He'd ride to church before taking his seat in the court. One morning they were waiting for him in an oak grove by the river.

Plant Mat.

'Took him down,' Vaughan said. 'Murdered him.'

'*The King's justice?*' Dudley finally driven to outrage. 'Was there no retribution for that?'

'They knew where to hide, Master Roberts. It's their country. There may've been a hanging or two, but no one knew if they'd got the judge's killer. After that, it was deemed unsafe for judges to sit at Rhayader.'

'Driven out? Bowing to this scum?'

'So that was why the court was moved here. To the softer lands on the edge of England.'

'And this man Gethin is the leader of Plant Mat. Where's he caged?'

'A dungeon at New Radnor Castle. Not much left of the castle since the Glyndwr wars, but still the safest prison we have.'

'About an hour's ride?' I said.

'If that. But they en't gonner do it in this weather. They'll want to see where they're going, and who else is on the road. Or in the hills. If the rain en't over well before nightfall, they'll fetch him on the morrow. Won't please Sir Christopher if it prolongs his stay, but what can they do?'

'The Queen's judiciary running in fear of petty outlaws?' Dudley sat shaking his head in disgust. 'Am I alone here in finding that a complete humiliation?'

'This place might look like England, Master Roberts,' Vaughan said. 'But it en't.'

'Give us time, Vaughan.'

Dudley smiled, and I sighed and poured more beer for us all.

'Prys Gethin, Master Vaughan... Prys the Terrible, Prys the Fierce... is that his real name?'

'Probably some puny little turd with a withered arm,' Dudley said.

'Two good arms, Master Roberts,' Vaughan said, 'but only the one eye. His real name… well, who can say? But clearly he's too young to be the son or even the grandson of Rhys Gethin.'

Dudley looked blank-faced for a moment as the association of names registered upon him.

'Prys, Mr Roberts. *Ap Rhys*. Son of Rhys? Dr Dee your house – your family home, Nant-y-groes… under Brynglas? The hill of Pilleth?'

'Christ's blood, Vaughan…' Dudley slammed down his beermug. 'The Battle of Pilleth?

I didn't share Dudley's fascination with all manner of mortal conflict, human and animal, but I knew that an army hurriedly raised by Edmund Mortimer, the Marcher Lord, had been outwitted and crushed by the Welsh, with terrible carnage.

But all this was a century and a half ago.

'They're yet finding the remains of the Pilleth dead,' Vaughan said. 'Turned up by the plough. A dark place, it is. Holds terrors yet. I don't much like where *I* live, but I'd not live there.'

'And which side,' Dudley asked me, head atilt, 'was your father's family supporting, John? I do believe the Dees were there at the time?'

Oh yes, they must have been there. But, God help me, I didn't know which side they'd been on or if any of them had died in the Battle of Pilleth.

'Hill of ghosts,' Vaughan said. 'I've heard it called that.'

I wondered which side *his* family had been on. He sounded Welsh, spoke Welsh and yet the house, Hergest Court, was, if only by a short distance, in England.

'Beg mercy,' I said, 'but I don't yet understand how this is linked with Prys Gethin. Glyndwr's long gone. There's no Welsh army any more.'

'Not as such, no.' Vaughan drank some beer, wiped his mouth. 'But the ole Welsh families who ran with Glyndwr... they still dream. And some still hate the English. And don't feel obliged to live by English laws. Plant Mat, see, the first of them were likely men who ran with Glyndwr's army and, for them, it was never gonner be over. And as Glyndwr's general – the man leading the Welsh in the rout of the English on Brynglas – as his name was Rhys Gethin. See?'

The cold rain rolled down the panes, and only Dudley laughed.

'Small-time outlaw affecting the name of a famous warlord? Shrouding himself in old myth to frighten the peasants?'

No smile from Vaughan. The boy sat silent, watching the unceasing violence of water on ill-fitting glass. Me? I understood at once what local superstition this would arouse and didn't feel it misplaced. The land remembers. Only wished now that I'd listened harder to my father's tales, asked a few more questions. But then, I never thought I'd ever come here. I sought to quench it, all the same.

'One hundred and fifty years ago. This man must needs be... what... a *great*-grandson?'

'Or no relation at all, more like. Just a man who wants folk to think him possessed of a vengeful and still-active spirit.' Vaughan fingered his sparse gingery beard as if there was more he might say about active spirits. 'The thought of Gethin returned to the place where he slaughtered a thousand English – even if he's in chains – is bound to cause unrest among the

159

local folk. Not that it frightens the wool merchants. But they weren't raised yere.'

'And the judges from Ludlow and Shrewsbury fear only for their lives,' I said. 'After what happened twenty years ago.'

'Legge, however,' Dudley said, 'comes with sixty armed guards and has no fear that can't be overridden by his ambition. But you're right, only a good hanging can end this.'

Vaughan slumped in a corner of the parlour settle.

'You think?'

✝

A cattle raid one full-moon night in the Irfon Valley, the other side of Radnor Forest. This was how they'd caught him.

Been a few raids, and all the talk was of Plant Mat, so the local squires banded together and had all their men out – farm hands and shepherds, pigmen and rickmen. Long nights waiting in the woods, all armed with axes and pitchforks and clubs. The Plant Mat raiders, when they came, were badly outnumbered and taken by surprise, for once, and fled into the hills.

Except for their leader who caught his foot in a root and twisted his ankle, and the farmers' boys were on him. Two of the squires were summoned from their beds and came out and beat him about before having him tied, hand and foot, to a cart.

'They know who he was?' Dudley asked.

'They did when he told them. Stood there all bloody and told them his brothers would pay them well if they let him go. He'd get a message back and they'd arrange an exchange, and they'd be rich men and their stock would be safe forever.'

'Tempting,' I said, 'for a border farmer.'

'But an insult to a squire,' Vaughan said. 'These two, they both knew what had happened over at Rhayader, when Plant Mat were taking a slice of the farmers' meat in return for not firing their buildings. Forever's no more'n a year in Wales. You make a deal with these brigands, they leave you alone for a few months, then they're back, and worse.'

'Never bargain with scum,' Dudley said.

All they did, Vaughan said, was to have Prys Gethin tied tighter and gagged him so they didn't have to listen to any more of his babble. And then… a triumphal torchlight procession through the hills of Radnor Forest.

'The new sheriff, Evan Lewis, he lives at Gladestry, which was along the route, and they sent ahead to have him roused. And Evan Lewis joined them on the road to New Radnor Castle, where Prys Gethin was dragged down from the cart. Standing there, under the full moon, they were in high spirits, mabbe a bit drunk. As you might well be if you'd brought the bane of Radnorshire to justice.'

One of the squires, Thomas Harris by name, had stepped up and spat in the prisoner's eye. Well, not in his eye, exactly, as Gethin only had the one. What Harris spat into was the shrivelled skin around the empty socket of the eye that was gone.

Prys Gethin had not wiped it away. Although he could have done. They saw his hands were freed from their bonds. How was that possible?

Vaughan drank some beer and was silent for a moment, as if unsure how the rest would be received.

'Stood there, blood and spit on his cheeks. Pointed at the two squires who'd beaten him, tied him down, spat into his eye socket. Stood there in the light of the full moon and cursed them by turn, low in his voice, pointing with a curled finger.'

'Cursed in Welsh?' Dudley looked unimpressed. 'Terrifying.'

But I noticed Vaughan's eyes and the bleak way he was staring into his beer.

'Within a month,' he said, 'Thomas Harris was dead of a fever that came overnight. And the other, Hywel Griffiths, he drowned in the river, when a new footbridge collapsed in high wind.'

I hoped Dudley would not laugh, and he didn't. I'd be the last to deny the power of a curse, especially if the victim knows he's cursed.

'This wind,' Vaughan said, 'was sudden, fierce and unnaturally short-lived. Came and went in a matter of minutes. Taking with it the little bridge and a man's life.'

'And another myth was born,' Dudley said sourly.

'*Myth?*' Roger Vaughan, for all his schooling in London and Oxford, was a man of the border yet, his accent strengthening with his anger. 'That's how you sees it, is it, Master Roberts?'

'So' – I broke in – 'the charges will be cattle-thieving...'

'And witchcraft,' Vaughan said. 'Murder by witchcraft.'

Ha. So this was where Scory came in. What evidence, I wondered, would he give to strengthen the case against this felon?

'Not easy to prove,' I said. 'Not these days.'

The last Witchcraft Act, introduced by King Henry, having been repealed after his death. Everyone had expected it to be replaced by something less random, but it hadn't happened yet, whatever Jack Simm might say about the Queen's need to prove that she was not like her mother. Goodwife Faldo had been on firm ground when she'd said, in Mortlake Church, that she no longer feared imprisonment for inviting a scryer into her house.

But where a death was involved… well, I'd heard of cases where evidence of circumstance had been enough to hang a woman – it was usually a woman – where proof of dark threats had been given. And fear of witchcraft would never go away. Even in London, there would have been unrest under these circumstances. Out here, with all the terror of the Glyndwr war yet within local memory, it would have a considerable power to disturb.

'Glyndwr studied magic,' I said.

Vaughan was nodding.

'And is said to have used it with clear intent, Dr Dee. As you likely know, it was said he could arouse spirits to change the weather – arouse storms and the like – to gain advantage on the battlefield.'

'So a sudden wind blowing down a footbridge,' Dudley said. 'would suggest this man was simply calling on the same dark powers?'

'Not too difficult to make out a case for it, Master Roberts.'

'Especially before a man of Legge's abilities,' I said. '*Was* Rhys Gethin said to have dark powers?'

'I don't know. He was killed in battle three years after Pilleth.' Vaughan drained his cup. 'But what a victory *that* was. Against all odds. And he *was* Glyndwr's best general. And they *did* burn down the church of the Holy Virgin before the battle. Oh God, it's all a nest of wasps.'

'So you're saying the local judges… might be in fear for more than their lives?'

'Like I said, Dr Dee, this en't England. And it definitely en't London. Although Plant Mat's never been known to work so far east, the guard's yere to make sure Sir Christopher Legge stays safe before and during the trial. And the hanging, if he stays for it.

'As for any kind of danger that don't involve *physical* attack...'

'Legge has fairly advanced Lutheran leanings, as I understand it,' Dudley said. 'The Lutheran scholars are in the process of effecting a severe reduction of what we're allowed to be afraid of.'

'Aye, and the handful of men who own this town now are all firm reformers, too.' Vaughan stood up, peered at the window. 'It en't stopping, is it? Better face the wrath of Sir Christopher. Tell him his trial en't gonner start tomorrow.'

He flinched, as did I, at a sudden cracking of glass. The loose pane had fallen from its leading, or been blasted out by the force of the rain, and now smashed on the flooded stone flag. Shards of glass were skittering through the spill, as a second pane fell out.

'I'll send the innkeeper,' Vaughan said. 'If I can find him.'

None of us had commented on the uncommon ferocity of the rain which looked like preventing the sheriff bringing Prys Gethin from New Radnor this night.

It had, after all, been a wet summer.

XXI

Rowly's Boy

COLD IN THE parlour now, with that jagged hole in the window
and water beginning to pool around Dudley's fine riding boots.
When we were alone, he stood up, regarding me sideways, dark
eyes aslant.

'I don't think... that should we get involved in this, John.'

'Did I suggest we might?'

He snorted like a stallion.

'You eel! I was watching your face. All that talk of Glyndwr's
magic and altering the weather and the curse of Prys Gethin?
John Dee in the land of Merlin? A pig in shit. As for this boy
Vaughan...'

'Mmm.' I nodded. 'He's sitting on eggs. He's a lawyer, but
also border-raised, and he doesn't think free pies can cure fear.
Mortimer's army would have been drawn from places like
Presteigne. The presence in the town of another Gethin...'

'So *called*. And in chains.'

'Freed himself from his bonds on the road to New Radnor,'
I said. 'So that he was able to point the finger in malevolence...'

'Jesu, don't *you* start.' Dudley rubbed his hands together to
make heat. 'Gives me shivers, this place, somehow, even more
than Glastonbury. How far to Wigmore from here?'

'Seven miles. Eight? You weren't thinking of riding there in this?'

'First light, I was thinking,' Dudley said. 'Assuming we aren't all drowned by then.'

I shook my head.

'No real use in riding out to Wigmore until we have a better idea of exactly what we're looking for. I gather there are people we might talk to in this town first.'

It was the first chance I'd had to tell him what I'd learned from John Scory in Hereford. Dudley listened without interruption, only the occasional raised eyebrow.

'You saying the Bishop of Hereford knew of the stone?'

'But not where it is – or the former abbot. But he did say Presteigne would be a good place to start looking. Not least because much of the property here once belonged to the abbey.'

'And then gathered in by the Crown, and the Crown would sell it off. I don't see how there'd be a connection any more.'

'Just telling you what he said. He also thought it worth talking to my cousin Nicholas Meredith. Who also seems to be a substantial property owner.'

I was recalling how Scory had laughed on learning that Meredith was my cousin, when a man appeared in the doorway, bearing a broom and glowering at the remains of the window.

'God's blood! Profuse apologies, my masters. The glazier's art is yet in its infancy round yere.'

He began sweeping the shards of glass into a corner with his broom, then gave up and tossed the broom across the parlour.

'I'll have it shuttered. He'll not get paid for *this*.' Wiping his

166

wet hands on his apron, straightening up and jabbing a thumb at his chest. 'Jeremy Martin. Keeper of this inn.'

A powerfully built man of late middle-years. Dense grey hair winged back behind his ears.

'Least there'll be no broken glass in your bedchamber this night, my masters.'

'Although wouldn't that be because it's yet without any kind of glass?' Dudley said.

Jeremy Martin grinned.

'On the list, that is. Glass in all the windows next year, sure to be. Proper glass. I en't been yere long enough to do all as needs doing, but this'll be the finest inn in the west 'fore long. Can I replenish your jug, my masters? On the house?' Picking up the beer jug, he sniffed it with suspicion. 'Holy blood, you're drinking ale! You have a flagon of my ole cider, masters, and I'll tell you, you en't gonner go back to this bat's piss in a hurry.'

Dudley looked pained. One virtue of high social status, he'd been known to remark, was that it spared you the crude predations of the serving classes.

'Master Martin,' I said, 'would you happen to know where we might find Nicholas Meredith?'

'Won't be far away. He's in town. Friend of yours?'

'My cousin.'

'You're his cousin? From London? You en't a lawyer, then?'

'I… No. Not as such.'

Martin took a step back into the pooled water, inspecting me from head to feet and back again.

'Holy blood! You en't…?' His eyes widened, and then his arms were thrown wide as if he'd embrace me. 'Rowly Dee's boy? The man who… Holy *blood*…'

'You knew my father?'

'Rowland Dee? All the talk was about him at one time. How close he was to the ole King. How well-favoured. And now it's his son and the ole King's daughter. Holy blood! I tell you... Master Meredith, when the pamphlets come from London after the crowning, he's in yere reading it all out. His uncle's boy calculating the stars for the new queen. Well, well... Do he know you're yere?'

'I wrote to him but... no, he doesn't. Not yet.'

'Aye, I thought... He'd known you was coming, we'd never've yeard the last of it. So you en't nothing to do with the judge?'

I assured him we were merely travelling with the judge's company, while inspecting manuscripts from disassembled libraries. Taking the opportunity to make a visit to my family's old home.

'Nant-y-groes? Master Stephen Price, he's there now, see. You know Master Price? *He* was down London. MP for Radnorshire.'

'Why's he living at Nant-y-groes?'

'Building a new home down the valley, by the ole monastery grange. Gotter keep his family somewhere, meanwhile.'

'So he's only renting it.'

'Master Nick likely owns it yet.'

'And much of this town?'

'Not as much as Master Bradshaw – big wool merchant.' Jeremy Martin beamed. 'Wool, cloth and the law, my masters. As good a foundation as you'll find anywhere. Used to be religion, now it's wool, cloth and the law.'

✛

The rain stopped not long before twilight. Within half an hour, a piercing red sun lit the street, and Dudley and I walked out into a town that you could feel to be growing around you.

Signs of building on a scale I hadn't encountered since leaving Cecil's house in the Strand. Piles of bricks everywhere and frames of green oak for new houses. Poke into any alleyway, and you'd find old barns and outhouses being converted into business premises.

We edged around a puddle the size of a duckpond, the sun floating there like an orange.

'I don't see,' I said, 'why this town makes you shiver.'

Dudley looked across the street where the ground rose towards a castle, fallen into ruin on its green mound, much of its stone already plundered.

'I do mistrust sudden wealth.'

'As distinct from inherited wealth?'

He didn't rise to that. The sun spread a glowing hearthlight over a wall of new brick, and a stout man in clerk's apparel crossed the street in front of us, bearing a pile of leather-bound documents.

'It's in a hurry, this town, to leave something behind,' Dudley said. 'Don't you feel that?'

'Poverty, perhaps?'

He eyed me.

'Why so frivolous tonight?'

'That's frivolous?'

Dudley frowned. The ostler, who'd stabled our horses, led two more past us towards the entrance to the mews at the side of the Bull. It was not hard to imagine my tad here, carousing with his friends on the hot summer nights of old. I felt sad.

'Tell me about Cumnor Place,' I said.

No reply. Doors were opening, people threatening to throng the streets. I waited until we could no longer hear the clitter of hooves.

'Better here than back at the inn,' I said. 'You never know who's listening at the door of a bedchamber.'

We'd come to the corner of the wide street leading down to the church and the sheriff's house. All was yet quiet here. If they'd brought Prys Gethin from New Radnor, another crowd would have formed in no time, but the street was empty. At the bottom, just past the church, a stone bridge over the river carried a narrow road into the hills, where a castle occupied a gap in the forest. Probably back in England.

'I don't know what to do about it,' Dudley said.

'About what… exactly?'

He stopped, glanced behind him to where the lurid sun was down on the horizon, poking through the layered clouds like the tip of a tongue betwixt reddened lips.

'The murder of my wife. Beyond all doubt, now.'

XXII

So She Wouldn't Die

CUMNOR PLACE. BARELY three miles from Oxford. Hardly a demanding ride from Kew. And now his wife was dead and buried Dudley had finally made the journey.

I wondered how he'd felt, but didn't ask.

The house was a century old, but recently made modern by Dudley's friend and his wife's last host, Anthony Forster. It had been divided into a number of fine apartments, one of which had become the home of Amy Dudley.

Ten years of marriage, no country house of her own and unwelcome in London town – so that the Queen could pretend she didn't exist.

Not that she was alone at Cumnor. There were retainers, perhaps half a dozen of them. A small, itinerant household.

So where was this retinue on the day of Amy's death?

Why... at the local fair.

Amy, it seemed, had ordered everyone – *everyone*, women and men – to go to the fair. Would hear no word of dissent.

I'd heard about this before and had not liked what it implied.

It had been a Sunday and the day after the Queen's twenty-seventh birthday which Dudley, who arranged the festivities, might have claimed was also his. For his wife's birthday, he would have *sent a present*.

171

My mother had heard gossip in Mortlake village about Amy being so stricken with darkness of mind over her husband's neglect that she'd oft-times determined to make away with herself. And yet, not so very long before that, she seemed in good heart. Dudley had been told of a letter, dated August 24, which she'd sent to her London tailor, William Edney, with instructions for the styling of a velvet gown. She was not frugal with her clothing, having spent nearly fifty shillings on a Spanish gown of russet damask, and she urged Edney to make haste to get the latest gown to her.

Had she really wanted a new gown in which to throw herself down eight steps to a far from certain death?

Yes... a mere eight stone steps, and not even a straight flight – a bend in it, apparently.

The only sequence of events I could imagine begins in an instant of blinding despair, as Amy stands at the top of the stairs, maybe with an image all aflame in her mind of Dudley and Elizabeth dancing together on *their* birthday... and in her anguish she hurls herself, with some violence, from the top step to the stone flags below.

Which sat well with her ordering of everyone to the fair, so that she might be alone. No one to stop her.

'Broken her neck.' Dudley gazing down the sloping street and doubtless seeing stairs stretching away into a black mist. 'That's what I was told. What everyone was told. Including Tom Blount.'

His steward, whom he'd sent to Cumnor in his place, so that he might not be seen as attempting to interfere with the inquiry.

'*You* thought she'd killed herself?' I said.

'My first thought, yes.'

'Because she didn't want to stand in your way.'

His eyes closed.

'Yet you told me earlier this year that she believed herself mortally ill.'

'From what she told me. But what if she was lying?'

I thought that if a wife of mine had suggested she was dying of some malady, I'd not leave her side. Must needs stop thinking like this. I was not Robert Dudley. Had never been blinded by an all-consuming sense of destiny.

There was yet more to this. Some private matter which, even as one of Dudley's oldest friends, I'd never be told. Nor should be, I supposed.

'Did you tell the Queen what Amy said?'

In my head the voice of Bishop Bonner.

… heard that, some days before your friend Dudley was widowed, the Queen confided to the esteemed Spanish ambassador, Bishop la Quadra, that Lady Dudley would very soon be departing this life.

Dudley having told her was the only reason I could think of for the Queen's terrifying foresight. The only reason I dare allow myself to think of.

No reply. He'd gone to sit on the remains of a stone wall, where part of an old house was being taken down.

'Blount told me a report had been written about the state of the… of Amy's body. He couldn't get a sight of the document.'

'When it's put before the coroner, its content should be made public.'

'*When…* No date's set for the resumption of the inquest. Knew I could demand to see it, though. If I pulled rank.'

'And you thought that wise?'

'God no. Didn't even try. But did have a quiet meeting with Anthony Forster. Well, if it was your house, you'd want to know everything, wouldn't you?'

Forster, of course, had not been there either when Amy died but, yes, he'd want to know.

'We arrived the day after two servants had seen her ghost at the top of the stairs. Forster said the rest of them were afraid to go into that part of the house, day or night.'

'But you went there.'

'Oh yes. I saw the place. The chances of falling to your death from those stairs are... slight.'

'But her neck *was*—'

'Broken, yes. And she was found at the bottom of the stairs. But there were...' He thought for a moment. 'What's never been talked about is that there were other injuries. Dints. In her head. Which may have been caused by hitting the stone, but one was a good two inches deep. What does that suggest to you?'

'Something sharp. Maybe the sharp edge of a stair?'

Had the feeling I was clutching at reeds here.

'Oh, John, come *on*...'

'It might also suggest she was struck. A two-inch dint... speaks to me of a blow from a... a sword blade.'

'If you saw that stair, then you'd know nothing else explains it. And yet... Tom Blount says he understands, from his inquiries, that the jury is not disposed to see evidence of evil.'

Dudley stood up and faced what remained of the sun. I only hoped he wasn't seeing it as I was. The clouds like reddened lips had become the slit of an open wound, so that the sun – a sun which this day had scarce lived – looked to be dying in an ooze of sticky blood.

I said, 'Anyone seeing the entire household, apart from Amy, at the fair… would have a good idea that she was alone. Might this be a robbery? Was anything taken?'

'No. I'm telling you, somebody killed her, John. Somebody went into Cumnor to kill her. No doubt left.'

His face looked very dark against the low light. The gipsy, they called him, those who sought to dishonour him, and the change wrought by the butchery to his beard and moustache made this seem not unjust. Without those trademark facial twirls, even a friend might take some time to recognise Lord Dudley.

'Let's bring this into the air,' I said. 'You think someone killed her to damage you.'

'I *know* it.'

'Who?'

'Make a list.'

'But if it was someone who wanted to make sure you would not wed the Queen, surely it were better than Amy lived.'

'Ah, well, you would think that, wouldn't you? But then… perhaps you wouldn't.'

He turned sharply and began to walk quickly away, back along the route we'd come, across the street towards the castle mound, me striding after him.

And then he called back, over a shoulder,

'Suppose someone killed her… so she wouldn't die?'

'*What?*'

He stopped, panting, at the foot of the castle mound.

'Yes, all right… I may have told Bess what Amy had said.

175

About having a mortal illness. Maybe a sickness of the breast, I don't know exactly what I said. But why the *hell* she had to tell that scheming bastard la Quadra, who yet wants her for the King of Spain… or some muffin appointed by Spain to snatch England back for Rome…'

'She'd have told the Spanish ambassador simply to give Spain the message that marriage to you might no longer be out of the question. She probably regretted it as soon as it was out.'

Both of us knowing the Queen was sometimes inclined to speak with insufficient forethought, even on matters of world significance.

'And meanwhile la Quadra blabs,' Dudley said. 'The man has a mouth like a slop pail. How many people have told *you* what the Queen said?'

He'd started to climb the castle mound between shadowy stacks of broken masonry and bushes of broom and gorse, snatching at handfuls of grass, calling back at me.

'Jesu, John, are you not seeing this yet? If my wife had died of natural cause…'

Close to dark now, bats flittering overhead, and…

… and dear God, yes, I *was* seeing it now. I followed him up the mound, tripping over a slab of masonry, picking myself up, my hands slimed with mud and dew, Dudley shouting back at me, too loud.

'If it was a *natural cause*, then I'd be not only free but *blameless*.'

Yes. For his enemies, the worst of all situations. So if Amy was to die in an *un*natural way before her time – however short that time might be…

I reached the flattened top of the mound just as the last of the sun, dull as an old coin, slid down into the western hills. Soot-dark hills which gave a sense of the real Wales, its isolation, its secrecy.

… killed… so she wouldn't die.

God…

Dudley was facing me with hands on hips.

'If her death is unnatural, then I'm yet free but, in most people's eyes, far from blameless. Even if nothing can be proved against me.'

'What are you going to do, Robbie?'

'Try not to get killed as well, I suppose. A good many men would feel justified in doing it, if I'm seen to have escaped justice for the wilful murder of my wife.'

If someone had killed Amy expecting Dudley to be held responsible and then to walk away in shame, retire to the country to live out his years in the comparative seclusion of the English squirearchy… then they knew him not as I did.

He ran fingers across the wreckage of his beard.

'Life seems as dark to me now as when I was in the Tower awaiting the block.'

'But if you were to find out who killed Amy…?'

'How? Through a fucking shewstone?' He raised both hands. 'Ah… mercy. Look… even if it were possible to discover the killer, it would rather depend, methinks, on who it was.'

There were names I wouldn't say out loud beyond the walls of my own home. What a wasp's nest this country was become.

It was cold on that mound. I knew not who'd built the castle or who had destroyed it – maybe Glyndwr. But there was a feeling of hostility here; we were not wanted. I looked down at

Presteigne. How tidily it sat. Glimmerings, as tapers were lit behind the windows of the wealthy.

'Let's go back,' Dudley said.

I followed him, feeling sad to the soul. What if Amy *had* been lying about her illness to see what response she'd get from Dudley? What if she was suffering from no more than a malady of the mind, grown out of a profound loneliness?

A plea for love answered by death.

XXIII

Dark Alleys

WE WALKED BACK into the town, me in a grey fog, to find that a crowd was gathered around the sheriff's house. Pitch torches blazed either side of the gates, their reflected flames riffling like lilies on the puddles where a group of men had dismounted, ostlers hurrying to take the horses.

The sheriff's company was back and without Prys Gethin. I saw Vaughan addressed by a red-faced man in a muddied jerkin and moved closer to listen.

'... his humour, Roger?'

Vaughan muttered something, and the red-faced man groaned, threw up his hands, then turned and addressed the crowd.

'Too foul, it is, see. Not safe to make the journey before nightfall. Not with a prisoner the Welsh want back.'

Evidently this year's sheriff, Evan Lewis. His promise to ride out again to New Radnor on the morrow brought a sour response, a man asking, with sarcasm, what would happen if it was pissing down again.

'Let him go, is it, Evan, so he'll catch a cold?'

A rope of damp pennants fell from the darkening sky, evidently cut down. Made a mocking garland around the sheriff's hat, Lewis wrenching it away, shouting over a river of laughter.

'We'll hold the trial at New Radnor, then. That what you want? *Is* it?'

I turned to Dudley.

'That even possible?'

'He's jesting. You think he'd deprive the goodfolk of Presteigne of an entertainment they'd waited twenty years for?'

'This talk of curses...'

'*Talk of curses*? God's bollocks, John, looks to me that Plant Mat's brought nothing but good fortune to this town. Given it the Great Sessions, and now a good hanging? They should throw a feast for the bastard before he dangles.'

I'd found it interesting, though, the way the sheriff had said *the Welsh* wanted Gethin back. As if it was accepted that Presteigne was not truly Wales. Admittedly, we hadn't been long in the town, but I'd yet to hear someone speak the language.

Evan Lewis, scowling, passed through his own gates to face the judge. Dudley turned away, in the direction of the Bull, and I was about to follow him, when someone stepped purposefully between us.

'Dr Dee?'

By a torch's fizzing light, I marked a man of about my own height, perhaps a few years older and fairer of hair and skin. Clad as a country gentleman in fine leather jerkin and boots that stood well in foot-deep puddles.

'Nicholas Meredith,' he said.

'My God, we were trying to find you...'

I held out my hand; he didn't take it, and it was knocked aside by a fellow pushing past. Nicholas Meredith braced himself against the sheriff's wall. I smiled.

'Good to meet you at last, cousin.'

'I received a letter from you this morning, Dr Dee.' The border accent was in his voice, but so also was an education. 'Replying to it at once, with proper civility.'

'Well, yes—'

'Evidently a waste of my time. Why would you write to me, knowing you were coming here? And saying nothing of that.'

'Cousin Nicholas, I wrote before I *knew* I'd be coming.'

Telling him about the providence of the judicial company. Thinking he'd understood when the dazzle of the pitch torch made it seem as if he was smiling.

In fact he was not.

'You've made me look a fool, Dr Dee. Fetching up without a word, taking a chamber at my inn.'

'*Your* inn? I didn't even know that. We were simply told it was the best inn in Presteigne. My...' I made a gesture towards Dudley. 'This is my colleague, Master Roberts, an antiquary. We were both—'

'Your letter' – my cousin didn't even look at Dudley – 'suggests you're here in search of treasure.'

'Of a kind.'

'Well, well...' Nicholas Meredith jutted his chin. His short beard was combed to an elegant point. 'How like your father.'

No mistaking his expression this time; I'd seen too many sneers. A low growl from Dudley.

'That knave,' my cousin Meredith said.

I had no response, was held in shock. Not two hours ago, the innkeeper had talked of my cousin's pride in my father's position at King Henry's court. *All the talk was about him.* And me too. All this man's letters to me had been invariably cordial.

181

'I don't understand,' I said at last. 'The innkeeper said you spoke well of my father. How close he was to the old king.'

'I'm sure he was,' Nicholas Meredith said. 'Close enough to pocket the spoons.'

A long hissing breath came out of Dudley, but he was yet ignored. A few men had made a half circle around us, in the way that men do, scenting the approach of violence. Meredith raised his tone.

'You think we're so removed from London, Dr Dee, that we hear nothing of what goes on there? You think we know nothing of your father's crimes? You think we weren't dishonoured by him?'

'I know not what you're—'

'In your ill-writ letter,' my cousin said, 'you ask if I know of the whereabouts of a gemstone, formerly the property of the Abbey of Wigmore. Possibly misappropriated. Hah, methinks, how can this man talk so loftily about the misappropriation of church treasures when his own father—'

'My father was a kind man,' I said softly. 'A generous man.'

'Particularly with the property of others.'

I'm not good at conflict, have no ready store of oiled ripostes. I stood in silence, aware of a greater gathering of onlookers and Dudley at my shoulder.

'Forgive me for intruding, John, but why don't we just beat the piss out of this muffin?'

I could feel how badly Dudley wanted this to become a fight, if only to relieve himself of weeks of stored-up rage. And still, Nicholas Meredith behaved as if he wasn't there.

'Were you about to deny that Rowland Dee, when churchwarden at St Dunstan's in London, stole church plates left in his charge?'

Dudley's right hand was at his belt, where he'd keep a dagger.

'No,' I said quietly.

Dudley stiffened. Nicholas Meredith smiled.

'You asked about Abbot Smart? My letter, when you receive it on your return, will tell you he's long gone. Probably into France. You'll learn that nobody here has seen him for years. So if you've somewhere else on your treasure-hunting itinerary, I suggest you depart for it at first light.'

As he turned away, my hose was soaked at the groin by a splash of fire-bright water thrown up by his boot.

✢

In my haste to avoid a further exchange, I'd walked the wrong way, and we found ourselves down by the church and the river. A mean river compared with the Wye, and the bridge was wooden and creaked when I stood upon it, but at least we seemed to be alone.

'... doesn't matter if it's true,' Dudley was hissing. 'You don't let any man who spoke thus walk away undamaged.'

'It does matter,' I said. 'Matters to me. My father sullied his status as churchwarden at St Dunstan's. He sold plate that certainly wasn't his to sell. He'd lost his place at court and his business was ruined – through no fault of his own, I'd guess. I'm sure he... would have made good, when his fortunes improved.'

'Oh, for God's sake, John, every family has *some* knavery to hide.'

183

I looked down at the moonlit river, swollen by the downpour and not far below the bridge timbers.

'He was not a thief. He was a proud man. And he paid for the best education I could've had. I wish I'd been able to earn enough money to ease his old age. But he died. And now I don't earn enough to support my mother in the way she once was used to.'

'You've not done badly under the circumstances. Given that he doesn't seem to have left you any money... or even a house.'

'He left me an education.'

'Which you spend all your life expanding. *Is* that life? Come on, let's get back. See how this looks in daylight.'

Dudley began to walk back up the street, quieter now, fewer lights.

'I no longer feel happy to pass the night in my cousin's inn,' I said.

'We'll we're not spending it in a fucking field. Besides, another word with the smarmy innkeeper might not go amiss, methinks.'

'Why would he lie?'

'It's what innkeepers do when you're paying for meals and a bedchamber. But it would be worth finding out if Meredith's been blackening your name all over town.'

Only two of the judge's guards stood, with their pikes, outside the sheriff's house. No one troubling them. The pitch-torches were burned low, the ropes of pennants gathering into loops and thrown over the wall.

Near the top of the street a man walked past us and sniggered. Dudley lurched towards him, and I seized his arm.

'No—'

184

'You want a reputation as a fucking Betsy by morning, John?'

'Must needs think.'

'Or will we even still be *here* by morning? *Think?* Well, of course. Why don't you consult one of your *books* on how best to respond to an insult to your family?'

Never going to let this go, was he? But I was thinking of something else.

'He said Abbot Smart had not been seen here in years. That he was probably in France.'

'Would indeed have been useful to know that before we came.'

'It's not the impression I had from the Bishop of Hereford.'

I recalled John Scory's words exactly: *I don't know where Smart is, though I do hear word of him from time to time.*

'You think Meredith was lying?'

'Scory was spare with actual facts, but more generous with hints. He implied that my cousin might have things to hide. He said Presteigne, despite its appearance, was... a place of dark alleys.'

'I told you there was something wrong here. You lose religion and let a town become ruled by commerce and greed...'

'Dr Dee...'

A man drew level with us at the corner of the street. Dudley's elbows bent, one hand forming a fist.

'This one,' he said, 'I'll deal with now.'

'If I may have a word, Dr Dee?'

The moon showed me a man who, though shortish, was yet built like a brick privy.

'Make it *very* quick, fellow,' Dudley said.

185

The man didn't move, as though the word quick had little meaning for him.

'Only I overheard your cousin's tirade, see.'

Dudley starting forward, but the man was standing his ground, like a bull in a meadow.

'And was surprised,' he said, 'at how he spoke. Seein' as when I was in London, I heard naught but good words of you. And knew of your father when he was at Nant-y-groes and I was a child down the valley. He was ever merry and, as you said, generous – especially with apples, as I recall.'

'Thank you,' I said. 'Thank you, Master...'

'Stephen Price.'

'Then you...'

'Lease Nant-y-groes from Nicholas Meredith, and I wondered... Well, it would seem a pity if you'd come all this way without seeing your father's birthplace.'

Found myself nodding, grasping at a friendly hand.

'And as I'll be riding back there at dawn... no wish to watch all the paid-for glee at the arrival of the Welshie in chains. So if you wanted to ride back with me, I'd deem it an honour to show you around the place. And your companion, of course.'

✝

'He wants something,' Dudley said in darkness.

The shutters were up at the window but left open. Dudley had the four-poster. I'd taken – by choice – the truckle pulled from under it, though he'd tossed me an extra pillow in a bere.

'I doubt Price means us ill,' I said. 'And I *would* like to see the house and its situation. Maybe the only chance I'll ever have if it's owned by my cousin. Don't mind riding out with

186

him alone. It's but a few miles. Could be back soon after noon.'

'I was about to suggest it. Let Meredith think he's driven you away. Would give me chance to ask a few questions while the town's in holiday mood over the trial. Be a pity to leave empty-handed.'

'You're yet determined to have the stone?'

'I've faith in your learning, John. And if France's poisonous prophet's making use of scrying, it's our duty. I'll let it be known I'm an antiquary collecting gemstones and prepared to pay good money for intelligence about Smart.'

'Well, keep away from my cousin.'

'I could deal with the likes of your cousin in my sleep. It's interesting, though, John. What's behind it? Why's he want you out of here? What's he not want you to find out? Is there money here you're entitled to? Property?'

'Don't raise my hopes. Money and the Dees—'

'His approach to you seemed a little too *conspicuously* aggressive. As if he sought to draw you into public conflict.'

'I should call him out?'

'Big books at dawn?' Dudley said. 'Goodnight, John.'

✠

I lay in the truckle bed next to the door. A haloed moon was visible where the shutters had been left open so I'd awaken at first light, and I looked for known stars. Wondering why we were here, what the future might hold for Dudley. If he'd ever find out how Amy died and at whose hands and if that would free him or expose him to more threat. On the rim of sleep, I found myself considering if it might even be true that the

Queen carried Dudley's child. So many months had passed since she'd summoned me. How many others had seen her in that time?

Among the stars, I saw images of Elizabeth walking alone in the private gardens of Richmond, all big of belly, gazing out to the fabricated island where Robert Dudley had lain his head betwixt her feet.

If he'd stopped at her feet. I saw him as he was an hour ago, when first he'd seen the ripe-bosomed young woman who had shown us to our chamber and turned out to be the innkeeper's wife. A movement in his jaw, a tightening of wires.

I shut my eyes on the stars, wrapping the sheets twice round me because of the cold. Knowing not that I'd slept until I awoke to Dudley's scream.

XXIV

All Heavy with Old Death

THERE WERE TWO families of ducks on the good-sized pond in front of Nant-y-groes. Sheep grazed the land down to the river and more sheep were on the opposite bank until the valley floor was lost into woodland.

Beyond which was the hill, a pale and almost luminous green under the heavy sky.

The hill of ghosts.

'Be glad when I don't have to see it every morning,' Stephen Price said. 'Or watch it under the last lights.'

'And when will that be?'

'One year, mabbe two. Fair bit of work to be done on the new place yet.'

He stood firm on this land. Short, thick-built, weathered of face, and showing more confidence than he had in Presteigne last night, as he spoke of the house his family was rebuilding in the next valley, a former abbey grange, Monaughty, from the Welsh for monastery.

An easy walk from here, but its aspect was different.

'Keeping an air of the holy,' Stephen Price said. 'We'd like it to be…' He glanced back at Nant-y-groes. '…three, four times this size. Bigger families in the years to come. As you doctors learn to stop disease leaving empty cribs.'

'Not that kind of doctor, Master Price. Or... well, not beyond a small knowledge of anatomy.'

'Ah.' He nodded his big, squarish head and led me along a path towards the river and a new barn of green oak. Though obviously of the gentry, he spoke simply, in a farmer's way, as if with an inborn sense of the rudiments of life which the time he'd spent in London could not take away.

'If the new house was a monastery grange,' I said, 'would that mean for Wigmore?'

'No, no. Abbey Cwmhir in the west. Wigmore land stopped at Presteigne. That's English, see – wherever they draws the boundary. This... is where Wales begins.'

✝

I'd tried to feel it. Tried to feel the weight of my ancestry, back from my grandfather Bedo Ddu – an ebullient man whom, my father said, had ordered the font filled with wine at the baptism of his first son. Back through Llewelyn Crugeryr, who had a castle, and Prince Rhys ap Tewdwr, which would give me common ancestry with the Queen... all the way back, my tad would insist, to Arthur himself.

Out of Presteigne, the country had changed: a darkening of the soil but a lightening of the hills, close shaven by sheep. Although there were no jagged peaks, you could sense the rock under the green, the bones of the land. The ruins of a small castle stood like a skeletal fist across the river, and a small grey church was tucked into the hill of Pilleth with a cluster of mean houses below.

I saw all this, but felt no pull of the heart.

Found no sense of my tad in the house which lay behind us,

190

a solid dwelling of timber and rubblestone, with a good hall and inglenook and a new chimney. An old housekeeper had been making flat cakes on a bakestone, with dried currants and shavings of apple. Welsh cakes, I guessed – my tad used to say proudly that he'd taught the King's cooks how to make them for the royal table. I'd told the housekeeper this, and she'd given me one to eat and said she remembered Master Rowly when he was a boy, him and all his jests. But the taste of the Welsh cake brought back only memories of Mortlake.

At the riverside, I turned to Stephen Price.

'You said you recalled my father?'

'I well recall him. Too young, mind, to know him as a man. I was sent away to an uncle up at Llanbister, to be tutored, as you might say, in the arts of marketing and butchery. When I came back, Master Dee was gone to London. Sought to look him up when I was down there for the parliaments, but he was dead by then.'

'Must have been strange,' I said, 'coming back from London to this...'

'Wilderness?' It was the first time I'd seen him smile. It found shape as slowly as his way of speech. 'Never thought of it that way, Dr Dee. Not till I came back that first time after three weeks in London. Couldn't settle back to it, not for a while. So quiet after London that you were listening to your own breaths.'

'Did Nicholas Meredith ever live out here?'

'Not that I'd know. Presteigne boy, see. Presteigne... it en't London, but it aims to be.' He sighed. 'I don't enquire into the doings of Master Meredith or how he got his money. En't my business, and I'm living in a house that belongs to him and plan to carry on leasing the farm after we moves out to Monaughty. But the way he was to you last night… spoke of more than I could understand.'

I looked him in the eyes.

'Left me mystified, also,' I said.

'Injured, too, I'd reckon. Come all this way, and your own family don't wanner know you.'

'I suppose.'

A pensive tightening of Price's lips.

'You must needs have care,' he said at last. 'Big man in Presteigne now. Him and Bradshaw. Ole John Bradshaw, down from Ludlow with all his wool money and the lease on most of the abbey property from the Crown. So Presteigne's yet owned by England, and the Council of the Marches gets its bidding done by the wool men. Who are also the magistrates, and so on. You getting the picture?'

'Do you know anything at all of the last Abbot of Wigmore? John Smart?'

'You keeps coming back to that, Dr Dee.'

'He's the reason I'm here. He's said to have in his charge a gemstone – a crystal stone, a beryl, I believe, which I and my colleague hope to acquire from him. For my research.'

'On the Queen's behalf?'

'Everything I do,' I said honestly and more than a little sadly, 'is for the Queen's Majesty.'

'What you do… relating to the Hidden?'

'One day it will no longer be hidden. Open to everyone. That's my hope.'

Thinking of my library, which anyone who could read was free to consult, not that many did.

'You think that's wise, Dr Dee? That all should be known?'

Stephen Price was watching me. It seemed that Dudley had been right, this man wanted something from me – perhaps what Vaughan had hinted at on the road to Hereford – and, in his border way, was taking the long route. I, however, continued to be direct and honest.

'What I'm seeking, Master Price, is a stone through which I believe knowledge can be obtained. The kind of knowledge that can't be learned from books or tutors, only by the lifting of the mind. It's said to have healing qualities. And is in the possession of John Smart. *Do* you know him?'

'Knows *of* him, that's all. A holy knave, by all accounts. Babbies everywhere.'

'You know if he's yet about?'

'Never had cause to. He don't enter my life. I got enough troubles. Some of the ole monks, they never went away. Abbots, you don't see much of them, but he could be around.'

If Price knew more, it was clear he felt not safe in the discussion of it. He folded his arms, rocking to and fro at the river's edge. Looking up for a hint of sun, to work out the time.

I said, 'You think they'll have brought their prisoner from New Radnor?'

'Sure to.'

'You said last night that you had no wish to watch all the glee. I think you said *paid-for* glee.'

'Time off work, free pies. A holiday. A fair.'

'To cover up fear?'

He eyed me.

'Feel it, did you, in Presteigne?'

'Not to any great extent.'

'Pies are working then, ennit?' He looked up at the hill, a pale green wall before us: steep sides, a flat top. 'Nothing works yere.'

'Brynglas Hill?'

'And Pilleth. The village. What's left of it.'

He took in a long breath, as if he was absorbing something of the humour of the place.

'There was no village left even before the battle, see. Just Nant-y-groes and a couple more farms, a way off. When they thought the battle was forgot, my ancestors set aside some ground east of the hill to build houses for a blacksmith, and woodsmen, cottagers to work the land. Then they rebuilt the church that was burned down, and Pilleth was become a proper village, mabbe for the first time. Seventy folks there at one time, they reckon. Mabbe twenty-five now.'

I waited in silence, recalling Vaughan's words.

A place where a thousand men have been slaughtered is not exactly the easiest place to make a home.

Price looked up the hill towards the church, which Brynglas held, as it were, to its breast.

'When I was told, as a boy,' he said, 'that you wouldn't find no sheep up there after sundown, I never questioned it.'

'The sheep won't sleep on the hill?'

'Nor anywhere 'twixt the hill and the river. As a man, riding to London, I never thought about it. It was just ole country lore. In London, I'd be with men who'd laugh. Or mabbe men such as yourself, who'd say, but *why's* it true?'

'And?'

'In Pilleth, it just *is*.' Price stood solid as a boar, his back to the river. 'This is a hard place to live. I been told nobody should be living yere at all. But the folks at Pilleth, they've learned how to withstand what has to be withstood. And I thought they were stronger for it, but now I en't sure. I never quite seen the truth of it till I went away and come back. And even then it took a while. Well, London – *you* know what that's like.'

'The biggest, noisiest city in the world.'

'Aye, and back from London, you think you're a big man – MP for Radnorshire. But what's it mean? Less than it sounds. You're rarely called to Parliament, and your vote don't count for more'n a fart – Privy Council opens a window and it's gone. And then you come back home, with all your big ideas, to find they'll pay more heed to an idiot boy as talks to the dead. 'Cause that's real, for them. That's *there.*'

What?

I said carefully, 'Some matters... some matters are as hard – if not harder – for men of intellect to discuss as they are for the uneducated.'

Looking out over the pale brown river and thinking of Dudley, as he'd been this dawn as I dressed and prepared to leave for Nant-y-groes. Dudley mumbling about bad dreams, but sleepily.

Not in the way he had some hours earlier. No screams, no sweat, no panting. No...

✠

Jesu... he's gone.

Who?

Sitting up on his high bolster, clutching the bed curtains.

You didn't see him? Standing beside your bed?

195

No.

Holding death, John. In his hands.

And me – I was no better. Keeping my voice steady, the words coming out as if spoken by someone else.

It was... a dream. A bad dream, that's all.

Knowing then, rolling over, staring out at the cold stars, that he'd be back to sleep long before I would.

✠

'Who's the idiot boy, Master Price?'

The sky hung low, like a soiled pillow that might suffocate all below it. Twenty people left in that grey community under the hill. And one of them talking to the dead?

Price stood beside the brown and roiling river, breathing heavily.

'This boy... latest in a long line of strange folk as fetches up in Pilleth, like it was ordained. But I chose not to believe. Big man, back from London, full of new ideas, man with his eyes open full wide. We... got ourselves a new rector and his eyes is full open, too. Least to some things. To others, his eyes is shut tight. One of the new breed.'

'A Bible man?'

'Lutheran to the core, and he don't like what he sees. Most of all, he don't like the boy. The idiot. I call him an idiot because there's no harm in an idiot. But, to the rector, he's gone to Satan.'

'Because he talks to the dead?'

'Because he finds them, Dr Dee. He finds the dead. On the hill. He puts out his hands, and the ole dead... it's like they reach out to him.'

196

'You mean the dead... from the battle?'

Stephen Price stared down into the muddy river. A mewling hawk glid over us.

'The battle... when it was fought, 1402, they reckon it was a summer just like this. Not much of a summer at all. The ground all waterlogged. Not much of a harvest. Omens. Folk seeing omens everywhere. Like they're seeing now, with the return of Rhys Gethin.'

'*Prys*. And he's—'

'A common bandit, aye. But *is* he? I don't see omens, but I don't feel good about Pilleth. And I'm the squire of yere, and my family goes back likely longer than yours, and it's my responsibility. And it en't Presteigne, it's a lonely place, all heavy with ole death. You can't buy off fear in Pilleth with free pies.'

Oh God. Here it was, coming out backwards and sideways and from under the feet, in the old Border way.

I made a stand.

'Master Price, some people think... In truth, I'm not a priest. I'm a scholar, a natural philosopher, a man of science. I study. I can't—'

'I know what you do, Dr Dee. I once talked to... another MP who knows you. Francis Walsingham?'

'You talked to Walsingham?'

'He came to me one time. Asking about your family.'

Well, the bastard would, wouldn't he? Francis Walsingham traded in intelligence, most of it passed to Cecil in the event of it being required to measure me for the gallows drop.

'Most complimentary about you, Dr Dee. Told me how much the Queen relies on your advice.'

Reassuring only to a point; if it had suited his or Cecil's purposes, Walsingham would just as easily have painted me black.

'I'd thought to write to you, as a local man, kind o' thing,' Price said. 'And then... yere you are, like you been sent by—'

'No!' Flinging up my hands. 'I came in search of a stone, for my experiments. For knowledge... for healing.'

'Healing. Aye. That's what's needed.'

Dear God, I was digging my own pit.

'Master Price, I have to say this oft-times, but... I don't... undertake the cure of souls.'

The Squire of Pilleth stood with his back to the flat-topped hill, a stubble of thorn bushes around its summit, half concealing the tower of the church. A church my tad had said was dedicated to the Virgin Mary, whose role was now reduced by the new theology as represented by this new vicar. But not, I guessed, for Stephen Price, clearly much heartened by the thought of a new family home grown from a monastery grange.

Keeping an air of the holy.

'All I'm asking, Dr Dee, is for advice. Like you give to the Queen.'

'You're a clever man, Master Price.'

'No. I'm a worried man. There's things I don't understand. And the dead are rising as never before. A place with more dead than living. Is that good?'

I stared at the ground.

'Probably not.'

'Come with me,' Price said. 'Come with me up the hill at least.'

198

XXV

Thrown From the Body

MY TAD HAD entertained me, as a boy, with tales of the Glyndwr wars. I can see his face now, reddened by the fire, his eyes bulging like a clown's as he relates how the rebel leader calling himself Prince of Wales rose against the English King, Henry IV, destroying all the border castles in his path. Oh, the romance of it.

A romance conspicuously missing from Stephen Price's account of the Battle of Brynglas as we set off up the hill, Price making a hand-gesture at the steepening slope before us.

'Imagine a thousand dead and dying men. Hear their hoarse whimpers. Many more dead men than there are sheep yere now. Arms and legs and guts. And hogsheads of blood. Imagine the sorely wounded crawling through the plashy pools of blood.'

Tad had claimed once that the Dees were descended from the same family as Glyndwr – well, who of note were we *not* descended from? But why don't I remember him ever speaking of the Battle of Brynglas?

'In a way,' Stephen Price said, 'it was almost separate from Glyndwr's campaign. It was about the Welsh and the Mortimers – the arrogant Norman Marcher lords with their impregnable castles and their contempt for the Welsh – the last true Britons. The lowly Welsh hated the Mortimers. Hate beyond our understanding in these modern days.'

'If the castles had been impregnable,' I said, 'would there be so many bald mounds the length of the border?'

'Or so many well-built stone farm buildings.'

Stephen Price chuckled bleakly. Looking back, we could see my father's birthplace, seeming the size of a candle box, and a smaller farmhouse the other side of the bridge, both part of the original Nant-y-groes estate. The English army on that June day must surely have assembled somewhere close to whatever kind of wooden bridge had crossed the river there.

And the Dees... had they just sat and watched from their farms? Or had they taken part? The previously unconsidered question of whose side my family had been on was writ now, in illuminated script across the deep grey sky.

'They say Edmund Mortimer's army was a ragbag of peasants, hastily recruited,' Price said. 'But that wasn't it. He knew the Welshman was on his way down from the north and reckoned to crush him for good and all. Grind him into the ground. Mortimer had two thousand in his army, including a core of well-trained fighting men – his own and the men brought along by the knights supporting him. And then there were the archers. Welsh archers, many of 'em – Mortimer pulled his bowmen from both sides of the border. No, it was at least a halfway-proper army.'

'Yet slaughtered by half as many Welsh?'

'Don't sound likely, do it, till you know what happened. Rhys Gethin, he had his own archers. And rage on his side, see. And cunning.'

Price pointing to the rounded top of the hill, almost

violently green now against the charcoal sky. Evidently, no hay crop had been taken from Brynglas this year.

'No armour to slow them up,' Price said. 'Fast on their feet. Mountain men, like goats. Over the hill, by there, I can show you a dip you can't see from this side, all full of trees and bushes. And that's where they hid out the night before. With their women, too. Day of the battle, they all come to the top of Brynglas. But they didn't come down, see. Didn't charge. If they'd charged into Mortimer's army they'd've been carved up into pieces and it would have ended here.'

'They simply waited?'

'Forcing Mortimer's boys to charge up the hill to attack, and it don't matter how strong your legs are, a charge up yere...'

'Steeper than it looks.'

Feeling the pain in my bookman's calves already. What in God's name was I *doing* here?

Price looked back the way we'd come.

'A full charge up yere in full armour, on a day in June – even a bad June? Full into a hailstorm of arrows with the slope behind them. Havoc, boy. Bloody havoc.'

I began to see it. I could see dead and wounded men falling back on those behind, who could only go on, their faces soaked with the spurted blood of their falling comrades.

'And then what happens?' Price stopped. A sheep track had become a muddied footpath. 'This is the worst of it. As the dead Englishmen start to fall back in greater numbers, Mortimer's *Welsh* archers, marching with the English, of a sudden they all turns round, these Welshies, bowstrings pulled hard back...'

He did the motion, one arm outstretched, the other withdrawn to the shoulder.

'And they all put their arrows… into their own side. And at that range, boy, they don't miss. They *does not* miss.'

I must have winced, as if an arrow had rushed with crippling force into my own chest.

'A planned treachery?'

'Some say that, some say they just seen the way the battle was going and changed sides. Yet… all at once? As if they was all moved by the same muscles.'

I was glad he didn't ask me what, other than an act of pre-arranged military precision, might have caused several dozen Welsh archers to act as one.

'Several of the knights died and Edmund Mortimer himself was taken prisoner when the Welshies finally come charging down. Hacking through what was left. Oh, the bitterness and shame of the all-powerful Mortimers. The only time the name of Pilleth has ever been yeard in London. All of Europe, come to that.'

'And the Dees… Which side were they on?'

Price shrugged.

'Never that simple. Even the Norman, Mortimer… after he was took prisoner, the King of England wouldn't pay the ransom, so all Mortimer done, he just changed sides. Married one of Owain's daughters, in the end. No border easier to cross than this one.'

On which side might Elizabeth's own family have fought? With which side would it look best now for my kin to have allied itself?

'The big, old families, they just goes on,' Stephen Price said. 'The small men, the farmers and peasants forced into fighting – they're the ghosts as walks the battlefields and the sad dreams of the widows, for as long as they lived.'

We were nearing the church now, a squat grey tower and nave, hard against the hill.

'The bones are everywhere in the soil,' he said. 'Down the valley, far as Nant-y-groes, as I discovered quite recently. Far as the mortally wounded could crawl. Like farming a church-yard, it is.'

'What do you do when you find the bones?'

This was like pulling rotting teeth. How he'd ever debated in Parliament was a mystery to me.

'They gets buried again,' he said. 'With suitable prayer and litany. We have a place, just by yere.' Pointing to the side of the church, where the land was level. 'Men of either side, they goes in together. With prayer upon prayer.'

'And do the dead then rest?' I asked.

He looked away. I wondered about the betrayed dead, impaled on the arrows of their comrades. Imagined myself, blood welling in my mouth, helplessly gazing over the reddening shaft of the arrow through my throat... into the merciless face, already misting over, of a man I'd marched with up this hill.

'Nobody likes to dig out a ditch up yere for fear of what they'll find,' Price said. 'If a man's bones are unearthed, all work stops till the whole body's been dug up and reburied.'

'Or...?'

'Or the ghost will haunt the man who fetched up the bones. If so much as a sheep-shelter is to be built, efforts are made to be sure it en't built on some man's bones, else there'd be no luck there, neither. And that's when they send for the boy.'

'To find the bones before they rise? How often does this happen?'

'The dead rising? Of late... too often. This summer, in all the rain... thirty or more.'

'It's the wet bringing them up now? The swelling of the... ground?'

My voice tailing off. There would have been many a wet summer since 1402.

The track had steepened under the church, and I stopped on a small promontory, offering a vast far-reaching aspect to the emptiness of the west. I marked two horsemen down near Nant-y-groes. Not moving, as if they were watching us. They might have been outriders from some long-gone army. How would you know when a man was a ghost?

'Is it easy,' I said, 'to separate one body from another?'

'Not really. Not much else left apart from ole brown bones. All the valuables would've been stripped off the corpses where they lay within days of the battle. And that wasn't all.'

Price sucked in his breath, stared up at me almost angrily.

'The matter of it is, Dr Dee, some of the dead... they weren't whole, that's what's said. Weren't whole for very long after they died.'

XXVI

Blade's Edge

STANDING BY THE sheriff's gate, Dudley finds himself meeting the sardonic gaze of the outlaw, Prys Gethin, as the prisoner is conveyed to one of the holding dungeons behind the court.

Other men, knowing the story of the curse and the subsequent deaths, might look away at once, but Dudley is Dudley. The role of Master Roberts dropping from his shoulders like a cheap cloak, he's giving the man a hard stare, a falcon watching a pigeon.

Except this man is not a pigeon. Anyone can see that.

✟

It's market day in Presteigne. Soon after I left with Stephen Price, Dudley heard the sounds of stalls being erected in the streets and went out to find the sheriff's men assembling at the junction for the ride to New Radnor Castle.

The sheriff's men and more. The judge was obviously taking no chances. This time, he'd sent most of his guard with them.

Roger Vaughan was watching them set off, and Dudley went across the street to join him.

'If anyone's planning an ambush, Master Roberts, they'll

need a small army. Aim is to start the trial this afternoon. Swear the jury in, at least.'

'Not wasting any time.'

'Would you? Where's Dr Dee?'

'Gone to find his family.'

'Master Meredith?' Vaughan looked surprised. 'Only what I yeard…'

'Not a big town this, is it?'

'Wasn't gossip, Master Roberts. I was there, near enough. Not as you had to be that close – Master Meredith sounded like he wanted it to be yeard far and wide.'

'So I noticed.'

'Also mabbe letting it be known that this is no time to have a… natural philosopher in town.'

Dudley smiled.

'That was the phrase he used – natural philosopher?'

'Conjuror,' Vaughan said.

Makes me sick to recount it but, because it's of some importance, I'm putting this conversation together from what Dudley has told me. Trusting that he was as strong in his defence of my profession as he insists. Not that this was necessary with Roger Vaughan.

'It's used in contempt, that word, but it—'

'*Conjuror?*'

'Bad word in London. Meant badly by Meredith. But it en't always bad in these parts. Hides a deep need in… mabbe not all of us, but enough, yet. We got a few working conjurers round yere, Master Roberts, and even more the further you gets into Wales. What en't always easy is to find the ones as knows what they're doing. Seems to me a man like Dr Dee who approaches it with learning and also has… the ole skills… Mabbe that's exactly what we need right now.'

'Old skills?'

'Way I sees it,' Vaughan said, 'a man wouldn't study the hidden as assiduously as Dr Dee does unless he was trying to make sense of his own strange… qualities.'

Dudley, who knows better than anyone the sad truth of this, tells me he held his silence.

'The conjurors and the cunning men, they yet make a good living in these parts, no question,' Vaughan said. 'Better now than before the Reform, I reckon. This was always a Catholic town, see, and the Catholic Church carried some of the old traditions along with it. Least, in these parts it did. The Protestants, the Bible men, in particular, they makes fewer allowances for us to know what's happening to us. Just accept it, it's the will of God. The cunning men and the wise women, they provides what we used to get from the Church.'

'You employ one yourself, Master Vaughan?'

'No. But I'm hoping that Dr Dee will be able to give me some advice when this is over.'

'And what… what think you he can do here?'

Dudley marked the way Vaughan was looking around before he spoke, for this was not safe talk, not even on the edge of Wales. But there were only the market traders assembling their stalls for the sale of fresh meat and fruit and fruit pies and honey, fish from the rivers, wool, fleeces and woollen garments from the local workshops. He saw men rehanging the ropes of pennants pulled down last night by those angry at the delay in bringing Prys Gethin to justice.

Mainly men on the streets, few women, fewer children. Despite the flags, there was no conspicuous gaiety.

'It's on a blade's edge, ennit?' Vaughan said.

Dudley, a man who ever relishes a blade's edge, tried not to show his heightened interest.

'How so?'

'En't sure, Master Roberts. I was born and raised yere, and it en't... stable. It en't balanced. You goes away and you comes back, and somewhere 'twixt Hereford and yere, the air changes. Things happen as don't happen anywhere else. Or they happens faster, so you don't see it coming. The way sometimes you don't see a storm till it breaks. Things yere can change in a lightning flash. So if you got a circumstance...'

Dudley says Vaughan had begun to look flushed with embarrassment. Having, perhaps, started something he no longer wanted to finish. Dudley prompted him.

'The trial of a man linked – or felt to be linked – to local history?'

'Aye. Recent history and not so recent. It all stirs something inside... not just people's feelings, but the feeling of the whole place.'

'Does a place have feelings?'

'Some places you can sense it more than others,' Vaughan said. 'Dunno why. Mabbe Dr Dee can tell you. But when you try and cover it up with new ways – industry, trade, too much wealth too quick, you're risking something going off like fireworks. The Ludlow men, the Bradshaws, the Beddoes, they come in, pulling men like Meredith behind them – the ambitious local families... and the greedy.

Keeping the Church out of it, far back as they can. That en't good.'

Maybe Vaughan was raising matters with Dudley with the intention that they should get back to me.

'John's gone to his old family home,' Dudley told him, 'with the man who lives there now.'

'Price. He's got a good head on him. The people of Pilleth need that. En't easy living on a battleground. Not that one, anyway.'

'Battle like any other,' Dudley said. 'I've seen—' Stopping himself, thinking that no antiquary would have seen nearly as much fighting or as much death as Lord Robert Dudley. 'That is, collecting documents takes me to places that've seen conflict. I know what happened at Pilleth.'

Vaughan looked at him.

'Do you? No offence, Master Roberts, but I doubt you do. This was a border battle, in every sense. The Welsh, they knew what they were fighting for. The Mortimer army didn't. Put that together with… the power of the place, and anything can happen. And it did. Why did the Welsh bowmen on Mortimer's side start killing their own comrades?'

Because they were fucking Welsh, Dudley thought.

But said nothing.

'If you ask them even now,' Vaughan said, 'they wouldn't be able to tell you.'

'Easy to say that, Vaughan. No one likes to admit to plain treachery.'

Dudley marked a quick and angry movement in Vaughan's eyes.

'Master Roberts, I once talked to a man whose great grandfather was a soldier at Pilleth – an archer. A legend in the family. After the battle, he went back to his farm and never picked up his bow again. Didn't trust himself, that was what was told to me. Didn't trust himself to fit an arrow, draw back his arm and know where that arrow was going.'

Dudley would have smiled, making no comment. But don't think he'd dismiss this as folklore and nonsense. I know this man, and his mind is far from closed to matters of the hidden.

'I think,' he said to Vaughan, doubtless with a deceptive diffidence, 'that you spoke of… the power of the place?'

If you ask me, I'm also sure that Roger Vaughan had a good idea, by now, of the true identity of Master Roberts. I don't believe that Judge Legge would have gone out of his way to conceal it.

'A holy hill,' Vaughan said. 'Brynglas.'

'What's it mean?'

'The blue hill. Behind the church there's a holy well, dedicated to the mother of Our Saviour. Many people have been healed there.'

'And even more killed,' Dudley said brutally.

'Well, there you are, Master Roberts. Healing power can be turned around. Dr Dee would know that.'

Dudley frowned.

'You… seem to know a good deal about it. For such a young man.'

Vaughan laughed, and Dudley tells me there was a high, wild edge to it.

'I'm a Vaughan,' the boy said. 'My whole family's haunted.'

✝

Three hours have passed. It would not have been the plan to bring Prys Gethin into Presteigne on market day, Dudley

210

thinks. But after losing a day to unforeseen rain they could hardly afford to lose another.

The cart, high-sided, is close to the front of the procession. Hands and feet in rusting manacles, he's sprawled lazily in the straw at the back, as though it's a royal coach.

With his grey-black hair back over his ears. His one eye cold and steady; only taut skin and a ridged scar where the other one used to be.

Dudley, for a moment, admires his nerve. The way, he tells me, he once admired a one-eyed stag, cornered by the hunt, returning his gaze with an old warrior's arrogance that Dudley recognised at once, and let him escape. With a kind of joy that surprised him.

Prys Gethin's one eye has a rare brilliance and intensity, as if it no longer ever blinks. He looks at Dudley as though they're old friends.

Dudley is aware of the smell of hot pies and gravy. He can hear whoops and cheers and halloos from the people assembled for the arrival of the prisoner. The crowd is swelled by those here for the market, many from out of town. But the whoops and cheers and halloos seemed muted compared with yesterday, when there was no prisoner to hear them.

Two men colourfully dressed as jesters, wearing masks, arrive out of the throng, carrying ropes woven into hangman's nooses which, hopping like frogs, they dangle in front of the occupant of the cart.

One of them is so encouraged by the mild, uncertain laughter that he leans into the cart, tightening and loosening his noose and then tightening it again and cackling.

Until Prys Gethin inclines his head and smiles gently.

'You'll die within the week, friend,' he says drily, in the perfectly rounded English of a priest making a pronouncement from his pulpit.

But he hasn't even looked at the sneering clowns.

His gaze has not shifted from Dudley.

XXVII

Likely a Sin

'THERE'S A STORY mabbe you'll've heard? How the Welshie women who followed Rhys Gethin's army, they come down from the hill when it was all over? With knives. Come with knives. All gleeful and laughing. Set about the remains of the English.'

Stephen Price gazed over the humps in the field bordering the church where the risen dead had been laid to rest. Below us was the cluster of houses I'd seen from Nant-y-groes, with pens for chickens and pigs, and a handful of people about their tasks and all the distant sheep, like maggots on decaying meat.

'Normal enough to cut the apparel from the slain,' Price said. 'Take the weaponry and the leather.'

Maybe I knew what was coming. Maybe I *had* heard it somewhere.

'The privy parts.' He looked away, down the hill. 'Stuffed them into their mouths, so they're hanging down, kind o' thing. A mockery. If there's any worse humiliation for a man, then I en't yeard of it.'

I winced.

'Hatred of the Norman Marcher lords, see. Taught, from birth, to hate. And the hatred hangs in the air, yet. Close your eyes by yere and stare into the full sun and all you see is black. That's what they say. Never tried it myself.'

I kept my eyes full open. Not that there was sun this day.

'When did the church catch fire?'

'Before the battle. Glyndwr would burn any church as paid tithes to England. And the English seen the smoke and flames from the house of God, like a sign before the battle. Rebuilt now, but it's a sad place.'

I'd marked how, the more he spoke, the more his accent deepened, as if he was retreating not so much into his own past, but Pilleth's. He looked into his hands, as if the geometry of the land was etched there.

'Used to be a place of pilgrimage. Shrine of the Virgin behind the tower, next to the well – the holy well. A healing place. For the eyes, mainly. For clear sight.'

'No one comes now?'

'No one gets near the well. The rector don't hold with it. Papism.'

I sighed. Thinking there should be a middle way. Hearing Bishop Scory in Hereford talking of how old beliefs yet held sway on the border. *It seemed to me that one could either respond with a Bonner-like ferocity or with a tolerance bordering on the spiritually lax... I chose tolerance.*

'Isn't this yet Bishop Scory's diocese?' I said to Price. 'Scory's a man of moderation. Why would he appoint a Puritan?'

Stephen Price's laugh was arid.

'Mabbe he didn't. Belief can change in a blinking. Mabbe the rector had a moment of revelation. Educated man, used to be a canon in Hereford. The ole boy who was yere before him, Father Walter, he used to have to hop over the big words in the Bible but, by God, he was the man for this parish. He'd do a Sunday worship with hands still wet from pulling a new lamb in your barn.'

'A practical man.'

'Aye. New rector talks of a calling. First sign of the way things were going was when an ole boy – widower, living alone – goes to him real scared by… what he seen. Asks for the ghosts to be sent away from his door. Rector shows him a face like stone and tells him the devil makes them see things as don't exist and to fall down on his knees and pray for the forgiveness of his sins.'

'He must be an inspiration to you all,' I said.

Price sat down on the little promontory, the hills around him like rough blankets, the horizon broken by the distant castle mound, with its forked fingers of stone.

'See, this… this en't a bad place, that's the thing. Good light, good shelter and you can see the weather coming. And all the families yere owns their own land. Village as should be five times the size it is, but folks don't come and the folks that's yere… there's no good fortune.'

Price looked up the slope of Brynglas towards the little church tower.

'Take the Thomas boy. Fine boy, good farmer, and then he's telling his mother he can't see no future yere. Hangs himself in the oak wood. Rector denies him burial in the churchyard for his sin. Now he lies with the ole warriors and no cross. Well, that en't right. That makes nobody happy.'

'Except the rector.'

'He don't know what happiness is. Likely a sin.' Price raised his eyes to mine. 'I'm the squire. What should I do?'

I'd seldom felt more useless. A student of the Hidden who observed and took notes for all the books he'd one day write. A collector of manuscripts, an aspirant to alchemical

215

transformation and a maker of owls that flapped their wings and went *woo-woo.*

'Look,' I said. 'It's a battle site. When men die in fear and torment, embittered by treachery, and then their bodies are abused and left to rot where they fell… then spirits may linger and there's an air of unhappiness which might last many years.'

'It's come back,' he said.

'What has?'

'We… buried another. Few days ago.' He'd dropped his gaze to the ground and his voice to a murmur. 'Buried him at night. Me and Morgan, the shepherd. Well… I had to do most of it. Pedr Morgan, he wouldn't touch it, but he done the digging. Never told the vicar. I said a few prayers, for what that was worth.'

I came down from the mound. Stephen Price kept on talking softly to the grass.

'I was thinking at first as we'd do what we sometimes does when it's more'n a few bones. When it's a man. Put him on an ole bier and take him into the church. We leave 'em there overnight covered in sacking and then take 'em out for burial. Well… clear soon enough we couldn't do that with this 'un.'

'Why?'

'Normal thing's to alert the coroner. And the sheriff.'

'About old bones?'

'And mabbe the sheriff'd raise the hue and cry, kind o' thing, and it'd be all over the county and beyond. And nobody'd get caught, and that'd only make it worse.'

Price looked up.

'All torn as if killed in battle, this man. But dead no more'n a day. Naked. We never found his apparel. Or his cock.'

'You hid a murder?'

'All gone,' he said, as if he hadn't heard me. 'A bloody, black hole. Nothing in his mouth. Not much mouth left. Face was carved up. Beyond recognising.'

'Master Price, let me get this right. You *are* saying this was done by human means.'

'Not crows, nor foxes. Well, God's blood, what was I supposed to do, Dr Dee? Nobody knowed about him except Pedr Morgan and Mistress Ceddol. And no local man was missing, far as I could ascertain, not yere, not in Presteigne, not in—'

'Who's Mistress Ceddol?'

'Sister of the mad boy who finds the dead. *She* en't mad, not by any means. Her and Morgan comes to me. Me. Stephen Price of Pilleth, the squire. Bad summer, nights full of ghosts, best tell Stephen Price, of Pilleth. Ask Stephen Price of Pilleth what he's gonner do about the man carrying the spirit of Rhys Gethin back to Brynglas. Ask him what he's gonner do about a dead man with no cock...'

'Master Price—'

'What would *you* do, Dr Dee?'

I didn't know. I yet couldn't think why he was telling me, a stranger. A student of natural philosophy.

'There's nothing of the Hidden about a man fresh-killed,' I said. 'Though, given what was done to him, and given *when* it was done, you might be talking about supporters of Plant Mat out to revive old fears.'

Price nodded soberly.

'A good reason, it seemed to me, not to go to the sheriff. Hue and cry, the spreading of terror...'

'*Is* it your feeling that this might be Plant Mat? Putting out a warning of what might happen if Gethin hangs?'

'If nobody knows, there won't be no terror.'

'So you buried him.'

'Drags him into the ole sheep shelter, covers him with straw. And then we… we come at night and takes him out and Pedr Morgan digs a grave by candlelight and we buries him, and yere he lies.'

'Here? Where we stand?'

'Not yere. Be too obvious. We couldn't leave no sign of a burial.' Price considered for a moment, before jerking a thumb behind him, down the valley towards the river. 'There's an ole tump down there beyond the trees. Nobody goes there.'

'Tump?'

'Grave of the ole Britons, down by the river.' He pointed. 'Other side of the wood down the western slope.'

'An ancient burial mound?'

'Nobody goes near *them*. You know that.'

Always been superstition about ancient mounds, warning tales of what had happened to treasure hunters who had plundered them – usually finding nothing.

'We dug a deep hole in the side, put him in.' Price's voice, of a sudden, was raw as bone. 'Pedr Morgan, he was frit to hell, but we didn't have no choice.'

He was still turned away from the river as if he could not bear to remember what he'd done. It was yet unclear to me why I'd been told. Why share the secret of a misdemeanour with a stranger?

But Stephen Price wasn't letting go. He insisted we should walk to the village, or what remained of it. Leading me on the path towards the church until it divided and the cluster of grey cottages was revealed gradually, through thinning trees already shedding their rusty leaves.

And at last, with a strange heart-lurch, I saw it.

Rowland Dee's Wales, where men were bent to the wind like thorn trees, their skin scoured raw, while the light – ever-changing but ever cold – was chopping their world into jagged shards of anguish.

XXVIII

The Jury

A CRAB, WHEN threatened, may move sideways.

Dudley, disgusted to find himself alarmed, slips into an alleyway, pulling out a kerchief, scrubbing at the unexpected sweat. Hands flat on a stone wall, forehead pressed into a patch of damp moss, he draws long breaths until his foul fear is reborn as fury.

But the single eye of Prys Gethin is yet boring through him, a dark diamond turning in bone.

It's not the *you'll die within a year* that's affected him. There have been times when he's been told he'll be dead within the hour. It's the words that followed, none of which he understood. He's been cursed in French and cursed in Spanish, and the spittle-slicked tirades barely reached him before they went to vapour. Gethin's language, he knows, is far older in these islands than his own and comes out like clotted honey, every opaque sentence an incantation.

It annoys him, the way a common brigand hides his villainy under a cloak of false patriotism, assuming a resonant name and the glow of dark magic around a long-dead national hero.

Dudley reminds himself why he's here. Prays silently, feeling around himself – as oft-times I've advised him – a white-gold protective light. I hold this to be angelic light but Dudley, I suspect, sees the glitter of the English crown. He and the Queen, twin souls, born – he yet insists – in the same hour of the same day, under the sign of Cancer, the crab. Dancing together with effortless elegance, iridescent like dragonflies on the water, peering with delight into the pools of one another's minds.

But Dudley never wants to hear Bess using words like those which issued from that prison cart. Regardless of the trail of horseshit left behind by her grandfather, he doesn't want to believe that the woman he desires more than long life is, in any respect, Welsh.

Prising himself from the stone wall, he stands warily at the top of the alleyway, watching a goodwife of Presteigne bartering for bruised apples. A foretelling of his death will ever send him in angry pursuit of something life-affirming.

Within moments, he's marked the woman wearing a green velvet gown, easily the most expensive in the market, and the kind of French hood once favoured by the Queen's mother. Carrying an empty basket over an arm, buying nothing.

Dudley watches this woman for no more than a minute before wandering over to stand quietly next to her at a stall selling pomegranates from the Holy Land.

At once, she's aware of his presence and, with a twist of the hips, is looking up into his eyes.

'A true feel of autumn today, master.'

'Yes,' Dudley says. 'It may rain again.'

'A good day to be indoors.'

'Preferably upstairs,' Dudley says, 'in case of flood.'

'Ever a sensible precaution.'

Dudley nods soberly at the wisdom of this.

'Are you with an attorney, mistress?'

'Not at the moment. They haven't caught me yet.'

She looks him up and down, her gaze lingering on those exceptional riding boots. Now he can smell her perfume. And her interest.

'You live near here, mistress?'

'Within a short walk.'

She smiles. The condition of her teeth suggests she's no older than he is. He moves his purse around to the front of his belt.

'It's a good day for a walk,' Dudley says.

And off they go together, Dudley priding himself on his ability to mark a whore from thirty paces.

✝

'You know what's different about you, master?'

'Modesty forbids me to ask.'

'You can make a woman laugh. That's rare.'

She's not the first to have said that.

'Yet I feel' – she lays a finger on the tip of his nose – 'that something unfortunate has happened to you today. Did you quarrel with your wife before you left London?'

'I don't have a wife.'

'Ever?'

'Any more.'

'Oh. Well…' She strokes his cheek. 'You'll find another.'

Dudley is lying on his back. He can't place her accent. It isn't local to the area, but he thinks it's Welsh and, in view of what they've just been doing, that pleases him.

'What's your name?' he says.

'Amy.'

When his muscles lock into rigidity, she leans over him in the bed.

'What did I say?'

He doesn't answer. He looks up into her face. She's nothing like his dead wife. Her eyes are far apart, her mouth is wide and her hair, hanging now over his cheeks, is more the colour of the Queen's. He lets out his breath. He smiles.

'A good living, is it, mistress – with all the attorneys and the judges at the Great Sessions?'

'Some sessions are greater than others,' she says.

Clever, too.

'And who pays for your time, apart from attorneys?'

'You ask a lot of questions.'

What about the wool merchants from Ludlow? You ever had Old Bradshaw up here?'

'Him?' She gives a yelp of amusement. 'He won't even be seen walking past my door.'

'What about Nicholas Meredith?'

'Master Roberts,' she says, 'if it's intelligence you're seeking, which may be used for some nefarious purpose… you must needs know I'm a woman who keeps her secrets. An element of mystery, in my trade, is' – she touches the tip of her nose with a forefinger – 'of the essence.'

Her house is 'twixt two workshops down an alley close to the centre of town. The ceiling of her bedchamber is very low and, of a sudden, in the scored and fissured black beams, he sees the dark, leathery face of Prys Gethin. A knot in the wood has become that one eye. Dudley feels a pressure in the centre of his forehead. He turns away, towards Amy the whore, pulling the sheet from her left breast and lowering his face.

'You only paid for once,' she reminds him. 'Not that it lasted particularly long.'

'I'll pay for thrice if you talk to me.'

She pushes him gently away and sits up, her smile fading.

'Who are you? I don't think you're an attorney.'

Dudley says. 'I'm an antiquary.'

'What's that?'

'A man who likes old things.'

'Well, thank *you!*'

'And you, mistress... are too clever to be a nun.'

'No,' she says, pushing back her ginger hair. 'I'm simply too clever to be a nun in Bristol or London. Here, I'm like the iron-monger, the apothecary, the blacksmith, the fruiterer.'

'Yes, I did mark your ability to squeeze a pair of plums.'

'That's a common farmer's jest.' She rolled away from him. 'In a few years I'll be forced to marry a farmer or somebody and the past will be the past. But if that doesn't happen... I'll always have money. And the means to make more. I might start a school. My father was a schoolmaster in Brecon.'

That would explain much. Dudley persists.

'What about priests?'

'Find absolution by marrying a *priest*?'

'Or a former monk? Have you known monks – in the biblical sense or otherwise? What about the former Abbot of Wigmore?'

He's approached it too quickly. Her eyes narrow. The chamber is lit by a single glazed pane under the eaves, and she blocks it with her body, rising up.

'I'm an antiquary,' Dudley says. 'I'm told he may have some... relics. For sale.'

'You would expect...' She laughs, incredulous. 'You'd expect the abbot of a monastery taken by the Crown to be selling holy relics twenty years afterwards?'

Dudley's at once excited. *The man's about.*

'Not a holy relic, mistress... as such. I and my friend have an interest in a certain gemstone which we believe the former abbot has. Its value is purely... historical.'

'You have the money?'

'You know I have the money.'

'How long,' she asks, 'will you be here?'

✛

An hour and a half later, with a sense of returning strength and well-being following a lunch of beef and gravy at the Bull, Dudley walks back into the marketplace and marks Roger Vaughan entering through the sheriff's gates, with documents under an arm. Hurries to catch him up.

'It's beginning, Master Vaughan?'

'Jury's being sworn in. You want to see?'

The guards are preventing people from using the main entrance, lest the entire town should come to watch. Vaughan leads Dudley down an alleyway, and soon they're in a cloister-like passage, where the slit windows are barred down the middle. At the end of it, an oak door hangs ajar and there's much commotion.

The courtroom is bigger than he'd expected in a place like Presteigne. Like to a barn, with low-hung rafters, as though a loft has been removed. Perhaps a barn was what it used to be.

A one end, steps lead to a structure like to a long pulpit where, presumably, the judge will sit, although there's yet no sign of Sir Christopher Legge. Or, indeed, the prisoner. Vaughan guides Dudley to a corner near a platform with bars around it which extend well beyond head-height. It's empty. A procession of men is winding from a doorway halfway up the courtroom.

Vaughan says, 'He'll leave it to one of the local JPs to swear in the jurymen.'

And so it turns out. The JP is snowy-haired and vague and barely looks at the members of the jury as, in turn, they swear upon the Bible that they will consider all the evidence laid before them and return a fair and honest verdict.

The JP looks uncertainly around the court, and an attorney in robes leans over and whispers something.

Dudley is marking each of the jurymen with a slow and faintly incredulous smile as the old JP announces that the trial of Prys Gethin for murder by witchcraft and cattle theft will commence on the morrow at ten of the clock.

'Hmmm,' Vaughan says, as the courtroom clears. 'They're taking no chances, are they?'

'I counted seven,' Dudley says.

'That would be about right. A safe majority. The fear is that a jury of all local men… that their families would be threatened. That retribution might be made against them, even years later. Never feel safe again.'

'Also, I expect that seven extra members of Legge's guard will come in quite useful if Gethin tries to escape.'

However important it may be that all possibilities of an acquittal for Prys Gethin should be sealed like cracks in the masonry, Robert Dudley, as an English gentleman, yet finds it distasteful that Sir Christopher Legge should feel the need to bring his own jurymen.

And however much he now wants the swift disposal of the man who slipped him a smiling curse from the back of a cart, Dudley begins to wonder, for the first time, what might be hiding behind the façade of this small, provincial trial.

XXIX

Betwixt the Living and the Dead

DEAR GOD, MY father had me trapped. Walking towards the village, he was with us all the way. I saw him sitting before our Christmas fire, mellowed by good wine, telling me about my forebears, all the way back to Arthur. All for Wales, my tad.

All for this?

Jesu.

Poor Pilleth, all grey and cowering. Huddled under the hill, waterlogged paths separating the mean, sunken homes with their mud and rubblestone walls, their rotting roofs, smoke-holes in the ridges and maybe a dozen small, shuttered windows.

There *was* a glow of life here, but only as from a rush-light which burns feebly and lives not long. And the shade of Rowland Dee.

'Said he'd be in London for five years at the outside,' Goodwife Thomas laughing shrilly. 'Just enough time for him to scrape some of the gold off the streets, he used to say. Scrape the gold off the streets!'

Oh, I could hear that, the way he'd say to my mother, *A proper tapestry, one day, Janey. Telling you now, I am, as God's my living witness, you'll be ripping down the ole wall hangings by New Year, you mark my words, girl.*

My tad, a good-looking, lively boy for whom, everyone knew, Pilleth and even Presteigne were too small.

'And then he'd be coming back, see, to put glass in all our windows,' Goodwife Thomas said. '*Glass*, master! Glass for the likes of we! Well... we knew we'd never see him again, but he was never thrifty with his dreams.'

How true that was. I brushed aside a small, bitter tear as if it were a fly. Goodwife Thomas, sparse-haired and thin as a rib, was laughing again, saying she could see some of him in me, so mabbe he'd come back after all, Master Rowly.

'My, but you're a good-looking boy, too, Dr Dee. Have you no wife?'

Trying to press upon me a slice of her *bara brith* but, seeing how little of it remained and knowing how few berries the summer would have yielded, I refused, with many thanks, saying I'd eaten too well at Nant-y-groes.

A mean wood fire burned beneath a stewpot. Children's faces peered out of the smoky gloom. Stephen Price had said the Thomas family lived in Pilleth's best house – a long house with barn attached for the animals, not that there were many now. When a dwelling was abandoned its fabric was plundered to strengthen the others.

'Dr Dee advises the Queen,' Price said. 'He can help us.'

I felt near-sick. What the hell had Walsingham told him about me?

'Tell him about your grandson.'

Wariness washed over me with the realisation of who her grandson must be. The old woman bowed her head.

'He don't want to know our troubles.'

'I want him to know,' Price said. 'He's one of us. Rowly's boy.

He's studied these matters, he can see what we can't because we're too close to it.' He turned to me. 'In the weeks before his death, the boy's dreams were troubled. He saw the church afire again and the graves—'

'Stephen,' Goodwife Thomas said. 'No more.'

'Didn't he say he saw the old graves opened and awoke and wouldn't go back to sleep for fear of what he seen coming from the graves?'

'Please, Stephen...' The old woman leaning forward on her bench. 'The rector, he said the devil had got in him and we must not speak of it. The boy took his own life and that's one of the worst of sins.' Wiping her eyes with a cloth. 'And I want to pray for his soul. But I don't... I don't know where it is.'

Behind her, a child had begun to sniffle. From outside in the misty distance, there came a yelping cry. Like to a vixen, but I knew it was human.

✝

'You see?' Price said, as we walked to the wooded end of the village. 'You see how things are? They're afraid even to call out to God.'

We passed two ruined hovels, whose roofs had long ago been burned, only the blackened walls remaining. I was thinking that nobody I'd met in Pilleth, not the Thomases nor the Lewises nor the Puws – none of the small farmers who had known him – had made reference to my tad as a dishonest man. Nobody gave indication that they had any knowledge of what I'd been doing in London, only – *well, well, Duw, Duw* – this slow-smiling surprise at meeting Rowly Dee's boy after all these years. Gareth Puw, who was also the village blacksmith, said he'd heard the new Queen was oft-times to be seen around London and was very friendly to the people, and had I ever seen her myself? I admitted that I had, said she was fair of face and full of good humour… and left it at that.

There was a quiet civility amongst these people, a hospitality I knew they could not afford. But no merriment. Even the children looked wan-faced and listless, and the air was chill, and the clouds hung like smoke from a damp fire. The sense of a community closing in upon itself. I guessed doors would be barred at sunset, tapers lit in windows, for those who could afford them.

But they would not talk about what Stephen Price wanted them to talk about.

'The whole village will die around them,' he said, 'and they won't question it.'

On the edge of the village, a door opened as we approached it, and we heard a thin wailing from within, and then a man emerged, a narrow man in a long coat.

'Child's gone, Master Price,' he said without preamble.

He was built like a broken archway, face white as plaster.

Stephen Price sighed.

'One left.' The narrow man's voice was from his nose. 'The one they thought would go last year, but yet hangs on. The Lord God decides, as ever.'

I saw Price's body quake.

'And that's all you got to say, is it?'

'What would you have me say?'

'Mabbe the Lord God got more time for some places than he got for others,' Price said with bitterness.

A distant smile.

'I'll pray for you, too, Master Price.'

The man looked briefly at me and pulled his black coat around him and moved away with high, pecking steps, like a raven, as the door was barred from within.

I said, 'That's your rector?'

'Matthew Daunce. Gone back to his lair, in the trees above the village.'

'God,' I said.

✛

It was set tight into the hillside itself, framed by thorn trees whose twisting branches were grown over its walls. Its roof was well mossed and its open doorway like to a crack in the rockface.

This squat and crooked dwelling had not been visible during our ascent of the hill. We'd had to pass through the village and stand within a small wood of stunted oak to see it unobserved.

'Was this here when the battle was fought?' I asked Price.

'Here, but not lived in. It's said once to have been the cell of an anchoress, living alone here for many years. But that was long before the battle, when there was just a shrine. The anchoress looked after the shrine, and when she was gone, the brambles took over.'

'That's what it's called? *The Bryn*. As if it's part of the hill itself?'

His face twisted.

'For years, it was *Ty Marw*.'

I looked at him.

'The house of death. Charnel house. When someone went

in, after the battle, they found it filled to the rafters with dried-out bodies. In the end, they got taken out and buried with the rest, but nobody wanted to live there… until Mistress Ceddol came yere with her brother. I was in London at the time, learning about Parliament and how it all worked.'

'Was this woman told of its history when they came to live here?'

'You've met the local people, Dr Dee.'

I nodded. They'd tell her, of course they would.

'She must be a remarkable woman. Or very desperate for somewhere to live.'

'Made it habitable mostly by herself, last summer. A better summer than this. She and the boy lay nights under bent-over saplings covered with sheepskins, while she worked. Had I been here, I'd've found them shelter in the outhouses at Nant-y-groes. I think it was the Puw brothers who came to help in the end – first Pilleth people to go inside the Bryn for generations. And then gradually more of them came to help. She'd insist on paying them with what she was earning through the sale of potions and ointments she'd made from herbs and sheep fat, to sell at the apothecary's in Presteigne.'

'Where did they come from, the woman and the boy?'

'Somewhere north of here, Shropshire mabbe. Driven away from home, she'll readily admit, because of her brother. Her father couldn't live with his wailing, his sudden rages, ramblings in the night. Especially when their mother died not long after he was born.'

As if to prove the nuisance of it, there came that vixen shriek from within the little house – within the hill, it sounded like – followed by a woman's laughter. A smittering of slow rain began to rattle the crispen oak leaves, and Price led us into deeper shelter.

'Her patience with him appears endless.'

'The sister brought him up?'

'No choice. People are afraid of him. Stricken from birth with some malady of the mind. And yet… possessed of this… talent.'

He told me how the boy had found a skull in the foundation for his new barn, Price dismissing it as rookery until, just over a week later, he'd given instruction for a new field drain to be dug, and nobody would sink a spade until Siôn Ceddol had been sent to walk the pegged-out route. The boy had stopped three quarters of the way to the last peg where, subsequently, a whole skeleton had been unearthed.

In the oak wood, I carefully prised away a bramble which had coiled like a monk's manacle around my wrist. The path through the wood ended at the Bryn. It was all too clear that this was our final destination and the reason I'd been brought to Pilleth. The Bryn was either the cause of the sickness or, in some strange way, its possible solution. Whatever Siôn Ceddol was possessed of, Price didn't understand it and was afraid of where it would end, especially under the eyes of the new rector, Daunce.

'Whenever the boy's called out to search for bones, he'll know, and he'll go there first and mumble his prayers into the ground and then walk away and have no part in what follows. Preaches on a Sunday about the devil in our midst, but he don't name names. Not yet. But he sows unrest where once there was acceptance.'

'Acceptance?'

'There's always been a wise woman yere, or a cunning man.

The last one died about five years ago. Mother Marged. Blind in both eyes. Blind to the world, but there was a calm around her. After she died, her ghost was said to walk through the village every night just beyond sunset. Me, I think they just wanted to see her, with her hands out in benediction. A comfort. But when the boy came, she was seen no more.'

'A successor.'

'Most of the cunning people, they got something wrong with 'em. Blind or deformed. They need your help, and they give it back in kind. Siôn Ceddol, he can't talk, in English or Welsh. The sounds that come out of him, all with dribbling and swively eyes, people say it's the faerie tongue. Most of the time he can't even walk a straight line. But he walks 'twixt the living and the dead, and there's no fear in him.'

'Finds the bones.'

'En't only the bones, he'll show you where to dig for a well. You tell his sister what you need, she gets through to... to where he is. And when he understands, he's straight to it, like a digging dog. And they're paid in meat and clothing and a few yards of land and the help to manage it. And if he won't go in the church after he shit hisself in there once... well, they'll stand outside and she'll join in with the hymns and prayers, and the boy's scampering around the churchyard like a rabbit, making his noises. A harmless idiot.'

'The rector won't see it that way,' I said.

'No,' Price said. 'He don't.'

I looked out between the wet trees at the low crooked rock-house once called Ty Marw. Built into Brynglas Hill. *Grown* into the hill. A slow spiral of smoke curled from the hole in the roof, meeting the steady rain.

Now I wanted badly to know about this boy. If he did what they said he did, and how.

'I can make an introduction, if you like,' Price said.

I sensed he didn't want to. Didn't even want to be here, now that he'd shown me the place.

'Have you ever been in there?' I said.

He shook his head.

'Foolish, ennit?'

'I'll go alone,' I said. 'See what I can see. And come back to you.'

I felt I was misleading him because this was little more than scientific curiosity on my part, a scrabbling amongst the thickets of the hidden. I marked the relief in his eyes with a certain horror.

The door of the Bryn was black with damp. It was opened as if I'd already knocked upon it, and a woman stood there. As if she knew I was here, though I was sure she couldn't see us for the trees.

And, oh my God, why had no one warned me about *her?*

XXX

More Than Water

WE ARE MOVED – I know this – according to the configurations of the stars and the interplay of planetary rays. We are moved like chesspieces on a board, and oft-times I think of myself as the knight, placed with an oblique mathematical precision, but unpredictably. The knight, who never knows which direction he'll be made to face next.

'My name's John Dee,' I said.

Standing betwixt the oak wood and the doorway. Anna Ceddol looked at me with small curiosity. Siôn Ceddol scowled and picked up a stick. The rain fell upon the chessboard.

'My father was born down at Nant-y-groes.'

'I know,' she said. 'They've talked about you in the village.'

'My… my tad left many years ago, to live in London. It's the first time I've been here.'

'The royal conjuror, is it?' Anna Ceddol said.

No apparent malice or even an awareness of saying anything that might cause offence. Of a sudden, I was weary of denying it. I may even have nodded.

The rain was seeping uncomfortably through my jerkin. Anna Ceddol held the door wider.

'You'd best come in. You'll be soaked.'

'Thank you. I... left my wizard's hat in my saddlebag in the stable at Nant-y-groes.'

She didn't smile. The boy, Siôn Ceddol, kicked sulkily at a thorn-tree root. About half an acre of ground beside the cottage had been cleared of brambles, bushes and undergrowth. Some of it had been cultivated for vegetables, with rotted horseshit spread on top before the winter. Some appeared good pasture. But there was no stock on it. No chickens pecked the ground.

I went in. The boy followed me, picking up a bundle of small sticks from beside the door. He wore a bright red hat pulled down over his eyes.

'I... went into the wood to shelter,' I said. 'Seeing the rain about to come on.'

She shook her head, as if disappointed that I'd lied so glibly. I felt a weight of shame. I'd not lie again.

'Stephen Price brought me,' I said.

The Bryn was even lower than it had seemed from outside. My height, which comes from the men of Kent on my mother's side, made it impossible for me to stand even with bent neck.

Anna Ceddol pointed to a three-legged stool by the fire, which was on a raised hearth, against one wall, with the smokehole above. Two large upright stones backing on to the wall might have been supports for an ingle beam, had there been one. Rainwater fizzed on the red embers, although I guessed the hill rising so close behind the cottage would be shielding us from the worst of it.

'Master Price thought I might talk to you,' I said. 'And your brother.'

For a moment, Anna Ceddol appeared to smile, and then it was gone, fleet as a clouded moonbeam.

'Well perhaps not your brother,' I said. 'That is—'

'Master Price doesn't come here. His wife would not like it.'

'I've not met his wife.'

'Me neither. A quiet woman. Or so they say. Sits before the kitchen fire, goes out to listen to the priest on a Sunday and then goes home and worries. Quietly.'

No particular expression in her voice, except maybe a resignation. Her overdress was the colour of sacking, its hem frayed and flaked with mud. God's tears, why had no one warned me about her? I'd seen women this lovely at court, but their faces were paled, their lips reddened like cherries. They were ladies; this was a woman, with all the timeless beauty of an unadorned statue. Long face, full lips, heavy hair. A sense of grace about her... and, although she was slim and lithe, a certain weight.

She said, 'Can I fetch a drink for you, Dr Dee? We have good water, from a spring. I... regret if I insult you, but they say that the water in London...'

'No, no, it's true. The water in London kills.'

She inclined her head. Her eyes were vividly blue, although her hair, all bound into a thick braid, was dark as rich earth. I was somehow glad when she turned away and went to a pitcher which stood amid the rushes on the floor, leaving me sitting in the feebly sparking firelight listening to my own fraught breathing.

The Bryn: from the outside, it had looked like the worst of hovels, but as my eyes grew accustomed to the dimness I saw that the inner walls were all scrubbed and the rushes on the

239

floor clean and dry. The boy sat in a corner beyond the fire, quiet now, but watching me, the way a cat does.

The chessboard expanded and shrank in my fogged head.

'Mistress,' I said at last, 'I confess I know not what I'm doing here.'

'Surely,' she said, 'you were sent to see if we're drenched in evil?'

'Mistress, I—'

'Sooner or later, wherever we go, this is what happens. All's well till something goes amiss and we're blamed. And then we'll move on. They're good people here, but it can't be long now before we're made to go. Not without regret, mind, after all the work we've done to make this a home.'

She gave me water in a wooden cup. I drank, tentatively at first, and then… Jesu, liquid alchemy from the rocks, water from Eden.

'Your brother found this?'

'One of his less disturbing skills. And our most gainful, I suppose.'

'He has an instinct for where best to sink wells?'

'Farmers ever think they can do it, but not many can. Anyway,' she shrugged, 'the rector won't have it in his font.'

'Ah,' I said. 'The rector.'

'Anything that can't be explained, it's either the will of God and must not be questioned, or the work of Satan… and must be destroyed. And he's our closest neighbour.'

I watched her solemn face. There was a silken calm behind it that I found almost eerie. What also surprised me was the eloquence of her speech. I'd expected a woman living in such humble circumstance, with an idiot brother, to be uneducated, barely coherent. It was clear now why Stephen Price found her alarming and the rector, held in the ligature of Lutherism, feared the demonic.

'Listen,' I said. 'I know not what they say about *me* in the village. What you're told to your face is seldom what's in people's minds. But my tad came from here, and I doubt they'd mean me harm. And Stephen Price, against all his inclinations, he believes this place cursed by its history. And thinks, with all my fabled learning, that I might at least be able to direct him to a cure. I doubt I can do that, but now I… I do feel driven to try.'

Found I was leaning from the stool, my voice rising in urgency. Anna Ceddol stared at me, with an evident consternation that reassured me of her humanity. I fell back under the weight of my own inadequacy.

'I consider myself a natural philosopher. A man of science. Half of London – maybe more than half – yet thinks me a sorcerer, and not so many years ago I was close to being burned for it. And you know the bitter truth of this, Mistress Ceddol? I can rhyme off the theory for hours… but I can't do what your brother's said to do. Nothing approaching it.'

'Then perhaps,' she said, 'you should thank God for that.'

'Mistress, I *don't* thank God for that. My whole life is focused towards a need to enter the Hidden. And I know now that it can't be done by books alone. Not by all the books in the libraries of the world. All that the books can hope to do is make sense of it.'

I drained my cup of the sublime water that Siôn Ceddol, the idiot, had found in the rocks of Brynglas.

'I yet need something of which to make sense,' I said.

Some of my long-held despair doubtless showing itself – to a stranger in a house like a cave.

'My brother?' She smiled at last, though it was smirched with rue. 'Does it not occur to you that when the circumstances of birth leave a child damaged or crippled in his body or his mind then sometimes God will make amends by giving him other gifts?'

'I think,' I said carefully, 'that this is not always true.'

'No.' She looked into the fire. 'I suppose not. Sometimes I wish God had left him alone with his ills. We've been driven from too many towns. At first they value him and then, when there's water enough for everyone...'

'It's more than water, isn't it?'

Mistress Ceddol drew a bench across the rushes, so that she sat opposite me, the fire betwixt us. The boy crawled across the floor and nestled close to her skirts, looking at me, wide-eyed but silent.

'The dead?' She tossed back her dense, braided hair like a ship's mooring rope. 'What do you want me to say? That the dead have been kinder to him than the living? Look... what happens with the bones... that's not happened before. Only here.'

'The obvious explanation being the large number of bones here,' I said. 'So close to the surface.'

Now looking away, though, because I knew it was more than the physical fact of broken bodies absorbed into the hill. This countryside reeked of the numinous. Why else had it been chosen for a shrine to the holy virgin, its spring sanctified, probably to more than one god?

'What I'm saying...' Anna Ceddol squeezed her eyes shut,

242

her calmness lost for a moment to exasperation. '…and what I've said to others… is that the bones are not the dead. Only what's left.'

'But what of the man who was found more recently dead? And… cut about.'

With no warning, the boy let out his vixen shriek, and I sprang back in alarm, almost toppling the stool.

Siôn Ceddol grinned. Anna Ceddol pressed down upon his red hat, and he squirmed and giggled, and she laughed for his benefit but addressed me in a darker humour, her eyes steady and intense.

'He didn't find that man. He wouldn't even come out that day. He was afraid and clung to the fire.'

'But—'

'No, look at him. He's ever in his own place, and a big part of him is missing. He feels no responsibility, no obligation to any of us. When he shits, I wipe his arse and change his napkin. He expects it and always will. He doesn't understand. He feels no need to understand anything beyond his own needs. Other people don't matter to him – never have, never will. Not the living, nor the dead.'

Her face as calm as ever, but behind it pulsed an old and constant sorrow, always on the edge of despair. Sweet woodsmoke caught in my throat and made me cough, and I felt sorely shamed by my concern with – in comparison – such small frustrations.

'Listen, he's tired now,' she said. 'Maybe, if you can come back tomorrow…'

'Here?'

'If you come back in the morning, I can show you what he

does and you can judge for yourself whether it's the devil in him.'

Siôn Ceddol was sitting up now, still giggling. Reaching out his arms – I thought at first to me, but his eyes were on something to the side of me, where smoke hung over a stack of cut logs.

The boy reached out to the space above the logs, making kittenish noises. If there had been heat from the fire there was none now.

Anna Ceddol said sharply, '*No.*'

Her brother began to pant, his hands held out before him as though he held a holy chalice. The fire's cold red embers shone in his eyes.

'He's tired,' Mistress Ceddol said. 'You should go.'

✝

Another oak wood bearded the lower western slope of Brynglas. An old wood, where some trees had boles with the girth of the late King Harry.

I hesitated on its threshold. If there had been a path through it, it was long obscured.

The sky would go dark soon. I should collect my horse from Nant-y-groes and ride back to Presteigne. But the rain had stopped and something beckoned, something beyond the wood.

I went in, as to a country church, the branches above me like twisted rafters, the crunching of acorns under my boots. There ought to be pigs here, but nothing moved except a man who felt himself drawn deep into something he did not understand, surrounded by people who thought he should.

Anna Ceddol: I felt a profound sadness for her situation. And more than a little desire of her body, which I could only regret for she was in need of better than that.

And I had a sense of what this boy was about and, if only for Mistress Ceddol's sake, must needs prove it.

Tomorrow.

Who was I fooling? It was as much for my own sake, or – as I might claim – for the furtherance of learning. The boy had found a link to the land, something of another sphere that was channelled through him.

The oaks shone dully from the rain, and the old churchiness of the wood was as strong as if it were perfumed with incense. I thought of priests, ancient priests *in robes of deathly black, with hair in disarray*, as Tacitus would have it.

The Druids, the priestly class of ancient Britain. Made demonic by the invading Romans who would slaughter them on the Isle of Mona in the north-west of Wales – surely demolishing a shining spiritual engine, for was not Merlin himself a Druid?

Ever the fate of the magician, to be demonised and put to the sword.

Sooner than I'd expected, I emerged from the wood's cloister onto a plateau of land overlooking low ground suggestive of marshland, to which I at once slid down.

For, against the darkening sky, I'd seen it.

Normally, I'd need no alerting to a man-made bump in the land. Oft-times they hold a promise of treasure which, as I've said, almost always comes to naught.

This tump was low and regular, too small and shallow to be a castle motte. It was nothing in itself and yet, as I crossed the low ground towards it, it seemed to sing to me. That is, I was sure I could hear a low humming in the air. Maybe the sound of my own excitement, for ancient earthworks tantalised me, made my hands tingle, and I knew not why.

Found myself murmuring a prayer in Latin as I stood at the foot of the tump. The grass on its sides was clearly of a different colour to the turf of the land on which it sat.

I stood looking up to the summit, where another oak tree grew, like an emissary from the wood.

What was it about these lonely old graves? The graves of men who were here, I believe, before the Romans, before Arthur. Of a race who lived according to an old magic linked to an arcane knowledge of the sun and the moon and the planets... but who lacked the means or the ability to write any of this down. These were men whom I'm sure would have known some of what Pythagoras knew, but by instinct. Men whose remains – oft-times no more than cremation dust in a pot vessel – were too meagre for such an upheaval of earth.

This was the treasure: the old knowledge, the ancient wisdom. The tumps were like books made of soil and turf, if only we could read them. Whatever guardian rose up to frighten those who would dig into the tumps in vain search of gold – and I'll confess that I was once inclined to be amongst them – was perhaps in defence of old secrets.

It was easy to climb to the summit, where the oak tree stood like a bent old blackfriar. I stood with a hand on the tree and looked all around, and my breath caught in my chest.

Even from such a modest height, the view was immoderately enhanced. The shape of the nearby river could now be

246

seen, a gleaming eel, brighter than the sky, gathering light from a source I could not see.

The River Lugg.

Lugg?

How might this be spelt? Could it not be a local pronunciation of Lugh, an old British god of light and the harvest? *Was this the holy river of Lugh?*

Was the sloping oak-wood the remains of a sacred grove of the Druids?

The presence of a holy well near the church on the hill that rose before me was a further indication that this had been a place of worship older than the Christian church. And I could see now that the tump on which I stood was set into a curve of the river – the *sacred* river? – which, it seemed to me, was like to its own shape.

Indeed, it seemed, at that moment, as if the whole valley had been formed around this tump. When I came down, it was on the other side, nearest the river, and I was marking the dints where it had been invaded by Stephen Price and Morgan the shepherd.

A body introduced where a body was not meant to lie. A violated body.

A kind of sacrilege, I thought, as the air of the place was pulled around me like a damp old cloak.

XXXI

A Popular Knave

IN PRESTEIGNE, THE night was alive with lights and the wailing of a fiddle and flute band which was led, I saw, by the chief ostler from the Bull, in a yellow hat with a feather, plucking at a battered lute.

And so many more people this night. The constant clatter of shod hooves. Messengers, likely from the Council of Wales at Ludlow, coming to feed and water their horses and take meat before going back on the road. New pitch-torches were set to burn all night outside the sheriff's house, and extra guards had been posted outside.

The roistering was not a paid-for merriment; something had taken fire. If all this was over the trial of one man, it still made not full sense to me, despite what Roger Vaughan had said about the scratching of an old itch. I wondered, as I led my horse into the mews at the Bull, to what extent the wound had been inflamed by the manner of the deaths of the men who'd brought Prys Gethin out of Radnor Forest.

Lights against the perceived darkness of witchcraft?

'*Sorcerer!*'

At the entrance to the mews, something stinking slapped into my left cheek. A child's screech was followed by an ooze of grown man's laughter, as I winced, plucking at the mess of rotting fruit on my face. Clearly my cousin Nicholas had not been inactive this day.

Quick footsteps behind me in the mews, and I froze, my horse's hot breath on my neck. No way of knowing how many of them were in the shadows, or if they were all children.

'No use in hiding...' A voice more Welsh than any I'd heard in Presteigne or Pilleth. 'Seen your faces now, boys.'

A voice familiar to me.

'And here's the thing,' it said. 'If I see your faces again this night and there's no one about, I shall have no choice but to drown the both of you in the river. Leave you floating faces-down all the way to Hereford. A pity, but there it is. Can*not* abide impoliteness in the young.'

Silence, then the voice came back quieter, with perhaps an edge of amusement.

'I think there's a horse trough just behind you, John.'

God's blood. I found the tank and bent to it, splashing the cold water on my face and rising, dripping.

'*Thomas Jones?*'

'The small surprises life throws at us, eh? Keep me going, they do. How are you, boy?'

This was a man high on the list of people I'd not expected to meet in this town. But then again...

'You're here as a friend of the accused?' I said.

'Ha!'

'To plead for his life, perhaps?'

Thomas Jones, who was betrothed to my cousin Joanne, peered at the approaching ostler.

'Lying with the horse tonight, is it, John, or have you come into money?'

'Living off my rich friends,' I said. 'As usual.'

'I thought maybe it was that. You can buy me dinner, then.'

+

I'm yet unsure how my cousin Joanne, whom I'd encountered but rarely, had come to be enamoured of the man known in his own country as Twm Siôn Cati.

Thomas, son of John and Catherine, is all it means, but it's said to ring like mocking bells in west Wales, where he was known as a scholar. And also a thief.

Thief? Listen, I know not – and take care never to ask – what he stole. According to the legend, his victims tended to be knavish landowners. Some of the proceeds of his crimes were, it is said, fed to the victims' hard-pressed tenants... while leaving some behind for the purchase of his books, I'd guess, though never asked.

Especially since Thomas Jones – *Dr* Jones now – had, with little explanation, been granted a pardon by the Queen. Maybe through petition of his family to Cecil or even Blanche Parry. Who really knew how or why such pardons were granted? But Robert Dudley, when introduced, was predictably sceptical of the provenance of this one.

'You expect me to dine with this sack of shit?'

Glaring at Thomas Jones from a corner of the parlour at the Bull, where candles flared from the walls and men I recognised as Legge's attorneys were pressed amongst well-dressed men with a merchant air, and serving girls bore jugs of ale and cider.

Twm Siôn Cati looked hurt. He'd gained some weight since last I'd seen him, and his hair was longer, his beard shaven close. His doublet, of a warm, russet colour with threads looking suspiciously gilded, was the kind of garment that Dudley himself might have worn were he not in mourning or the guise of Master Roberts.

I did not know – and yet don't – if there was history common to these men or whether Dudley's disdain might even hide a well-buried respect. I might even have derived some amusement from it, had circumstances been different, for it was clear that Thomas Jones had a good idea of my companion's identity. And Dudley's attitude would confirm it.

'This man's a renowned knave. You do *know* that, John?'

'Former knave,' Thomas Jones said stiffly.

'And you're telling me this piece of gangrenous Welsh pus is your *cousin*?'

'Soon to be, Master Roberts, by marriage.' Thomas Jones tossed a handful of groats on to a tray and snatched up a mug of cider. 'And may I say, John, your antiquary's manner of speech—'

'Tutored him myself,' I said.

'—is sadly typical of the vulgar way the grasping lower orders, when exposed to a little learning, choose to express themselves these days. Thank God, I say, that such a man will never be seen within a mile of the Queen's Majesty.'

'If I were in a position to order it,' Dudley murmured, 'I'd be obliged, for the good of the country and all of us, to see you hang.'

'You'll stay for that, masters? The hanging?' The big, shiny face of the innkeeper was before us. 'Likely no more than a day after the trial. And then we'll sell some ale, sure to.'

Thomas Jones looked dubious.

'Won't they torture him first? Find out where the others are? Won't they want to crush what's left of Plant Mat once and for all?'

'You could be right, master, could be right. Likely be dusting off the rack at New Radnor as we speaks. Might have to build the gallows a few inches higher.'

The innkeeper was near doubled up with merriment.

☩

Dudley said, 'You actually trust this man Jones?'

'In a way, I probably do. But I wish I knew why he was here.'

It had not been possible, in the suffocatingly crowded inn, to discuss anything of significance. Dudley had said hardly a word. Soon after our supper, Thomas Jones had disappeared to wherever he was to lie this night and Dudley and I had taken a jug of cider to our chamber, lit a candle, closed the shutters against what remained of the revelry.

'He's here,' Dudley said, 'because he knows Prys Gethin. Why else?'

'Robbie, he was pardoned by the Queen.'

'Only because she likes to appear magnanimous towards the Welsh. And because he's a popular knave. That, of course, is assuming it was her own decision, which I tend to doubt. And who can be sure that Jones isn't one of them? Plant Mat.'

Dudley had told me about coming face to face with Prys Gethin, chained in his gaol cart. Of his conviction that he'd been cursed by the man. I knew not what to think. For any number of reasons, Dudley was in a peculiar state of mind.

'I just… I don't like the feel of this, John. I'm yet failing to understand why a judge of the eminence of Legge is sent here, complete with jury, to make sure that one man is seen to be tried and goes to the gallows with all ends tied. It's too much. There's something happening behind it.'

He'd also told me about the whore he'd lain with – why was I unsurprised to hear of this? – and his belief that she might lead him to Abbot Smart and the Wigmore shewstone.

'And you trust *her*?' I said.

'I know women. She'll want more of me. What are you doing?'

I'd found paper and ink in my bag and spread them out upon the board under the candle.

'Drawing a map, from memory, of Brynglas Hill and the valley leading down to the River Lugg.'

Wishing I was in my library, with Leland's maps, where all might be measured against what was known and recorded. So many possibilities here. Did the ancients believe that dedication of the river to the god of the harvest might ensure fertility in the valley? I drew the ancient burial mound in the river's curve and the church with its pre-Christian well and shrine. And betwixt them the oak grove. Dudley was peering over my shoulder, a mug of cider in hand.

'What's it mean?'

'All these heathen sacred places all clustered together. The river and the hill. It's clear that in the time before Christ some places were seen as more suited to worship and communion with the beyond. Places where there might be passage through the spheres, one to another.'

Dudley took a step back, cider spilling over his wrist.

'Beg mercy, John, I may have asked the wrong question. What I meant was, *what the fuck does any of this matter?*'

I looked up at him, perhaps vaguely.

'I don't know. I need to think on it. But it's clear, is it not, that the battlefield was chosen by Glyndwr and Rhys Gethin? And Glyndwr studied magic and would see the power in this place.'

'Jesu,' Dudley said wearily. 'You never change, do you? This is all because some failed MP from the rear benches asks you to explain why his village is dying on its feet.'

'My father's village.'

'Your father's *dead*! And it was so much his village that he took the first opportunity to put it a three-day ride behind him and never go back to the dismal hole.'

I shook my head. I'd fought against it and lost, for reasons I'd refused even to explain to myself.

'I felt no particular kinship with it at first. Felt nothing of my tad there. And then mysteries appeared. As important, in their way, as... as the shewstone, I suppose.'

'As important to the Queen?'

'Possibly not.'

'Your mysticism leads you by the nose,' Dudley said. 'So Pilleth's dying. Villages die all the time, from the plague, or the river dries up, or—'

'One more day.'

'You're going *back*?'

'Maybe not more than *half* a day.'

Dudley thrust his face up to mine.

'Can it be that you've forgotten why we came here? You're leaving me to find the shewstone, while you waste another day trying to restore the reputation of the fucking Dees?'

'Give me one day, Robbie,' I said. 'Just one day.'

Maybe I should've told him about the Ceddols. Maybe if he'd known there was a startlingly beautiful and mysterious woman in Pilleth he would even have come with me.

Maybe some people would not have died so cruelly.

Maybe.

But I said nothing. When I crept from my truckle at first light, my head was all full of writings about a man called Agricola who I thought might answer the mystery of Siôn Ceddol. And Dudley was yet sleeping in the high bed.

The early ostler was saddling my faithful mare when, of a sudden, he climbed the ladder to his loft and returned with a fold of stiff paper.

'Left for you last night, master.'

John, the message said. *We must needs talk, boy. Alone. And with some urgency.*

Had there been any sign of Thomas Jones on the streets of Presteigne as I rode out, I would of course have stopped.

Maybe I should have asked him where he was lodging.

Maybe, maybe, maybe…

Dear God.

PART FOUR

... that he the said abbot hath lived viciously,
and kept to concubines divers and many
women that is openly known.
... that the said abbot doth yet continue his
vicious living, as it is known, openly.
... that the said abbot hath spent and wasted
much of the goods of the said monastery
upon the foresaid women.

Articles to be objected against John Smart,
Abbot of the Monastery of Wigmore, in the county
of Hereford, to be exhibited to the Right Honourable
Lord Thomas Cromwell, the Lord Privy Seal

XXXII

Given Back

NOW THAT WE were well into autumn, the mist was dense and speckled with white and gold, showing that the sun was yet alive somewhere. The boy was running ahead of us into the mist, arms flung wide, flapping like the wings of a ground-hopping bird.

Not entirely of this world, I'd have sworn that.

'Sometimes,' Anna Ceddol said as we pursued him up the hill, 'I think I can see lights around him. Little winking lights at his shoulders.'

People talk of foreshadows of the End-time. Lights in the sky. Prophecy in dreams. Voices in the night. Footsteps in empty rooms. The dead among the living. I hear of these things all the time. I draw glyphs and sigils and mark wondrous geometry in the night sky to calcule how celestial configurations might alter our humour. Yet how can I know what is real and what is imagined?

He spun, red-crested, amongst the curling leaves, swirling in the energy of autumn. He was of nature, she said. The woods would feed him. He would wind himself around the twisted trees, occasionally snapping off twigs which would come alive like extra fingers, twitching and dipping.

Although not so much now. He seemed to find that

unnecessary now, she said, as though he could conjure invisible twigs and follow where they led.

Natural magic.

'You took it up there?'

Anna Ceddol had stopped halfway up the slope, drawing her woollen shawl around her. The church tower had appeared above the trees. I looked at her, worried.

'I thought to take it somewhere he might not normally go. Was that wrong?'

The secret, she'd said earlier, *is in making him want to do it. He has no care for how you regard him. Will show no real love for any of us. Only need, which is not the same. He feels only for himself, and oft-times, it's hard not to think the worst of him.*

'Not,' she said, 'if it proves something to you.'

But I saw she was anxious.

Once you understand, you can feel only pity... the pity that you know he'll never feel for you. You can't teach him to obey commands, like a dog, because a dog wants to please and he doesn't care. You have to know when to catch his attention and point it at what you seek.

What he was seeking now, on Brynglas Hill, was an earth-browned thigh bone.

Anna Ceddol had presented it to me while he was outside.

His favourite bone. The first he found here, a few feet from our door. I could never take it to be reburied because he won't be parted from it. Sometimes he holds it next to him as he sleeps.

I'd asked her what she wanted me to do with it, and she'd bid me take it and hide it. Anywhere. Then come back. Which was what I'd done. It had felt unreal walking through the mist carrying a thigh bone before me like a talisman, to leave in a place where I'd felt it would be in the care of a higher presence.

Returning to the Bryn, I'd heard his vixen scream and the angry toppling of wood from the fireside pile and wondered how Anna Ceddol could go on living with this, year upon year. He was already near as tall as her, would soon be bigger, a grown man with a grown man's urges and living alone with his sister. *Dear God in heaven.*

When he'd registered that the bone was gone, I'd watched him running from the hovel, hands clawed, face contorted in rage, staring at me with a clear and focused hatred, Anna Ceddol watching him, impassive. Used to this – his humours changing faster than clouds in a windy dawn.

We stood and watched his red hat bobbing in the grass.

'Do you never go to town, mistress?'

'When I've something to sell.'

'You have no cart… no horse.'

'Nor stabling for one. No need. Horses won't rest at the Bryn. Ewes won't graze. Chickens escape. When I go to town, we walk. It's not far. On a fine day.'

'Why won't animals live here?'

'At the Bryn? I'd have thought you'd know, master.'

'I'll put it another way, then – how can *you* live here? You're clearly an educated woman. How came you here?'

'I…'

She bit her lip. Her hair was not braided this morning, and the breeze blew it back. I drew breath; her beauty unnerved me.

'You don't have to tell me,' I said.

'Beg mercy,' she said. 'I called you master. It's doctor, isn't it? You treat the sick also?'

261

'I… treat nobody and nothing,' I said. 'And cure even less. The doctorate's something I picked up in the course of a long education. Which will never finish.'

'No,' she said. 'I don't *have* to tell you anything.'

✝

Tomos Ceddol, her father, had laboured on her grandparents' farm. Good looking, and her mother had fallen for him and determined to marry him against her own father's wishes. Anna's mother had been the youngest of six.

Had Tomos Ceddol expected some kind of dowry? Had he expected to be rich, wed to a big farmer's daughter? Whatever, he was soon embittered.

'Not a good marriage,' Anna Ceddol said, 'and my mother, as soon as I could understand, was telling me I must never make the same mistake, to marry below me. My father had to go farther away to find work. My grandfather wanted nothing to do with him. While he was away, my mother taught me to read. Secretly. If he'd known, he'd have beaten her. And then my mother died of the summer plague, and we were left alone with him.'

'How old was your brother?'

'Very young. We didn't know then that he wasn't… as he should be.'

Some time had passed before it became clear that Siôn was not as other children. Crying in the night… that didn't stop. Nor pissing his bed. His sister washed his sheets daily and made more in secret, or her father would have had him sleeping on straw. Soon Tomos Ceddol was become ashamed of his son. Could not bear to look at him.

'Spent as much time away from the house as he could. He'd come home drunk – so as to get to sleep, he said. But oft-times, the noise was too much. He'd awake in a tearing rage and... hurt Siôn. One night he took him out to the barn. I found him kicking my brother where he lay, and I pulled him away, and he hit me until I knew not where I was. The next day, I loaded a handcart and took my brother away.'

'Where could you go?'

She shrugged.

'Kept on walking until we were too far away for my father to find us. I'd robbed him, see.' She looked at me, eyes wide open and unmoving. 'Took all the money he had in the house. Well... he'd no cause for complaint. It would have cost him more if we'd stayed.'

'Where was this? Where did you live?'

'A good distance away. You'll excuse me, Dr Dee, for not saying where. If he hasn't drunk himself to death in a ditch by now, I don't want him finding us.'

'Did you know by then of Siôn's... qualities?'

She shook her head.

'We came down the border, village to village, for some years. For some time I had work caring for the small daughters of a widowed gentleman who paid a village woman to look after Siôn by day. It seemed a good situation until I learned that I was expected to marry him. He was older than my father, and I... Anyway, it was back on the road until the money was all gone.'

I waited.

'Then another rich man took us in.'

Looking at her, was it any surprise? All the rich men would be waiting in line.

'He gave me money and offered me a house to live in. In Presteigne.'

'Generous,' I said.

'It was a good dwelling, behind one of the clothing work-shops. Too good to be given without demands on my... time.'

They were walking out of town when a man and his family stopped and gave them a ride on their stock cart. Pedr Morgan, shepherd of Pilleth, returning from taking fat lambs to market. They'd spent the night in his stable. She'd asked if there was anywhere she might find work and somewhere to live for a while.

'The rest... is of small import. Save that it took time. The people here are slow to befriend a stranger. But at least there are no rich men, save Master Price. Rich men have not been good for me.'

'Nor poor men, it sounds like.'

'Except for Pedr Morgan.'

Who had lost his finest fleecing shears – must have fallen off the cart in one of the fields, he had no idea which. Been searching for a fortnight and more. Taking Anna's advice, he'd shown his old pair to Siôn Ceddol, who had found the missing shears within an hour. Within a week, he'd found two new springs in the hillside. Wells were sunk, the Ceddols given food and offered dry barns to sleep in. And then Anna Ceddol had happened upon the Bryn, where nobody wanted to live and could be hers, for nothing.

And then Siôn Ceddol had found the thigh bone. The first of hundreds of body parts.

✛

'Where's he gone?' I said.

All the time she'd been talking, the red hat had been bobbing above the yellowing grass. No sign of it now.

'He won't be far away,' she said. 'Where did you put the bone? You might as well tell me.'

I told her I'd gone up to the little church, finding it empty. And then, walking around the side, had come upon…

'Oh Jesu,' Anna Ceddol said.

Already she was running up the hill, lifting her skirts, her breath coming hard.

I caught her up.

'Mistress, it was the best test of him I could think of. A place he's not used to going – a place he might avoid – though quite close. I needed to know how—'

'I thought you understood!'

It was almost a scream. The most emotion I'd seen her show, and made me sick to my heart.

'Listen,' I said, running alongside of her, panting. 'Please… I think I do understand. I think your brother possesses rare natural skills of a kind which are yet… fully explicable by emerging science. I'd like to… to help him develop them.'

'That's not possible.'

She stumbled on, the mist gathering more densely around us. Her head was lifted to the obscured sky, and her lips were moving in what looked to be rapid prayer, as we came up to the church's grey walls. The tower was darkly garlanded in mist which seemed to hide no sun, trees bending away into the sloping churchyard. A cawking of crows and ravens, intimate in the fog, and, mingled with them, a kind of liquid wailing which sent Anna Ceddol, sobbing in relief, forward in a rush,

265

to follow the church wall to the holy shrine of Our Lady of Pilleth.

I'd been in a hurry when I'd brought the bone and now saw the shrine and holy well as if for the first time: the green-slimed rocks, the steps down to the spring-fed pool, the stone wall built around it making it look like an open tomb.

On her ledge against the church walls, the mother of our saviour was smirched by the grime of neglect. Abandoned. Behind the body of the church, almost certainly older in its origins, the shrine of the holy virgin had been given back to nature.

And the bone given back to Siôn Ceddol.

He sat with his legs overhanging the pool, rocking from side to side, the dripping thigh bone in his arms, a gurgling in his throat.

He *could*, I suppose, have found it by accident, but why would he even come this way? And I'd hidden it close to the edge of the well, where bushes concealed the shallow water, and covered it over with silt and sodden leaves.

It was conclusive enough for me. I turned to his sister.

'I do understand him. I know what he does.'

As if this were all that mattered.

Oh, the blindness of science.

I went down to the holy well, where rough steps sank towards the water, the mist gathered above it like a soiled veil. Siôn Ceddol clutched his bone to his chest and looked up at me as though he'd never seen me before and snarled, his face twisting like to a gargoyle's.

And then...

'*He makes mockery of God!*'

Christ, *no.*

Turning slowly to see the rector, in his long black coat. Everything happening as though darkly ordained for my undoing.

'He is a walking blasphemy,' Matthew Daunce said.

Anna Ceddol's eyes closed, her shoulders falling, the shawl dropping to her elbows. Oh, dear God, oh, Christ, what had I done? What had I set in train here?

'No,' I said. 'You know not what you're saying.' I stood up. 'Mistress Ceddol. It's best if you go. And the boy.'

Her eyes moved from the rector to me, and she took the boy's arm and pulled him to his feet. He writhed, and she held him and the bone and dragged him away and looked at me.

'Please,' I said. 'Go.'

'You also.' The rector's face was a ball of white light in the mist. 'Now I know who you are. You are not wanted here. You're filled with dark sprites. The filth oozes from you.'

I said nothing. Watched the Ceddols backing away, Anna dragging the boy with his thigh bone bumping off the trees, leaving me staring into the rector's pointing, rigid finger.

'Go with your whore and her demonic sibling.' His forefinger twisting as if to bore a hole between my eyes. 'Go on! Before I call upon the Lord God to hurl you out.'

'No,' I said.

The word emerging fainter than I'd wanted, for I found I had no breath. Could almost see it leaving me, fading into the mist as, from the woods below the church, the horrific, faerie, vixen shriek of Siôn Ceddol tore the morn into dark strips.

XXXIII

The Single Eye

DUDLEY HAS TRIED several times to meet the single eye of Prys Gethin, determined to send back the curse to its source by force of will.

Like most of those around the Queen, he's seen the advantages in a mild study of practical magic and is prepared for an exchange of black chemistry across the already tense courtroom.

But never once does he entrap the Welshman's gaze.

Gethin stands limply in a corner of the prisoner's dock, which is close to the centre of the courtroom, hands manacled behind him, two armed guards his companions in the wooden pen, the jury seated along the wall to his right.

Access to the court, not surprisingly, is limited. Dudley has gained his place by following Roger Vaughan into the attorneys' enclosure. Five of them in there, with their books of notes. Hard to see what function they each perform, but the judge will have his reasons. Sir Christopher Legge is nothing if not coldly efficient, and such men as him, Dudley freely admits, are necessary.

The law is not about humanity.

Already, the rough-beamed former barn has taken on an air of London. Banners are hung on the wall behind the judge's

268

bench of green oak, reflecting the Queen's Majesty, a royal authority. Something to be feared.

Yet it's all too big for this petty affair, and Dudley is tormented with suspicion.

The judge's bench rises several feet higher than the attorneys' to its right and the seats to its left which soon begin to be occupied by a handful of men who Vaughan says are the JPs from Radnorshire and neighbouring counties.

'Come to see how it's done?' Dudley whispers. 'How real justice is administered?'

'Certainly, no one will have seen it done like *this* before,' Vaughan tells him. 'A trial here rarely takes longer than half an hour. Twenty cases might be heard in a morning. I'm thinking this will go on most of the day.'

God's bollocks, Dudley thinks. Only a royal trial matches this.

He draws in a steadying breath and tries again to catch the eye of Prys Gethin, but Gethin is looking down, his face without expression. Has he been tortured, Dudley wonders, for the names of his fellow brigands in Plant Mat? Is he cowed from a night of beatings?

Nothing evident.

Outside, the sound of a massing of people, a dull roar, but in here the public gallery along the back wall is big enough only for about two dozen – Dudley marking one of them at once: Thomas Jones of Tregaron. Why *is* this bastard here? What's his interest? Who let him in?

'What have they told you, Vaughan?'

'I'm a child in this. They tell me nothing. Only ask me questions about local matters and how people feel about them.'

They are at one end of the attorneys' bench and Vaughan glances warily towards the other, where one of the older lawyers might only appear to be consulting his notes.

Dudley gets the message and keeps quiet, observing a man in a bishop's mitre, attended by two clerics, entering through the main doors and approaching the bench, where two men in dark robes are arranging large books before the judge's throne.

The bishop inclines his head and... hell, it's John Scory of Hereford. They've brought the Bishop of Hereford here to represent God. Whose judgement is yet final, of course, in an English court. As if to confirm this, the morning sun at last breaks through, filling one of the high windows, and the air shimmers with dust motes.

The bishop goes out again. A robed usher enters, calls for silence and for every man to stand, and there's a communal shuffling, and then Sir Christopher Legge slips in through a small Gothic-pointed door behind the judge's bench.

✠

Only after the prayers to a just God are delivered and the charges read out, is Prys Gethin's red-stubbled chin seen to rise from his chest.

And through witchcraft did bring about the deaths of Thomas Harris and Hywel Griffiths in the county of Radnorshire on the night of September 20th, in the year of Our Lord 1560.

There were other charges relating to the stealing of cattle. Enough, on their own, to stow Gethin in the deepest cell for many a long year. Perhaps even hang him.

'How do you plead, Master Gethin?'

Legge barely glancing at the accused. The sunbeams from

the high windows create dusty cloisters in the air above the dock and the jury box.

A silence. Legge looking mildly irritated.

'What have you to say, Master Gethin? If you wish to make plea in your own tongue, we have an interpreter.'

Glancing at Roger Vaughan.

Prys Gethin looks the judge full in the face.

'I'll not require an interpreter, my Lord, having spent considerable time in England. I plead not guilty to all charges.'

Legge nods. What else would he expect? The prisoner clears his throat.

'And if I may be permitted to say, at this early stage, my Lord, my name is not Gethin but Gwilym Davies, gentleman farmer of Carmarthen. Something I've been trying to tell your minions, who seem strangely predisposed not to listen.'

Dudley sits up hard and, for just a moment, his eyes meet the prisoner's one eye, where he sees laughter flaring like raging flames.

XXXIV

Adversary

SUCH WAS THE density of the fog now, it was as though the rector and I were set in wax. His body was like to a scarecrow's, but his face shone as marble. I looked at him and saw an effigy from a tomb dressed in cast-out apparel, and his eyes were lit, I'd swear, with madness.

The air was grown thick as a damp, grey blanket around the forlorn shrine. The walls of the church were now as far as I could see. Shivering in my cheap jerkin, I felt that this was no longer a normal autumnal mist but a fogging of the senses. I breathed in its bitterness and spoke with insistence.

'Let me tell you… about Siôn Ceddol…'

'There is *nothing*' – his voice coming back at me like a horse-whip – 'that you can tell me about Siôn Ceddol. Nothing that will change my opinion of him as an inhuman carrier of demons, who should never have been born into this world.'

'You're wrong.'

'Who are you to tell me—?'

'What Siôn Ceddol does,' I said, 'religion has no bearing upon it.'

'Religion has a bearing on everything. Are you a fool as well?'

'As well as what?'

Standing at the top of the steps, where Siôn Ceddol had sat, my breath was coming harder. If a place of healing is a place of inherent power, there was no sense of healing here now. Only the power, and that was a cold power with none of the promise of transcendence implied by an old sacred site. Within the quaking mist, I was aware of an ancient conflict, shafts of darkness and light twisting like blades.

'As well as what?' I said quietly. 'Say it.'

'I shall not. You know what you are and appear to live with it. But *I* don't have to. I do not have to tolerate your presence here. Get yourself away from my church, *conjuror*.'

'There,' I said. 'That wasn't so hard, was it?'

'*Get out of here!*'

His narrow body jerking in fury, elongating like a shadow.

'No,' I said. 'Not before I tell you the truth about Siôn Ceddol.'

He'd turned away from me, so that I was speaking to his back.

'How much do you know about water divining?'

'Of the devil,' he told the fog.

I shook my head with confidence.

'A human faculty, known since early times, which may soon be explained by science. But only now are scholars finding it can be applied to more than the finding of water. Though the fact that Siôn Ceddol can find water as well as bones is surely proof—'

'That he's riddled with demons. Don't waste my time.'

I would not give up. Spoke to the rector's back about the great natural philosophers – Paracelsus, whom he'd have heard of as a healer, even if he disapproved. And the German, Georgius Agricola, of whom he probably would be ignorant.

'This is the man who's become the best known diviner in

273

Europe. Who began with water, but then extended his art to finding metals and ore for mining. Using the same fork of hazel, which twisted and turned in his hands when he stood over an underground spring.'

I'd learned about Agricola at Louvain and, of course, had tried it myself, to no avail, before sending a report on it to Cecil, suggesting he might strike a bargain with one of the German experts to establish a mining enterprise in England. Cecil had seemed interested, but I'd heard nothing since and assumed he'd dispatched spies to Europe in the hope of acquiring the knowledge for no cost.

'You don't see it, do you?' Daunce said. 'You do not see the obvious. A demon enters a man and gives him knowledge he could not otherwise possess. Causing his limbs to move on their own. Snatching his body from the reins of his mind. I've watched that creature, seen its eyes go white as its hands burrow in the earth to bring up the dead.'

'It's becoming known that the mind can be attuned to whatever it needs to unearth.'

'And what if there is *no* mind?' His rage throwing him back to face me. 'The brain of that monstrous boy will ever be in ruins, and ruins are where demons walk unchecked.'

Turning away his head again, in contempt. It was like talking to the rocks. But at least I'd told him what I believed to be the truth; maybe he'd think about it.

Though probably, he wouldn't.

I said wearily, 'What are you *doing* here, Daunce? You hate this place. You distress its people. They're not theologians eager to embrace the rigid tenets of Lutherism. They're not going to change their ways with a snap of the fingers.'

'The word of God will change their ways.'

It had long seemed to me that the word of God as filtered through a Puritan's rigid liturgy would change nothing for the better.

I thought of the boy who hanged himself because he could see no future here. Who might normally have gone to his priest for advice. And the old man who did go to Daunce, with his fears of night walkers and was told it was the devil making him see what was not there.

I said, 'Does Bishop Scory know of your... way of thinking?'

But if I thought to put him in fear...

'Scory? That heretic? A man who worships the lewd and the sacrilegious in a secret chamber *in the Cathedral itself*?'

I realised he must mean Scory's treasured map of the world, Scory himself having said some canons had been in fear of it and wanted it burned. Daunce, unsurprisingly, must have been one of them. I didn't pursue this, but I'd not give up.

'What progress can we ever make if we put everything we don't understand at the door of the devil? If a man sees the ghost of his dead wife and we tell him, that was not your wife, that was an image wrought by the devil to torment you...'

'The truth is not always easy to face,' he said calmly. 'But faced it must be.'

'And there can be no ghosts of the dead because the Lutheran faith has decided there's no purgatory?'

'All papist myth and must be revealed as such. Stripping away these fondly held archaic beliefs is bound to cause a small period of pain, before the clear light is seen.'

Well, of course, he'd see it as a challenge, a mission. Slicing through all the layers of the place with the clean, cold butcher's blade of the new Puritanism.

I glanced at the statue of the Virgin in her grotto in the rocks above the water, marking the green slime on her brow and her robes all smirched with slug-trails and dead insects. Whatever power was here now, the Virgin was no longer the source of it.

'You can't be said to have taken care of her, Rector.'

He didn't look at the shrine. Or I don't think he did; his eyes were no more than smudges in the fog.

'A papist conceit, perpetuating an old evil. I'd have it smashed. Maybe I will. I'll certainly be erecting a barrier to keep people away. Let the brambles and thorns do the rest.'

'Isn't she the reason for this church? Our Lady of Pilleth?'

A silence, and then he eyed me, a slight smile on his dry, pale lips.

'And who is *she*? Who is the lady?'

'Who do you think she is?'

'Can you not feel her?'

I said nothing.

'I've never felt her so strongly. *Our Lady of Slime.*'

Dear God.

'I found here a long tradition of dark worship which had never been challenged. This well was made by the old Britons, doubtless in veneration of some predatory water goddess. They would have performed sacrifice here, thrown the heads of their enemies into the pool.'

I could only nod. This married with my own findings from old English manuscripts.

'The papists take a pagan well,' Daunce said, 'and claim it for the Virgin and nothing changes… because the practices of the Catholic Church, like those of the heathens, like those of the Druids, are founded upon magic and sorcery. You, of all people, should know that.'

Well, of course I knew that. Bishop Scory knew that. The Queen herself would acknowledge that high magic was a ceremonial gateway to knowledge.

And was a simpler magic so wrong for a place like this, the valley of the river of the god of light, dotted with ancient mounds, scattered with the remains of the violently killed? A place where a careful balance must needs be maintained?

'I presume you know that Owain Glyndwr worshipped here before the battle,' Daunce said. 'In his desperate need for a great victory. But did he worship at the church? No, he burned it down. He worshipped *here*, at the pagan shrine. Glyndwr invoked the heathen goddess – the devil, in other words.'

I said nothing. Given Owain Glyndwr's knowledge of magic and that he or Rhys Gethin appeared to have chosen this site for the conflict, I'd come to a not entirely dissimilar conclusion myself. But was disinclined to voice agreement with anything this man came out with.

'Invoking the power of Satan,' Daunce said, 'and it was given to him. His name was exalted all over Europe. For a while – the devil's favours last only so long. As you're probably already finding out.'

I was feeling very cold now in my thin jerkin, with no hat, but felt that Daunce was not. That he was, in some twisted way, beginning finally to relish this encounter. He came closer to me, his coat hanging limp around him like damp and blackened leaves.

'And they worship here yet. This so-called holy well dedicated to the Virgin Mary, who's but a screen around the heathen goddess... is yet a shrine to evil. For I've seen— I have *seen* them anointing themselves here at night, in the heathen way.'

'Who?'

'If I'd gone close enough to see they would have set on me and killed me. God told me this. I've heard God's voice in the night.'

'How do you know it was God's voice?'

'You'd try and make me doubt it?' His whole body shaking. 'You'd make me out a madman?'

'Father Daunce, you're alone in a place you don't understand and maybe never will. You're prey to divers fears and fancies. You believe everyone's your enemy—'

'I've only one enemy, though he wears many faces, and I'm looking into one at this moment, asking myself is it a coincidence that England's most famous sorcerer should arrive here... *now*? The adversary?'

I reeled back.

'*Adversary?*'

'Oh, I was warned in my prayers that one would come. I'd thought it was the demon inhabiting the boy. But it's a subtler devil. A manifestation of one that's been here for generations. Dee... *ddu*... black! All black as sin.'

His face was blanched and his lips were parched. I began to see where this was going.

'Rector, you're—'

'Your grandfather... was he not Bedo Ddu, who filled the font with wine? No sacrilege worse than that at the baptism of a child, when all evil's expelled.'

'It was done in merriment, it—'

'And the tainted wine flowed in the blood of your father, who went on to steal from the Church.'

Jesu, who'd told him that? What had I walked into?

'But it found its full flowering...' The rector folded his arms, as if sitting in judgement. '...in his heretical son...'

So close now I seemed to see a white light in his eyes.

'... who stood trial for sorcery... and was saved by Satan in the guise of a papist monster who made him his *chaplain*.'

Bonner.

'Are you yet a priest of the papist church, Dr Dee?'

He'd done his studies and found the most vulnerable part of my skin. There was nothing I could say that would not make this worse. How easy it must be to see everything in black and white. But there was no black here and no white. The mist would tell you this.

His finger came up.

'Let not this place be tainted by your presence. Take yourself away from here while you can. Crawl back to your London lair. And when the Welshman's sentenced, I'll visit the sheriff and have charges of witchcraft brought against the monster and his sister, the Great Papist's whore.'

What?

'There's no workable witchcraft law in this country,' I said. 'The Plant Mat case was only set in train because it was an accusation of murder by sorcery and two men were dead. There's been no murder here. Only a mass slaughter a century and a half ago.'

A silence, then Daunce walked away, turning back to face me only when he reached the church wall.

'I think,' he said, 'we both know better than that. And what lies in an ancient grave.'

I rose up, would have raced after him, grabbed him, maybe thrown him in the pool.

But what use would that do?

The balance was tipped against me. He knew about the mutilated man secretly buried by Stephen Price and Morgan the shepherd.

And he was mad enough to loose a witch-hunt upon Pilleth.

A weight of weariness came over me, and I sank to my knees in the mud.

XXXV

The Etiquette of Cursing

THE PRISONER SAYS,

'*They* told me my name was Prys Gethin.'

He sounds bewildered, as if the name has no significance for him. The judge leans back in his oaken chair.

'Who did?'

'The gaolers at New Radnor Castle, my Lord. When they overpowered me and took me to New Radnor, kept telling me my name was Prys Gethin, they did. All the time Prys Gethin. Would not have it any other way.'

The court billows with whispers, which are only hushed when the pikes are lifted and Sir Christopher Legge turns his anvil head, under its triangular black hat, towards the prisoner.

'So… you accept that you *were* the man taken to New Radnor Castle by the sheriff and constables.'

'I do, my Lord, but—'

'Enough! You have pleaded not guilty to the offences with which you are charged, and that's all the court wishes to hear from you until the case against you has been heard. You will, therefore, be silent until then. Is that understood?'

The prisoner nods his head with, Dudley notes, conspicuous courtesy and a certain grace. The clever bastard. It could be that his real name is indeed Gwilym Davies, that he's known only within Plant Mat as Prys Gethin. It ought to change nothing. He glances at Vaughan, who looks a touch apprehensive, as though wondering if there's any way he might be blamed for this oversight.

✢

Evan Lewis, the sheriff, is called to give evidence. He is a bulky, brown-haired man who, unsurprisingly, appears slightly in awe of the London court visited upon Presteigne.

Legge has before him the sheriff's written account of what occurred when the farm workers, who had lain in wait for many a long night, finally surprised the band of cattle raiders.

'And how did they know, Sheriff, that these cattle thieves were the brigands calling themselves Plant Mat?'

The eyes of Evan Lewis flicker from side to side with transparent uncertainty. Dudley casts his own gaze to the ceiling, despairing of the quality of men responsible for upholding the law in these distant counties. They just wait in line, these farmers, for their turn at being sheriff.

'Perhaps,' the judge says helpfully, 'these brigands were known to boast about their activities in local taverns. Determined to perpetuate their... legend?'

'Exac'ly, my Lord.' The sheriff's body sags in his gratitude. 'That's as I believe—'

'Yet, in the end, only this one was apprehended. How many others escaped?'

'Hard to say, my Lord. Could have been a dozen or more. But they were fortunate that the one made lame by a fall readily identified himself to them as the leader, Prys Gethin.'

'How very generous of him.'

'My Lord, this was to open the way for a bargain. He said his fellows would pay handsomely for his release and if he was freed they could count on their land being safe from raids in the future. While if anything was to happen to him...' The sheriff pauses and looks around the court. '...then every man who'd laid hands on him would be cursed to hell.'

A communal indrawing of breath in the courtroom. The judge holds up papers.

'I have here statements taken down from four of the farm men which confirm what the sheriff has just told the court. I see no point in having each of them read out, but they are available for inspection, signed with the marks of the named individuals... whom I understand, Sheriff, were reluctant to appear before this court in person.'

'My Lord. These are men who fear for their lives and their families.'

'That they might be made targets of Plant Mat?'

Dudley smiles at Legge's affected, faintly Gallic, pronunciation of the words – *Plaunt Met*.

'And also they fear... his eye,' the sheriff says, his cheeks turned a little pink.

Legge peers, in an exaggerated fashion, towards the prisoner's dock. Laughter from the jury's box. The prisoner looks down.

'So,' Legge says. 'What was the response to this offer of a *bargain*?'

The sheriff straightens his back.

'The landowners were summoned from their beds and would hear none of it, my Lord. No one should make deals with notorious thieves. They had him tied to a cart and taken to New Radnor. Calling in at my farm, where I was roused and, realising the importance of this arrest, sent at once for constables.'

'And while you were waiting for the castle dungeons to be unlocked and prepared, I gather there was intercourse between the prisoner and the landowners, Thomas Harris and Hywel Griffiths?'

'My Lord...' Roger Vaughan comes hesitantly to his feet. 'It's, um... it's pronounced Howell.'

'What is?'

'Hywel Griffiths, my Lord. Pronounced Howell. I just thought—'

'Very useful, I'm sure, Master Vaughan,' Legge says with venom. 'Let us proceed.'

Vaughan sits down, eyes closing in embarrassment. Dudley smiles. Legge pretends to have lost the thread of his questioning and consults his papers, turning back a page.

'How would you describe the nature of this intercourse between the prisoner and the owners of the cattle he's accused of attempting to steal?'

'Well... heated, my Lord. The prisoner, having failed to make a deal for his release, tried to escape and was restrained. It was then that he... uttered curses.'

'Hmm.' Legge pinching his sharp chin. 'Consider, for a moment, your use of the word "curses". In the heat of the moment, a man might shout abuse...?'

'No, my Lord. This was delivered in what I can only describe as cold blood.'

'You were witness to it.'

'Indeed I was, my Lord. I saw and heard all of it, although –

my Welsh having fallen away in recent years – I was not able to understand every word.'

'You're saying that the alleged curses were phrased in the language of the Welsh?'

'They were. With finger pointed, under a full moon, which is said to give more power to—'

'Yes, yes. I believe we shall shortly be hearing more expert testimony as to the, ah, etiquette of cursing. Was *any* of it delivered in the Queen's English?'

'Enough to convince me of the nature of it.'

'Which was?'

'That my neighbours, Thomas Harris and Hywel Griffiths would be dead before the new moon.'

'And indeed there seems little doubt that both men… were.'

'No doubt at all, my Lord.'

'In ways… unexpected?'

'One of a sudden fever.'

'Hardly uncommon in itself, Sheriff.'

'The other drowning when a sudden, ferocious wind smashed an old and narrow footbridge over the River Irfon as he was crossing it.'

'You were not there at the time, I take it.'

'I was not. However, I was summoned within hours, after the dead body was recovered from the river. My home is but a few miles away, see, and I can testify that this particular day was one of an unusual stillness. Not a breath of wind in the Radnor Forest.'

The judge nods, extracting a paper from the pile before him.

'I also have a statement here, signed by the son of Master *Hie-well* Griffiths' – flinging a cold glance at poor Vaughan –

'giving testimony that he was at that time burning twiggery from a tree-felling not two fields distant from the point in the river where his father met his death and felt no hint of a breeze. Saying the smoke from his fire rose steadily throughout the morning.'

Strong evidence, Dudley thinks. In the absence of a specific Witchcraft Act, cases of causing injury or death by force of magic are become difficult to prove. Given her own interest in magic and alchemy, Bess might dither for years over this issue. Meanwhile, the power of malevolence conjured through focused thought and satanic ritual will go unchecked.

Dudley, who more than once has felt himself to be the target of a distant hatred made toxic by dark arts, is himself convinced that Prys Gethin, or whoever else he claims to be, does indeed have a stare of practised malignancy through that one eye.

And Dudley also knows that, where the use of magic is concerned, a sense of self-belief takes the practitioner more than halfway along the shadowed road. He stares hard at Prys Gethin.

Look up, you bastard, look up.

'These two deaths,' Sir Christopher Legge says. 'How far apart were they, in time?'

The prisoner makes no move. His head is bowed, as if for the rope, as the sheriff replies.

'My Lord, the fever struck the night before the collapse of the bridge.'

A hiss rushes round the old barn as if a cold river has been directed through it.

'I think,' the judge says over it, 'that it is incumbent upon this court to learn more about the practice of witchcraft along this border. After our midday meal, I shall call the Lord Bishop of Hereford to give evidence. In the meantime, Sheriff, perhaps you might enlighten me as to the significance for this county, of the name *Prys Gethin*.'

XXXVI

In Dark Arts

JOHN SCORY HAS removed his mitre and wears a small hat of an academic kind. He takes the oath with a knowing half-smile. Legge consults his papers, then sits back in his big chair and looks up.

'My Lord Bishop, you are, I believe, my last witness.'

Scory looks perturbed.

'Not the last *ever*, I trust, Sir Christopher. One would hate to think the fear of a Welsh curse might drive you from the Bench.'

Legge scowls. Dudley grins. He rather likes Scory, a bishop in perhaps his last see who gives not a whit for anyone, least of all an ambitious judge from London.

The light in here has gloomed since midday, the banners fading into shadow, the old barn's beams and pillars giving the court the illumination of a forest clearing.

The judge starts again.

'You've been Bishop of Hereford since…?'

'Last year.'

Legge frowns. He evidently thought it was longer.

'But in that time,' Scory tells him, 'I've studied in some detail the religious beliefs and practices on the fringes of the diocese.'

'By which you mean the area in which we now sit?'

'And some regions further west.'

'You're saying that beliefs in this area may differ in some ways from the accepted faith of the land?'

'Only in the way that faith might be interpreted,' Scory says. 'Wales and the Border country are not noted as areas of religious rebellion, but old beliefs die hard.'

Legge waits. Now Dudley begins to see where the judge is going with this. He'll have the court presented with clear proof that Wales is yet riddled with witchcraft and that it's entirely reasonable to suppose that a man like Prys Gethin was schooled in dark arts.

It should make for an entertaining hour or so. Dudley has eaten passably well in the Bull, drained a flagon of the innkeeper's finest cider and then emerged to find the whore, Amy, waiting for him in the marketplace. Telling him that if he comes to her after court's out, she may well be able to point him towards the man he seeks.

Perfect. With any luck they could be out of here on the morrow, with the Wigmore shewstone all packed away. He has the money… and the menace, if required, as it usually is.

'Coming out here,' Scory says, 'was a rather bewildering experience for someone used to softer climes. I found things remarkably different from Chichester in the south-east, where I was bishop in… in earlier times. There, for most people, worship was seen primarily as essential preparation for the life which is to follow.'

'And is it not, my Lord Bishop?'

A suitably pious consternation creasing Legge's brow.

'Oh, most certainly it is, my Lord,' Scory says. 'However, in the wilder country, worship and ritual are seen also as serving a practical purpose in the surviving of *this* life. Isolated country people depend far more than do we upon a relationship with the land and its elements… perceiving themselves closer to the, ah, spirits which – under God – maintain the fertility of crops and stock, and hold the seasons in place.'

Legge's eyes close in upon the blade of his nose.

'*Spirits?*'

'Country people, inevitably, are closer to what you may prefer to think of as the elements of nature. Not as close as our ancestors might have been but closer than most city people can imagine. Few have not had some experience of natural powers which have raised them up or – more often – reduced them to fear for their livelihoods. And life itself.'

Scory pauses, casts his gaze around the rustic courtroom as though it were become his cathedral. The air is clouded in here now, but not dark enough for candles.

'My point is that they are constantly aware of the fragility of their lives and why a balance must be found and held. And, in finding this balance, are oft-times inclined – by instinct – to mingle the rituals and liturgy of the modern Christian church with the time-honoured customs of the area. Which some may see as witchcraft, but these simple folk—'

'What are you saying, Bishop?' the judge demands irritably. 'That witchcraft is so deeply embedded in the religious practices of these counties that it goes unrecognised as heresy and blasphemy?'

Scory beams.

'Precisely, my Lord. Were every man or woman who practises what we might consider a form of witchcraft to be brought before a court, most villages would be left derelict and the land untilled.'

Legge sits up, his chair creaking. This testimony has not taken the path which he – or Dudley – would have wished.

'And what of curses?'

'As old as time.'

'And in your experience of this area, can curses yet kill?'

'In my experience...' Scory wrinkles his nose. '...a countryman believing himself cursed will oft-times curl up and die.'

'You are saying the curse works.'

'I believe that, in the right circumstances, some curses do indeed work. Especially, as I say, if a man knows himself cursed. If he falls ill, he'll be inclined to believe the curse is come upon him.'

'And the inflictor of the curse may issue it with this intent?'

'Indeed,' Scory says, gazing into the air. 'However, I confess I'd find it rather harder to explain how such a man may seek to persuade let us say a bridge that its timbers are fatigued to the extent that the said bridge gives up its struggle against collapse just as the recipient of a curse is passing over it. Probably a gap in my occult knowledge, my Lord, which I must needs address.'

Silence, and then the sound of laughter.

Which, Dudley is dismayed to discover, comes from his own throat.

Scory retains his solemnity as the laughter spreads in slow ripples through the court.

'Thank you,' Legge says coldly. 'I have no more questions for this witness and will shortly adjourn this hearing for a period to consider all the evidence before addressing the jury.'

He glances disdainfully at the prisoner, who yet stands as though a noose is already in place. Dudley eyes the doors. No better time, as the judge prepares to rise, for a rescue attempt.

Legge delves among his papers.

'But before I adjourn… I had considered giving the prisoner an opportunity to speak for himself – on the understanding that it would be in English – but now see no need for this. However, a written statement has been presented to the court *by* the prisoner, writing in the name of Gwilym Davies, the substance of which I shall now disclose.'

The judge tells the court that the man calling himself Gwilym Davies and professing to be a farmer of Carmarthen, claims that, on the night in question, he and his fellows had driven a herd of black cattle to the London markets and were returning through Radnor Forest when they were set upon in darkness.

'Believing their assailants to be murderous robbers, they fled,' Legge said. 'But Davies, being lame, was captured and thrown into a cart. Being much beaten about by men who, he says, gave no evidence of being officers of the law, he admits to subjecting them to a tirade of abuse after one of them spat into his empty eye-socket. He denies issuing a formal death curse. Claims he…' The judge sniffs. '… would not know how to.'

In the dock, the prisoner is nodding very slowly.

What unmitigated shit. If there was anyone more practised in the art of cursing than this one-eyed man, Dudley has yet to encounter him. Deserves to dangle for these lies alone.

'He also repeats his assertion,' Legge continues, 'that the name Prys Gethin was pressed upon him by his captors. This being a name which, as the sheriff has told us, is calculed to spread a particular fear in this area of the borderlands.'

The judge smiles thinly and sceptically before adjourning the hearing for two hours – an extraordinary amount of time for such a petty case, Dudley thinks.

He leaves the court and walks down to piss in the river.

Only wishing he could have taken the stand himself and declared how the man had cursed *him*. Here in the market-place without a second thought, the malevolence springing full-formed to his lips as if directed from some outside force.

But then, what nest of wasps might Dudley have kicked if he were to have given evidence as Master Roberts, the antiquary?

Walking back up the street in the dimming afternoon, he marks a tall woman in a dark green cape, gliding towards him from the centre of town.

By the finery of her apparel alone, it can only be the whore calling herself Amy.

They draw level in the marketplace, now filling with people awaiting the conclusion of the trial that will scratch a twenty-year-old itch. The piemen gathering.

Amy smiles, reaches up quite openly and touches Dudley's cheek.

'Now, my Lord?'

The title delivered in a coquettish, mocking way, but Dudley still can't help wondering if she knows who he is. All the men of influence she must bed. And introducing herself as Amy. Could that...?

Enough. She's a woman. Dudley can handle women.

'You can take me to him now?' he asks.

'Of course.'

'Then I'm in your hands.'

'Time for that as well, if we're quick,' Amy says.

XXXVII

Falling Away

I MUST HAVE gone stumbling down the path like a hunchback, and the hunch was Brynglas Hill itself and all the weight of worship piled upon it – one religion grinding against another, the fog before me lit with frictive sparks. Why is it that all faiths founder upon the jagged rocks at their extremities?

Towards the foot of the hill, the fog thinned to a mist again before revealing a sky of amber-grey and the smoke from the Pilleth fires which I hurried towards… and then cried out as the path crumbled before me.

Losing my footing, and the land was all atilt. Then came the shock of cold water – treacherous mud had flung me headlong into a brown, stagnant puddle.

God *damn*. I lay soaked, twisted and dazed, close to weeping in frustration like an infant. Jesu, what was I become? *The adversary?* Truly, I've never in my life wanted to challenge God, only to understand some small part of his mind. Is that the worst kind of heresy?

Blinking away the dirt in my eyes, I thought for a moment that I saw my tad with that expression of both sympathy and scorn which all good fathers wear when a child falls and explodes into self-pitying tears.

And then found I was looking up into the calm, weather-browned face of Anna Ceddol.

'Mistress...' Coming at once, red-faced and dripping to my feet, brushing wet earth and slimed leaves from my sopping jerkin, feeling more foolish than I could ever remember. 'Oh God, Mistress Ceddol... what have I done without thinking.'

Or, more likely, while thinking too much.

Anna Ceddol nodded towards the boy, who was scrabbling among the damp ashes on the midden.

'He does everything without thinking. Or, at least, not as we know thinking.'

Yet still achieved more than me, for all my years of study. A bookman who thinks only of how his learning might grow. Making him more of scholar, but less of a man.

Anna Ceddol took my arm.

'You're shivering. Come by the fire.'

Leading me inside the Bryn, where she propped three logs in conical shape upon the smouldering hearth, drawing me towards the new flames.

'It was coming, anyway,' she said.

'What was?'

'The rector. Sooner or later he was going to move against us. He was only gathering kindling for his blaze.'

'We can stop him.'

'Don't waste your time, Dr John.'

'I'll find the sheriff tonight,' I said. 'Before Daunce gets to him. And bring Stephen Price down from the wall, on your side. He's halfway there. Can't deny the malady affecting the valley. Can't be the political man turning from the old ways. If he's to have the rest of his life here, he must needs face...'

I knew not how to put it and fell back on Price's own words.

'He must needs face what *is*,' I said. 'And that the Pilleth ills will never be cured by a Puritan whose answer to anything he doesn't understand is to condemn it as satanic and shut it out.'

In that enclosure of firelight and shadows, it was all very clear to me now. I saw the shrine left to crumble and rot, the holy well overgrown, sucked back into the earth which gave out old corpses in profusion.

'I'll tell the bishop he has the wrong cleric,' I said.

Yet I knew how hard it could be to remove a priest. Especially one who knew where a murdered man's body lay and who put it there. I closed my eyes.

Then opened them quickly.

'What are you doing?'

Perhaps I'd gone rigid, still lacking confidence in the close company of a woman, especially when she was...

... undoing my jerkin.

'Jesu—'

'They'll dry more quickly if you take them off.'

'Mistress, is this...?'

'Seemly?' Peeling my shirt from my skin. 'Who can ever say? Does it matter?'

Drying my chest now with a cloth of sacking, both her hands moving under it. She'd closed the door so the boy was shut out, and also much of the light. The smoke from the fire was sweet-smelling. Apple wood, clouding the air with fragrance, filling the head.

'The hose?'

'I—'

'I'll need your hose.'

Her long hands gently fumbling at my waist.

'Now I'm all wet, too,' she said.

Oh, dear God.

'These things happen,' Anna Ceddol said.

Her voice small now. I could barely draw breath. In the dimness, I saw her overdress falling away. Gave in to the smoke and the soft weight of a breast falling forward into my palm.

✛

I slept. It was a mistake. When I awoke, on the pallet amongst the rushes, there was a smell of stew and herbs from the pot over the fire, and the door was open to the dusk.

Sitting up, I marked my apparel hanging from a beam and Anna Ceddol full-dressed watching the boy playing with his favourite thigh bone on the edge of the hearth, rolling it along the stones, humming to himself like a drone of bees.

She smiled.

'Is it your wish to pass the night here, Dr John?'

'I... can't. I'm expected back at the Bull in Presteigne. And I must needs find the sheriff.'

Thinking I could reach him through Roger Vaughan. That Vaughan would surely vouch for my sanity.

I stretched out my legs, feeling warm and fulfilled in the simplest, most physical sense. She was only the second woman in this world I'd lain with, and my life was turned over again. I couldn't look at her without wanting her again, wanting her forever.

How easy it is to fall into love.

'Yet I don't want to leave you,' I said. 'I'm afraid of what the rector will do. The rector's mad.'

'I've faced worse.'

'I'm not sure you have.'

She looked at Siôn Ceddol, rolling his bone from one side of the hearth to the other, the eerie drone never ceasing.

'People like to say he's of the faerie. When he wants to find something, the faerie tell him where it lies – or the dead. Some say it's the same thing. That the faerie are the spirits of the dead.'

'I doubt that.' The mingling of spheres – this I felt, but what did I know? 'I think the faerie are the essences of things. The spirits of life in the land – in the trees and the rivers and the rocks.'

'The rocks live?'

'Some rocks, you can see the life in them. Crystals. It's my aim to study this for myself. Make experiments.'

I thought of the scryer, Brother Elias, in Goodwife Faldo's hall, how my attempts to observe and understand had led me only further into darkness and confusion. The perceived shade grown from the shewstone that night... the mention of bones drawing me at once to my guilt over Benlow, the Glastonbury boneman, when it might have been some strange foretelling of my encounter with Siôn Ceddol. The trickery our minds perform.

And then I thought of something else that Matthew Daunce had said.

'Anna...'

She was carefully detaching my jerkin and hose from the nail in the beams, shaking them out as if they were apparel of quality rather than the rubbish I wore.

'You needn't worry you might've given me a child,' she said. 'I'm barren.'

'I wasn't—'

'And glad of it. I've been raped twice. Would have been three times, but the third time I agreed, and then he couldn't do it.' She took down the items of apparel and laid them by me on the pallet. 'A young woman alone with an idiot boy, it's the least a man expects.'

'You can't go on,' I said. 'You can't go on with this life.'

I looked at Siôn Ceddol who seemed to have fallen to sleep with his arms around the bone. With closed eyes he looked like any other boy and harmless.

'Come back with me,' I said.

'To London. With him?' She laughed. 'They'd have him in Bedlam before the week was out. Don't you see? We can only ever live in places like this.'

'He has a skill. An important skill.'

I had a momentary crazed vision of presenting Siôn Ceddol to Cecil as the only dowser I'd known who might be able to replicate the wonders of Georgius Agricola.

'Don't even think of it,' Anna Ceddol said. 'The city would terrify him. Me as well. We're country people. If he wanders out in the night here, as oft-times he does, I know he'll come to no harm. What were you about to ask me?'

I ached in my breast for her and the gloomed years ahead. Changing his rag every day, washing the shit from him in the stream. Worst of all, never letting him be alone with those his age, particularly the maidens. None of this would be so bad if she wasn't educated. If she hadn't the wit to imagine what her life might have been.

I let go a sigh.

'When Daunce... when he was in full, abusive spate, he spoke of you as... the... the Great Papist's...'

'Whore?'

Her eyes were like rock.

I nodded, turning away from her, beginning quickly to drag on my apparel.

'It's not true,' she said. 'But it might have been.'

I stopped dressing.

'I think I told you of a rich man who offered me a home in Presteigne. I'd spent one night with him. Or half a night. He gave me money. He'd been… a monk. At the head of a monastery.'

'*John Smart…?*'

I stumbled, half into my hose. Could hardly say the name.

'He had a reputation,' she said. 'Even when in Holy Orders. Could not keep it in his robe.'

I sat down on the stool by the fire to put on my boots, shaking my head. How could this woman consider herself so worthless that she'd give herself to a man such as this even for one night?

Siôn Ceddol, awake again, came and sat on the rushes a few feet from me. He was looking to the side of me where the tall stones rose like the remains of an ingle.

As if watching something.

He smiled.

'He likes you,' Anna said.

'How can you tell?'

Thinking he hadn't liked me up at the holy well, when he thought I'd stolen his thigh bone.

'He's within a few feet of you,' she said, 'and he isn't screaming the walls down.'

'Where…' I didn't really want to ask her. 'Where was he when you… were with Smart?'

'There was a housekeeper. A young woman. She survived the night by plying Siôn with sweetmeats. My feeling was that she was one of several woman who… worked for him.'

'And this was all in Presteigne?'

She nodded.

'He's still there?'

'They say he pulls a good income from Presteigne. That's what's said. Only gossip, but the same gossip from different ends of town. Yes, he's there.'

'Tell me.'

While she told me what she knew and what she'd heard of John Smart and his dealings, Siôn Ceddol gazed placidly into the smoke. Holding out his hands in it, as though to accept a gift. But, conspicuously, not from me. His white hands swam up in the blue-grey smoke like flatfish and seemed to grasp something.

Something heavy.

Holding it up to look at it.

Holding up nothing.

Of a sudden there was no heat from the fire.

Anna Ceddol said quietly, 'There's someone with you.'

I stiffened. The fire burned white.

The boy turned and picked up his beloved earth-brown thigh bone and laid it on the hearth and then pushed it forward as if he were offering it for inspection to whoever sat next to me.

And then sat back and waited as I shivered.

✝

I should have gone then to Stephen Price, told him what had happened this day – some of it, anyway – but I couldn't face it.

Needed some time to separate the truth from the madness. Besides, I knew I had to reach the sheriff before Daunce could get to him, although I couldn't, at this moment, even remember his name.

I stole around to the stables at the rear of Nant-y-groes and found my mare. She knew me at once and was silent as I nuzzled her and saddled her and led her quietly out of the stable and down to the road. I'd come back tomorrow. By tomorrow I would have thought of something. Some way of persuading Anna Ceddol to return with me to London. What did it matter to me that she was incapable of childbearing? There was neither time nor money in my life for children.

I mounted up and followed the silvered ribbon of road with ease, giving brief thought to what I'd do when we arrived at my mother's house. How my mother would react to my appearance in Mortlake with a beautiful woman and an idiot. The truth of it – I didn't care. The moon rose, close to full in the clearing sky, and I felt hollow and sad and yet exalted.

We'd covered the few miles to Presteigne before I knew it, the mare and I, pounding the moonlit track.

As if she knew I was trying to shake something off.

Someone.

✛

Even the mare knew something was wrong in Presteigne, starting and throwing back her head as the town houses sprang up to either side.

Most of them with light inside, even the poorer homes on the edge of town, where you'd have expected the families to settle down for their first sleep.

I dismounted and led the mare slowly toward the market-place, now abuzz with groups of people, who spoke in low voices. No piemen. No merriment. The town was aslant, its balance altered, the sheriff's building in darkness, all the pitch-torches snuffed, while only the inns were ablaze with hard light and the jagged air of a pervading rage.

XXXVIII

Unholy Glamour

THEN I SAW men with lanterns, horses saddled. Men with swords strapped on and hard faces, some gathered in small groups, as if waiting for a leader.

I espied Roger Vaughan walking alone, seeming to be going nowhere. The white, fattened moon illumined the sweat which spiked his hair and smeared his face like melted tallow. He looked like a man newly claimed by the plague, trying to absorb the awful knowledge of it.

'I've just ridden from Nant-y-groes,' I said. 'What's—?'

Vaughan shook his head, blinking, kept on walking until I could position myself and the horse in front of him. He stopped by an abandoned stall, the smell of fruit about it, slippery skins underfoot.

I waved a hand at the crowd.

'A hue and cry?'

'You could very well say that, Dr Dee.'

A young man came shouldering betwixt us, sliding his sword in and out of its sheath, shouting back at someone.

'Be dead before midnight, if *I* finds him, tell you that much, boy.'

'Who's he talking about?'

'You don't know?'

'If I *knew*—'

'The one-eyed man,' Vaughan said.

'Gethin? Hell.' I took a step back. 'He's *escaped*?'

'You could say that, too.'

'What about all the guards?'

His smile was crooked.

'Dr Dee, the damn *jury* freed him. Under the explicit guidance of Sir Christopher Legge. The jury was as good as ordered to acquit him of all charges, and that's what they did.'

A moment of waxen silence, like when an ear pops. The night took on a strange, spherical quality, as if I'd stepped out of it like a bubble.

'Forgive me. The judge was sent from London with the specific purpose of convicting Gethin.'

'That did seem to be the plan.'

'Where is he? Where's Legge?'

'Gone. Ridden out within minutes of the verdict, with a small guard and no carts to delay them. Before the local people could storm the court.'

'*Jesu*, Vaughan…'

'Don't try to make sense of it, Dr Dee. There en't none.'

'Where's Dud— Where's Roberts?'

'Wouldn't know. He was with me in earlier in court.'

'Then where…?'

'There was an adjournment while Legge considered the evidence. Mabbe he couldn't get back in through the crush to hear the death sentence.'

Vaughan laughed dully, bent and picked up a stray plum and hurled it at the nearest wall, making a sucking *phat*.

'Death sentence.' He made gesture at the horsemen, beginning to move off in groups. 'They think to catch Gethin on the road. Bring him back and have their own trial. Or mabbe just hang him theirselves.'

'They won't find him, I'm guessing.'

It was just young men with a need to turn anger into action – the twenty-year-old itch violently inflamed. They'd rampage across the hills for an hour or two, until the drink ran out, and stagger back into town, while the lights were gradually doused and the muttering about betrayal died until morning.

I pointed Vaughan down towards the river and the church, where it looked to be quieter.

'Tell me about this, would you? In detail.'

He shrugged and followed me and the mare.

'Some of the ole boys are even saying the judge was bewitched,' he said.

☩

The man known as Prys Gethin... he'd be well away, back into the heartland. Even if the angry men of Presteigne had caught up with him, who among them would have risked his own life administering rustic justice to a man so firmly acquitted by the Queen's court?

Vaughan leaned over the bridge barrier, staring down at shards of the moon in the swirling waters of the River Lugg.

'The judge told the jury that a hundred years ago – even fifty or less – they wouldn't have had to think twice about their verdict. But the world was in the throes of mighty change and such matters as witchcraft were become subject to new thought.'

'Legge said that?'

He must himself have undergone mighty change since the days when he'd conspired with my enemies to get me burned for using dark magic against Queen Mary.

'He said that the two principal witness were also the victims, so called, and therefore dead. Told the jury that, as none of the men present had a proper knowledge of the Welsh speech, there was no evidence that a death curse had been delivered. But that it was reasonable to suppose – as implied by the Bishop of Hereford – that being abused in Welsh might have led Thomas Harris to believe that he *was* cursed.'

'The Bishop of Hereford? Scory?'

'Scory as good as said that witchcraft was the religion of Radnorshire. As for the collapse of the bridge in a sudden high wind… while there was much evidence of places nearby where there was no wind, what testimony was there to show there *had* been a violent storm in such a confined area? Only one man could say for certain, and he was drowned.'

'Where did the story of the wind come from?'

Vaughan shrugged.

'Legge asked that. To which there was no firm answer. It was all round the villages at the time but they clearly couldn't find anyone to describe it to the court. The truth is, it was an old bridge. The judge said the jury would have to decide whether it believed that bitter words spoken by one man could cause timbers in that bridge to weaken it to the point of collapse. Drawing here on the evidence of Bishop Scory.'

'Why was Scory even called?'

'Ah…' Vaughan pushed himself back from the bridge. 'Now *that*… is of interest in itself, ennit? Sounded like Legge'd been expecting Scory to paint a dark and damning picture of Wales as a stinking midden of sorcery. Instead we heard of an almost benign heathenism which, enmingled with the Christian faith, gave country folk their own *practical* religion.'

'Which is true, to an extent, is it not?'

'Aye, course it's true. But it en't what you say to a court when you're bent on getting a bad man hanged.'

'A judge like Legge,' I said, 'never calls upon a witness without knowing in advance the nature of his testimony.'

'Oh, he was heard to try and prod Scory back on to the path. And then ending his testimony at a stroke when it was clear he wasn't gonner play ball... but too late. Clever, eh?'

'You think Legge *knew* that Scory would be showing witch-craft in a different light... but pretended he didn't?'

'We had it all wrong. From the start. Assuming he was sent here to make sure of a conviction which a local judge might be affeared to preside over... when in fact he was sent to... make sure of an acquittal?'

'But why?'

Well, that's the big question, ennit? A few are saying it was done because the Queen seeks to hold favour with the Welsh.'

'The victims were Welsh.'

'Not as Welsh as the accused.'

'It's still against reason,' I said. 'Saving one man, only to make an enemy of a complete county? That makes not a whit of sense.'

'Gotter be something we don't know, ennit? See, even if Legge hadn't brought half a jury with him, he could've turned it either way. He could have asked why there were no state-ments from Gwilym Davies's fellow cattle-drovers to support his story of returning from London.'

'And why were there not, do you suppose?'

'Because all of them knew that if the case went against Gwilym they would have identified themselves as members of Plant Mat.'

I nodded.

'Legge commented on the fact that neither the sheriff nor any of his constables were there when the ambush was laid. Wouldn't it be normal, if a trap were laid, to include constables? The truth is that it's a big patch and there en't enough constables to send out night after night, week after week, when there's no proof a raid's to take place. Gethin could've been convicted. Easily. All the evidence was there, and all the focus of Legge's questioning was upon conviction. Nobody was even called to say cattle had been stolen – well, none had, they'd been discovered in the act. Ah... cleverest piece of double-twist I ever saw... and the horses all saddled up in the street at the back.'

I stood at the edge of the bridge.

'What about you? Where does this leave you?'

He shrugged.

'I came down with Legge. I was his interpreter. His guide to the thinking of Radnorshire folk. *And* he used what I told him. Oh hell, aye. Used it to aim his final bolt at us. Right at the start, the prisoner – before he was shut up – told the court *they* gave him the name Prys Gethin, see?'

'His captors? The sheriff?'

'Who knows? But Legge, in his address to the jury, came back to that. Saying the name carried what he called *an unholy glamour*. Particularly in this county. As if it had been introduced deliberately to give the capture of a common thief a significance it wasn't worth. As if it was all a piece of elaborate theatre to heighten the status of Presteigne as county town. In the west, see, they've ever resented it. Despising this place as an offcut from England.'

I could see the logic here. But why had Legge become such an enemy of this town?

'You had no opportunity to question, if not Legge himself, then, one of the other attorneys?'

'They'd cleared off within minutes of the verdict. The guards and jurymen split up into pairs and took off separately. Me...' Vaughan drew a rough breath. 'Two of the local boys had me up against a wall, would've beaten the shit out of me if a couple of Evan's constables hadn't come over, dragged them away.'

'He'll look a fool, too.'

'The sheriff? Aye, nobody'll come out of this unsullied. They think we're all in it. And half of Wales here to see the humiliation. A man was even pointed out to me as Twm Siôn Cati, the famous robber of the west – and he got away with it, too. They're laughing at us, Dr Dee. Mabbe I'll take the coward's way out on the morrow. See the kin at Hergest then ride back to London.'

I sighed.

'Twm Siôn Cati is to marry my cousin. He's a scholar now. I, um, try not to think about his past.'

He was silent a moment, then he smiled.

'No offence meant.'

'Nor taken. You believe Gethin was wholly guilty?'

'*I* believe he was, Dr Dee, I've looked into the bastard's eye. I believe there's evil in him. But then... I'm a local boy.'

XXXIX

Property of the Abbey

GREEN OAK AND clean new brick were aged by crowding shadows, alleyways become caverns. Behind the gloss of commerce, this was an old town with old ways.

We walked back towards a quietened market place, where you could smell the pitch from the dead torches. No lights in the sheriff's house. He'd be back in his farm, the other side of Radnor Forest, nursing his wounded reputation. Lights could yet be seen in the hills where the young men of Presteigne pursued a quarry they must have known they'd never find. I guessed it was become a game now, Prys Gethin already become a phantom.

I said, 'How did *he* get out of the court unmolested?'

'Mabbe the same way they got the judge out.' Vaughan stared ahead to where the castle mound loomed grey in the moonlight. 'There's a yard at the back, with a gate to an alley… and back to the road out of town. You'd expect him to take one of the two roads west, but who knows? He'd be safer in England tonight.'

'It deceives you, this town,' I said. 'So many alleyways, so many hidden houses.'

'England. Welsh towns are simpler.'

'Many of the houses and workshops were once owned, I'm told, by Wigmore Abbey.'

'Much of the town was owned by the abbey,' Vaughan said. 'It was how a wool merchant like Bradshaw could buy into Presteigne so quickly. Grabbing the old abbey property from the Crown as soon after the dissolution as deals could be done.'

'And is it possible,' I said, 'that deals may have been done *before*—?'

'Dr Dee!' A shout. A man approaching us briskly out of the shadows. 'Forest, Dr Dee. John Forest.'

Dudley's man, who we'd left behind in Hereford to intercept any significant messages from London. When the devil had *he* returned?

'My master, Dr Dee... he's not with you?'

'No, I... haven't seen him since this morning. I had business at my family's home, I—'

I saw the serious, gaunt-faced Forest glancing warily at Vaughan, who at once held out a hand for the reins of my mare.

'Take your horse to Albarn, Dr Dee?'

'Mercy?'

'The ostler at the Bull?'

'Oh... yes... thank you.'

He'd yet go far, this boy. Knew when to fade into shadow. When we were alone, Forest placed a hand on his leather jerkin, at the breast.

'I've a letter here – for my Lord Dudley. From Thomas Blount. His steward?'

'I know.'

'I'm given to understand that it...' He hesitated. 'That is, I think it's of considerable import. In relation to the continuing inquiries into the death of Lady Dudley.'

'You've been to the Bull?'

'He's not at the inn, although his horse is. No one there I spoke to can recall seeing Lord... Master Roberts. Not tonight, not this afternoon. I've since been all over the town.'

'He was in the courtroom earlier.'

'Then where in God's name is he? God's bones, Dr Dee, this is *Lord Dudley*— Master of the Horse.' Forest smashed a fist into a palm. 'I warned him – tried to – against this folly. Felt better when I saw all the armed men with the judge, but now...'

'You know what's happened here?'

'Be hard not to. The place is collapsed into insanity! Do you have *any* idea where he might have gone?'

'He'd be furious at the verdict,' I said. 'He'd want answers.'

'You think he went after the judge? With one of the hunting parties?'

I hadn't thought of that. In normal circumstance, Dudley would have been *leading* them.

'I don't know.' I spun around wildly. 'He's less driven by impulse these days, but... you said his horse was still stabled at the Bull?'

Of a sudden, none of this looked good.

'Let's go back to there,' I said. 'Make sure he hasn't returned.'

Yet knowing he wouldn't be there. Thinking now of Dudley telling me how the whore had implied she could put him in touch with Abbot Smart. When he'd told me, I hadn't been too convinced. But that was before I'd spoken with Anna Ceddol and drawn certain conclusions about the abbey property.

✠

It took not long to find the narrow house in the alley, dark workshops either side of it. Glass in its windows, the moon in the glass.

John Forest beat upon the door with a gloved fist, then again, louder and harder, until an upstairs window set into a small gable was pushed open with some difficulty.

'Come back tomorrow!'

Her face was furrowed with shadows in the moonlight; she pulled hair out of her eyes.

'We're looking for Master Roberts,' I said.

'Who?'

'Master Rob—'

'Never heard of him. You have the wrong door.'

'Tall,' Forest said. 'Not yet thirty years. A fine, handsome man such as you won't see around here too often.'

'Then I'd remember. Go away.'

You could hear the woman battling to close the window, its iron frame grinding.

'Wait,' I shouted. 'Amy...'

No reply, but she left the window ajar.

'Your name *is* Amy?' I said.

'My name,' she said, 'is Mistress Branwen Laetitia Swift. Ask anyone in this town.'

'You told Master Roberts your name was Amy,' I said, thoughtful now. 'How came you by that name?'

'I never came by it, for, as I've just told to you, it's not my name. Now leave me alone. You're both in your cups. Get off to your homes and sleep it off.'

'He came tonight, didn't he? You told him you might help him in his search for a man who was called John Smart.'

314

'You're at the wrong house.'

'Is Master Roberts in there still?'

'Must needs we break down the door?' Forest said.

'Holy Mother, do you want me to shout for a constable?' She turned her back to the window, speaking to someone in the room, not bothering to lower her voice. 'You… show them your face… another half hour if you show them your face.'

The face that came eventually to the window was plumpen, white-haired and stayed there not long. I looked at Forest. I thought we could take it that Dudley would not be in there with another man in her bed.

'*Was* he here earlier?' I asked. 'The man we're seeking.'

'I swear I know not what you're—'

'This house, mistress. Was it once the property of the Abbey of Wigmore?'

'You're drunk.'

'To whom do you pay a portion of your earnings for its use?'

'I bid you goodnight, masters,' the woman who was not called Amy said.

And the window slammed and rattled.

'Amy?' Forest said.

'Dudley told me that was what she called herself, when he… when he spoke with her. She was lying, of course. She knew who we meant.'

It all seemed less innocent now. For the first time this night, I began to fear for Dudley's welfare. We came out into the alley, Forest resting a hand on the hilt of his sword.

'Where now?'

I was not confident about this, but saw no other way.

'I think… the abbot himself.'

XL

Paper Kites

WITH THE YOUNGER men out on the hills, the main parlour of the Bull was only half full, but the power behind the new Presteigne was here, its red-veined faces flushed in the creamy light of stubby candles on a round board.

Many a sideways glance for Forest and me, as we drank small beer served by the innkeeper, Jeremy Martin, whose agreeable manner was, for once, muted. For I, too, had journeyed here with the judge's company and my name would, by now, have been well blackened by my cousin, Nicholas Meredith, who sat amongst his elders and did not acknowledge me.

Half a dozen of them, all well dressed and drinking French wine.

Forest and I took stools at the serving board and drank silently, listening, but our entry had dampened their discussion. Then the urgency of the situation broke upon me and I gave Forest a nod.

He stood up.

'I come from Hereford with a letter for Master Roberts, the antiquary. I'm unable to find him. Does anyone here know where he might have gone?'

Nobody replied. None of them said a word. As if we might simply disappear if they made no response to us.

I looked at the innkeeper.

'Martin?'

'En't seen Master Roberts since he broke his fast. Off to the court, he reckoned.'

'Looks to me like the court's over,' John Forest said.

'With a unfortunate verdict for this town,' I said to the company at the candlelit board.

A heavy-set man with crinkled grey hair set down his goblet, his voice a reluctant, weighted drawl.

'An unfortunate verdict, one might say, for the superstitious.'

'By which you mean the local people?'

'We,' he said, 'are the local people.'

'My name is John Dee,' I said. 'And you are?'

'Bradshaw.'

I nodded. The wealthiest wool merchant in Presteigne, the owner of many of the one-time abbey properties.

'Half the townsmen are out on the hills,' I said, 'thinking to recapture Prys Gethin. What think you of that... as a magistrate?'

'What I'm thinking, Master Dee, is that while we may not agree with the verdict, no one can deny that the trial was good for the town. Never done better trade. More lawyers than we've ever seen. Guards, attendants. Every room taken at every inn.'

'Better than a visit by the Queen.'

'The lawyers,' he said sourly, 'pay for *their* accommodation.'

'Tell me,' I said. 'As a man of stature here, did *you* know how it might end? Did you have a meeting with Sir Christopher Legge before the trial?'

Bradshaw sniffed.

'Your knowledge of the processes of the law seems somewhat lacking, Master Dee.'

My cousin, Nicholas Meredith, stirred, his beard jutting, anger deepening the lines of wear on his otherwise bland face.

'You accuse his worship of irregular conduct?'

'Is that what it sounds like, cousin?'

He rose.

'Why don't you just go back to London? You've seen your father's place of birth, what else is here for you?'

'I'd hoped,' I said, 'before I left, to meet the former abbot of Wigmore, of whom I wrote in my letter to you.'

'And I told you I knew not where he was.'

I placed both hands on the round board.

'And I don't believe you. Cousin.'

Meredith turned to Jeremy Martin.

'Innkeeper, this man offends me. Perhaps you might summon a constable.'

I smothered laughter.

'Now I know,' I said, 'that my mention of John Smart was the main reason you were less than joyous at my arrival...'

Only gossip, Anna Ceddol had said, *but the same gossip from different ends of town.* Taking me back to the guarded words of Bishop John Scory as we walked by the Wye. *The abbey owned most of it at one time. And Meredith... owned the rest. And now appears to own even more. Oh, yes, he might be a very good man to talk to.*

'Having done business with Smart,' I said. 'Around the time of the dissolution of the abbey.'

'Have a care, Dr Dee,' Bradshaw said.

'Who *does* own this inn,' I asked Meredith. '*Is* it you?'

'Of course it's me.'

'In your own right… or as his guise? What I'm told is that the good abbot, knowing what fate was to befall the abbey at the hands of Lord Cromwell might have sought to dispose of certain abbey property—'

'Get yourself off my property,' Meredith said. 'Conjurer.'

'—by sale or rent, before the axe, as it were… fell.'

Bradshaw grunted.

'What drivel is this? Nothing got past Cromwell.'

'Divers deals were done in the confusion of Reform,' I said. 'Deeds of property discreetly transferred, oft-times with the cooperation of the local gentry who told themselves they were only helping the true Church from being plundered by the Protestants. The word is that Abbot Smart was already proficient in… matters of finance. After a while, I'd guess, it would not always be easy for the agents of the Crown to work out precisely what the abbey owned. Especially out here.'

'Where's your proof of that?' Bradshaw said. 'For if you don't want to spend the night in the sheriff's dungeon—'

'The sheriff's gone home to sulk. Now listen to me. Although I'm good with numbers, the fiscal side of them is not my country. But I'm sure the office of Sir William Cecil, scenting riches which should be in the Queen's treasury, would waste no time in appointing accountants to unravel what we might call the discrepancies in Presteigne.'

There was a long silence, tense as a bowstring. What the hell kind of place *was* this, where a disgraced former abbot could be running whores and collecting money for the tenure of houses he'd corruptly removed from the ownership of the

Church? I was aware that John Forest had his hand upon his sword. I had, in truth, never thought it might come to this.

'I don't believe,' Bradshaw said to Meredith, 'that this man knows anything. I think he flies paper kites.'

'You'll have noticed,' I said, 'that I put my questions to you, rather than the abbot himself. Knowing of his obvious need to walk in stealth in order to live a full life. Which, for the lascivious former abbot, must needs include a ready supply of woman's crack.'

Throwing down the vulgarity like a stone into a placid garden pond, watching Bradshaw wince.

'While deriving a little extra income from whorehouse takings,' I said.

'What do you want?'

I turned slowly, the question having come from the serving board behind me.

'Where's my friend?'

'I've already told you. I know not where he's gone.'

But I'd not previously seen the plumpen, brown-faced innkeeper, Jeremy Martin, so far from a smile.

'Earlier, he was with – I think I have this right – Branwen Laetitia Swift? One of your whores?'

'Letty? Keeps her own affairs, Dr Dee. A clever woman, whom men pay for more than her body.'

'Which men?'

'Not my affair,' Martin said.

Had I misheard, or was his cheerful border-country accent fallen away?

No matter, this was going not as well as I'd hoped. What if these knaves truly had no knowledge of Dudley? I moved myself further away from the innkeeper, so that I might see every man in the well-lit parlour.

My cousin watched me in silence, his face in collapse. What must his thoughts have been when he'd received my letter asking if he knew the whereabouts of the former Abbot of Wigmore? And then, when I arrived without warning, a man with links at the highest level of government, who might shatter his little world like poor glass.

But how dare the bastard point the finger at my father for the foolish and desperate sale of church plate in a time of dire need?

I stood up.

'Think on it,' I said. 'If anything useful occurs to you, we'll be in my chamber.'

On the way out, I looked at the hands of Jeremy Martin – hands too plump and smooth to have spent years hefting barrels from a cellar.

Thought of those hands on Anna Ceddol.

Turned away.

XLI

Personal Dressmaker

'Oh, that was a mistake,' Forest said. 'And coming up here was an even worse one.'

He went to the window, pushed open the shutters to look down into the moonwashed mews.

No one there, not even the ostler.

'We can get out this way, if needs be. Not much of a drop. Grab hold of the ivy, you'll be—'

'They're merchants and dealers,' I said, 'not men of violence.'

Forest swung round to face me.

'Such men live only for money. And you've threatened their life's income, Dr Dee. Not to say their freedom. Even their necks. You're alone in a strange town in the midst of nowhere. If you fail to arrive back in London… well, anything could've happened along the road. That's what they'll say when nobody even finds your body.'

He went to make sure the door of the bedchamber was bolted. I recalled the parting words of John Scory.

… worth remembering that Presteigne still has its share of dark alleys.

Was all this well known? Or only to a circumspect and pragmatic bishop.

Forest slumped back on to the truckle bed, rubbing his eyes. Cold in here, but he was sweating.

'Did I understand that aright? It's your opinion that the fat innkeeper is the former Abbot of Wigmore?'

'He didn't deny it, did he?'

'God's blood.' Forest was shaking his head. 'How's he got away with it for so long? It's not as if he's invisible.'

'No better place to hide than in full view. And if a man's added immeasurably to the prosperity of a town and all who live there, a wall of silence will be erected about him.'

'A whoremaster, too?'

'Well qualified,' I said, recalling Bonner in the Marshalsea. *Poking maids and goodwives over quite a wide area.*

'If even half of what you came out with down there is true,' Forest said, 'it's clear you can't lie here tonight. Nor anywhere in this town. You have to get out, and soon. And I mean *soon*. Might be the best thing if you were to ride back with me to Hereford, after—'

'What about Dudley?'

'—after we make full sure that Lord Dudley is not here.' Forest wiped sweat from his brow with a sleeve. 'Jesu, how can he be away from here without a horse? This looks not good, Dr Dee. Is he robbed? Is he beaten? Is he…? What can we do? You know this shithole better than me. Where've we failed to search?'

'I think, for a start, we might open his letter.'

'No. Never. I'm entrusted to bring it to him.'

'I say this not lightly. What if it offers some possible reason for his disappearance? Or suggests something we might do… somewhere we might look?'

'I've never opened my lord's correspondence.'

'Then I'll open it,' I said.

I took a candle on a tray, went out and fired it from the sconce on the landing, glancing down the oaken stairs to the lower hall, where another single sconce lit an oak pillar.

All was quiet down there.

Too quiet, maybe.

☩

It made little sense at first.

There was a letter within a letter, the outer and shorter of which was to Dudley from his steward, evidently written in haste and signed *TB*.

May it please your lordship, I enclose correspondence recently discovered by Sir Anthony Forster between the pages of a book in his library but not disclosed to the coroner whose inquiries were deemed to be completed.

I broke the inner seal and uncovered a bill of work from Lady Dudley's London dressmaker, William Edney, for the alteration of two gowns.

Well, I knew of this from Dudley. One of the best indications that Amy had been in relatively good heart within days of her death was her continuing interest in fashionable apparel. The only other possible explanation was that she'd wanted her corpse to be found well and elegantly clad.

Attached to the bill was a note from Edney on which some lines had been underscored in thick ink strokes, presumably by Blount.

My lady's personal dressmaker will attend upon her, as arranged, on the first Friday of next month, September 6.

It was dated August 27.

This, to me, was new. There had been no suggestion of Amy receiving any visitors on that last weekend.

There was another short note to Dudley from Blount which I read twice before passing the bill to Forest, who stared at it for some moments as if it might break into flames. I opened my hands, helpless.

'I think you should read it. All of it.' Pushing the candle towards him. 'Did Lord Dudley have any idea that his wife was to be visited by a dressmaker two days before she died?'

'Not to my knowledge. Can that be true?'

I passed him the small paper attached to the bill.

My Lord, Edney tells me that the personal dressmaker was unable to visit Lady Dudley, being ill with a fever during the week of the appointment. You will know of my Lady's fondness for the Spanish styles and it seems the personal dressmaker was a well qualified Spaniard who had been in Edney's employ these past five months and made other apparel for Lady Dudley but has since returned to Spain. I was therefore not able to establish the severity of his fever, if fever there was, during the first week of September.

Forest, looked up, squeezing his dark-bearded jaw.

'What does it mean?'

'Dressmaking is… a regrettable gap in my knowledge. What think you of Blount's final sentence? "If fever there was". It seems Blount may have had cause to think that the dressmaker might have lied about his fever to cover the fact that he made that journey to Cumnor after all. Perchance arriving...' I broke off to read the note yet again, to be quite certain '...two days later than arranged.'

Forest thought on it longer than was necessary.

'No one would know, if that were the case,' he said at last. 'The entire household having gone to the local fair.'

'The entire household having been virtually *dispatched* to the fair. By Lady Dudley.'

Closing my eyes upon a hollow expulsion of breath. It was all too clear that Amy had gone to some considerable effort to make sure that she'd be alone in the house that day.

For the visit of a Spanish dressmaker? For the purpose of him measuring her for a gown?

'Listen, I—' Forest was coughing from a parched throat. 'I can't... can't discuss this any further. We should never have opened it.'

'Was Edney deceived by the Spaniard? We must needs consider the possibility of the Spaniard acting independently of Edney, having feigned a sickness to cover his movements.'

But maybe not independently of his country, its king... or his ambassador, la Quadra. And others I could think of who were not Spanish. The implications were like to a blade in the gut, and each name that arose in my mind was another savage twist.

Forest's face was yet a mask of bewilderment as I gave voice to the unspeakable.

'Why would Amy have gone to so much effort to make sure she was alone in the house for the visit of a Spanish dressmaker? Because, as Blount's letter says, she knew him. He'd made gowns for her before. She was fond of the Spanish styles. So… how *well* did she know him?'

'Stop!' Forest cried out. 'For Christ's sake, Dr Dee, go no further with this madness until we find Lord Dudley. There's true darkness here. Darkness on every side.'

'Well enough to *wish* to be alone with him?'

'We must needs leave this place. Without delay. Those bastards downstairs, they'd rather burn it down with us inside—'

'A woman alone in someone else's house?' I couldn't stop now. 'A woman who'd not seen her husband for a year, only heard the persistent rumour about him siring the Queen's child?'

'I pray you, Dr Dee, get out of here.'

Even as Forest snatched up the letter and the bill, bundled them together and thrust the packet inside his doublet, a knock came on the door of the bedchamber.

One knock. Truly, no more than a tap but in our present mood it had the impact of a mace. A hiss issued from Forest.

'Don't open it.'

I said, 'Who's that?'

My heart leaping at the thought that it might be Dudley.

But there was no reply, only the padding of soft footsteps, I thought receding down the stairs, but could not be sure. I waited until I could hear nothing outside then brought the candle to the door. As I drew back the bolt, Forest pulled his side-sword, whispering.

'Open it no more than an inch. Keep your hand out of the opening. Stand hard against the door.'

So I might slam it in a face?

But there *was* no face.

I peered through the widening gap. The only movement was the flame from the sconce on the landing slanting in the draught from the opened door. I went out, lifting the candle into the corners. No one there, no one on the stairs.

'Nobody,' I said.

Stumbling, then, as my left foot prodded something on the floorboards, sending it skittering.

I crouched with the candle: a sackcloth bundle, no more than a few inches wide. Unexpectedly heavy. I brought it back into the chamber and closed and rebolted the door.

Placed the bundle on the board under the window in full moonlight.

'Careful.' Forest laid his sword on the truckle, pulled on his leather gloves. 'Let me do this.'

'You think something might spring out at us?'

'And *you* think it's a bar of gold as a bribe, do you?'

I supposed that any man who'd been with the Dudley family as long as Forest would, in any situation, fear a blade from out of darkness. He pulled at the sackcloth, which came easily away, revealing another cloth underneath. Black.

'Holy God,' I said.

Gently lifting away the corners of soft black cloth.

What lay beneath welcomed the moon.

Forest stepped away.

'What is it?'

Despite the circumstances of its arrival, I was stricken with awe.

'This,' I said, 'would seem to be... what we came here for.'

328

XLII

Contempt

UNDER THE CANDLE, it was a rich dark red. A swollen blood-drop.

Less than half the size of a tennis ball, but more perfectly spherical. After I blew out the candle, there were yet lights in it.

Lights that moved. A sprinkling of them. More lights than I could see in the air around us or the night sky, where the moon was so close-pressed by clouds that few stars were in evidence.

Only here in the inner firmament of the stone: points of white and piercing blue and a lambent orange, all in fluct.

As I looked at it, it seemed to breathe.

Easier than could I, who dared not touch it, this precious portal to the Hidden. Wondering: if I could have sat in this window-space, alone and concentrated, with the Trithemius manuscript and the whole untroubled night ahead of me, might I then find one of those fragments of light projected into the chamber in angelic form?

Whatever planet rules in that hour, the angel governing the planet thou shalt call,

sayeth Trithemius.

Raphael... Uriel...? I had no books or charts here. I didn't know. Couldn't think. And the night was far from untroubled.

'So you *were* right,' John Forest said.

'Mercy?'

'Everything you said to them. They're in so much fear of how much you might know and who you might tell that they think to pay you off. Send you on your way with what you came here for.'

'Yes. So it would appear.'

I took a last long look at the Wigmore shewstone before covering it over with the black cloth. A cloth of velvet like the one Elias, the scryer, had kept around his.

I could not believe they'd let such a treasure go so easily.

'It must go back,' I said.

'*What?*'

Forest had snatched the stone from the boardtop, clutched it ridiculously to his breast.

'No spiritual device should ever be acquired this way,' I said. 'It's corrupted from the start. No good will come of it. Not for me or Dudley. Or the Queen.'

'Are you gone mad?' Forest thrust the stone at me. 'Take it, for Christ's sake! They'll think you're silenced. It's your talisman. It'll get you out of here. When you're well away, throw the damned thing in the river if that's what you want.'

'I pray you, put it down,' I said quietly.

John Forest weighed the stone in one hand before tossing it to the other and then he shrugged and replaced it on the board. Looking, for a moment, almost grateful, as if it had been too hot or too cold or he'd felt its alien energy racing up his arm.

'You'd best ride back to Hereford,' I said. 'Where Dudley knows he can reach you. Where other letters may be waiting.'

330

'And you?'

'As you said, maybe they think I'm bought off with the shewstone.'

'Dr John, they want you to take it and *leave*.'

'I can't leave. Not without Dudley. But you can.'

'And leave you alone with these bastards?'

'If I'm troubled by Bradshaw or Meredith or Martin, I'll say I've written an account of all I know about property theft from the abbey and you've ridden with it to London. And if I'm not back there in a week, you'll put it before whoever in the Privy Council deals with such matters, and Presteigne will be overrun with accountants. Now... go.'

Forest pulled on his leather gloves.

'And what will you do?'

'I'll find him. Somehow I'll find him.'

Hoping this sounded more confident than I felt, I dragged the board away from the window. Forest swung himself up on to the sill, looked down into the mews then back at me, his head bent under the lintel.

'All right, I'll go. But I'll ride not to Hereford. Ludlow's the place. To the Council of the Marches. Where I'll rouse people, identify myself as Lord Dudley's man. Tell them he's missing within twenty miles of their stronghold. Return with a hundred armed men, at least, before sunrise. Take this town apart.'

'And if all the time he's with some other whore?'

He stared at me.

'You think that, *now*?'

'No,' I said soberly. 'Have a care. God go with you.'

I watched him lower himself from the window, gripping the

ivy, his feet kicking against the wall until he could jump to the ground. Watched him leading his horse to the opening of the mews without looking up. Listened to the hooves as they gathered pace.

I'd never felt so alone, so useless. Twisted by contempt for myself and what drove me – a thirst for secret wisdom disguised as love for queen and country. I thought I might never unwrap the stone again.

The stone I'd thought to deliver to the Queen, with the promise of angelic advice on how best to exalt her majesty. The stone which might procure knowledge of which islands remained to be discovered beyond the known world, which unknown natural forces might be harnessed to the Queen's cause.

What had led me to think that a man who could not see might walk in celestial light? The only man in the Faldos' hall who'd caught no glimpse of even the boneman's ghost, if such it was.

And worse, how could I have brought Dudley into this? A man with more enemies than he could name in a year. No matter that he'd leapt at it like a dog in a butcher's shop, I was the one who'd laid the scented trail.

Hear his voice from that moment of engagement:

We'll make a good bargain with this man, in the noble cause of expanding the Queen's vision.

It had come too easy. The bargain was a black bargain, founded upon threats, and no good could come of it.

I gazed, without hope, at the shrouded stone. My Christian cabalism, that shield against the demonic, had been compromised by the means of its acquisition.

To begin with, how had John Smart known of my desire for it? As I'd not mentioned it in my own letter to my cousin Meredith, it surely could only have been through the whore, who'd learned of it from Dudley. The whore whose fishmonger, as we say in London, was Smart. I wondered how many bawdy houses in Presteigne were owned by this man, whose shrill laughter I could almost hear.

Go on... take the stone... for all the good it will do you.

Tainted.

I flung myself on the floor by the truckle, my teeming head buried in my quivering hands. Filled with dread, now, over Dudley who, in pursuit of my own ends, I'd left alone in a town full of hostile strangers. Where might I even begin to search for him?

Friendship apart, the thought of returning to London without him made me cold to the spine. I'd tell the Queen almost everything – for how could I not? – and be lucky to escape with my head, let alone my occasional place at court. For even though she'd ever dithered over his suitability as a husband, Dudley, beyond all doubt, was the only man she'd ever loved.

Maybe the angels could tell me where to find him. I stared at the black-wrapped stone and began to laugh, in a crazed way which could only break asunder into weeping, and then I was down on my knees in a vault of moonlight, praying for inspiration to a God who seemed this night to be very far away.

And then the King made God smaller.

Not the first time that Goodwife Faldo's words in Mortlake church had come back to me.

XLIII

Graveyard Mist

No memory of falling back across the truckle, but that was where I lay until the moon, having shed all its cloud, awoke me with its brilliance. Or maybe it was the whispers rising like hissing steam from the mews.

The light was so bright that I sprang unsteadily to my feet, at first thinking in panic that morning was come. Slowly realising, as the moon's position in the window was unchanged, that I could only have slept – thank Christ – for an hour or so. There was a pain in my chest from how I'd lain as I leaned out into the chill night and took breath after long breath, hanging over the sill, my hair fallen over my face and eyes.

'John, boy...'

'Huh?'

Raking away my hair, as he came out of shadow and stood looking up at me, removing his green, small-brimmed hat and holding it in both hands at waist level.

Thomas Jones.

Twm Siôn Cati. Plump, very Welsh, ever half-amused.

'The inn's all locked up. What kind of bloody inn's all locked up before midnight?'

'What the hell are you doing here? Time is it?'

'Maybe not yet midnight, maybe just after. You mean you didn't get my message?'

Oh God, it all came back, the note he'd left for me with the ostler. Seemed like weeks ago.

'I… left very early this morning.'

'You should know I'm not a man to waste paper, John.'

'Beg mercy. Listen… my friend… Dudley…' No point at all in maintaining the *Master Roberts* conceit. 'You seen him this night? Or earlier?'

'You mean he's not here?'

'Missing.'

'Since when?'

'Not sure.'

He was silent for a moment. I looked over to the stables; we must surely have disturbed the night ostler in his loft.

'All right,' Thomas Jones said. 'As you seem to be wearing your day apparel, if I were you, I'd come down.'

'From the window?'

'Unless you want to rouse everyone. We can't talk like this, people will think we're lovers.'

I raised myself up in the window, threw a tentative leg over the sill and then slid back into the bedchamber and grabbed the shewstone from the board. Stowed it away in my jerkin, and then, before I could think too hard about it, was out into the night, holding to the ivy.

Which came away in my hands, halfway down, and I tumbled to the cobbles, stifling a cry.

Thomas Jones stood looking down at me, not assisting.

'Not used to this, are you, John?'

'Not broken into as many houses as you.'

Picking myself up, hoping the moon would not expose my swollen eyes or any other evidence of how close I'd been to parting with my mind.

'Fetch your horse,' Thomas Jones said. 'Quietly.'

'Where are we going?'

'To begin with, somewhere we can talk in normal voices.'

'In relation to Dudley?'

I must have sounded like a child.

'Who knows, boy? I fear we're close to the heart of something quite unpleasant.'

☩

We *had* disturbed the night ostler, but half the money in my purse secured, I hoped, his silence. He helped me saddle up and we went out to where Thomas Jones's horse was tethered at the entrance to the mews. Riding out of Presteigne on a moon-barred road that now was become all too familiar to me.

'Would've told you this the other night,' Thomas Jones said, as we dismounted a mile from town. 'But not in front of that cocky scut.' He sniffed. 'Even if he's dead, I might not take that back.'

'*Dead?*'

'I don't *say* that he's dead, but these are not the kindest of men.'

'Who?'

He made no reply, leading his horse along the side of the road. Without too much reference to Dudley's private and public troubles, I'd explained to him why we'd come here. His only reaction had been a slow nodding of his head.

Could I trust this man, you might ask. Well... he was betrothed to my cousin and had been pardoned by the Queen. There were those I'd trust less.

'Men?' I said. 'Not the kindest?'

'I'll get to it.'

If you're wondering about the true nature of his knavery, I know little, preferring the legend of a Welsh Robin Hood who, for a brief period, would prey upon the Norman dynasties holding the best farmland in the far west of Wales. All of it stolen, Thomas Jones would allege, and who was I to argue? Wales was, they said, a land ruled at every level by brigands. Some of them in London now.

He tilted his hat over his eyes, for the moon was become oppressively bright.

'Some of the company I kept in my former life, John, was, ah...'

'You need not explain,' I said.

'Kind of you.'

'Get to the point.'

'The point is that there is no such thing as a free pardon.'

'You mean you once thought there *was*?'

'I was therefore quietly approached for intelligence about our friends in Plant Mat.'

'Who made the approach?'

'I won't answer that, and it matters not. Suffice to say that some of your masters in London have kin this side of the border. Let's say I was approached by a friend, who has... other friends.'

'Sir William Cecil has family in Wales.'

'Does he?'

'You're now *a spy for Cecil*?'

'How would I know that?'

He wouldn't. I'd thought of Cecil several times on the way here, my mind more alert in the open air, under stars. Thoughts turning, inevitably, to the content of the letter from Amy Dudley's London dressmaker. It was said there had been a number of meetings over the past few months between Cecil and the Spanish ambassador, la Quadra. Who, if they had but one aim in common, it would be to keep the Queen and Dudley out of wedlock.

But, dear God… to have Amy murdered lest she suffered from some fatal malady or was of a mind to take her own life?

And why, in God's name, would Cecil want to know about Plant Mat? I stared up into the night for enlightenment. Compared with the twisting mesh of London politics, the formation of the stars seemed constant and reassuringly familiar.

'And were you able,' I asked, 'to supply the intelligence?'

Thomas Jones blew breath through his teeth.

'Why does every bastard think that if you have a history of thieving you're part of some hidden body of neckweed-contenders, all known to the others? Even *I* wouldn't have dealings with Plant Mat.'

'So you had nothing to tell them?'

'On the contrary, boy, I had a great to deal to tell them. Particularly about Gwilym Davies, who likes to call himself Prys Gethin. Who also calls himself a gentleman farmer and collects land with the alacrity of a Norman baron after the conquest. Well… buying some of it, of course, but where's the money come from? But I'll get to him. Plant Mat, yes… oh, how the romantic legends are formed around them. Like graveyard mist, boy.'

'Do Plant Mat even exist, now? Legge's verdict might suggest not.'

'Indeed they exist. And profess themselves driven by love of their country. Don't fool yourself, boy, there's a good deal of hatred in Wales for the English. And for so-called Welsh towns like Presteigne, where the old language is let rot by English pouring in, looking to increase their ill-grown wealth.'

'Hatred? Despite the Tudor line? Jesu, Jones, we're all of us ruled by Welshmen, now.'

'Ach!' He waved a hand as if to swat a fly. 'What a prime piece of English rookery that is. Even though most of us are content to float with it. Arthurian descent? Bollocks. The truth is that Wales is yet a Catholic country, and as long as little Bess permits Catholic worship, she'll get no shit from this side of the border.'

'Except from Plant Mat?'

'All right, let me tell you.'

The original Plant Mat, he said, were the three children, two sons and a daughter, of an innkeeper in his own home town of Tregaron. The family had become famous robbers, gathering others to them and inhabiting a cave, with an entrance so narrow that only one man at a time might pass through. A cave in a place laden with legend, which people kept away from because it was said the devil himself climbed those rocks.

'The cave was their... what's the word in English... *temple*? Certainly of some almost ritual significance. They were inside the land, see... in the heart of Wales. I don't know what they did in there, maybe just got drunk. But the legend of that cave grew – that they drew their power from the land around them. Thus, out of the past. Out of their heritage.'

They'd use a glove to identify themselves, passed one to another. Always a sense of ritual, a mystery which they encouraged. For years they'd been simply robbers, even if some victims had lost their lives as well as their goods. But when it came to the planned murder of a judge at Rhayader…

'All wrongdoers in the heart of Wales were pleased to have the assize court in Rhayader, see – where they had control, justices in their pockets and no jury that did not include a few of their own. Maybe they thought that if they killed an English judge the judiciary would get the message and leave them alone, I don't know. Madness.'

'And they paid the price.'

'Martyrs. The sons telling glorious tales of their dead fathers and all they'd done for Wales. And the name Plant Mat was anybody's now – any band of brigands who wanted to wear it like a black cloak. A cloak with all the weight of heritage. See?'

'They yet live in a cave?'

'Pah! Who lives in a cave? They live in good houses – some with big halls and spare chambers and a *bwddyn* or two in the grounds for the servants – like the estate of our friend Gwilym Davies. Or Prys Gethin.'

'He claimed in court,' I said, 'that the name was pressed upon him by the Sheriff of Radnorshire.'

'Which your English judge never questioned. Curious, that.'

The road was passing through what had been a long wood, sporadic trees on either side and behind them, thickets, the stumps of felled oak and heaps of discarded twiggery all caged in brambles.

I stopped walking.

'What's this about? Help me. Why are you telling me this now, and how does it relate to Dudley?'

Thomas Jones took off his hat.

'Don't think me self-righteous. *I* stole. I stole as a boy because my friends stole, and I stole as a man because I found I was good at it… and if I spread some of the proceeds among the needy it didn't seem so bad to be saving some aside to spend on books. To acquire an education. But don't think me *self-righteous*. I'll do my years in purgatory, resigned to it, boy. But Prys…'

He stood in a shaft of moonlight betwixt the trees. He yet wore the russet doublet with the gold thread.

'Prys,' he said, 'will one day be in the deepest chamber of hell. Though not, it seems, soon enough.'

XLIV

Monstrous Constellations

'THEY SAY HE once killed a man just to rape his wife.'

Thomas Jones was sitting amidst the fungus on a tree stump, legs apart, bunched hands swinging between his knees.

'Not his first rape. Nor, needless to say, his first killing.'

I did not ask how the man known as Prys Gethin had remained alive and free. *This is Wales, boy.*

'Then he choked the life out of the wife.' He shrugged. 'Well, why not? Killing and rape are as natural to him as taking a piss. Would have been a soldier, if there was a Welsh army. Like the man he believes possesses him.'

'Possesses?'

'It's just a word, John. I only met him once, see. Some years ago, in an alehouse, both of us well into our cups. I recall that he invited me to join him in his work.'

'Plant Mat?'

'I suppose. Who knows where I'd be today if I hadn't, at that moment, been compelled to go outside and throw up my supper? Never went back. Never saw him again.'

'Then how,' I asked, 'do you know all this?'

'Common knowledge where I come from, boy. Some of it, anyway. No one'll touch him, see. He knows too much and he's done too many favours. This is not London. Middle Wales is a big village, full of mountains and rivers and lakes and water-falls and miles of emptiness, around which the legends echo. Vast whispers in the wind.'

'Jesu, Twm, is this a matter for poetry?'

'I'm Welsh. It's in the blood. His wife, now – did I tell you about his wife? Said to have fled within a month of their wedding. To England, I believe, which did not improve his love of our neighbour. Word was that he liked to do her while covered in pig blood, still wet. She seems to have been a religious woman who would not have a child conceived in pig blood.'

'Did she also put out his eye before she left?'

'Put it out himself, they say, in a drunken rage. Tell me when you've heard enough of this?'

'Sounds like horseshit to me.'

'Who am I to say otherwise? All right. In truth, little is known about the man. I do not, for example, believe that Gwilym Davies is his name any more than is Prys Gethin. The legend says he was born in Tregaron, where Plant Mat began, all those years ago. I can tell you, boy, that he was not. He acquired an old farm in the hills near there, which he claims as his ancestral home. It is not. I'm from Tregaron and I know.'

'Where's he come from then?'

'Don't know *that*. By his accent, I'd say north rather than south. But Welsh is his language and thieving is certainly his trade. He inspires fear and respect over a wide area, and not only through his looks. And the killing and the rape, that is not *all* legend.'

'He *lives* by thieving?'

'Lives by farming, now. Oh, and slaughtering. So loves to

slaughter stock – anybody's stock, and not quickly. After a successful cattle raid, he'll sacrifice one of the beasts on a hilltop under a beacon fire. I know this, I've seen the flames from afar.'

'Sacrificed to God?'

'Some god. Or the demon he's invested with the spirit of Rhys Gethin. Who knows? He was rambling over all this as we drank. Full of the Old Testament.'

Thomas Jones sat very still in the grey light, his habitual levity long shed. I waited for him to continue, but he said nothing.

I said, 'So the curse…'

Thinking not only of the two dead men but of Dudley in the marketplace in Presteigne.

'Cursing… we might consider that to be a woman's preserve,' Thomas Jones said. 'Also the Sight, and yet he has that, too, or so it's claimed. Styling himself as a man who walks with his ancestors. Journeying to the wild and barren places to meet with Owain and Rhys. The time I drank with him, he told me what they looked like now, how they'd not aged. How, in the other world, all the grey had gone from Owain's forked beard and his powers were there to be called upon in the cause of Wales.'

'He's mad?'

'Increasingly, I'd say.'

'So the bridge from which the farmer fell—'

'Ach, let's not get swept away. It might just as easily have had an axe taken to it by Gethin's followers in the Plant. Who then drowned the poor old boy and left him all entangled in the ruins of it.'

'How many followers does Gethin have?'

'Hard to be sure. But two of them were in Presteigne – the day I found you at the inn. The Roberts brothers, this is, Gerallt and Gwyn. That is, I've known them only as woodsmen and hunters on his estate and both are men of violence – short-temper, alehouse fights. But not high in intellect.'

'Just the two?'

'May have been more I didn't recognise. I thought at first there might be some plan to free Prys from the gaol or the court. So I followed them, keeping a safe distance behind. They took this road. All the way to Brynglas Hill. Where they stopped.'

I may have blinked.

'What did they do there?'

'Didn't go close enough to find out, boy. Remembering too well the face of a man beaten in Tregaron town by Gerallt Roberts. Most of his teeth gone and his jaw too close to an ear than a jaw was ever meant to be. However... I did see two other men on the hill, one of whom bore a close resemblance to my old friend John Dee.'

'When was this?'

But I knew, recalling two horsemen I'd noticed down by Nant-y-groes when I was on first the hill, with Stephen Price.

'The same Dee I saw again that night, in Presteigne,' Thomas Jones said. 'Well, well... why then was the Queen's conjurer in town? Was he there to give evidence to the court on aspects of the Hidden relating to Prys Gethin and death by cursing?'

'No,' I said with caution. 'He wasn't.'

'Anyway, it seemed useful to seek you out. I even wondered if you'd been followed to Brynglas by the Roberts brothers.'

'Not to my knowledge.'

'So I left you a message, which you, with your renowned intelligence, contrived to ignore.'

'Consider my head hung in shame,' I said. 'But the Roberts brothers had no need to free Gethin from the court.'

'None at all.'

'And you think they knew this?'

Thomas Jones shrugged.

'What's *happening* here?' I said. 'How could the truth about Prys Gethin have failed to come out in court?'

'Because it was an English court.'

'Not good enough. Legge knew. Legge knew everything before the trial began. You'd told... whoever you told. You'd told them all about Prys Gethin – no such thing as a free pardon? I don't understand. Why did you even come to the trial?'

'Not such a long ride from my home.'

'That's no answer.'

'No.' He looked down at his enfolded fingers. 'I suppose not. Does it make more sense that I came to court because I was most explicitly warned not to?'

'In truth?'

He looked up at me.

'You think I would not like to see an end to Prys Gethin? Look, the woman... I'll tell you... the young woman who was raped and then choked to death and her husband killed, that was no myth, they were neighbours of my aunt at Llanddewi, not far from Tregaron. Everyone knew who'd done it, but it

346

would never be proved, so I… Thinking it cowardly to finger Prys from behind, I offered to give evidence to the court regarding his reputation.'

'But you—'

'And was told, boy, that it *would not be necessary*. Told my presence *would not be useful*. Told to keep my head down in the west and forget the foregoing conversation had ever taken place. So why, after that, would I not come to the trial?'

Movement overhead – a bat flittering tree to tree, followed by another. Thomas Jones leaned back, hands clasped behind his head.

'Does all this then suggest anything to you, John?'

The wood all around us let off a smell of voracious decay. I sat down upon a stump with a jagged edge that hurt my arse. I didn't care; pain sharpens the senses.

Monstrous constellations, like the grotesque creatures on Scory's map, were finding form in the firmament of my head, and it felt as if the cold moon itself were lodged in my breast.

XLV

Cold Geometry

IT FELT LIKE they were here with us now, skulking and scurrying amid the rotting trees: Cecil in shadow, long-nosed and mastiff-eyed, with his intelligence gatherer Walsingham running hither and thither, ratlike, getting things done.

Getting things done.

And, of course, none of it would ever lead back.

Nothing ever did.

Hell, I didn't even know if this *was* Cecil. Felt my fists clenching and unclenching, my body all aquiver. Asking Thomas Jones when he'd been approached by the man he would not name who might have been of Cecil's Welsh kin.

'Ten days ago… a fortnight?' he said. 'A messenger came to me with instruction to ride to… a certain place.'

'And what was required?'

'I told you. As much intelligence as I could provide on the man calling himself Prys Gethin. And speedily.'

Yes, it would need to be, else how could all this have been arranged in the time?

Easily, when you thought about it. Dudley had never explained fully, but I guessed that, not wishing to attract attention by assembling his own travelling party, he would have instructed his steward Thomas Blount to cast around for a discreet but secure company journeying to the Welsh border.

And Thomas Blount being a lawyer well known in the inns of court... they would have found him. How fortunate that this should coincide with the most unusual circumstance of a London judge being sent to try a Welsh felon for a most uncertain offence.

My thoughts curled in upon themselves like eels in a bucket, and I fought to untangle them.

'The idea of the border judiciary in fear of a band of brig-ands – that seemed unlikely to me from the start.'

'If the word came down from London,' Thomas Jones said, 'they'd be forced to swallow their pride. Still hard, it is, to believe London would go to all that trouble, all that expense. All that *connivance*.'

The question of Robert Dudley and the Queen... this was the most crucial matter in England. Nay, in all Europe. A decision had therefore been taken to dispose of a man, at whatever cost.

I recalled the urgency in Cecil that day I'd been brought to him. The day it must have begun to look as if Amy's suspicious death had not been enough to finish Dudley as a suitor. The day Cecil and Blanche Parry had conspired to ensure that she failed to deliver the message to me from the Queen seeking a suitable date for a royal wedding.

I have no doubts about your ability in this regard. Which is why I don't want you and your fucking charts within a mile of the Queen at this time.

Watching me. How long had they been watching me? I recalled a flitting glimpse of the black-clad Walsingham, mothlike in the Strand as I was leaving Cecil's house.

Watching Dudley, too. Well, of course. Watching Dudley,

the most hated man in all England, and all his household – in particular his principal retainers, Blount and Forest.

I said, 'How would they get to the prisoner in New Radnor castle?'

'It's hardly the Fleet, John.'

And if it *had* been the Fleet, they'd have got to him easily enough. Even quicker at Marshalsea, though it might cost a groat or two more for the guards. New Radnor castle, inside curtain walls, would be a fine place for comings and goings. Certainly better than Presteigne, with its gaol in the middle of the town, where all could see.

'So men came to Prys Gethin's dungeon at New Radnor, with a proposition.'

'He'd be suspicious, of course, at first,' Thomas Jones said, 'if the men who came to him were English.'

'And if they were not? If he was addressed in Welsh?'

'*Duw*, you're right. Who thinks of all this?'

I'm sure we both saw the dimensions of it now, the plan laid out with all its Euclidian precision.

The alarming thought came to me that there would have been no one better to put the proposal to Prys Gethin than Thomas Jones – Twm Siôn Cati himself.

No such thing as a free pardon.

But, no, his pardon had come from the Queen, and this plan was the most savage thrust into Elizabeth's heart. He wouldn't do it and they wouldn't demand it of him for fear that he'd go along with it and then, with typical cunning, damage it at the eleventh hour.

Or was that what he was doing now? Dear Christ, I was out of my head, dizzy with imaginings.

'Just say it, John,' Thomas Jones said wearily.

I nodded, closing my eyes.

'A bargain is cut. Against all reason, Prys Gethin walks free. While Robert Dudley – Master Roberts – never comes back across the border.'

I felt myself sinking inexorably into the most treacherous political marsh in the world, full of rapids and sucking pools, dark water, hanging weed.

✝

'Fortunate that you were out of town, when they took him,' Thomas Jones said, 'otherwise, they'd've had you as well, and we wouldn't be sitting here working it all out. And you, I'm guessing, would have been long dead. Your value being – beg mercy, John – negligible by comparison.'

I could not argue with this.

'They took him, how?' I said. 'Where?'

No sooner was the question out than I knew.

My name is Mistress Branwen Laetitia Swift. Ask anyone in this town.

Maybe a sleeping draught in a cup of wine he'd not refuse. Perhaps poison.

I stiffened.

'I should also have told you,' Thomas Jones said, 'that while discreetly following the Roberts brothers around town before their departure for Brynglas, I was led to a warehouse on the outskirts. Gwyn let himself in and then came out quite quickly. I think he was just making sure it was still there. Would still be there when it was needed.'

'What?'

'A cart. Wooden frame and a cover. As much of it as I could see.'

'How would they know what was required of them?'

'I imagine a message was conveyed to them from Prys. By mouth – I'd doubt either of them can read. Likely whoever went to Gethin at New Radnor would then have conveyed instructions to the brothers.'

'Gethin would have revealed their names to him?'

'If his life depended on it, he'd certainly take the chance with *their* lives. *I* don't know how it was done – likely the man would go alone, unarmed, as a sign of trust. I don't know. All we can be sure of is that none of them will know who authorised the bargain. How high it goes. And the beauty of it, when you think about it, is that they know that Prys, as a devout Welshman, will never – not even under the most imaginative of tortures – reveal a deal struck with the English.'

Perfection. I stood up.

'So they have Dudley. Alive or...'

'I think we must assume they have him,' Thomas Jones said.

Apart from the scratting of rats or badgers in the wood, there was silence.

So here it was: for the sake of England, or someone's idea of what was best for her, it had been agreed to spare a killer. A many times murderer who relished the slick of blood upon his skin and believed himself justified... driven by the ghosts of Glyndwr and Rhys Gethin. This man released to rob and kill and rape again at will.

'Though Gethin might end up quietly dead,' I said. 'Knowing what he knows.'

'If they ever find him. And I doubt they would.' Plump, Welsh Thomas Jones was leaned back, looking at me, his eyes

352

slitted. 'There we are. I've told you all I know. What happens next is for you to say.'

'How sure are you that they've taken Dudley to Brynglas?'

'It's no more than an astute guess, John. Though what I might add is that, before he disappears forever, it strikes me as likely that *Prys* will want to come to Brynglas. I do think he believes that Rhys Gethin is within him. Is part of him. And this is Rhys's place... the citadel of his highest triumph. So... a final pilgrimage. A meeting with Rhys.'

'Or whatever demon he's invested with the spirit of Rhys. You said that. What did you mean by it?'

'Ah, well... I think we may have read some of the same books.'

'But you more than—

'*Hush.*'

Thomas Jones was on his feet. The sound of a distant horse, moving at speed, was no longer so distant.

XLVI

Portal

HE'D BEEN AFRAID to sleep lest they came for him, the local men who sought Gethin.

Roger Vaughan: also a local man. The only local man within the judge's company. Therefore, the local man who had let it happen, the young pettifogger raised beyond his abilities in return for selling his county town down its mean river. The cry of *traitor* resounding from an open window as he returned to his inn after taking my mare to the ostler. A big, sharp stone glancing from a wall by his head.

'I was watching by my window, see,' he said, 'for those fools to come back from the hills. Trying to stay awake. Which is how I saw the arrival of Dr Jones at the Bull, and then the two of you leaving along the Knighton road, and I... felt less secure.'

He truly thought he'd feel safer with us, a conjurer and a pardoned felon, than left alone in Presteigne?

'We're all gone from there now,' the boy said. 'Every one of us who journeyed with the judge.'

A sheepish shrug as he stood there, holding his horse's bridle. I explained our situation, telling Thomas Jones he could say what he wanted in front of Vaughan. Didn't know how wise this was, but it was too late for secrecy. I suppose I was glad to have Roger Vaughan with us, a lawyer, with a lawyer's sharp mind, but also a local man alert to the snares of the Hidden.

'There might be a hundred armed men in Presteigne by morning,' I said, 'if Forest gets to Ludlow unharmed. But it would be foolish for us to wait for them.'

'I know my way around Brynglas,' Vaughan said.

'We don't *know* Dudley was taken there,' I told him. 'Or if he was, where exactly he might have been taken... But if these brothers have him, they're likely to want proof that Gethin has been freed, before... they fulfil their side of the bargain.'

It was my only hope for Dudley, but I saw Thomas Jones shaking his head.

'It's Gethin who'll want the proof of his freedom. The knowledge than no one is on his trail. And also, from what I know of him, he'll want to... well, an Englishman of Dudley's status, he'll want to finish it himself. In some...'

He tightened his lips, half turned away.

'Ritual fashion?' I said.

'He has a legend to support,' Thomas Jones said. 'And that's another reason why he'd want it to be done here.'

Looking between the trees to the moon-grazed hills, I experienced that momentary sensation of being separate from the physical: the uncomfortable feeling of following yourself, just one step behind, which always comes when there's no time to contemplate its significance.

And then it was fading, and Thomas Jones was untying his horse from the tree.

'He may not even be there yet, especially if he's on foot. You have weaponry, boys?'

Vaughan produced a stubby dagger. I had nothing.

'Only your magic, eh, John?'

Thomas Jones smiled, more than a touch ruefully.

✝

Whitton Church lay by the side of the road, amid ancient yew trees, about half a mile short of Pilleth. It was two or three hundred years old and not in good repair. But it gave us some concealment as we looked out towards Brynglas, upon whose slopes the moonlight gave the illusion of a first fall of quiet snow.

'Been here in my dreams so often,' Thomas Jones said. 'Every Welshmen is inclined to venerate Owain Glyndwr.'

Was this a time for following such dreams? I wondered again how far I might trust him. What if he played a double game, with his veneration of Glyndwr?

This is what the night does to you.

'If we go directly up the hill, we'll be seen for miles,' Vaughan said. 'Better to follow the river, where it winds behind the trees.'

He led us out past Nant-y-groes, where one small light shone in a downstairs room – or was it the moon's reflection? And then we left the road to follow the River Lugg… the river of light living up to its name this night, still as a cold, white, twisting road. Behind us, a multitude of sheep lay close-packed in a corner of the pasture, like frogspawn on a pond.

'They come down before sunset,' I said. 'They don't like the hill at night.'

We kept, as far as possible, behind the trees. The ground was rough and sloping. We went carefully, passing under the

356

towering motte of the long-ruined castle, overgrown now, the river forming a natural moat.

The moon was high and white and the clouds were rolled back, and the side of Brynglas shone now like a polished breastplate, looking bigger than I'd ever seen it. I thought of Anna Ceddol sleeping in the house that was half inside the hill – if ever there could be sleep with the mad boy in the house. Pushing back the thought, I called softly to Thomas Jones.

'So how was it in your dreams?'

'Brynglas? Like Jerusalem. A shrine. It makes me tremble.'

His voice low and sibilant as the wind through dead foliage.

'There *is* a shrine up there,' I said, as we stopped. 'To the Virgin Mary. And, um, I suppose what came before her.'

'I know.' Thomas Jones gazed up, between tall trees, at the silvered hillside. 'The heathen well, where nymphs would bathe. A portal to the otherworld, the land of the dead, of the ancestors.'

'So they say.'

'They also say Owain went there on the night before the battle, did you know that? There'd been this huge and savage storm, the sky ripped apart with lightning.'

'Weather again.'

'Indeed. His war began with a fiery star crossing the heavens, followed by thunder, and so it went on. And in the silence after this fierce storm in the summer of 1402, Owain and Rhys Gethin ascended the hill to the holy well. It was June the twenty-first. Midsummer. The old festival.'

'And the next day they set fire to the church,' I said. 'They stood and watched the church burn.'

Glyndwr had fired several churches on the way here,

supposedly because they paid tithes into England, but I said nothing about this.

'The new Rector of Pilleth, he'd say Glyndwr and Gethin had sold their immortal souls to the devil that night.'

'And a goodish deal it was, boy. Imagine the terror when word of the victory reached the English court. Wondering if, by year's end, they'd all be learning Welsh.'

'But short-lived. Like all deals with the devil. Whatever he invoked here deserted him when he entered England. He died unfulfilled as, presumably, did Rhys Gethin.'

'*If* he died.' Thomas Jones reined in his horse. 'Don't make dust of this, boy. Owain's death was never recorded, nor his burial place ever found. He simply disappeared. Oh, I'm not saying he *lives*… but something of him does. And, if it's anywhere, it's here.'

He turned slowly in the saddle to face me, his round, pale face shining like a smaller moon.

'Look at me, boy – fallen Welshman, recipient of an English pardon. See what it does to *me*, this place. Oh, they all come here, at least once. Not just the handful of mad old ragamuffins in Plant Mat, but all those who yet dream of an exalted Wales. They come here to seek… renewal. And they keep coming back, oft-times for reasons they'll never quite understand. The men I drink with in Tregaron, the poets and the dreamers. They come quietly, and quietly they leave, at dusk or before dawn. Sometimes journeying all the way on foot.'

I thought of the rector: *I have* seen *them anointing themselves here at night, in the heathen way.*

'So this is the place for them, isn't it? The shrine. The most likely, anyway. Where might they take him? What hiding places are there? How far is it from the village?'

'Not within sight of the village at night,' I said. 'And no one comes out of there after dark. The church itself… the shrine's behind it, and the well, a long hole in the ground, with a pine wood behind.'

And below it… the Bryn. Half sunk into the hill itself.

Like a cave.

I said nothing of this, but it would be the first place I'd go, to warn the Ceddols. I kept my voice steady.

'There are wide views from the church,' I said. 'Especially on a night like this. You'd see anyone coming.'

'Especially three of us, on horseback. If we ride directly up the hill, we're meat. Is there another way?'

'There *is* another way,' I said. 'With good tree cover.'

'Fit for horses?'

'If we dismount and lead them. I'm sure we could leave them in the stables at Nant-y-groes, but… Stephen Price is a cautious man, and the explanations would take time.'

'We'll continue,' Thomas Jones said. 'See what there is to be seen. If anything.'

'Wait,' I said. 'How much do you believe? *Is* there magic?'

'There's magic everywhere on a night like this, boy.'

But I had little faith that there was anything of the Hidden here. So many legends were woven with hindsight, to light mere coincidence with glamour: strange weather, moving stars, earth-tremors.

'You feel a softening of the ground?' Vaughan had dismounted and was tying his horse to a young oak. 'We should be able to get through this way and up the hill from behind but not if we're in bog.'

Damn. I should have thought. When I came down the hill,

through the oak wood, I'd only gone as far as the burial tump. Now I only wanted a swift and discreet way to the church and Dudley, if Dudley was there. And also to the Bryn.

'I'll go through on foot for a short way,' Vaughan said. 'See how firm it is for the horses.'

I watched him vanish into a thickening of undergrowth, wishing there were more of us, then looked up at the hill and the moon. You could make out the grey tower of Pilleth Church, halfway up. A marker for the shrine. Of the village you could see nothing.

'I've never asked,' Thomas Jones said. 'But why *were* you here when I followed the Roberts boys? I presumed just to visit your old family home, but...'

'It's dying,' I said, not wanting to mention the peculiar talents of Siôn Ceddol and the lure of his sister. 'The village is dying.'

'I'd almost think you cared.'

'It's the old home of my father. My tad.'

'Tad? That's what you called him, in the Welsh way?'

For years I hadn't even realised it *was* Welsh. I said nothing.

'Ah, you're one of us more than you know, John Dee. Why's the village dying?'

'Weight of too much killing. The dead outnumber the living, and the dead are rising. It oppresses them. There were always priests of the old kind to help them cope, but now they're told it's their own fault for not praising God enough.'

'My,' he said. 'You *do* care.'

'I hardly know anyone here. My tad told them he'd come back, when he was rich. But he never was, not for long. And he never did come back. Tell me... do have any idea how practised Gethin believes himself to be... in the ways of magic?'

'I doubt he's read the books, John. But he's said to have the Sight. And the desire. And what some might call the courage... and others the madness of—'

Thomas Jones breaking off because of a sharp cry from down by the river. He began to turn his horse.

'He's in the marsh?'

Twisting in the saddle, I saw the water's glitter, sword-bright through a line of trees.

'We should all have gone.'

I slid to the ground and tied the mare to the slender trunk of the oak. Aware again of that feeling of separation from the physical, a shudder going through me, like you sometimes get in sleep – as if I were snatched out of my body and then flung back. The mare flinched, as if she'd felt it, too.

'He's here,' Thomas Jones said uncertainly.

I spun round, thinking for a fearful moment that he meant Prys Gethin, then saw Roger Vaughan fading up greyly from the riverbank, the shape of him imprinted on the night, but blurred in my sight, as if the ink had run. I moved towards him.

He was limping. Not looking at either of us, only at the ground, as if he might sink into it.

'I'm all right, Dr Dee. I'm not hurt.'

His voice was cracked like old parchment. He was not all right. He was far from all right.

XLVII

Orifice

VAUGHAN'S HORSE, QUITE a big grey stallion, was straining at his tether, panting and blowing, and I saw that the others were become restive, too, their eyes all aflare.

I said to Vaughan, 'What happened down there?'

'I don't know.' He clearly was shaken. 'That is, I'm not sure. I think… I think there might be something dead down there. The smell. Might just be a sheep, but I… It don't feel right in any way.'

He went to soothe the stallion, putting his hands on it, I'd swear, in search of warmth and life, but the horse sheered away from him. I looked down towards the river.

'I'll go,' I said. 'Find out.'

'Leave it, John,' Thomas Jones said. 'We're better moving to higher ground, where we can see anyone coming. If Dudley's only been missing since this morning, it's not likely that—'

'His body will yet stink? That rather depends, doesn't it?'

I knew not what it depended on, but must needs be sure. And I was weary of unexplained fears and shadowplay, nature's marked cards and loaded dice. Before I could think better of it, I was scrabbling down the way Vaughan had come, over short turf which suggested the sheep had been here in profusion in daylight hours. The sheep which fled at sunset.

Divers trees sprang up around me, from half-grown saplings to old oaks with bloated, cankered boles and branches like fingers with the gnarling sickness. The river was no longer to be seen – too close, or the bank had been raised up against winter floods.

You might conclude that, on this hard moon-flayed night, I was not fully in my mind, and maybe I wasn't. I'd experienced this in Glastonbury and other places where Christianity and old magic were interwoven – the air unsteady and full of sparks, and sometimes you thought you could hear it like the hum of bees or, indeed, smell it in a sudden rank, richness of earth.

... you're one of us more than you know, John Dee.

I wondered now, if my tad's evocation of Wales – the men bent like thorn trees, their skin scoured – had not simply been intended to keep me away from here, plant some deep revulsion inside me. Maybe some dark memory had lived inside him and the last thing he wanted was for his son to become *one of us.*

But now I was here, whether by destiny or conspiracy, an educated man grown weary of the pinches and taunts, the mists and flickerings. I wove between the trees, looking for the river, recalling my own drawing of the valley, a place given form by ancient ritual. But the river was hidden now by the earth, of a sudden, rising before me, all humped like a deathbed.

How our night-minds ever find the most sinister of likeness. It was only raised earth, an upturned bowl. Made bigger by enclosing shadows than it had looked by day, and the trees growing out of it turned into a conference of witches, one of them long-dead, naked boughs clawing for the moon. But it wasn't the tree that stank.

In the windless night, it seemed as if the smell was all over the tump. A raw essence of decay, of corrupted flesh, sharp and hideously sweet. Stephen Price and Pedr Morgan had secretly buried a new corpse here, which by now would indeed be in a ripe condition, but... *buried.*

Under the moon's lamp, I rounded the tump to where they'd dug and was driven back, as if struck, by a reek so insidiously putrid that I felt as if my own body were rotting in its blast. Was sent reeling away, a hand cupped over my nose, my feet slithering and...

Christ...

A blow – a battlefield blow. A bright, ripping pain in the back of my head had me tumbling, flung around and thrown down, my stricken head jouncing from the bole of the tree behind me, legs slithering into a bed of twiggery and stony soil.

I lay for long moments, benumbed, the night in spasm around me. I must simply have backed hard into a tree with a low and knobbled branch which had scored my skull and put me down. But it had felt like an act of violence.

Reaching up a hand, I hissed in pain on finding a flap of peeled flesh, warm blood flooding through my fingers, my hair already thick with it.

Embedded in tree roots, I stared through the pain into a blackness, as if into the cave where the children of Mat met – *entrance so narrow that only one man at a time might pass through.* And the devil. The hole gaped at me like an open mouth, and its breath was foul. No escape from the stench of bloating flesh from… not a cave…

…but it *was* an orifice in the tump's flank, where none had been when I was here before. When I opened my mouth to call out for Thomas Jones and Vaughan, something at once rushed in, foul as returning vomit.

How can I tell you this? How can I describe the horror of closing my mouth on a mess of putrid flesh? Trying to retch, but finding no breath for it. Beginning to choke, the panic throwing me on my back amidst bone-hard roots, knowing full well that, although my throat and gut were tight with revulsion, there was *nothing* in my mouth.

Nothing anywhere. No air. The moon gone, darkness absolute.

Know that I *like* darkness. Nights when I can lie on my back, and planets and stars are laid out for me in strings and clusters like an intricate garden whose patterns I know with an intimacy as if I'd cultivated them myself.

This was a solid darkness, like stilled smoke. Should I have formed a prayer, holding it inside me, or inscribed a protective pentagram on the air? We don't think, even those of us who've pored for years over the Cabala and ascended, if only in our minds, the angelic stairways. In cold life, magic has a tendency to shrink back into the books. In the struggle against hungry death, we fall back on the physical.

With the running blood pooling on my face, I pushed against the roots, dug my boots into soft earth, coming up very slowly, my back against the tree. But my body felt too heavy, and I was aware of something pulling me back.

365

Fighting it, cold sweat welling from my skin to join the blood, but it was too much for me and I slid back into the gleefully crackling leaves, and felt a presence, a nearness, an active *resentment* fast hardening into hatred as I realised I must needs go into the hole.

XLVIII

Not in a Goodly Way

A LOG THE size of a side of mutton was in slumber in the ingle at Nant-y-groes. I bent over the meagre glow from its under-side, needing bodily heat more than ever I could remember. But Stephen Price was a farmer and wouldn't even think to awaken his fire before morning.

'Not that I sleep much these nights,' he said. 'Three or four hours, then I'll awake and get dressed, have a bite to eat, and then mabbe doze till dawn, if I can. And tonight, with this Gethin let loose…'

'You know about this?'

'The whole country knows of it by now.'

I looked around. The moon was a wavering lamp in the poor, blued glass of a deep-hewn window. I could hear Clarys the housekeeper clattering somewhere. In the brightness of pain, my thoughts were voiced, fast as arrows.

'Where's your wife? Why do I never see your wife?'

Price shuffled uncomfortably on his stool.

'Gone.'

'I'm… very sorry to hear that.'

'To Monaughty farm. To stay with my brother's family.'

I'd thought he'd meant dead. *A quiet woman*, Anna Ceddol had said. *Sits before the kitchen fire, goes out to listen to the priest on a Sunday and then goes home and worries.* Well, I was glad she wasn't dead, but why had she gone to stay at another farm, not even two miles away?

Stephen Price was asking me if I wanted to lie down. I shook my head... but slowly, the pain scraping ceaselessly at my head like a wind-driven bough against a window. I'd bathed it in the holy well and again with well-water in the yard at Nant-y-groes. The good housekeeper, Clarys, had applied a nettle balm, but it had begun to bleed again.

'I'll recover,' I said.

Looked like you were rehearsing alone for some Christmas play, Thomas Jones had said, shaken. *Pretending the other actors were there all around. Frit the hell out of me, boy.*

'I did not mean for this to happen,' Price said. 'I didn't think it would happen to you.'

He hadn't even asked why I, accompanied by two others, had come this night to Brynglas, seeming only grateful that I was attempting, in my way, to uncover what was wrong here. And if he hadn't *thought* that anything would happen to me he seemed not unhappy that something had.

'Didn't think such things could happen to me either,' I said dully.

And had once been foolish enough to think that if they ever did I'd feel... *favoured*? Maybe one day I'd be far enough removed from it to consider the science, but not now, when I felt as if my very soul had been snatched out and left to go cold.

Could not smother another spasm of shivering, and at last Stephen Price pulled down an iron poker from the wall and raised the log until a flame came tonguing through.

'I… was not as forthright with you,' he said stiffly, 'as I might've been. Never told you nothing wrong, but could've told you more.'

There was a clopping of hooves from the yard outside. The horses still were edgy, frit and sweating. I'd asked if we might leave all three at Nant-y-groes for a while, to calm down while we considered our situation. And so Vaughan and Thomas Jones had followed Price's sons to the stables. Leaving us alone, Price and me.

+

We'd moved on, widely skirting the tump and the marshy ground. Leading the horses, at last, through the oak wood and up to Pilleth church.

Jones and I had waited in the trees while Vaughan crept up alone to the church, where it took him not long to establish that the building and surrounds were deserted. He said later that he'd stifled a cry when, on peering around the wall of the tower, he'd encountered the stone virgin on her plinth, her face so tainted that she seemed to sneer into his eyes. I think he meant to pray to her and could not.

But at least the cold virgin was alone, so we came down from the hill the more direct way, veering from the path only once, so that I might be sure that the door and shutters of the Bryn were closed tight against invasion.

At first despondent over our failure to find Dudley, I was briefly lit by a small hope that we'd been wildly wrong and that he was back in Presteigne in some other whore's bed.

But that light soon went out.

'Thing was, I was affeared she'd die.'

'Your wife?'

I looked blearily at Price, my hair and face stiff with dried blood.

'Couldn't sleep, would not eat. Would not go out, not even in daylight. Gone thin as a rib. Sent her down to Monaughty farm to be cared for by my brother's wife. Mabbe she won't be back. It's all different down there, see. Not much more'n a mile, but it lies easy.'

'A monastery farm.'

'A safer air. She never liked this house, or this valley, that's what it come down to. Couldn't wait to move to Monaughty where there'd be more company. More company... and less company.'

He looked down at the fire, shaking his head.

'Wanted me to spend more money on the building work, finish the extension at Monaughty, so we could go. It led to much quarrelling at first. I was glad to get away to London, truth be told. You know what women are like, think you're tight with money, don't understand what you gotter spend keeping your ground in good heart, and...'

He looked up, stricken, his face all creased.

'Truth of it is, *I* never want to go to Monaughty. Two brothers, one farm, divers sons, it don't work. Stephen Price of Pilleth, that's me. Was gonner make Meredith an offer for this house.'

'It's all your land down here?'

'Most of it. But no house. Joan was all, "Oh thank God it's only rented. We can be out of yere." We'd signed for the place for two years. I thought to… mend things, somehow. Thought mabbe ole Walter, the priest, could change it for us. When we first come, if my wife or anybody seen anything, we'd send for Walter. And sometimes Marged, the wise woman. Mother Marged and Walter the priest… they had an understanding.'

'What did they think was the problem here?'

'Never listened much to ole Marged, it was all mumbles and spells. Father Walter, he'd say that, if you had the Sight, living yere you'd ever need the Saviour's protection.'

'What did he mean?'

'Shrine to the Holy Mother, place of pilgrimage – you come, you pay your respects and then you leave with faith renewed. No one should live too close to such places, Walter said, 'cept mabbe monks and hermits trained to thrive on spiritual agony. The ole priest, you never knowed when he was serious, but he knowed what he was about. And then he died. And then ole Marged. Both gone, one after the other.'

'And then all you had,' I said quietly, 'was a boy who brought death out of the earth but could not talk. And a new priest, all for the Bible.'

'Had hopes for Daunce at first. That he'd bring some sense, with the new religion. Plain talking. But, in the end…' Price stabbed the poker into the heart of the fire. '…putting it all down to the devil, that was the last thing we needed.'

'So you came to me.'

'You were sent to us. That's how I seen it.' He leaned away from the fire. 'The boy with you out there. Was that young Vaughan of Hergest?'

'And the man with him is my… my cousin, Thomas Jones, from the west of Wales.'

He and Vaughan had said they'd stay outside, watch the night, watch the hill for movement. Anything.

'My wife's been like this all her life,' Price said. 'Some has it, most of us en't. I thought it didn't bother her much any more.'

'But it was different here?'

'She liked to walk. In the evening, when the air was soft.'

'Not any more.'

'No. Never any more.'

His accent was thicker this night, but his voice was higher, querulous.

'What did she see?'

'The dead?' He prodded at the fire. 'But not in a goodly way.'

'You mean from the battlefield...'

'Confused. Looking for a home. Fragments of them. She'd be walking through them, like they were part of the wind, blowing down the hill, scattered like leaves – that was how she described it. After a while, she wouldn't go up the hill at all, except to church, in a group of us.'

'Where did she walk then?'

'By the river.' He looked uncomfortable. 'Quieter down there, see, until—'

I leaned forward, driven by sudden and powerful insight.

'Until you buried a man's body in the old grave mound?'

I sat back, into shadow. Felt I was close to the very heart of it. If it was just the fears of villagers, he'd pass it off as the superstitions of the uneducated. But his own wife... domestic troubles, matrimonial strife. His desire to remain here, in his own place, tempered by that fear that his wife, if they stayed, might even die of it.

I said, 'Did she know what you'd buried in the mound?'

'Christ, no.'

Of course not. It was even possible that his wife's fear of Brynglas had been another good reason to dispose of the remains… before she could find out about it. The thought of what *that* might do to her.

'Why did you bury him there?'

'*Why*? Because it was the only place I could think of where the mad boy wouldn't find him. Or, if he did, nobody would dig there because they all knowed it was an ole grave. Nobody disturbs a known grave.'

'No.' I nodded. 'Can you tell me what happened down by the river… with your wife?'

Price sat staring at the window and the smeared moon.

'Gone to walk. Around dusk. Pleasant, warm evening. Come back not an hour later… worst I've ever seen her. Close to swooning in distress. Face white as clouds. Took until next day 'fore she could even tell me.'

'What was it she saw?'

'Saw… smelled… felt.'

I nodded. I'd thought the smell would cling to my apparel, but when I left there it was gone. The smell had been part of the place. Part of what was there. And for the first time I'd been thankful that I did not see, like Mistress Price.

'No more'n a white mist, at first,' her husband said. 'Drifting across the marsh. Taking shape when it got close. Too close to run from.'

'What shape did it take?'

'A man.' He swallowed, shifting on his stool. 'Clothed only… only in his rage.'

'You mean naked?'

'Violence.' Price poked angrily at the log. 'She felt the violence in him. A *dirty* violence. She *felt*... what he wanted to do to her. Felt it inside.' He threw down the poker, turned away from the fire. '*Inside*. You know what I'm saying, Dr Dee? You know what it felt like? You heard of anything like that before.'

'No.'

Though maybe read of it. I wasn't sure. Horrified, I sought to reassure Price, telling him that no one was mad, that the old priest had been right about the peculiar air of a place of pilgrimage which might have its origins long before the shrine of the Virgin. That it seemed to me the tump had itself been placed in geometric accordance with the hill, the river, the shrine's heathen precursor and perhaps other monuments now vanished – even the sun and moon and the stars – to give this place a certain mystic resonance. Maybe empowering the spirit of whoever lay within the tump. And anyone who disturbed it... might themselves be disturbed.

All of this unloaded unrefined from my hurting head. Years of study might make it no clearer. And I knew that, but for my own experience at the tump this night, I'd be inclined to say that Mistress Price had created the whole story in her head to persuade her husband to turn his back on Brynglas Hill.

'We buried a naked man in the tump,' Price said. 'A man whose spirit did not rest. Who walked, and... more.'

'And what did you do?'

'She hadn't been out of her bed for three days. After I'd spent the day with you on the hill, came back home and Clarys said Joan hadn't been able to keep food down. Death was coming for her. Got the ole cart out, and we carried her on it, me and

Clarys, took her down to Monaughty. And later, when all were abed, I went to the tump.'

'On your own?'

'With a lantern. And the bier from the church.'

I sought to frame a question; it would not come.

'It was my fault,' Price said. 'My wife had been near death. My fault to put right. Like you say, it was the wrong place.' He wiped his brow with a sleeve. 'Not the pleasantest task. He stank to deepest hell. He was… green and going to fluids. Pieces were coming away from him. But I done it.'

'What?'

I'd reared back.

'Dug him out and took him away. Buried him the other side of the hill, behind the pines. Laid the turf on top and packed it tight. And said what prayers I could think of over him.'

'No one saw you?'

'Not as I know of. Doubt if I cared by then. Had to be done. Why? Was it wrong? Against the laws of God? I think not.'

'Only the laws of man.'

'Aye. Mabbe. But what choice did I have? Tell me that.'

I leaned forward, looking into Price's round, firelit face.

'So there's nothing in there now. Nothing in the tump.'

'Only what was there before. Whatever that may be.'

'And the hole,' I said. 'The hole remains.'

'No hole. I filled it in. Who would not?'

I gripped the wooden seat of my stool, my aching head all aswirl. I'd gone most of a day and a night without sleep, had little to eat and taken a blow to the head.

But I knew that I'd gone into the hole and… nothing there but a foul miasma and a swirling hatred and—

'John, boy?'

Thomas Jones standing in the doorway, hands behind his back. How long he'd been there I knew not, but I knew the tilted smile on his face was no portent of good fortune.

'Beg mercy if I interrupt you, John, but I thought you might want to know that at this moment there is a man walking quite openly along the road towards us, from the direction of Presteigne. Evidently making for the hill.'

I stood up.

'Someone you know?'

'Well... he's yet some distance away, so we cannot be entirely sure. But, Vaughan and I are in general agreement that it might well be the man who likes to call himself Prys Gethin.'

I stood unsteadily, a hand on the ingle beam.

'John, you look worse,' Thomas Jones said. 'You should stay here. Vaughan and I will follow him.'

'I'll come,' I said. 'I must needs come.'

For I was hearing his voice from earlier.

Killing and rape... as natural to him as taking a piss... O liked to do her while covered in pig blood, still wet... the demon he's invested with the spirit of Rhys Gethin...

I stood pushing my hands back through my blood-stiffened hair, regardless of the pain, and then turned to Price and asked him what I'd thought, as a bookman and a philosopher, never to ask any man.

'Master Price,' I said, 'have you weaponry here?'

XLIX

Skin of the Valley

AT FIRST SIGHT, looking down, you might almost have thought him drunk. Trying to stay upright, hands extended either side of his body, upturned as if weighing the air.

It was the first time I'd seen him.

We watched from a small orchard growing on a shelf of higher ground behind Nant-y-groes, standing inside a lattice of shadows and speaking in low voices. Stephen Price had offered to come with us, bringing both his sons, maybe rousing some of the local men. But Thomas Jones had pointed out that too many of us on Brynglas would only draw attention.

Besides, I'd no wish for too many people to know about Robert Dudley.

'If it *is* Gethin,' Vaughan said. 'How did he avoid half the men of Presteigne?'

'They'll have given up long ago,' I said, 'though that doesn't tell us how they failed to see him on the road.'

'Unless,' Vaughan said, 'he was given help. Nobody saw him leave the court. He may have been smuggled away later than we think.'

'It being important that he reaches his destination,' I said.

It was all aglow again. The night alive and me half dead.

'We have a choice,' Thomas Jones said. 'We could simply wait here until he goes past and then follow him in the assumption that he'll lead us to wherever your friend is held. If he still lives.'

'We'd have the moonlight on our side, so we could leave a reasonable distance between him and ourselves.'

I pointed to a line of pines on the eastern side of Brynglas Hill, which hid the village and would offer us some cover.

'More copses and dingles up there than you'd imagine,' Roger Vaughan said. 'Plenty of places he can disappear if he *does* see us. Especially if he knows the hill.'

'I think we can take it he knows the hill all too well,' Thomas Jones said. 'Having been here many times, following in the steps of Rhys Gethin, calling Rhys's spirit into him. Rhys in the time of triumph.'

I said nothing. None of my mentors – Agrippa, Trithemius – would deem it possible for a man to summon another's ghost into himself, except in his imagination. Which would have more effect on himself than upon others and should not be too much feared.

We could see him more clearly now, a sprightly puppet-figure under the moon, and sometimes it looked as if he was almost dancing and then his pace was slowed and he was walking down the middle of the road as if in a procession. As if he was not alone.

I felt Vaughan's shudder.

'Something unearthly about this.'

'He's happy, that's all,' Thomas Jones said. 'He's walked free from the highest court ever held in Presteigne. And he's on his way to do a killing.'

'Something even more than that.' I marked how his hands seem to gather-in the bright night. 'He feels himself entranced.'

The arms of the figure on the road were opening and hands reaching out, as if he might clasp the hill to his bosom.

'We might simply go down to him,' Thomas Jones said. 'Present ourselves. Three against one and we have… this.'

The blade of the butcher's chopping knife was near two feet long. Stephen Price had handed it to me as we left and I'd unloaded it upon Thomas Jones at the earliest opportunity. He held it point down behind an apple tree so that its blade should not reflect the moonlight.

'A scholar,' he said, 'a lawyer… and a man who, since his pardon, has become rather too fond of his meat. Against a man of considerable strength who's driven to kill. Yes, I suppose we could do that. Demand he tells us where they have your friend. And, when he refuses, lop off one of his hands.' He ran a tentative thumb along the blade. 'Sharp enough, certainly. Will it be you, John, to do the first hand?'

'We'll follow him,' I said.

✝

Nearly halfway up Brynglas, not far below the church, Prys Gethin stopped and sat down on a small tump in the grass. To gain the cover of the last stand of pine before the church wall, we'd had to creep, one by one, to higher ground and so looked down on Gethin now.

Both Thomas Jones and Vaughan had been able to verify to their satisfaction that this *was* Gethin. And there was confirmation for me, too, when he turned his head and the moon lit the grim cavity where an eye once had lodged.

I looked at Thomas Jones in frustration. He shrugged. There was nothing we could do but wait. After several minutes, Gethin had not moved, sitting quite still, as though in meditation. Or was *he* waiting for someone? I leaned against one of the pines, fatigue weighting my legs. The only warmth came from the new blood on my brow, the deep gash in my head having opened again, tributaries channelled either side of my nose.

Vaughan raised a hand, making motion towards the church. I looked at Thomas Jones and he nodded: we might as well take this opportunity to leave the pines and reach the cover of the church wall, for if Gethin rose now and moved ahead of us, he'd have an open view of the whole valley and might well mark us.

We moved, as before, one by one. I waited another minute before running in a crouch, half blinded by the blood-flow, to join the other two behind the low trees and bushes which enclosed the church on three sides. Below us to the left, the village lay lightless and silent.

We approached the church itself with greater caution this time, but a window of plain glass showed that there was still no one inside, only a sheet of moonlight over the altar. The raised churchyard gave us a plateau from which we could watch Prys Gethin, still as a monument and far enough away for us to commune in whispers as we crouched among outlying tombs behind a loose wall of bushes.

'You might almost imagine that he knew he was watched,' Roger Vaughan said.

'I doubt that.' Thomas Jones prodded the earth with the butcher's blade. 'It seems more likely that he's waiting for someone. We could be here until sunrise. Let me think on it.' He sat down on a low tomb, the blade across his knees. 'Go and bathe your head in the well, John. If he moves we'll come for you.'

'I'll go with you,' Vaughan said. 'It's on the dark side of the church, and the steps to the well are worn.'

An owl's call across the valley was returned, as I followed Vaughan around the body of the church. The area of the well was darkened not only by the tower but the line of tall pines on the other side. Vaughan stopped, stood with his back against the church wall. I could not see his face, only hear the desolation in his voice.

'The truth is, I must needs pray to the holy mother.'

'Vaughan—'

'I've no confidence in surviving this night.'

I stopped under the grey diamond panes of the steep end window, and sighed.

'Because of what you saw down by the tump.'

'And felt. And smelled.'

'A man?'

'Mabbe. Came and went. In a blinking.'

'Listen,' I said. 'Sometimes we throw pictures from our thoughts into the night air, and in some places the air is more receptive. If the ancient Greeks and the Egyptians before them were so far ahead of where we are, even now, in matters of the Hidden… then we mustn't be too quick to dismiss the ancient Britons with their standing stones and their rough, earthen monuments. More than just graves.'

It seemed a rare madness, delivering a lecture on antiquities to a gathering of one in a moonlit churchyard. But it was clear to me now that the skin of this valley and the fabric betwixt the spheres must be rendered muslin-thin.

'It would have…' Vaughan held his back against the church wall. 'If I'd died from the fear of it… I felt it would've relished that. Do you see?'

No, I did not *see*.

But I nodded.

'Look,' I said. 'Pray to the Lady. If you dip your sleeve in the holy well and wipe the grime from her brow, she might even respond.'

If his glance at me was in search of irony, he'd find no sign of it this night.

'Roger,' I said. 'Don't dwell on it and it won't reach you.'

He nodded and picked his way to where the sad, smirched Virgin stood atop her ridge of rubble-stones, watching over the stone-lined vault in the earth which held the holy well. A well older than Christianity, where the heads of dead enemies would have been sunk in veneration of some forgotten druidic deity later, perhaps, invoked by Owain Glyndwr and Rhys Gethin.

And then Prys Gethin, too, on one of his dark pilgrimages to Pilleth, betwixt cattle raids. No one more likely to have murdered and mutilated the man twice buried by Stephen Price, in grotesque and would-be magical re-enactment of the events of 1402. What I could not yet imagine was how the unknown man's unquiet spirit had been invested with the base instincts of his killer.

My split head could hold no more. All logic and learning was collapsed into the midden of superstition, as we returned to the tomb. Watching Prys Gethin, so still on the hillside below us, small as a toad from here, as Venus gleamed, first signal of the coming dawn.

In my old life, which surely had ended this night, ghosts were neither good nor bad, and all they could give me was the knowledge of their existence. Fear had no role to play, for I'd not been able to understand fear of the unknown which, to me, was a wondrous thing which I'd approached eagerly with my arms spread wide.

I looked at Thomas Jones, the butcher's knife betwixt his knees, his hands on its string-wound wooden hilt.

He leaned back, stretched, sighing.

'He doesn't know, boy. Doesn't know where they are. He's waiting for them to find him. That's why he made no attempt to conceal his arrival. When they know he's free, they'll know it's not a trick and their side of the bargain can be met without fear of reprisal.'

'Meaning Dudley yet lives?'

'Who can say? We don't know where they might have him. We don't know how many of them are holding him. If we wait for them to find him and take him to the place, yes, we can follow them. But how do we stop them putting an end to it? Prys's moment of blood-drenched triumph. What do we do about this, John?'

'Can only wait,' Vaughan said, returning from his prayers. 'What other choice do we have?'

'The other choice is to make sure they *never* find Prys. Go down there now, three against one. And this...'

Thomas Jones thumbed the butcher's blade. Roger Vaughan drew back in alarm with a rattling of bushes.

'I'm a man of the *law*.'

'So's Legge.'

'Master Jones, it's one thing for a man to be legally hanged—'

'Heroes we'd be, in Presteigne.'

'*Jesu!*'

Only a hiss from Vaughan, but it was too loud, and I thought I saw Gethin's head move, though he was too distant for me to be sure.

Thomas Jones held out a dagger to me. I took it. I saw Roger Vaughan's eyes close momentarily.

'Roger, you know this place. Go around the church, into the pines, wait for a while to be sure you're not seen, then quietly follow the path back.'

'To Nant-y-groes?'

'Indeed,' Thomas Jones said, catching on. 'Fetch Price and however many sons he has over the age of six.'

'What about you?'

'Just do it, eh?'

Vaughan hesitated for a moment and then turned and was gone. Thomas Jones took a long breath, parted the bushes separating us from the pale hillside, peered through for a moment then let the bushes swing back and picked up his butcher's knife from the tomb.

'This is it, then, boy. Don't forget your magic.'

✢

White and amber strands in the east suggested that the moon's dominion would end before long, and I was glad of this. The moon might be your friend on a night ride, but it meddles too much with your mind and senses.

We'd moved about fifty paces to the other end of the churchyard before easing ourselves through the bushes, so that he would not at first see us. Walking slowly towards him, for a swifter pace might have implied an attack.

Thomas Jones plucked off his green hat.

'*Bore da*, Prys.'

Good morning.

A thin white line on the horizon, but the morning must be more than an hour away.

L

Courtly Dance

A SILENCE FORMED, allowing me to observe Gethin for the first time.

He was perhaps a little over medium height with long, tangled, greying hair and a face like from a misericord, its lines chiselled deep in varnished oak.

My gaze was drawn inevitably to the open cavity where the left eye had been, a knot hole in the wood.

'Twm Siôn Cati,' he said. 'Well, well.'

His wide lips fell easily into a loose smile, and then he spoke in Welsh so rapid that I could understand not a word of it.

Thomas Jones nodded.

'Indeed,' he said. 'However, in the presence of an Englishman, I ever think it polite – for those who *can* – to use his language. Indeed, I'm told that Owain Glyndwr himself, when he was at the English court, was oft-times *mistaken* for an Englishman.'

'While Elizabeth of England, who claims descent from Arthur' – Prys Gethin speaking rapidly, as though his mastery of the neighbouring tongue had been impugned – 'speaks not a word *yn Gymreig*.'

His voice was unexpectedly high and surprisingly melodious, like to a bladder-pipe.

'Not entirely true,' I said.

Foolishly. In truth I was far from sure that, for all her linguistic skills, the Queen had more than a few words of Welsh, but I'd always instinctively take her side.

'Is it not?' Prys Gethin glanced across at me. 'And who are you to say, sirrah?'

Thomas Jones threw a swift warning look in my direction, but I caught it too late.

'John Dee.'

'*Oh.*' Prys Gethin's one eye lit up and, for a moment, I had the disturbing sensation that I was also viewed by some organ of perception behind the empty socket of the other, a secret sight which might penetrate my thoughts. 'Her *conjurer.*'

I shrugged.

'So the Queen of England saw fit to dispatch her sorcerer to Wales… along with the father of her bastard child.'

'She doesn't have a—' I shook my head, and my lips tightened with the pain. 'No matter.'

No matter, indeed, for I knew that in one sentence he'd confirmed what, until that moment, had been only an elaborate theory.

'Where is he?' I said.

He glanced briefly at me then looked away.

'Where are you holding Lord Dudley?'

No reply.

'We know why you were freed,' I said. 'We know about the agreement.'

Gethin spoke in Welsh to Thomas Jones, who at once translated.

'John, he invites us to kill him.'

Gethin smiled.

Thomas Jones raised the butcher's knife. Gethin did not flinch.

The whole texture of the night was altered. I watched the start of a dangerously delicate courtly dance in the remains of the moonlight: Prys Gethin tossing a question in Welsh at Thomas Jones, who gave no answer, Gethin then addressing him at length, still in Welsh, Thomas Jones listening without a word, hands on hips, then turning to me, his voice mild.

'Prys wonders, John, why I'm working with the enemy.'

'And he is not?'

Realising, too late, my possible mistake. If Gethin believed his task had been assigned by Cecil, then he might see it as some peculiarly Welsh alliance between the two of them. How much he knew of Cecil's reasons for not wanting the Queen wed to Dudley, an Englishman, I could not say. Nor whether, from a Welsh standpoint, a Spaniard or a Frenchman would be preferable as a consort.

More Welsh from Gethin, Thomas Jones listening, then slowly shaking his head.

'No, boy. Myself, I've never considered that accepting an English Queen's pardon was any kind of treachery. But equally, I'm under no illusion about the continuing Welshness of the Tudor line.'

Silence for a while, only the call of a distant owl at night's end. Then Gethin brought his attention to me.

'Do you know where you are standing, Dr Dee?'

'I believe so.'

I took an instinctive step back, down the hillside, for Prys Gethin, even after walking from Presteigne, gave off such animation, such an energy. Perhaps the energy of freedom after a long captivity. Or perhaps something more. There was little doubt he knew where *he* was standing. Did he believe the spirit of the man whose name he'd borrowed had come into him while he sat waiting on the hill?

A spirit now burning inside him?

Not possible. An occupying spirit could not be of human origin, only demonic.

Christ.

I felt my own energy seeping away into the ground. I was near exhaustion and, despite the extreme danger here, felt I might fall to sleep on my feet like a horse. We were in Gethin's hands and he knew it.

Time passed, the voice piping on, as if delivering a sermon, the Welsh rising and dipping like a liturgy, and then Thomas Jones replying, this time also in Welsh, still now, looking beyond me down the hill, his eyes black. I felt like a watcher from another, smaller world.

Thomas Jones was nodding now, a faint smile upon his plumpen features.

'*Da iawn,*' he said.

Very good. Both men smiling.

All three of them.

Jesu.

The third man was unknown to me. He was a large man. His hair was short and crinkled, his beard grey, his arms bare and muscular. Silver sweat shone from his face and a dagger from a fist.

Thomas Jones nodded to him.

'John, this is Master Gerallt Roberts.'

Oh God, he must have moved silently out of the pines, lower down the hill from where we stood, and simply walked up, silently over the sheep-cropped turf.

We were equal in number now, but you only had to look at Gerallt Roberts to know that, in truth, we were outnumbered.

A long silence, and then Prys Gethin spoke again, in Welsh.

'John...' Thomas Jones looking down the slope at me. 'Prys tells me we are upon the very spot at which the Welsh archers hired by the English were caused to turn and loose their arrows into the English army. Thus redeeming their heritage.'

'And how can he know that?'

Nobody replied. Having retreated a little way down the hill, I had my back to those first pale lights of pre-dawn, looking up at two men who were still in night.

'A place of redemption indeed.' Thomas Jones approached me, looking sorrowful. 'It's been conveyed to me that this may be my last chance to regain my honour.'

'Honour?'

'After my cowardly acceptance of mercy from a woman who will never be Queen of Wales.'

I looked for a smile, but his face was empty.

'We'll never be part of that. Of England. Owain, with his English education and his smooth English speech, made that all too explicit.'

'My father achieved it,' I said.

'Traitors don't count, John.' Thomas Jones sighed. 'Prys says that redemption requires of me one simple, perfect act.'

I heard his kindly voice as if from a great distance.

'Your decapitation,' it said.

I said nothing. It was a play. I was not part of it. The only reality was the ache in my head and even that was dulled now.

'How can we let you live, knowing what you know?'

We?

I saw that he'd plucked the dagger from my belt. I stared into his eyes, but they would not meet mine.

Look at me, boy – fallen Welshman, recipient of an English pardon. See what it does to me, this place.

Thomas Jones brought up the butcher's knife, ran a thumb along the blade.

It *was* a play. It could not be happening. I must endeavour not to make him laugh. I turned to Gethin.

'The sheriff's men will be here soon. You do know that?'

'The sheriff.' He smiled patiently. 'The sheriff, at whose behest I was comfortably accommodated for a few hours, until all the hotheads waiting to kill me had dispersed. In whose covered cart I was safely conveyed beyond the boundaries of Presteigne. *That* sheriff?'

'How many murders do you want to be tried for this time?'

'This is murder?' Gethin spread his hands. 'Oh, I think not, Dr Dee. Not in my country.'

I saw that only he and Thomas Jones were standing on the higher ground. The big man, Roberts, was gone.

And then I heard his slow breathing from behind me, even smelling it. Foul. The reek of betrayal. Or did that come from the ground, where a history of it glittered in the very dew?

'Where's Lord Dudley?' I said. 'You might as well tell me. You owe me that much.'

'I owe nothing… to you or any man of your mongrel race. No one will ever know where Lord Dudley died, and all that will remain of his body will be his cock – the cock which impregnated the English queen—'

'For God's sake, the Queen—'

'—to be dried and powdered and sold to make fertility potions for old men. In England, of course.'

'The Queen,' I said, 'has not given birth to Dudley's child… and neither did his wife, after ten years of marriage.'

He seemed not to hear me, nodded to Thomas Jones, who looked uncomfortable, weighing the long knife in two hands, one clasped over the other because of the shortness of the wooden handle.

'Wouldn't be the first time, would it?' I said to Gethin. 'I'm thinking of the man you killed and chopped off his privy parts and cut off his face?'

'He talks drivel,' Gethin said. 'Position him.'

Something spoken in Welsh, Thomas Jones nodding, then gesturing toward an area of turf a yard or so out from his boots.

'I am… required to invite you, John, to kneel and bow your head.'

I looked at the selected turf and backed away from it, into the arms of Gerallt Roberts who pulled me close, sharply, and I felt what could only be his head butting the back of mine, bursting open my wound, and I must have screamed as I sank in agony to my knees.

'What a night for this,' Prys Gethin said. 'Did you see the star earlier? I witnessed it as I walked here. Crossed the whole of the sky, like the one which fired the heavens just before the start of Owain's war. You'd know of that, as an astrologer.'

Through the pain came outrage. In 1402, a comet widely

seen across Europe had been viewed as a portent of the End-time but hailed by Glyndwr as inscribing across the night sky the trajectory of his campaign. I'd charted the frequency of comets and if there'd been one this night I was no astronomer. This man was mad, and I could not believe that someone at the highest level of English government would bargain with him. Maybe it was the French or the Spaniards or some unbalanced independent contender like the preening Earl of Arundel.

'When you are ready,' Prys Gethin said, 'it will be easier for all of us if you pull your hair to one side to enable a clean cut. Don't think to further demean your race by attempting to run, or to struggle. The end of it would be the same, only bloodier.'

For just a moment – as I came stubbornly to my feet, yet refusing to believe – by some trick of the paling moon, his empty socket seem to glow, as if this imaginary comet burned inside his skull.

In such a man it could only portend horror and tragedy.

As it would.

LI

Ragged White

I STOOD, SWAYING, hands on my gut where the Wigmore shew-stone swelled out of my jerkin like a cyst. Thomas Jones bent and laid down the butcher's knife.

'Let me talk to him,' he said to Gethin. 'With some small privacy. He was, after all, to have become my cousin.'

Gethin picked up the long knife.

'Make it swift.'

He stood back and signalled to the big man to do the same. Thomas Jones came forward, not a weapon betwixt us. I wondered if, as a known sorcerer, a curse from me might have any effect. In such moments, you'll consider anything.

'Kneel, John,' Thomas Jones said. 'If you please.'

'Piss off.'

'There's no way out of this,' Thomas Jones said. 'And yet you know there is. You know of these matters. If you go quietly—'

'That will not happen.'

'You *know*... that if you go quietly and with humility, your soul will slip away from this place in peace and grace. Whereas if you resist and must needs be ignominiously cut down, your embittered ghost will join all the other unquiet spirits which crowd Brynglas like crows.'

I would have had an answer for that, and a good and informed one, but then Thomas Jones was stepping away, holding out a hand to Gethin for the butcher's knife. Hefting it from hand to hand, testing its balance. The big man, Roberts, was come close behind me again. The smell of his breath was worse at this moment than the stench of rotting flesh from the hole in the tump by the river.

I couldn't speak. I stood swaying, new blood stiff on my cheeks. I was aware of Gethin walking over. Heard his rich, bladder-pipe voice, in Welsh, and then it broke off.

'Translate for him,' he said.

With no expression in his voice, Thomas Jones did as bid.

'John, the Prince of Wales is with us now. He who could never leave while the English yoke lies heavily upon us.'

More Welsh, but all I heard was the voice of Thomas Jones from earlier.

…not saying he lives… *but something of him does. And, if it's anywhere, it's here.*

And now, having watched Prys Gethin sitting upon the hill, as if in silent summons, I was afraid.

I cleared my throat.

'He was, in his way,' I said, 'a man of honour. I believe my family might even have supported his cause. And yet…' I looked into the powdery night 'twixt Thomas Jones and Prys Gethin. '…he looks not happy. And who *would* be, knowing that his only representative on the hill of his finest day was a one-eyed, twisted scut who—'

A grunt from behind, and an agony as if my skull were cleaved open, but this time I stayed on my feet.

'—who cares not a toss for the future of Wales, but only to satisfy his need for—'

'Do it,' Prys Gethin said.

When I knelt, every muscle and sinew in my legs was straining against it. The body fighting to live, the mind in furious, bitter conflict with itself over what to believe, who to trust. The need to hold on to the last small hope that a man you'd liked, who'd oft-times made you laugh, was not, after all, to be your murderer.

His voice at my ear.

'I'm trying to help you, boy. To give you the quick and merciful passing that's mete for a man of your standing.'

Shifting his gaze when I looked up at him. I knelt in the wet turf, and they stood in silence around me. With my head bowed, all I could see was their boots – one pair, worn by Roberts were all smirched with mud and pine needles but not enough to obscure the fine leather and good stitching and—

Oh God. Robbie…

When my head jerked, the wound under my hair sprang apart yet again and blood begin to run, down into my eyes. When the head was severed it would stop.

I let the breath go from my chest to my abdomen, beginning to pray, and in my head, against a cloth of deep blue, the sigil of St Michael appeared for a moment – Michael who brings courage.

Michael who is also the angel of death, weighing the soul, conveying it to where it must go.

Out of the corner of one eye, I saw the knife leave the ground. Then I saw, on the grey grass, the shadow of a raised blade extended from bowed arms.

Breath froze in my throat, silence roared in my ears. I saw

the shadow of the blade at an oblique angle. Not the slender, fine-honed blade that beheaded Anne Boleyn in one stroke, but a rude butcher's knife, made for mutton. I fell into prayer, as the shadow-blade twitched once and then fell with the echo of a cry across the night. Then came a brutal blow, my body tipping sideways, my head fallen heavily into the grass.

All shadow. Moments of emptiness, then wet splatter. Hot blood on my cheeks, in my mouth, in my eyes.

Through it, I saw the blade falling again and again and again. More blood flying up.

Up.

✟

'Up, John!'

The hand of God reaching down for me.

I didn't move. Lay on my side, looking up through the blood into the face of Thomas Jones, his panicked eyes under a blur of madness and tears, as he kicked me over on to my back.

'Get up, John… *Get the fuck up…*'

I could feel my hands, fingers flexing and then moving with an exploratory slowness to my neck, which somehow seemed yet to be held 'twixt my collar bones. Sitting up, now, in a pond of blood, looking down on the body of the big man, Roberts, heaving and squirming in the grass, his face a dark red carnival mask, and then flinching away from the sight of the thick blade coming down on him, and I heard Thomas Jones sob and, over the sickening splinter of bone, I heard the vixen shriek.

It came down the hillside with all the force of an arrow that would pierce my heart and, in a blinking, I was struggling to my feet. Fresh blood was slicked under my boots, and I stumbled and fell, dragged myself up again, scraping the salty blood from my eyes as I clambered up into the dregs of the night, and there was Prys Gethin creeping through the muddy dawn.

Quite some distance ahead of me, close to the church, something up there having trapped his attention.

A pale fluttering.

Gethin still now.

Standing, dagger in hand, feet apart. Waiting for the figure in the ragged white nightshirt to come down from the hill like a summoned ghost.

Oh, no. Oh dear God, no.

I ran crookedly up the steepening side of Brynglas. Stumbling twice and clawing at the grass. Knowing these two, black and white, would come together long before I could reach them, I began to cry out urgently and was answered, the way one owl answers another.

The nightshirt billowed. The long bone was raised. The vixen shriek resounded down the valley.

I saw what might have been the first pale rays of the rising sun in Prys Gethin's blade as it was drawn quickly back and then pushed, with a practised ease, under the boy's jaw.

Saw Gethin wipe the blade in the grass and stride away, not once looking back at any of us.

LII

The Wasting

I KNEW HE was gone before I reached him. The old white night-shirt lay around him like the flaccid feathers of a dead bird, slowly turning red under the bloody light of early dawn. His throat was laid open, as were his mad, unseeing eyes, to the awakening day.

Sick to my soul, I came to my knees beside him. He was quite still; his spirit had flit as lightly as a moth's. I looked up, in dread, through the dimness for sign of his sister, but there was none, only her voice in my memory.

We're country people. If he wanders out in the night here, as oft-times he does, I know he'll come to no harm.

I threw my fist with savagery at the turf, grief and pity turned into a useless rage, as Thomas Jones arrived at my shoulder. I looked up at him and at Brynglas, a melancholic grey without even the mystery of mist. As though the last small hope of spiritual relief for this damned hill had lodged for a while in Siôn Ceddol and now was snuffed out.

Thomas Jones was painfully panting, florid-faced, still holding the butcher's knife, reddened to the handle.

'Who's this?'

'Boy from the village. Armed—' My voice choked on the senseless, wasteful cruelty of it. 'Armed with a...'

I picked up the age-browned thigh bone from where it lay, close to Siôn Ceddol's half-curled left hand. I'd not noticed he was left handed, a sinistral – though doubtless the rector would have. Another unfailing sign of the demonic. To Gethin, he'd have looked unearthly in the half light.

Like an angel.

'He'll kill anyone in his path, now,' Thomas Jones said. 'You know that...'

Then he was bent over, coughing wretchedly, his hands bloodied to the wrists, the cuffs of his doublet blackened. He came up pointing towards the thickness of pines to the left of the church.

'Went through there. The woods, not the churchyard.'

This brought me to my feet, dizzied for a moment, too long without sleep and bleeding from the head. The sky was the colour of ale. No sun yet. I looked down at Siôn Ceddol and his favourite bone, his open throat. I swallowed bile.

'I'll go after him.'

Took the butcher's knife, its handle all clammy with blood and worse.

'*We'll* go.' Thomas Jones had me by the shoulders. 'Listen... remember this. Don't think to appeal to his reason. It's gone. In the ruins of his mind, all is justified.'

'What did he say to you? In Welsh.'

'He said that only one of us need die. I weighed the odds and they weren't good. I've seen Roberts take three men down in a street brawl. I did all I could think to do, which was to go with him... until the moment came.'

And what if the moment had *not* come? What if Gethin's attention had not been snared by the vixen shriek and the fluttering figure in white who, unknowingly, may have given his life for mine?

I turned back towards the upper part of the hill, the high pines still black on the skyline.

'What's up there?' Thomas Jones said.

'I'm not sure. I don't know. Maybe the Rector's house.'

Along with the wasting of an innocent life, maybe the most innocent, the thin brown light of dawn had brought a mournful uncertainty.

✢

The pines closed around us like the pillars of a rude temple. Wandering from tree to tree, apparel stiffened with dried and drying blood, saying nothing, we must have looked like war-sick soldiers escaping the fray.

Moving with caution now, as most of the trees were well grown enough to hide a man. I'd no wish for us to die foolishly at Gethin's hands. If he died at ours, I'd feel no regret, but how likely was that? We were soft-skinned men who lived in books – even Thomas Jones nowadays – and one of us vainly courted the angelic. The man we sought had skin like a lizard's, was well-practised in the art of killing, driven by devils.

The wood was deeper than it had appeared from the slope below the church. It crested Brynglas and continued down the northern flank. Could be that these pines had grown upon the land where Rhys Gethin's fiery army had waited for Edmund Mortimer's trained soldiers, yeomen and peasants. And the Welsh archers who knew – or yet did not – what they'd do. When the moment came.

Maybe this was also where the women waited. The women

who travelled with Gethin's heroes and were said to have come scurrying down, after the battle, with their little knives.

Standing in that clearing, under a whitening sky, I threw down the butcher's knife in horrified realisation of the recent carnage it had performed in the saving of the unworthy life of a conjurer who might never know what he'd conjured... a seer who saw nothing beyond the physical. The Wigmore shew-stone was a useless weight in the front pouch of my jerkin. Had it not been for my futile pursuit of advancement and the engines of creation, we would not have come here and Siôn Ceddol would yet live. *Let not this place be tainted by your presence*, said Rector Daunce, perhaps, after all, with prescience.

I kicked the knife away, and the blade came to rest at the bottom of one of the pines, around which a...

'John—'

... rope was tied.

I felt a drumming in my chest. This was not the old and rotting hemp you might expect to find at the heart of a wood, but new rope, strong rope. Bending to it, I saw that other, shorter lengths lay nearby, tossed among the needles and cones – on top, not embedded.

'Someone was roped to this tree... and then cut loose.'

'And not long ago,' Thomas Jones said.

'Was this it... Dudley's prison?'

I picked up a strand of rope. Its ragged end was brown with blood, and almost at once, across the clearing, I saw the reason.

✠

He lay 'twixt two young pines on the edge of the clearing, where it was beginning to thicken into something approaching forestry.

He was most conspicuously dead, face down in a bolster of browning needles, a pond of blood beneath and around him.

And barefooted.

I shut my eyes in anguish. Close to weeping with despair, I followed Thomas Jones across the clearing to the corpse. He took a breath of pine wood and bent among the day's first flies.

'Stabbed in more than one place.'

'But not freshly.'

The pond of blood beneath him was congealed, like a black-berry preserve.

'Or efficiently. Looks to me, like the mortal injuries inflicted in a fight.'

Pine needles glued together by black blood, a trail. Thomas Jones stood up then bent and turned the body over, stood looking down, hands on hips.

'John, if you thought this was…'

I turned slowly in the oily light.

The dead man's eyes were open. An ooze of blood linked nose and mouth. A young man, maybe not yet twenty-five. I'd never seen him before. The breath went out of me.

'Gwyn Roberts,' Thomas Jones said.

'You think Dudley…?'

'The rope's cut, Gwyn's stabbed to death in what looks like a fight. I don't—'

'And his boots taken,' I said. 'You may not have noticed, but the older Roberts was wearing riding boots of the finest quality. Dudley's. In one of which he keeps a blade.'

'In his boot?'

'Used to, anyway.'

He'd shown it to me two or three years ago, on an older pair: the thin sheath stitched into a seam of leather, to fit beside the calf. The dagger it concealed had been no more than five inches long, including the bone handle. New boots, but he wouldn't have abandoned an old precaution. Robert Dudley was as superstitious as anyone I knew.

'Maybe he guessed they'd take his boots, for their value and to render him more helpless. Maybe he retrieved the knife from the boot after they'd searched him. I know not.'

'So it's likely he lives,' Thomas Jones said.

'Or *lived*,' I said. 'If Gethin passed this way...'

I walked back into the clearing, wiping my mouth on a sleeve, not daring to think there was cause for hope. Finally snatching up the bloodied knife from which it seemed that destiny, that twisted joker, had decreed there could be no parting.

Flies sticking to it now.

✝

Coming out of the pine wood, some minutes later, we found ourselves closer to the church of St Mary than I'd expected. An ominous quiet was hung upon the air. Dawn bird-sound was distant and thin. Thomas Jones went to the holy well to wash, but I sank to my knees in the grass, sucking dew into my dry mouth. This was the second dawn I'd seen since sleeping, and I knew not when I'd ever felt as weary.

Wet faced, I walked around the front of the little grey church to the now familiar view over the cauldron of hills, down the battlefield of Brynglas, becoming aware of movement, villagers gathering. A dozen or more, including several women, on the hill, under the dirty-bruised skin of the sky.

I saw old Goodwife Thomas and Gareth Puw, the blacksmith, and others I recognised but could not name, but there was no sign of Vaughan or Price and his sons.

Only, some distance away, something still as a sculpted tableau in the grass which no one approached.

Siôn Ceddol's head lolled in his sister's lap, her own head bowed, her dense brown hair down around her face and his. She did not seem to see any of them, kneeling in an island of grief to which none could cross.

Stabbing the knife into the ground, I stood between the small trees on the edge of the churchyard, from where we'd watched Prys Gethin summoning his demons.

Maybe it was through fatigue or because I *did* blame myself for the boy's killing that I didn't go down. There was nothing I could say to her, not in front of the villagers. The boy was slain, and I could not bring him back.

'Who is she, John?'

Thomas Jones had come round from the well. He'd stripped away his ruined doublet, stood in his shirt, the sleeves rolled up, blood streaks not fully washed from his arms.

Anna let Siôn's head slip from her lap and, laying it tenderly in the turf, slowly arose. Her overdress was darkened at the thighs, her lips parted in a soundless distress.

'His mother?'

'Sister. He was... there was something missing in his mind. But something else there... that we don't have.'

A bar of sunlight split the fleshy cloud, lighting the hillside. I turned my head away, blinded for the moment, and then Thomas Jones was pulling me back 'twixt the trees, speaking quietly.

'Do nothing.'

A hundred paces below us, Prys Gethin had emerged like a sprite from the pines. I reached for the butcher's knife, but we were too far away and already it was too late.

LIII

Untethered

BLACK, NOW, AGAINST the rosening sun whose rays, for a moment, seemed to sprout from his shoulders like small wings of dark fire.

Dark angel rising.

His movements had been so swift and easy that he was already half a dozen paces down the hill, taking Anna Ceddol with him, the blade which had penetrated her brother's throat now at her own.

'Stay where you are, John,' Thomas Jones murmured, voice very low, heavy with warning.

Gethin had twisted her head to his chest, was pulling her backwards. One of the women cried out. I saw Gareth Puw, the blacksmith, taking steps towards him and then reeling back at what Gethin had done.

Anna's overdress was parted at the top, a single red petal blooming above her shift.

I drew savage breath as the blade was lifted, red-edged.

'Freshly-sharpened,' Gethin said.

The piping voice was light and clear, risen into a kind of rapture. I made out his fingers and thumb tight around Anna Ceddol's jaw, as if he were squeezing juice from an orange, as if his whole body was revelling in the sensation of it, bright bells pealing in his head.

'Who wishes,' he sang, 'to see the ease with which it severs a breast?'

'Do not move,' Thomas Jones hissed. 'If he sees either of us coming, he'll do it.'

'*Anyone?*'

Gethin's voice risen higher, and now he faced the pines, from which men were emerging: Roger Vaughan, Stephen Price.

'No further,' Gethin said. 'Or her lifeblood flows.'

'Harm her,' Stephen Price said hoarsely, 'and you'll be torn apart by all of us.'

'Not before she's dead. And more of you with her.'

Even from this distance, I saw Gethin's smile open up, a split in the wood. The silence around him was waxen, Price's round face was pale and sagging. Helpless. A whole community held at bay by one man, who believed himself more than a man. Who *looked* like more than a man. I sensed a demon moving inside a puppet of skin.

'Untethered,' Thomas Jones said, 'from all human constraint.'

Anna Ceddol sagged in Gethin's grip. My breath was rapid, my thoughts feverish. It would be unwise to kill her now, he'd know that, but I didn't doubt that he'd deform her and take pleasure in it. I wondered if I could cross from the church to the pines, go further down the hill from Price and Vaughan, maybe come out behind him.

Thomas Jones said, 'Whatever you're thinking...'

'I know. I *know.*'

He'd moved too far away from the pines; wherever I was coming from he'd see me running out, and his knife hand would twitch.

And then Gethin spoke, so quietly that I caught only half of it.

'—who I want.'

The sun had gone in. Gethin waited.

Until, out of the pines, not too far from the churchyard where we stood, came the ruins of a man.

✠

His long face discoloured, lips cut and swollen.

One eye enpurpled and abulge with blood. One arm bound up in a sling ill-made of rope. A man so beaten he could no longer stand aright.

It took me a moment. Even me.

'So let her go.'

The voice was a rasp against dry stone.

Prys Gethin said, 'Where's your blade?'

A stillness for maybe three heartbeats, then something dropped to the turf.

'Further out,' Gethin said.

Robert Dudley looked down for a moment and then stepped over the body of Siôn Ceddol.

'You.' With Anna Ceddol's head crooked in an elbow, Gethin pointed, with the tip of his blade, at Roger Vaughan. 'Come out.'

Even from here I marked the terror in Vaughan's face as he left the shelter of the pine wood, glancing behind him at Price's face, impassive.

'Take the rope from his arm,' Gethin said. '*Do it*, or she—'

'Yes...'

Vaughan put up his hands, found the knot in the sling. No

resistance from Dudley and no scream when his arm was freed, only a tightening of the mouth that might have cracked teeth. The way the arm fell from the rope made clear that it was broken. Prys Gethin pointed his blade at the rope where it lay on the ground.

'Pick it up. Bind his hands. Behind his back.'

Price said, 'But his arm's—'

'Do it!' The blade moved against Anna's throat. 'Bind it *tight…*'

Dudley's face creasing, pale as cloud, as he bit down on his agony whilst the binding was done.

'Now take his boots,' Gethin said.

Dudley sniffed, kicked off one of Gwyn Roberts's boots. It came easily from his foot. He said something that I took to be derogatory about Welsh leather, and I felt a foolish admiration for him. This absurd hauteur in the face of imminent death.

I'd kept looking down the hill and across the valley for a sign of the hundred armed men promised by John Forest. Nothing. Betrayal at every level. I felt the Wigmore shewstone pressing through the worn fabric of my jerkin into my abdomen, reminding me how all this had started. *In the noble cause of expanding the Queen's vision.* Would *she* ever know how it had ended?

Vaughan knelt and pulled off the second boot.

'You can go back now,' Gethin said.

With the tip of his knife, he beckoned Dudley forward. Some women were turned away looking at the ground, averting their eyes from an expected execution.

Thomas Jones looked at me, baffled.

'He can't kill Dudley whilst holding the woman. If he lets the

410

woman go, some of these men may try and take him. And succeed.'

But Gethin didn't let the woman go.

He pointed down the hill, towards the river, sent Dudley limping barefoot ahead of him.

'I hear anyone following us,' Gethin said, 'and you know what will happen.'

'His fucking mind's gone,' Thomas Jones said. 'He can't do this. He cannot do it on his own.'

The progress was slow and awkward, Gethin holding Anna Ceddol tight and the knife tighter, Dudley shuffling and stumbling a few feet in front, head thrown back in obvious agony.

'Then either he believes himself not alone,' I said. 'Or he isn't.'

As they crossed the hill and entered a small copse of birch and rowan, I saw that the petal on Anna's breast was become a rose in full bloom.

I seized the butcher's knife.

'Tell them where I've gone,' I said.

'Where? For God's sake—'

'You know where.'

LIV

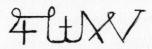

I RAN DOWN the oak wood's primitive cloister. Early light flickered amongst the dry leaves and acorns under what felt like someone else's racing feet.

Running against sombre reason and the cold denial of the Puritans. Running against a sorry sense of my own failings. Running hardest of all against the images crowding into the mind's poor glass: the blade at the woman's throat, the blooming of the blood-flower. At the start of a second day without sleep or much food, I was become a creature of little more than air, while the world was a faerie blur, the dark oaks swelling and then shrinking before me like illusions in the distorting mirror I keep in my library at Mortlake.

Emerging from the wood on to the sheep-cropped turf, I ran, in a fever, calling upon an archangel's energy, throwing his sigil into the air, pure white against the small pale sun and the still-visible moon, waxing close to full. I ran, panting like a hound and bathed with sweat and prayer, until I stopped before the alien green of the old tump in the river's bend, knowing I'd be here a good while before Gethin and his captives.

By daylight, it was clear the hole in the side had been redug in haste. The displaced soil lay in two heaps either side of it, the cut turves lain against the bottom of the tump. There was still a stench of putrefaction, but nowhere near as strong as it had been last night.

Who'd dug it out again? The Roberts boys? I could see no other explanation. It would be done here. The corpse tidily tucked into the earth. Then across the river they'd all go and away into the real Wales.

I prayed that Thomas Jones was assembling those who would understand, ready to move fast. I prayed that Dudley had some reserve of ingenuity. I prayed to God and Christ and the Holy Virgin and the Archangel Michael that Anna Ceddol would not lose her life.

Turning my back on the hole, I saw the bough which had ploughed the furrow in my head, upthrust from the twisted bole of a thorn tree grown from the foot of the tump. Picked up a forked twig, its bark stripped away by my head before the twig was snapped from the tree in my helpless writhing.

Only good can fight evil, and, God knows, there was little enough of it in me. Against all my rage, I sought to gather in all the good I'd met or heard around Brynglas hill: the souls of Father Walter and Marged the wisewoman and the unknown anchoress said to have lived where the church now stood, by the shrine of the Virgin, who I visualised unsmirched and shining, blessing the pure spring below. Conjuring a peace over Brynglas, a blue glow upon its slopes on which the sigil, in my mind, was etched.

The twig twisted in my hands, lit by a shaft of amber sunlight, my arms afire before the light was, in an instant, extinguished from above.

I dropped the twig.

'Who are you?' I said.

413

He came awkwardly down from the tump, as if his limbs were afflicted by the gnarling sickness, symptoms not apparent the last time I'd seen him. He wore a peasant's apparel, sacking around his waist, where the apron had been.

He looked tired. His grey-white hair, in disarray, was like to the tonsure he must once have worn. He was, I realised, much older than I'd thought – maybe seventy, maybe more. Too old for a satyr.

'Ah, Dr Dee,' he said wearily. 'I feel you're determined to do me harm.'

The local accent was all gone. I recalled that he'd been educated at Oxford. His background may indeed have been wealthy and privileged if, as Bishop Bonner thought, he'd actually bought his position of supremacy at Wigmore Abbey.

I followed him around to the sweeter-scented side of the tump, where the air was merely autumnally damp. In truth, I hadn't expected him. I'd thought it might be Daunce.

'You're all aglow, my boy,' he said. 'Look like a priest who's just celebrated the Mass.'

'Merely tired,' I said. 'Abbot.'

It was true that I felt light and separate from my body. Yet my mind, freed from its weight, had a piercing focus, and when John Smart raised his hands I felt it was in defence, rather than benediction.

'Call me Martin,' he said. 'Abbots are of the past.'

I looked around, warily.

'You're alone.'

'I thought we should talk. Somewhere only the faeries can overhear us.'

'Help me,' I said. 'Where are they?'

'Safe, I believe. Except for Gethin, who is dead.'

I stared at him, the former abbot who'd stolen Church gold, sold the buildings around him, ran whores.

'It's too late for lies,' John Smart said. 'I can show you his body, if you like, though I'd guess you've seen enough of them for one morning, and it's not pretty. He put out his own eye with his dagger. The last good eye. With some rage, so that the blade would seem to have proceeded into his brain. A swifter end than perhaps he deserved.'

And too easy.

'Where *was* this?'

'In a dingle about half a mile from the hill, not ten minutes ago.'

'Why would he?'

'The Presteigne boys. Out all night in the hills and angry. For some reason, he thought they were on his side, let them take the woman.'

'So Mistress Ceddol—'

'Safe. I believe.'

'You *believe*?'

'She ran away. She was not hurt. Not more than she *had* been anyway.'

'Master Roberts?'

'The so-called *Master Roberts* is taken by cart back to Presteigne, where I'll find a better bedchamber for his recovery.' A wry smile. 'With glass in its windows. As befits his status.'

I was watching his hands, both exposed, both empty. No sign of weaponry.

'I'm not *lying* to you, Dee.'

'Why would Gethin think that, Abbot? That the angry boys from Presteigne were on his side?'

'Call me Martin. Odd, is it not, the way men's minds work *in extremis*.'

'Jesu, Smart, you weren't even born here, and you can't give a straight answer to a straight question.'

'Met Scory last night,' he said, 'for the first time. Still in town, after giving evidence to the court. This was before you arrived, all full of wild accusations.' Smart chuckled. 'Poor old Bradshaw. He was far more surprised than I was.'

I sighed.

'What did you discuss with Scory?'

'Talked about the problems of survival in the Church in a time of constant change. Scory's less adventurous than me in my younger days, but he likes to, as you might say, put some modest items discreetly in store for his future comfort. But that's an aside.'

It seemed the Bishop of Hereford knew more about Abbot Smart and his circumstances than he'd confided to me. What a bag of adders the Church of England already was become.

'Good man, Scory, make no mistake,' John Smart said. 'But, as he may have indicated to you, working the Welsh border-lands does require a certain... adaptability. He's become quite exercised over the conduct of this man Daunce, who, it might be said, has too much God in him.'

More energy in Smart now, his cheeks pinkened.

I said, 'Once again, why *did* Gethin think the Presteigne boys were on his side?'

The sun had broken through again. Smart clapped his hands.

'What a fine morning this is become.' He peered at me. 'Are you sure you haven't performed some kind of invocation, Dr Dee? All manner of stories are told about you.'

'Most of them exaggerated.'

'I know the feeling.'

'I think you knew Mistress Ceddol?'

'Did I?

'But how well did you know Prys Gethin?'

I knew not where this question came from. Maybe I'd thought back to what Bonner had said about simony, the ordination of fifty paying candidates, *a small coterie of thoroughly reprehensible followers.* Or maybe it was given to me by the Archangel Michael.

'Was he at the Abbey of Wigmore?' I said. 'Was he given Holy Orders?'

Smart said, 'Gethin trusted the Presteigne boys because I'd told him he could. And because *I* was with them.'

'My thanks,' I said. 'Now to go back to my previous question…'

Smart's face had visibly darkened. His eyes grown still. He looked down at what I yet held: the butcher's knife, laden with dried blood. I let go of it and it fell to my feet, bounced and slid in the slick grass towards the foot of the tump.

'Thank you,' Smart said. 'This is very much not the place to keep a weapon too close.'

'Or an obsessive killer? God's tears, Smart, you can't just tell me what you want me to know and expect me to take my nose out of your stinking midden and walk away.'

Smart sighed at last.

'There were times, in the years before and during the

Reform, when an abbot of the Welsh Borderlands was in need of personal protection. I was, I suppose, threatened more than most. In divers ways.'

'You ordained him… as your guard?'

He shrugged.

'Knowing *what he was*?'

'All right, it was not my holiest act. Look, Dee, if you've seen the report made to Cromwell, that was not fully accurate, but some of it… had foundation. I knew it was coming. I knew Cromwell was committed to taking virtually all of us down; the abbeys, by whatever means, and I knew there'd be no great difficulty doing it to me. I'd already journeyed to London, *cwtching* up to the wily bastard, offering my services…'

'In what way?'

'Matter of survival, Dee. I'm not proud of it. Not my behaviour then, nor my behaviour now, although old Jeremy Martin…'

'Is a different man.'

'And a good innkeeper, generous with his ale and cider and ever offering a night's sleep to those in need.'

He smiled, and then it died.

'An innkeeper hears everything. An innkeeper with a host of old acquaintances and friends in London is able to form an impression of what's taking shape under his nose and… use it. When it came to my notice that certain men were entrusting the man now known as Prys Gethin with a task of considerable delicacy… let's say I thought it was ill-advised and might rebound.'

'On whom?'

'I remember what he did, in my defence, twenty years ago

when he was little more than a boy. In those days, his excuse would have been that he was doing it for the Church. Now he's been...'

'All for Wales?'

Smart sat down on the edge of the tump, as though the burden of his past were become too much to support.

'Once made the mistake of going whoring with him. Learning that we had... very different needs. Later, a particular canon who sought to gather evidence of my misconduct... had an accident. After a while, even I was in dismay over the depth of the boy's depravity. Quite relieved when our ways diverged.'

We sat in silence for a while. I knew that everything he'd told me might later be denied.

'I wanted him to hang,' Smart said. 'I did not want him back in my life. And when, after he was freed, the sheriff brought him to me, as he'd apparently requested...'

'What did you do?

'What do you think I did? I greeted him cordially, as an old friend. With great celebration. Fed him well and gave him drink. Told him how much I was in his debt for all he'd done for me twenty years ago. Said I'd help him any way I could.'

'Of course you did.'

'And, in time, he told me where he wanted to go, and I took him part-way there, hidden in my cart. Saying I'd return for him in the morning, with trusted friends. Men he could rely on.'

'The Presteigne boys.'

'Regular customers of mine, in the lower parlour. Roisterers, street-fighters. As I said, Jeremy Martin is ever generous with ale and cider and a bed for the night, and they were the first

419

hunting party to return to Presteigne – this was after you and your Welsh friend had left. Much competition that night over who'd find Prys Gethin. So I told them I'd received information as to his whereabouts and could perhaps lead them there. Giving them more drink before we rode off.'

'You know where he was going. You knew his plans.'

Smart smiled and tapped his nose.

'Best outcome, Dee. We don't need another trial. Not for a while. And you don't need to know any more about my role in Gethin's demise. Just as, in the matter of Master Roberts, I have no need at all to know who *he* is.'

✢

I walked with Smart to the Nant-y-groes bridge where the Presteigne boys waited with the horses and his cart.

The day was brighter now, though the sky was white. When we were in first sight of the company, I brought the shewstone from my bloodied jerkin, quite alarmed at how full of heat it was, having spent the whole night next to my lower abdomen.

Yes, I know… which is the home of the second mind where lie the deepest feelings, the unspoken perceptions. *There must needs be a close bond 'twixt the crystal and the scryer*, my friend Jack Simm, the apothecary, had said. I wondered if, at this moment, in its swirling depths, the sigil of St Michael would be aglow.

When I gave the stone back to John Smart, he accepted it without a word, and I was glad. The circumstance was not right. It was not the time, although in some odd way, it had served a purpose.

I said, 'You scry, Abbot?'

'Martin,' he said. 'Call me Martin. No I don't scry. That... was another of *his* tasks.'

'I— Gethin?'

'He saw. In the stone. He saw what would come. At my house in the abbey, we'd spend whole hours before the stone.'

Thomas Jones had said Gethin was reputed to have the Sight, but...

'God's tears. This was *his* stone?'

'No, it's mine. But he was the scryer. A scryer need not be a spiritual man. Or so I thought.'

I also thought to ask if he had acquaintance with a certain Brother Elias, but guessed there'd be no straight answer.

He stowed the stone away in his saddlebag.

'Should you ever have need of a scryer, Dee, I'd advise you to have a care over whom you choose.'

I did not look at the Presteigne boys. I nodded and turned away and walked back towards the river of light. I lay flat on its bank, hanging down, reaching to splash bright water on my face.

When I went back to the tump, the hole – the wound in its side – had collapsed in upon itself, and the stench had gone, leaving only the sharp, bitter essence of autumn.

LV

For Tonight

ALL WIDE AWAKE now and in need of someone with whom to talk it all through, I walked up, through the cloistered oaks, to the church and sat on the step below Our Lady of Pilleth.

Her demure, chipped face shone through a dappled haze and a rediscovered beatific smile, which led me to suppose that Roger Vaughan had been back.

There was no sign of Matthew Daunce, with whom I'd nothing to discuss.

I let my head fall into my hands. It no longer bled or ached so badly, but whatever part of it enclosed my creative thoughts felt beaten thin as an old drumskin.

I'd bathed my head and eyes again, this time with water from the holy well, unable to shake off the vibrant feeling that I'd been used... had been, for a short time, part of some engine of change.

Or was it illusion?

I saw how circumstance had completed most of the preparations required for an invocation: fasting, self-denial and the many hours without sleep that would separate me from this world, leaving me open to the higher spheres. And yet...

'There are things I still can't comprehend,' I told the Virgin. 'I know not what was here before you. How far it all goes back.

How Brynglas became a place of healing before it was a place of killing. *Where lies the power?'*

Was there some energy in the very earth which was released in places such as this for the healing of the body and the expansion of human thought?

Perhaps it had begun not here at all, but with the river and the tump that was raised within its curve. With whoever had been buried there at a time when there were no English and the word Welsh, meaning – obscurely – *foreigner* or *stranger*, had not been invented. Had that been Pilleth's golden time?

And when was it turned bad? When was the tump become a cauldron of spiritual pestilence from the second sphere? And the hill... was its natural vigour fouled by that single act of treachery by the Welsh bowmen? Or was this ruinous reversal of allegiance, as the church burned, itself effected by something here already become malign?

All I knew was that the roiling air of betrayal seemed to have become an engine in itself, a pestilence possessed of a dark intelligence which was become manifest in extremes of thought, extremes of behaviour only held in balance by a mingling of spiritual disciplines as divers as the pulleys that made my Mortlake owls flap their wings and make hoot.

I thought of the fevered swooping of the women with their knives, wondering if it was even true or just corrosive gossip of the kind that had the Queen pregnant with Dudley's child. How could it ever be proved when privy parts have no bones?

I looked up into the lowered eyelids of the stone mother.

'Are we able to reverse it?' I asked her. 'Is it in our power to restore life and health to this valley?'

A shadow was fallen across the Virgin and me, and I turned and looked up into open eyes the colour a sky is meant to be in summer.

'I was looking for you,' Anna Ceddol said.

Her wet hair hung black as a raven's wings. She pushed it back behind her ears. Must have washed it to be rid of the blood. In the river, or one of Siôn's wells.

'Too quiet, see,' she said. 'Too quiet at the Bryn. They told me to try and sleep, so I took a potion. But I could not sleep for the quiet.'

I rose to my feet. I understood. She faced me, wet-haired, dry-eyed.

'They say you saw it done.'

I nodded.

'It was... very quick. Gone like a... moth. A butterfly. I saw what might be about to happen and ran—'

'He's in the church,' she said quickly. 'On the bier.'

'Does Daunce...?'

'Daunce has been summoned to Presteigne,' Anna Ceddol said. 'Where the bishop lodges. I know not where Siôn will lie.'

'I'll talk to the bishop,' I said. 'If it's necessary.'

Knowing I must needs talk to him anyway. About many things.

'They say he's killed,' Anna said. 'The Welshman.'

'They say he killed himself. Were you not there?'

'When he let me go, I ran away. I saw no more of him.'

'It's as well,' I said. 'He... killed without a thought. He was driven by a demonic madness. The man who you and the shepherd found, all cut about... the man Stephen Price buried to prevent panic... he can only have been killed by Gethin.'

Anna Ceddol looked down at the stain on her dress, then up at the statue of the Virgin.

'No,' she said.

'Mercy?'

'No more lies. You've been good to me. I won't—'

'No,' I said. 'I may have brought a terrible sorrow to you and everyone here. Stephen Price saw me as a saviour but I think, in truth, that I'm just part of the curse.'

'I won't lie to you,' she said, as if I hadn't spoken. 'I know how that man died, and I know how he was cut about.'

I stared at her.

'Because I cut him.' Her voice was soft as moss. 'I took his apparel and then I set about his face with a spade.'

My body jerked back against the statue's stone robe.

'What are you saying?'

'So that no one would ever know who he was,' she said rapidly. 'That he was my father. And Siôn's father.'

'Listen,' I said. 'You don't have to tell me any of this. It'll go no further, but you still don't have to tell me. No one will ever know any of it from me.'

She looked up at the statue.

'The Holy Mother will know.'

☩

Tomos Ceddol. The man who, Anna had told me, had courted her mother but was deemed by her mother's parents as not of their level. Who, when Anna's mother died, had begun to drink to excess. Who had been driven to violence by the ravings of their youngest child, barely weaned when his mother had died.

'Not true,' Anna said. 'She was not his mother. When she died, I was already with child. I was twelve years old.'

Oh, dear God.

'She was unwell for nearly a year, my mother. After a while, he began to touch me. He'd get drunk on strong ale. He was a big man. Resisting him would only lead – *did* lead – to injury.'

She was hardly the first this had happened to. Hardly the first who'd gone on to give birth to her own father's child. I believed that most women stayed, made the best of it, at least until the child was old enough to leave home.

But this child would never be old enough to leave. And Anna would blame her father for the boy's idiocy. Her father... and herself.

'When I found out I was with child, I tried to... make away with him. Went to a wise woman in the next village, who charged me all I had for a potion that made me sick for days. But the babe continued to grow. It wasn't until he was nearly two years that I knew he must be damaged in the head. And knew why.'

'You don't know that,' I said, but she seemed not to hear.

She'd never let her father touch her again. She'd been sleeping with a kitchen knife since first learning there was a child on the way.

The night she'd found him kicking Siôn, to quieten him – that was true enough and happened just as she'd told me. What she hadn't told me was that, when they left home, taking all his money, Tomos Ceddol had gone in search of them. *This* was why they'd moved from village to village down the border.

'He found you?' I said. 'He found you here?'

'I'd become careless. It was over twelve years since we'd left.

426

I'd thought he'd surely given up, found a woman somewhere. I thought we were safe in the Bryn. The first real home we'd had.'

His approach had been slow and careful at first. He'd watched for whole nights from the oak wood – one of the Thomas boys had seen him twice, thought him a thief, though nobody was ever robbed... not then. I imagined Tomos Ceddol catching sight of his daughter – even more beautiful than he'd remembered. All the money he'd spent trying to find her. She was his daughter and the father of his child, who should have been disposed of long ago.

God's tears.

The night he broke in, he was drunk, having found a barrel of cider left over from the harvest festival. They heard later he'd been driven out of his own village after two rapes, although the women would not name him.

Anna Ceddol stopped, as though that were the end of the story.

'How did he die?' I said at last, in dread of the answer. 'Not that you have to—'

'Nor will I. I awoke and he was in my bed. Naked. And some men... some have thinner skulls than others.'

Siôn had done this? Struck his father...

... with the thigh bone?

'It took me about three hours get him out to the hill,' Anna said. 'I had to do it myself.'

He didn't find that man, she'd said, of Siôn. *He wouldn't even come out that day. He was afraid and clung to the fire.*

'I smashed his face with the spade. And then took the spade to him... down there. Bore it on the spade into the wood. I

427

suppose the pigs ate it. Pedr Morgan found him next day and his wife came to me to ask what we should do.'

I thought of Stephen Price who'd buried Tomos Ceddol, not knowing who he was. Buried him twice. In the tump.

Why? Because it was the only place I could think of where the mad boy wouldn't find him.

But no one lay easy in the tump.

She felt... what he wanted to do to her. Felt it inside.

I would talk to Scory. This was a matter for a priest of the old kind. Someone practised in the cure of souls.

'Come home with me,' Anna Ceddol said. 'Please come home with me. For tonight.'

PART FIVE

Here the vulgar eye will see
nothing but obscurity
and will despair considerably

JOHN DEE
Monas Hieroglyphica

LVI

From an Angel

He refused wine, accepting small beer. There was a ring of blood around the pupil of his left eye.

No longer wearing mourning, though his apparel was of earth colours, he'd ridden alone to Mortlake, and I wondered if this meant he no longer feared for his life… or if he no longer cared. I wondered if he'd been shown the letter from Thomas Blount. I wondered if he'd tell me if he had. I wondered too much.

There was an unseasonably close air for that time of year when late afternoon and evening are become one and the traffic of wherries on the river is thinned. Dudley leaned back on the bench in my workroom, the long board betwixt us, his shoulders against the wall.

'So you gave it back.'

Oft-times you don't choose the stone, Jack Simm had said, reporting the words of Elias the scryer. *The stone chooses you.*

I didn't remind Dudley of this: my feeling was that if that stone *had* chosen me it was not for anything good.

But it hadn't, anyway. It had been given either as a bribe for my silence or…

I didn't know enough about the properties of crystal, though I could almost feel its weight again, pressed against the bottom of my gut, the lower mind. Had my clumsy, if heartfelt, invocation of the archangel in some way altered its vibration? Altered *me*? For altered I was.

'Smart's scryer was Gethin,' I said.

'And that taints it?'

'Who can say what was invoked through Gethin's madness? Who knows what lived in him? You'd really want to risk loosing something… uncertain into the Queen's—?'

'All right.' A gloved hand was raised, a frown flickering across Dudley's damaged face. 'I understand. I'm already accused of carrying some satanic spore, so I'll bow to your superior knowledge of the Hidden.'

I sighed.

'For the first time in years I'm beginning to wonder if I truly—'

'You *do*.' His bloodied eyes hardened. 'Never forget that, or you'll be begging on the fucking streets.'

I said nothing. Could only wonder if such a simple life as that might not be preferable. Too many things which my poor mind was unable to arrange into the roughest of geometric patterns. I was humbled. I'd lost all faith in the power of my library. I lowered my hands and stared into them, watching them tremble.

'I suppose… another crystal stone will come. When I'm deemed ready. If ever.'

'Gethin,' Dudley said, 'fixed me with his eye and said I'd be dead within the week, and instead… he is.'

I said carefully, 'Did you see it done?'

'Saw his body. Saw it loaded on to a handcart.'

Not what I'd asked.

A silence. The air was like sand.

'I suppose,' Dudley said, 'that I owe you my life.'

'Not me. Thomas Jones, perhaps.'

'Tell me I don't have to thank him.'

'I doubt he'll be holding his breath in anticipation. How are you now?'

'Better.'

As good as his word, for once, John Smart had indeed provided, for Dudley's recovery, a good bedchamber with window glass. But not at the Bull.

'How you could stay with the doxy after what she...'

'Branwen Laetitia Swift,' Dudley said.

Almost fondly.

'*Did* she give you a potion? Did she aid in your abduction?'

All this yet worried me. How could Smart, in his role as her fishmonger and former associate of Gethin's, *not* have been part of it? The most likely explanation, it seemed to me now, was that Smart had not realised for a while how high the plot went. Maybe not realised that the target was Lord Robert Dudley, panicked when he found out. *Let's say I thought it was ill-advised and might rebound.* On him and his comfortable retirement.

'Who knows?' Dudley said. 'I was taken in the street. Hit from behind, thrown into an alley. Dragged out as if drunk. And then beaten, tied down in a cart.' He drained his cup. 'Don't want to talk about it. It demeans me.'

Did it? I was inclined to think that now he was out of it, he found it perversely flattering, the lengths to which they'd gone. And that coming through it had strengthened his cause.

He'd remained with Mistress Swift until he was fit enough to mount a horse his broken arm still bound. Three days – Dudley healed quickly. And ever thought the best of women, and they of him.

'She had new boots made for me,' he said. 'Man must've been working day and night.'

'With a sheath in the side?'

We'd not discussed this. For all his soldierly training, I suspected this might have been the first time he'd actually fought for his life.

'You'd taken out the blade after they searched you but before they stole the boots – as obviously they would, boots of such quality.'

'Secreted the blade into my sleeve. It took a couple of painful hours, but eventually I had the ropes stripped to a thread. When the older man left us alone, it was the obvious time. The boy had been taunting me in his halting English. How they'd be cutting off my cock and what they'd do with it.'

'So *they* knew who you were.'

'Evidently. It delighted them. Lost count of the beatings.' His jaw tightening at the memory. 'When the moment came, the boy made the first move. When his brother hadn't returned by first light, he was on his feet, blade out. I think he'd have cut my throat if I hadn't snapped the threads and… Not at my best, I have to say, but with surprise on my side…' He shrugged. 'You seen Cecil since your return?'

'He hasn't summoned me.'

Nor had his muscle come to snatch me into a barge. Cecil's silence had said all I needed to hear.

'However,' I said, 'a royal barge did arrive this morning.'

'Jesu!' Dudley sat up hard, with a clacking of the bench-feet on the flags. '*Bess?*'

My mother also had wondered as much and had been driven into a panic.

I shook my head.

'Blanche.'

My cousin. The Queen's senior gentlewoman and closest confidante. A social visit. Much circumspect Border-talk with never a mention of either astrology or wedding dates.

Dudley leaned forward across the board.

'You told her?'

'Everything.'

Dudley expelled a long long breath.

'Hell's bells, John.'

'Who better?' I said. 'She won't tell the Queen unless it becomes necessary. But she might have words with Cecil.'

'You clever bastard.' He sat back, smiling again. 'What about Legge? Did he know why he was sent to Presteigne?'

'Only to an extent, I'd guess. He'd simply know his duty was to see that Gethin was acquitted. He's not a fool. Had he asked too many questions, well… would he even have arrived back in London?'

'How would he not, with several dozen armed men?'

'It would take but one man,' I said, 'to smother him in his chamber during some overnight—'

'God's bollocks, John! I always took you for an innocent.'

'Me too,' I said ruefully. 'What will you do now?'

Soon wishing I hadn't asked. In some awful way, fortified, convinced that God had brought him through for only one purpose, what he'd do was to continue as before, in pursuit of his life's goal.

A spear of late sunlight lit the glass eyes of my finest owl, sitting stately on his window sill. The one that flapped his wings and said *woo-woo*.

As we walked down to the Thames, Dudley's limp was barely perceptible; he stood tall again.

Oh, dear God.

'Well, of course I won't give up,' he said.

I said nothing. The last barge of the day was returning empty to the Mortlake brewery as we went down the steps to the river's edge.

'Gather I'm to be honoured quite soon.'

'How?'

'Earldom. And if that doesn't make me more of a candidate for Bess's hand…'

'Or it might be a compensation,' I said.

'Bollocks.'

'You could waste your life.'

'John.' He turned to face me, his face half in shadow. 'It *is* my life. It's me or no one.'

'She's told you that?'

'Had it from an angel,' Dudley said.

✛

When he'd gone, I sat on the top step and watched an olive mist floating over the water.

He hadn't mentioned the letter from Thomas Blount. Even before this, I'd begun to wonder whether John Forest had even shown it to him. Perhaps Forest had been to Blount and cautioned against revealing intelligence suggesting Amy Dudley had been unfaithful to her husband and on the most intimate terms with her murderer.

That would most certainly demean him if it became public knowledge. And what would it achieve if Dudley knew? Murder by some Spanish assassin could never be proven now. There was little doubt that the inquest jury would return a verdict of death by accident.

Forest had perhaps reminded Blount that messengers were apt to be blamed. He himself had been embarrassed, on his return from Ludlow with twenty-five armed men, to find that Dudley was back in Presteigne and had commanded him, without explanation, to return to London.

My own greatest regret was that I'd not insisted on seeing Gethin's body. I did not trust John Smart, who only wanted to protect his business and the reputation of Jeremy Martin.

While I had no doubt that Gethin was dead, I realised that he was only dead in the sense that his hero, Owain Glyndwr, was dead. No one knew where his body lay and perhaps no one ever would. Which would make a legend of him – stories told to children that he would one day return, this black sprite, if the spiritual defences of Brynglas were ever lowered.

And how could they be lower than they were now?

While Dudley had lain at the home of Branwen Laetitia Swift, Roger Vaughan and I had met with Bishop John Scory in the privacy of the church in Presteigne. Scory, with many threats and much bad feeling, was in the process of prising Matthew Daunce out of Pilleth and would choose his successor with care. The statue would be scrubbed and the church lightened with more windows.

Daunce, he said, would doubtless go to London where he had friends at the heart – if you could ever call it that – of the new Puritanism. I suspected his clerical career would rise. It was the way things were going.

Pilleth, however, would require spiritual ministry, of a more traditional kind. An old magic. John Scory asked my advice, as he had about the mysterious map of the world. I'd told him that Brynglas and its environs were no less mysterious to me now.

A lesson to be learned. I said I'd write in some detail to Scory when I'd given it more thought. It's part of me now, that place, and I think I may have to return ere long.

✛

After Siôn Ceddol was buried, not far from the church, I'd sought to persuade Anna to return with me to London, but had known it was unlikely. By Christmas I'd learn, in a letter from Stephen Price, that she was betrothed to a schoolmaster in Hereford.

Within three weeks of my return home, Thomas Jones came to Mortlake with my cousin Joanne, and we discussed these matters in some depth. I was intrigued to learn that five parish churches in the area of Pilleth and the Radnor Forest were dedicated to the Archangel Michael, which made me wonder if I'd not been drawn, that strange and tragic morn, into some archaic circus of power, long buried.

Who can say? Yet while the Wigmore shewstone remained there, I did take something away, which I was able to demonstrate to Thomas Jones… and hoped one day to show to the Queen in the gardens at Richmond.

The first instinct of it had been beside the tump, when the twig which had scored my head had twitched in my hand.

In my mother's garden at Mortlake, I found forked twigs, of

birch and hazel, with which, to my great joy, I was able to discover a new well betwixt our orchard and the church.

On another occasion, when Goodwife Faldo lost not a ring (thank God) but a copper brooch, I was able to find it for her – in the hedge by the road leading to the brewery – by walking with the twig held out before me and awaiting its response.

Feeling my wrists seized by an unknown force. Learning, by trial, that I should simply let it happen, for, when I tried to study *how* it happened, it would not. It was about... *setting aside all intellect.*

Several times, I'd swear that when my wrists moved I would look up and think I'd caught a bright bobbing movement over a hedge or a wall, like the progress of a red hat.

But, of course, this was in my mind, for I do not See.

THE END

Notes and Credits

A YEAR AFTER it was opened, the inquest into the death of Amy Dudley did indeed end, as John Dee expected, with a verdict of Accidental Death. It made no difference. Dudley would never marry Elizabeth.

Most of the theories about Amy's death are explored in depth in *Death and the Virgin* by Chris Skidmore and *Elizabeth and Leicester* by Sarah Gristwood. A letter, dated August 24 – a fortnight before her death – from Amy to her dressmaker, places an order for the alteration of a velvet gown.

In these increasingly secular times, it's easy to underestimate the influence of religion, superstition and magic in Tudor England and Wales. Often, advances in science only added credibility to the concept of magic.

For anyone still sceptical, the classic *Religion and the Decline of Magic* by Keith Thomas and *The Arch-Conjurer of England* by Glyn Parry will explain everything in scholarly detail.

Once again, I also relied on *The Queen's Conjurer* by Benjamin Woolley, *John Dee* by Richard Deacon, *John Dee, The World of an Elizabethan Magus* by Peter J. French and *The Occult Philosophy in the Elizabethan Age* by Frances Yates.

Some informed speculation about the Dee dwelling at Mortlake can be found in *John Dee of Mortlake* by Nicholas Dakin, published by the Barnes and Mortlake History Society. Damon Albarn's music for his opera *Dr Dee* shows a sympathetic understanding of Mortlake's finest and is well worth a listen.

✝

Dee's abilities as a dowser are fairly well chronicled. John Aubrey records how he'd find missing items for his Mortlake neighbour, Goodwife Faldo. The Faldo family of Mortlake were long-time neighbours of John Dee and his mother. It may have been the daughter-in-law of the Goodwife Faldo mentioned in this manuscript, who, as an old woman, gave an account of the tall, good-looking and generous Dr Dee to Aubrey.

Dee's scrying sessions, in later life, with the medium, Edward Kelley, are well chronicled. He apparently told people his crystal had come 'from the angels' but where his scrying activities began is less certain. The Queen's interest is well known, as is her visit to Dee's house to examine his scrying equipment for herself. It's likely she was accompanied on this visit by Robert Dudley. The beryl in the British Museum may have been Dee's... or may not.

Dowsing is the only fringe-psychic gift he appeared to have possessed. Thanks to Ced Jackson, John Moss, Graham Gardner and Helen Lamb of the British Society of Dowsers for background. And Caitlin Sagan for the BM pictures.

The story of how Presteigne became the assize town of Radnorshire is well documented. The Mid Wales organised-crime syndicate, Plant Mat, based in a cave in the Devil's Bridge area of Ceredigion, accepted responsibility for the murder of a judge at Rhayader and some of its members were subsequently hunted down.

The Prices did finish their new home, still known as Monaughty and still the most impressive Elizabethan house in Radnorshire, standing alone, in a curve of the road from Knighton to Penybont.

John Dee is recorded as visiting Wigmore in 1576, when he found discarded manuscripts, which he considered to be of some value, in the remains of the chapel at Wigmore Castle, already falling into ruin. Today, the castle is far more visible than the abbey. The abbot's house is now the home of John and Carol Challis, who were kind enough to show us around… and put me on to Abbot Smart, more of whose alleged misdeeds were uncovered by John Grove, of the Mortimer History Society.

Roger Vaughan went on to become MP for Radnorshire and, in the 1580s, bought Kinnersley Castle, just over the English border, which he restored extensively, putting in large windows to flood its rooms with light. A ceiling, decorated with esoteric symbols in its moulding, is said to have been designed by John Dee. As Dee was not known as an interior decorator, it can only be assumed that, if he *was* the designer, it was meant to serve some protective purpose, but that's another story.

Five years later, in 1565, local merchant John Beddoes, after whom Presteigne High School is named, left an area of land, the rent from which is still used to pay for the ringing of the nightly curfew. But that was another book.

Twm Siôn Cati – Thomas Jones, of Tregaron – is still a well-known folk hero in south-west Wales, often celebrated as the Welsh Robin Hood. He was pardoned by Elizabeth not long after she came to the throne. And he did indeed become John Dee's cousin by marriage.

✝

It was Tracy Thursfield, student of the Hidden, who first told me about the shewstone (which was last heard of at Brampton Bryan Castle, home of the Harleys, who were also connected with Wigmore Abbey) and gave regular advice throughout. Mairead Reidy, ace researcher, found more details and provided a rich assortment of relevant literature. Keith Parker, author of *A History of Presteigne*, provided the background on Dee's family, Nicholas Meredith and Stephen Price, and Hilary Marchant suggested the sites of judicial premises.

Thanks once again to the present owners of the two houses at Nant-y-groes. Also Duncan Baldwin and Lucille, for legal advice. Apart from those involving royalty and high government figures, there's little evidence of the way Elizabethan trials were conducted, especially at assize level. It seems unlikely that there were barristers for the prosecution and defence, as we know them today, which suggests that most of the questioning of witnesses was done by the judge himself. The rights of the accused to offer up a defence were not automatic and might depend on the generosity of the judge.

Thanks to Sir Richard Heygate, co-author with Philip Carr-Gomm of (every home should have one) *The Book of English*

Magic for links to portals and John Dee; Ed Wilson for London geography and yet more legal assistance; Bev Craven, masterly graphic artist and connoisseur of the curious; Alun Lenny for the background on Plant Mat, Twm and Dee's Welsh roots; my wife, Carol, for the usual massive and perceptive edit; and Sara O'Keeffe at Corvus for a final overview... and a lot of patience.

+

Pilleth Church on Brynglas is well worth a visit. The holy well remains, if not the statue of the Virgin and – as someone said – it's so light and welcoming up there these days that it looks as if 'work' has been carried out there.

The name of Rhys Gethin, who achieved Owain Glyndwr's greatest victory, at Pilleth, is still remembered in Wales – most recently as the professed author of communications from the small terrorist unit, Meibion Glyndwr, who ran an arson campaign against English-owned holiday cottages in north Wales in the 1980s. The most intriguing account of Glyndwr's campaign and its aftermath is Alex Gibbon's *The Mystery of Jack of Kent and the Fate of Owain Glyndwr*.

My apologies to Nicholas Meredith, who may have been an entirely honest and decent businessman and property dealer.

The Mappa Mundi can be seen at Hereford Cathedral.

Legends of *guardians* of ancient sites are well known on the Welsh border. And some stories of guardian manifestations are rather too recent to qualify as old legends. An archaeologist once told me he'd been refused permission to excavate a Bronze Age mound on a farm in Powys because the farmer had himself once sunk a spade into it and seen something so dreadful he'd not gone near it since, with any kind of implement.

According to legend, the restless spirit of Amy Robsart at Cumnor Place was removed from Cumnor by ten priests with candles.

Poor Amy. That seems wrong, somehow.

Enjoyed *The Heresy of Dr Dee*?

The Bones of Avalon, Dee's first investigation,
is also available from Corvus

England, 1560

A country divided
Riven by religious strife and dynastic ambition

Elizabeth Tudor

The newly crowned queen
Twenty-six years old, superstitious and desperately vulnerable

Dr John Dee

The queen's astrologer
Scholar, suspected sorcerer and now investigator, sent to
Glastonbury to unearth the missing bones of King Arthur

The Bones of Avalon

Centuries-old secrets, unexpected violence, the breathless
stirring of first love… and the cold heart of a complex plot
against Queen Elizabeth I.

Read on for a taste of this exciting adventure!

Matters of the Hidden

A foreboding.

I MUST HAVE been the only man that morning to touch it. They'd gathered around me in the alley, but when I put a hand into the coffin they all drew back.

A drab day, not long after the year's beginning. Sky like a soiled rag, sooted snow still clinging to the cobbles. I'd walked down, for maybe the last time, from my lodgings behind New Fish Street, through air already fugged with smoke from the morning fires. A stink of sour ale and vomit in the alley, and a hanging dread.

'Dr Dee...'

The man pushing through the ring of onlookers wore a long black coat over a black doublet, expensive but unslashed. Mole-sleek hair was cut close to his skull.

'You may not remember me, Doctor.'

His voice soft, making him younger than his appearance suggested.

'Um...'

'Arrived in Cambridge not long before you left.'

I was edging a cautious thumbnail over the yellowing face within the coffin. All the people you're supposed to recognise these days. Why? They're something then nothing, here then gone. Waste of study-time.

'Quite a big college,' I said.

'I think you were a reader in Greek at the time?'

Which would have made it 1547 or '48. I hadn't been back to Cambridge since, having – to my mother's fierce consternation – turned down a couple of proffered posts there. I looked up at him, shaking my head and begging mercy, for in truth I knew him not.

'Walsingham,' he said.

Heard of him. An MP now, about five years younger than me, so still in his twenties. Ambitious, they said, and courting Cecil for position. His messenger had been banging on my door before eight, when it was yet dark. I hadn't liked this; it put me on edge. It always does, now.

'Lucky to catch me, Master Walsingham. I was about to leave London for my mother's house in Mortlake.'

'Not permanently, I trust?'

I looked up, suspicious. A week earlier, the tight-arse who owned the house where I was lodging had finally raised the rent beyond my means – maybe under the impression, as many now seemed to be, that I was a man of wealth. It was as if this Walsingham knew the truth of my situation. How was that possible? There was also an assumed authority here which I doubted that he, as a mere MP, had any right to exercise.

Still, this matter intrigued me, so I was prepared to indulge him for a while.

'Wax?' he said.

Squatting down in the mud on the other side of the coffin, which was laid across a stone horse-trough. Putting out a forefinger to the face, but then drawing it back.

'Let's see,' I said.

And then, impatient with all this superstition, placed both hands inside the coffin and lifted out the bundle, prompting a gasp from someone as I bent my head and sniffed.

'Beeswax.'

'Stolen from a church, then?'

'I'd guess. Shaped over a flame. See the fingermark?'

What had lain in the box was naked upon a cloth of dark red, edged in gold. It was a foot in length, three inches in thickness. The eyes were jagged holes, the mouth a knife-slit smeared red. The smudged print was on one over-plump breast and another small glob of red made a dark berry in the cleft between the legs.

'An altar candle?' Walsingham said.

'Could be. It was you who found it?'

'My clerk. I live not far away, along the river. He thought at first it must be some nun's still-born babe. When he—'

2

'Don't they usually just get dropped in the river wrapped in rags?'

'—when he finally found the balls to take off the lid, he returned at once. Had me roused.'

I looked around: two constables, a man of the Watch, a couple of whores and a vagrant near the entrance to the alley. A dying pitch-torch smouldered by the door of a mean tavern on the corner, but the buildings either side were all tight-shuttered, no smoke from the chimneys. Warehouses, most likely.

'Found exactly as . . . ?'

'No, no. The foul thing was in a most conspicuous position out on the quayside, where anyone might chance upon it. I had it moved here, then sent the Watch to knock on doors. A man walking the streets with a coffin in his arms can't have gone entirely unseen.'

I nodded. Probably some drunkard out there still fearing for his sanity. I laid the waxen effigy back in the box and hefted the whole thing. It was quite light – pine maybe, 'neath the tarry black.

'And then you summoned *me*,' I said. 'Can I, um, ask why?'

The question was left on the air; he tossed another at me.

'Dr Dee, given that we both know who it represents, how is it supposed to work?'

I eased what I now saw to be a wooden crown from the hair of plaited straw. I picked it up. Not well carved, but from a distance . . .

'And if it *is* fashioned from an altar candle,' Walsingham said, 'would that be considered to enhance its, ah, efficacy?'

'Master Walsingham, before we take this further—'

Walsingham raised a hand, stood up, waved to the constables and retainers to move further away and then made motion toward a doorway opposite the trough. I scrambled up and followed him. He leaned back into a door frame which was flaking and starting to rot. A man drawn to damp and shadows.

Who evidently thought the same of me.

'My understanding, Dr Dee, is that you're our foremost authority on what we might call *matters of the hidden*.'

A sudden skreeting of seagulls over the river. Walsingham waited, bony face solemn, eyes sunk into hollows. I was wary now. How I'd served the new Queen was no secret, but it carried more risk than profit; anyone given leave to part dark curtains inevitably drew the suspicions of the vulgar.

But what could I say? I shrugged and acknowledged an academic interest. Reticent, though, because he still hadn't given reason why a wax doll in a babe's coffin should be an MP's affair.

'Seems to me, Dr Dee, that in seeking the provenance of this artefact we have two directions.'

We?

'The first… some kind of papist pretence, to spread alarm. Hence its public display.' He nodded toward the two constables. 'See their faces. They fear for their very souls through being in its proximity.'

'Which you do not?'

Fairly sure in my mind, now, that the Walsinghams were a strong reformist family, with a link to the Boleyns and, presumably, a hatred of idolatry in any form. Hence his disdainful use of *nun* for a street-woman.

'And the second direction,' he said, 'would, of course, be toward Satan himself.'

✛

These midnight questions, I approach them daily. Yet with care.

Know this: a few of us are endowed with abilities like to the angels. Some can see the dead or pluck thoughts from the minds of others. And to some are gifted the means to bring about change in the natural order of things.

All this I know, and yet, if you thought to detect there an element of self-reference, then you must needs forget it. Mine's the scholar's way. A commitment to finding and charting pathways towards lights both beyond us and within us. Which, let me tell you, is never easy, for the paths are all overgrown with barbs and briars, and we are ever led by *false* lights.

I've oft-times followed them, too, those false lights, but I'm more cautious now.

✛

'What we both know,' I said, 'is that London's full of cunning villainy.'

Walsingham sniffed tightly.

'Quite. But does this thing have satanic power, or not?'

'It evidently has the power to arouse fear and anxiety.'

I looked at the constables, murmuring one to another now. Muted laughter to disguise a primitive terror. I wished I could take the effigy and its box for further examination but decided it was inadvisable to demonstrate too much interest.

'It's clear someone's gone to some considerable effort,' I said. 'The coffin's passably well made. The doll itself... hardly a work of high art. And yet...'

'What?'

'The one odd thing is that, apart from the fingermark, there's no... I mean, normally an image like this might be pricked with pins. The clear intention being to arouse pain, whether in mind or body, in the person it represents. There's nothing like that here that I can see.'

'It's laid out as a corpse in a coffin! How clear do you—?'

'Death, yes, sure, but what *kind* of death?'

'A prediction, then? An omen?'

'The quality of the cloth and the general workmanship suggest... well, a certain wealth and a serious intent. The crudeness of the eyes and mouth conveying, rather than a lack of artistic skill, a simple contempt for the subject. Which is further emphasised by that smirched finger-mark upon the, um, breast.'

No accident, that.

'It'll get back, of course,' Walsingham said.

'To court?'

'Too many people know already. I can swear every one of those men to secrecy – and I shall – but it'll still get back. Could be pamphlets on the street before the week's end.'

'I can be available,' I said, 'to offer some reassurance to the, um... should it be required.'

'I'm sure you can, Dr Dee. Meanwhile, what's to be done with it? Melt it on the fire?'

'Um... no.' I took a step back. 'I wouldn't do that. Not in the first

5

instance. I'd have its… its inherent darkness… dispersed. By a bishop, if possible. Do you know any bishops, Master Walsingham?'

'I will by tonight, if necessary.'

'Good. He'll know what to do.'

I nodded and was about to walk away, when Walsingham said, 'Suppose there's another.'

'Like this?'

'They could be all over London. A spreading rash of evil. Where can we find you?'

I couldn't see it; a multiplicity of effigies would somehow reduce the insidious effect.

'I'll be leaving today, as I said, for my mother's house. If you get word to Lord Dudley, he'll have a messenger sent to me.'

Taking care to throw in that mention of Dudley. Even though his odour was not good in certain circles, his was yet a potent name. Walsingham nodded and bent over to the coffin and this time he put a finger very close to the wax, as if he *might* be touching it, though I thought not.

'Is that blood?'

The smear of red across the knife-slit mouth. I'd wondered about that. And, more significantly, the glob of red between the legs – preferring to say nothing about this lest my supposition of its intent as regards future childbearing be wrong.

'If it's the blood of whoever made this,' I said, 'it might be thought to carry the essence of that person's hatred to… she who's represented here. Blood was also seen by the ancients as an agent for the, um, materialising of spirits.'

'For conjuring?'

Never my favourite word.

'It's a matter of will. The harnessing of the human will to something from another… level of existence.'

'Something demonic?'

'If the Queen's appointed by God…'

'*If*? You *doubt* that?'

The question lightly posed, his eyes half lidded.

Jesu.

'No, no,' I said. 'Obviously not. What I'm saying is that the corruption of an altar candle could, as I think you've already suggested, be an attempt to subvert the power of God in this respect.'

'Breaking the sacred thread within the line of monarchy?'

'Which might itself be considered already weakened by—'

'The *sex* of the monarch?'

This man thought too fast for my liking.

'This is only my own—'

'Of *course*,' Walsingham hissed. 'That's why you're here.'

I looked at him closely.

'Who *are* you?' I said. '*What* are you?'

'What do I look like?'

'You look,' I said, 'like walking darkness.'

And he smiled and nodded, quite clearly pleased at this.

✠

When I'm asked how it all began, this is the incident I recall: the first example, in my own witness, of a malevolence – an *intelligent* malevolence – directed at the Queen.

You must needs be aware of its effect on me. In my way, I've loved this woman for whom I'll part any dark curtains, seek answers to the most forbidding of midnight questions. For if this is the time for an uncovering of universal mysteries, then I'd like to think *she* has made that possible by displaying a manner of tolerance which many of us had feared we might never see again.

After all is said, should it not be man's most ardent desire to see into the very mind of God? Does not God himself challenge us to interpret His art?

A silence.

Heresy, you whisper.

Burn him.

As they nearly did. A few years ago, in another reign – you may know something of this – I was close to being left as cinders upon a hearth of baked earth. Thoughts of it still sear my dreams, lie smouldering in my lower mind. The charges were manifestly unjust, but when did that ever matter?

Yet I survived, and now the wildfire of another dawn is kindled over the river, and I sit here in my mother's parlour and throw up my hands – for what else is the charge of heresy but a brutal blindfold for the far-sighted?

And I must needs set down what happened. Recount the whole bitter episode before it's murked by memory and rendered impenetrable to the common man by my own exhaustive analysis – oft-times it being said that few can comprehend my writings, full weighted as they are with scientific terms, befuddled by diagrams and arcane symbols. The very tradecraft, some will say, of the devil.

So I'll relate this story as simply and directly as it comes to memory. I shall not, as is my usual custom, carefully dissect and prod over each sentence or avoid what it tells of my inner nature... about what I was and what I am become.

But, before I begin, know this...

...there *is* a shape and pattern to it all. A universal geometry, the changing angles and rhythms of which, through mathematics and the study of the stars, we're learning to calcule again, as men did in ancient times. Twin journeys: above and below, without and within. I try to chart them daily, whilst knowing that I am, in divers ways, no more than an onlooker.

And helpless.

For although some may have abilities like to the angels, yet they are *not* angels.

I've learned this, and in the cruellest of ways.